SNOW WHITE MUST DIE

SNOW WHITE MUST DIE

NELE NEUHAUS

Translated by Steven T. Murray

MINOTAUR BOOKS ✹ NEW YORK

SNOW WHITE MUST DIE. Copyright © 2010 by Nele Neuhaus. English translation copyright © 2012 by Steven T. Murray. All rights reserved. Printed in the United States of America. For information, address St. Martin's Press, 175 Fifth Avenue, New York, N.Y. 10010.

www.minotaurbooks.com

The Library of Congress has cataloged the hardcover edition as follows:

Neuhaus, Nele.
   [Schneewittchen muss sterben. English]
   Snow White must die / Nele Neuhaus ; translated by Steven T. Murray.—1st U.S. ed.
     p. cm.
   ISBN 978-0-312-60425-7 (hardcover)
   ISBN 978-1-250-01209-8 (e-book)
 I. Murray, Steven T., translator. II. Title.
   PT2714.E95S3613 2013
   833'.92—dc23

                  2012038365

ISBN 978-1-250-03977-4 (trade paperback)

Minotaur books may be purchased for educational, business, or promotional use. For information on bulk purchases, please contact Macmillan Corporate and Premium Sales Department at 1-800-221-7945, extension 5442, or write specialmarkets@macmillan.com.

First published in Germany under the title *Schneewittchen muss sterben* by List Taschenbuch, an imprint of Ullstein Buchverlage GmbH, Berlin

First Minotaur Books Paperback Edition: December 2013

10 9 8 7 6 5 4 3 2 1

For Simone

Prologue

The rusty iron staircase leading downstairs was narrow and steep. He felt along the wall for the light switch, and seconds later the twenty-five-watt bulb illuminated the space with a dim light. The heavy iron door opened without a sound. He oiled the hinges regularly so they wouldn't squeak and wake her up when he came to visit. Warm air, mixed with the sweetish scent of wilting flowers, rose to meet him. Carefully he closed the door behind him, turned on the light, and paused for a moment. The large room, about thirty feet long by fifteen feet wide, was simply furnished, but she seemed to feel comfortable here. He went over to the stereo and punched the PLAY button. The raucous voice of Bryan Adams filled the room. He didn't much care for this music, but she loved the Canadian singer, and he usually took her preferences into consideration. As long as he had to keep her hidden, she shouldn't lack for anything. As usual she said nothing. She never talked to him, never answered his questions, but that didn't bother him. He moved aside the folding screen that discreetly divided the room. There she lay, motionless and lovely on the narrow bed, her hands folded on her stomach, her long hair spread out like a black fan around her head. Beside the bed stood her shoes, and on the nightstand a bouquet of wilted lilies in a glass vase.

"Hello, Snow White," he said softly. Beads of sweat formed on his brow. The heat was almost unbearable, but that was the way she liked it. Before, she had always been sensitive to cold. His gaze drifted to the photographs that he had put up beside her bed. He wanted to ask her whether he could put up a new one, but he needed to save this request for the proper moment, when she wouldn't take offense. Cautiously he sat down on the edge of the bed.

The mattress sagged a bit under his weight, and for a moment he thought she had moved. But no. She never moved. He reached out his hand and placed it on her cheek. Her skin had taken on a yellowish hue over the years and now felt stiff and leathery. As always she had her eyes closed, and even though her skin was no longer as tender and rosy, her mouth was as beautiful as before, back when she still talked to him and smiled. He sat there for a long while looking at her. His desire to protect her had never felt so strong.

"I have to be going," he said at last, regretfully. "I have so much to do."

He got up, took the wilted flowers from the vase, and made sure that the bottle of cola on her nightstand was full.

"Tell me if you need anything, all right?"

Sometimes he missed her laughter, and then he felt sad. Of course he knew that she was dead, yet he still found it simpler to act as if he didn't know. He had never given up hoping for a smile from her.

Thursday, November 6, 2008

He didn't say "See you later." Nobody who was let out of the slammer ever said "See you later." Often, very often over the past ten years, he had imagined the day of his release. Now it occurred to him that he'd only thought as far as the moment he would walk out the door into freedom, which all of a sudden seemed threatening. He had no plans for his life. Not anymore. Even without the droning admonishments of the social workers he had realized long ago that the world was not waiting for him, and that he would have to deal with all sorts of obstacles and defeats in a future that no longer seemed so rosy. He could forget about a career as a doctor, which had once been his ambition after he passed his A-level exams for the university. Under the circumstances the training he'd received to be a locksmith, which he'd completed in prison, might come in handy. In any case it was high time he looked life straight in the eye.

As the gray, spike-topped iron gate of the Rockenberg Correctional Facility closed behind him with a clang, he saw her standing there across the street. In the past ten years she was the only one who had written to him regularly, but he was still surprised to see her. Actually he had expected his father to come. She was leaning on the fender of a silver SUV, holding a cell phone to her ear, and puffing nervously on a cigarette. He stopped. When she recognized him, she straightened up, stuck the phone in her coat pocket, and flicked away the cigarette butt. He hesitated for a moment before crossing the cobblestone street, carrying the small suitcase with his possessions in his left hand. He stopped in front of her.

"Hello, Tobi," she said with a nervous laugh. Ten years was a long time.

They hadn't seen each other in all that time, because he hadn't wanted her to visit him.

"Hello, Nadia," he replied. It was strange to call each other by these unfamiliar names. In person she looked better than on TV. Younger. They stood facing each other, hesitant. A brisk gust of wind sent the dry fall leaves rustling across the pavement. The sun had slipped behind thick gray clouds. It was cold.

"Fantastic that you're out." She threw her arms around him and kissed his cheek. "I'm glad. Really."

"I'm glad too." The instant he uttered this cliché, he asked himself whether it was true. Happiness was not the same thing as this feeling of strangeness, of uncertainty. She let him go because he made no move to return her embrace. In the old days she had been his best friend, the neighbors' daughter, and he had taken her presence in his life for granted. Nadia was the sister he'd never had. But now everything was different, and not only her name. The tomboy Nathalie, who had been ashamed of her freckles, the gap in her front teeth, and her breasts, had been transformed into Nadia von Bredow, a famous actress who was in great demand. She had realized her ambitious dream to leave behind the village where they'd both grown up, to climb all the way to the top of the social ladder. He, on the other hand, could no longer put his foot even on the lowest rung. As of today he was an ex-con. Sure, he had served his time, but society was not exactly going to welcome him with open arms.

"Your father couldn't get off work today." Abruptly she took a step back, avoiding his eyes, as if his feeling of awkwardness was contagious. "That's why I'm picking you up."

"That's nice of you." Tobias shoved his suitcase into the back seat of her car and got into the passenger seat. The light-colored leather didn't have a mark on it, and the inside of the car still smelled new.

"Wow," he said, genuinely impressed, casting a glance at the dashboard, which looked like the cockpit of an airplane. "Cool car."

Nadia smiled briefly and pressed a button without putting the key in the ignition. The engine sprang to life with a subtle purr. She expertly maneuvered the powerful automobile out of the parking place. Tobias glanced briefly at a pair of enormous chestnut trees that stood close to the prison wall. The view of those trees from his cell window had been his only contact with the outside world for the past ten years. The way the trees changed through the seasons was all that had remained of the world that had otherwise vanished in a diffuse fog beyond the prison walls. And now he, the convicted murderer of two girls, had to step back into this fog after serving his sentence. Whether he wanted to or not.

"Where should I take you? To my place?" Nadia asked as she turned the car onto the autobahn. In her most recent letters she had offered several times to let him stay with her temporarily—her apartment in Frankfurt was big enough. The prospect of not having to return to Altenhain and confront the past was tempting, but he declined.

"Maybe later," he said. "First I want to go home."

Detective Inspector Pia Kirchhoff was standing in the pouring rain on the site of the former military airfield at Eschborn. She had done up her blond hair in two short braids and put on a baseball cap. With her hands thrust deep in the pockets of her down jacket she was watching with a blank expression as her colleagues spread a tarp over the hole at her feet. During the demolition of one of the dilapidated aircraft hangars, a backhoe operator had discovered bones and a human skull in one of the empty jet fuel tanks. To the dismay of his boss he had then called the police. Work had come to a standstill for the past two hours, and Pia had been forced to listen to the insulting tirades of the ill-tempered foreman, whose multicultural demolition crew had instantly fled in alarm when the police showed up. The man lit his third cigarette in fifteen minutes and hunched his shoulders, as if that would prevent the rain from running down inside the collar of his jacket. He kept swearing to himself the whole time.

"We're waiting for the medical examiner. He should be here soon." Pia had no interest in either the blatant use of illegal workers at the site or the schedule for the demolition work. "Go ahead and tear down another hangar in the meantime."

"Easy for you to say," the man complained, pointing in the direction of the waiting backhoe and dump truck. "Because of a few bones we've got a big delay on our hands, and it's going to cost us a fortune."

Pia shrugged and turned her back on him. A car came bouncing over the uneven concrete. Weeds had gnawed through every gap in the taxiway and had turned the formerly smooth surface into a regular mogul run. After the airfield had been shut down, nature had emphatically proven its ability to reclaim every man-made structure. Pia left the foreman to bitch and moan and went over to the silver Mercedes that had pulled up next to the police vehicles.

"You certainly took your time getting here," she greeted her ex-husband, not sounding overly friendly. "If I catch a cold it'll be all your fault."

Dr. Henning Kirchhoff, acting chief of Frankfurt forensic medicine, appeared unfazed by her remarks. He calmly donned the obligatory disposable coverall, exchanged his shiny black leather shoes for rubber boots, and pulled the hood over his head.

"I was giving a lecture," he countered. "And then there was a traffic jam near the fairgrounds. Sorry. What have we got?"

"A skeleton in one of the old underground jet fuel tanks. The demolition crew found it about two hours ago."

"Has it been moved?"

"I don't think so. They removed only the concrete and dirt, then cut open the top of the tank because they can't transport those things in one piece."

"Good." Kirchhoff nodded, said hello to the officers in the evidence team, and prepared to climb down into the pit underneath the tarp, where the lower portion of the tank was located. He was undoubtedly the best man for the job, since he was one of the few forensic anthropologists in Germany; human bones were his specialty. The wind was now driving the rain almost horizontally across the open taxiway. Pia was freezing. Water was dripping from the bill of her baseball cap, and her feet had turned to clumps of ice. She envied the men of the demolition team who had been idled, as they stood around in the hangar drinking hot coffee from thermoses. As usual, Henning worked meticulously; once he had some sort of bones in front of him, time and everything else lost all meaning for him. He knelt down at the bottom of the tank, bent over the skeleton, and examined one bone after another. Pia stooped to look under the tarp, holding on to the ladder so she wouldn't fall into the pit.

"A complete skeleton," Henning called up to her. "Female."

"Old or young? How long has it been here?"

"I can't say exactly yet. At first sight there's no tissue remaining, so probably a couple of years at least." Henning straightened up and came back up the ladder. The men of the evidence team began their work by carefully securing the bones and the surrounding soil. It was going to take a while before the skeleton could be transported to the forensic medicine lab, where Henning and his colleagues would examine it thoroughly.

Human bones were always being discovered at excavation sites. It was important to establish precisely how long the corpse had been buried there, since the statute of limitations on violent crimes, including murder, ran out after thirty years. It didn't make any sense to check the missing persons files until they had determined the age of the victim at death and how long the skeleton had been in the ground. Air traffic at the old military airfield had ceased sometime in the fifties, and that was how long it had been since the tanks were last filled. The skeleton might belong to a female American soldier from the U.S. base located next to the airfield until October 1992, or it could have been a resident of the former home for asylum seekers on the other side of the rusty wire fence.

"Why don't we go somewhere and get some coffee?" Henning took off his glasses and wiped them dry, then peeled off the wet coverall. Pia gave her ex-husband a surprised look. Café visits during working hours were simply not his style.

"Is something wrong?" she asked suspiciously.

He pursed his lips, then heaved a sigh.

"I'm really in a jam," he admitted. "And I need your advice."

The village huddled in the valley and looming over it were two tall, ugly monstrosities that were built in the seventies, back when every community worth its salt had approved construction of high-rise buildings. On the slope to the right was Millionaires' Hill, as the old established families called the two streets where the few newcomers lived in villas on spacious grounds. He felt his heart pounding nervously the closer he came to his parents' house. It was eleven years ago that he was here last. To the right stood the little half-timbered house belonging to Grandma Dombrowski. For ages it had looked as though it was still standing only because it was squeezed between two other houses. A little farther on was the judge's farm with the barn. And diagonally across from it was the restaurant his father owned called the Golden Rooster. Tobias swallowed hard when Nadia stopped in front. In disbelief he surveyed the dilapidated façade with the plaster flaking off, the blinds pulled down, and the gutters sagging along the eaves. Weeds had forced their way through the asphalt, and the gate hung crooked on its hinges. He almost asked Nadia to keep going—*Quick, quick, just get out of here!* But he resisted the temptation, said a curt thank-you, and climbed out, taking his suitcase from the back seat.

"If you need anything, just give me a call," Nadia said in parting, then stepped on the gas and zoomed off. What had he expected? A cheerful reception? He stood alone in the small blacktop parking area in front of the building, which had once been the center of this dismal dump. The formerly white plaster was now weathered and crumbling, and the name Golden Rooster was barely visible. A sign hung behind the cracked milky glass pane in the front door. TEMPORARILY CLOSED, it said in faded letters. His father had told him that he'd given up the restaurant, citing his slipped disk as the reason, but Tobias had a feeling that something else had brought him to this difficult decision. Hartmut Sartorius had been a third-generation innkeeper who had put body and soul into the business. He had done the slaughtering and cooking himself, he pressed his own hard cider, and he never neglected the restaurant for a single day because of illness. No doubt the customers had simply stopped coming. Nobody wanted to eat dinner or celebrate a special occasion at an establishment run by the parents of a double murderer. Tobias took a deep breath and walked over to the courtyard gate. It took some effort just to get the gate open. The condition of the courtyard shocked him. In the summer, tables and chairs had once stood beneath the spreading branches of a mighty chestnut tree and a picturesque pergola covered with wild grapevines, and waitresses had bustled from one table to the next. Now a sad dilapidation reigned. Tobias's gaze swept over piles of carelessly discarded refuse, broken furniture, and trash. The pergola had partially collapsed and the unruly grapevines had withered. No one had swept up the fallen leaves from the chestnut tree, and the trash can had apparently not been put out on the street for weeks, because trash bags were piled next to it in a stinking heap. How could his parents live like this? Tobias felt his last ounce of courage fade away. Slowly he made his way to the steps leading up to the front door, then reached out and pressed the doorbell. His heart was pounding in his throat when the door was hesitantly opened. The sight of his father brought tears to Tobias's eyes, and at the same time a sense of rage was growing inside him, rage at himself and at the people who had left his parents in the lurch after he'd been sent to prison.

"Tobias!" A smile flitted over the sunken face of Hartmut Sartorius, who was only a shadow of the vital, self-confident man he had once been. His thick, dark hair had turned thin and gray, and his bent posture betrayed the weight of the burden that life had imposed on him.

"I . . . I really should have cleaned things up a bit, but I didn't get any time off and—" He broke off, his smile gone. He merely stood there, a broken, shamefaced man, avoiding Tobias's gaze, because he knew what his son was seeing.

It was more than Tobias could bear. He dropped his suitcase, spread his arms wide, and clumsily embraced this emaciated, gray stranger who he scarcely recognized as his father.

A little while later they sat awkwardly facing each other at the kitchen table. There was so much to say, and yet every word seemed superfluous. The gaudy oilcloth on the table was covered with crumbs, the windowpanes were filthy, and a withered plant in a pot by the window had long since lost the fight to survive. The kitchen felt damp and smelled unpleasantly of sour milk and old cigarette smoke. Not a piece of furniture had been moved, not a picture taken down from the wall, since he'd been arrested on September 16, 1997, and left this house. But back then everything had been bright and cheerful and clean as a whistle; his mother was an efficient housewife. How could she permit such neglect, how could she stand it?

"Where's Mom?" Tobias finally said, breaking the silence. He saw at once that the question caused his father more embarrassment.

"We . . . we wanted to tell you, but . . . but then we thought it would be better if you didn't know," Hartmut Sartorius said at last. "It's been a while since your mother . . . moved out. But she knows that you're coming home today and is looking forward to seeing you."

Baffled, Tobias stared at his father.

"What's that supposed to mean—she moved out?"

"It wasn't easy for us after you . . . went away. The gossip never stopped. Finally she just couldn't take it anymore." There was no reproach in his voice, which had turned quavery and faint. "We were divorced four years ago. She's living in Bad Soden now."

Tobias swallowed with difficulty.

"Why didn't either of you tell me about this?" he whispered.

"Ah, it wouldn't have made any difference. We didn't want you to worry."

"So that means you're living here all by yourself?"

Hartmut Sartorius nodded, shoving the crumbs on the tablecloth back and forth, arranging them in symmetrical patterns and then scattering them again.

"What about the pigs? And the cows? How can you do all the work yourself?"

"I got rid of the animals years ago," his father answered. "I still do a little farming. And I found a really good job in a kitchen in Eschborn."

Tobias clenched his hands into fists. How foolish he had been to think that he was the only one being punished by life! He'd never understood before how much his parents must have suffered too. During their visits to the prison they had always acted as if their world was intact, yet it had all been a sham. How much effort that must have cost them! Helpless fury grabbed Tobias by the throat, trying to throttle him. He stood up, went over to the window, and stared blankly outside. His plan to go somewhere else after spending a few days with his parents, so he could try to start a new life far from Altenhain, now disintegrated. He would be staying here. In this house, on this farm, in this crappy dump of a village where everyone had made his parents suffer even though they were completely innocent.

The wood-paneled restaurant in the Black Horse was jam-packed, and the noise level was correspondingly high. Half of Altenhain had gathered at the tables and the bar, unusual for a Thursday night. Amelie Fröhlich balanced three orders of jägerschnitzel on a tray as she made her way over to table nine. She served the customers, wishing them *"Guten Appetit."* Normally master roofer Udo Pietsch and his pals would have some dumb remark ready, aimed at her bizarre appearance, but today Amelie could have been serving naked and probably nobody would have noticed. The mood was as tense as during a World Cup game. Amelie pricked up her ears when Gerda Pietsch leaned over toward the next table occupied by the Richters, who ran the grocery store on the main street.

"I saw him arrive," Margot Richter was saying. "What barefaced impudence to show up here, as if nothing had ever happened!"

Amelie went back to the kitchen. Roswitha was waiting by the counter for the order for Fritz Unger at table four, a medium rump steak with onions and herb butter.

"What's all the uproar about tonight?" Amelie asked her older colleague, who had slipped off one of her orthopedic shoes and was discreetly rubbing her right foot over the varicose veins on her left calf. Roswitha glanced at the boss's wife, who was too busy with all the drink orders to worry about her employees.

"The Sartorius kid got out of the joint today," Roswitha confided in a low voice. "He did ten years for killing those two girls."

"Oh!" Amelie's eyes widened with surprise. She knew Hartmut Sartorius slightly. He lived all alone on that big, run-down farm of his down the hill from her house, but she hadn't known anything about his son.

"Yep." Roswitha nodded toward the bar where master carpenter Manfred Wagner was staring into space, his eyes glassy as he held in his hand his tenth or eleventh glass of beer this evening. Normally it took him two hours longer to get through that many beers. "Manfred's daughter Laura—that's who Tobias killed. And the Schneeberger girl. To this day he hasn't told anyone what he did with their bodies."

"Rump steak with herb butter and onions!" called Kurt, the assistant cook, shoving the plate through the serving hatch. Roswitha slipped her shoe back on and maneuvered her corpulent figure skillfully through the jam-packed restaurant to table four. Tobias Sartorius—Amelie had never heard that name before. She had arrived in Altenhain only six months ago from Berlin, and not by choice. The village and its inhabitants were as interesting to her as a sack of rice in China, and if she hadn't been turned on to the job at the Black Horse by her father's employer, she still wouldn't know a soul.

"Three wheat beers, one small diet Coke," shouted Jenny Jagielski, the boss's wife, who had taken charge of the drinks. Amelie grabbed a tray, set the glasses on it, and cast a quick glance at Manfred Wagner. His daughter had been *murdered* by the son of Hartmut Sartorius! That was really intriguing. Here, in the most boring village in the world, undreamed of abysses suddenly opened up. She unloaded the three beers on the table where Jenny Jagielski's brother Jörg Richter was sitting with two other men. He was actually supposed to be tending bar instead of Jenny, but he seldom did what he was supposed to do. Especially when the boss, Jenny's husband, wasn't there. She deposited the diet soda in front of Mrs. Unger at table four. Then she had time for a short pit stop in the kitchen. All the guests had their food, and Roswitha had gathered new details on a further round through the restaurant. With glowing cheeks and heaving bosom she now recounted to her curious audience what she'd learned.

Amelie, the assistant cooks Kurt and Achim, and Wolfgang the head cook were all ears. Margot Richter's grocery store—Amelie had been surprised to hear that everyone in Altenhain said "we're going to Margot's," although strictly speaking the store belonged to her husband—stood directly across from the former Golden Rooster. That was why Margot and the hairdresser Inge Dombrowski, who had stopped at the grocery that afternoon for a little chat, had been eyewitnesses to the return of *that guy*. He had climbed out of a silver luxury car and walked over to his parents' farmhouse.

"He's certainly got some nerve," Roswitha fumed. "The girls are dead, and this guy shows up back here as if nothing had ever happened!"

"But where else would he go?" Wolfgang remarked nonchalantly, taking a gulp of his beer.

"I don't think you get it," Roswitha told him. "How would you like it if the murderer of your daughter suddenly showed up right in front of you?"

Wolfgang shrugged indifferently.

"What else?" Achim pressed her. "Where did he go?"

"Into the house, of course," said Roswitha. "He must have been surprised when he saw what it looks like now."

The swinging door opened. Jenny Jagielski marched into the kitchen and put her hands on her hips. Like her mother, Margot Richter, she was of the opinion that her employees were going to rob the cash register behind her back or somehow pull a fast one on her. Three pregnancies in rapid succession had ruined Jenny's figure, who'd been of stocky build to start with. By now she was as round as a barrel.

"Roswitha!" she called sharply to the woman who was about thirty years older. "Table ten is waiting for the check."

Roswitha vanished obediently, and Amelie tried to follow her, but Jenny Jagielski held her back.

"How many times have I told you to remove those disgusting piercings and brush your hair properly when you come to work?" Disapproval was written all over her puffy face. "And a blouse would be more suitable than this skimpy top. You can't be serving food in your underwear. We're a decent restaurant, not some underground Berlin disco!"

"But the men like it," Amelie countered. Jagielski's eyes narrowed and red patches appeared like crimson brands on her fat neck.

"I don't give a damn," she snapped. "Take a look at the hygiene regulations."

Amelie had a bitter retort on the tip of her tongue, but at the very last second she managed to control herself. Even if she found Jagielski unpleasant, from her cheap perm down to her plump bratwurst calves, Amelie should keep her mouth shut. She needed this job at the Black Horse.

"And you two?" The boss glared at her cooks. "Don't you have anything you should be doing?"

Amelie left the kitchen just as Manfred Wagner toppled over and brought the barstool down on top of him.

"Hey, Manni," called one of the men from the table of regulars. "It's only nine thirty!" The others laughed good-naturedly. Nobody got excited about it; this same spectacle, or something similar, played out almost every night, but usually along about eleven. Then they would call his wife, who would show up within a few minutes, pay his tab, and steer her husband toward home. This evening, however, Wagner altered the choreography. This man who was normally so placid struggled back to his feet without anyone's help, turned around, grabbed his beer glass, and smashed it on the floor. All conversation stopped as he staggered over to the table of regulars.

"You assholes," he mumbled, his tongue thick with drink. "You sit here talking all kinds of crap like it was nothing! None of you give a damn!"

Wagner held on to the back of a chair and looked around wildly with his bloodshot eyes. "But I, I have to…look at this…pig…and think about…" He broke off and his head drooped. Jörg Richter had stood up and now put his hand on Wagner's shoulder.

"Come on, Manni. Don't make trouble. I'll call Andrea and she…"

"Don't touch me!" Wagner howled, pushing him away so violently that the younger man lost his balance and fell. He grabbed hold of a chair and pulled the man sitting there down with him. All at once, chaos erupted.

"I'm going to kill that pig!" Wagner kept bellowing over and over. He was thrashing all about; the full glasses on the table tipped over, their contents spilling onto the clothing of the men sprawled on the floor. In fascination Amelie watched the scene from the cash register as her colleague fought for her life in the midst of the melee. A regular old-time brawl in the Black Horse! Finally something was happening in this dismal dump. Jenny Jagielski dashed past her into the kitchen.

"A decent restaurant," Amelie muttered derisively, earning a dirty look. Seconds later the boss came storming out of the kitchen with Kurt and Achim in tow. The two cooks overpowered the drunken man in a flash. Amelie grabbed the broom and dustpan and went over to the regulars' table to clean up the broken glass. Manfred Wagner was no longer belligerent and let himself be led away without resistance, but at the door he wrested himself from the grip of the two cooks and turned around. He stood there swaying, with saliva running from the corners of his mouth into his disheveled beard. A dark spot was spreading on the front of his pants. He must be really drunk, thought Amelie. She had never seen him piss himself before. Suddenly she felt sorry for this man she had always secretly ridiculed. Was the murder of his daughter the reason why he drank himself into a coma with such persistent regularity every night? It was deathly quiet in the restaurant.

"I'm going to get that bastard!" Wagner yelled. "I'll beat that . . . that . . . fucking killer to death."

His head fell forward and he began to sob.

Tobias Sartorius stepped out of the shower and reached for the towel. He wiped off the steamed-up mirror with his hand and looked at his face in the dim light produced by the last functioning lightbulb in the bathroom. The last time he had looked in this mirror was on the morning of September 16, 1997. Later that evening they had come to arrest him. How grown-up he had felt back then, that summer after he'd graduated from high school. Tobias closed his eyes and leaned his forehead against the cold surface. Here, in this house, where every nook and cranny was so familiar, the ten years he'd spent in prison seemed to have vanished. He remembered every detail of those last days before his arrest as if it had all happened yesterday. It was incredible how naïve he had been. But until today he'd had those black holes in his memory, although the court had refused to believe it. He opened his eyes, stared into the mirror, and for a second was surprised to see the angular face of a thirty-year-old. With his fingertips he touched the pale scar that ran along his jawbone to his chin. The wound had been inflicted in his second week in prison, and it was the reason why he had spent ten years in solitary, with almost no contact with his fellow prisoners. In the strict hierarchy of prison life the murderer of two teenage girls ranked only barely above the lowest filth, the child murderer. The bathroom door didn't close tightly anymore; a cold draft struck his wet skin and made him shiver.

From downstairs he could hear voices. His father must have a visitor. Tobias turned away and pulled on underwear, jeans, and a T-shirt. Earlier he had surveyed the depressing relic of the big farmhouse and confirmed that the front part looked downright presentable in comparison to the rear section. He gave up completely his vague plans to flee Altenhain as quickly as possible. He couldn't possibly leave his father all alone in this mess. Since he couldn't expect to find a job any time soon, he might as well spend the next few days getting the farm into shape. Then he would see what happened. He left the bathroom, passed the closed door to his room, and went down the stairs, out of habit skipping the steps that creaked. His father was sitting at the kitchen table, and his visitor had his back to Tobias. But he recognized the man at once.

When Oliver von Bodenstein, the detective superintendent and head of the Division of Violent Crimes at the Regional Criminal Unit in Hofheim, got home at nine thirty, he found that his dog was the only living creature in the house. The greeting he received seemed more embarrassed than cheerful—an unmistakable sign of a guilty conscience. And Bodenstein smelled the reason why before he saw it. He'd had a stressful fourteen-hour day. First there was a tedious meeting at the State Bureau of Investigation; the discussion of a skeleton discovered in Eschborn, which his boss, Commissioner Dr. Nicola Engel called a "cold case"; and last but not least the farewell party for a colleague from K-23 who had been transferred to Hamburg.

Bodenstein's stomach was growling, because he'd had only a few chips along with a quantity of alcohol. Disgruntled, he opened the refrigerator and saw nothing inside that would gratify his taste buds. Couldn't Cosima have done some grocery shopping if she wasn't going to fix him any dinner? Where was she, anyway? He went down the hall, ignoring the stinking pile and the puddle the dog had left, which thanks to the floor heating had already dried to a sticky yellow spot. Then he went upstairs to his youngest daughter's room. Sophia's bed was empty, as expected. Cosima must have taken the little girl with her, wherever it was she'd gone. He wasn't going to call her if she couldn't bother to leave him a note or at least send him a text message. Just as Bodenstein had gotten undressed and stepped into the bathroom to take a shower, the phone rang. Naturally it wasn't in the recharger on top of the chest of drawers in the hall, but somewhere else in the house. With growing annoyance he began searching for the phone, swearing as he stepped on a toy that had been left on the living room floor. Just as he located the phone on the couch, the ringing stopped. At the same time the key turned in the lock of the front door, and the dog began barking excitedly. Cosima came in, carrying their drowsy daughter and a huge bouquet of flowers.

"Oh, you're home," she said. That was her sole greeting. "Why didn't you pick up the phone?"

His hackles rose at once.

"Because I couldn't find it. Where were you, anyway?"

She didn't answer, ignoring the fact that he was dressed only in briefs, and went past him into the kitchen. She put the bouquet down on the table and then held Sophia out to him. The girl was now wide awake and whimpering unhappily. Bodenstein took his little daughter in his arms. He could smell that her diaper must be full.

"I sent you several texts to ask you to pick up Sophia at Lorenz and Thordis's." Cosima took off her coat. She looked exhausted and frazzled, but he didn't feel guilty.

"I didn't get any texts."

Sophia wriggled in his arms and started to cry.

"Because your cell was turned off. You've known for weeks that this afternoon I'd be at the film museum for the opening of the photo exhibition about New Guinea." Cosima's voice had a sharp edge to it. "Actually you promised to stay home tonight and take care of Sophia. When you didn't show up and your phone was off, Lorenz picked her up."

Bodenstein had to admit that he had indeed promised Cosima to come home early. He'd forgotten, and that annoyed him even more.

"Her diaper's dirty," he said, holding the child a bit away from him. "And the dog pooped in the house. You could have at least let him out before you left. And would it be too much to ask that you do some grocery shopping so I could find something to eat in the fridge after a long day at work?"

Cosima didn't answer. Instead she gave him a look from under raised eyebrows that really sent him into a fury, because it made him feel both irresponsible and rotten. She took the crying baby from him and went upstairs to change her and put her to bed. Bodenstein stood in the kitchen undecided. Deep inside a battle was raging between pride and common sense, and at last the latter won out. With a sigh he took a vase from the cupboard, filled it with water, and put the flowers in it. From the pantry he got out a bucket and a roll of paper towels and set about cleaning up the dog's deposits in the hall. The last thing he wanted was a fight with Cosima.

"Hello, Tobias." Claudius Terlinden gave him a friendly smile. He got up from his chair and held out his hand. "Great to see you back home."

Tobias briefly grasped the proffered hand but said nothing. The father of his former best friend Lars had visited him several times in prison and assured him that he would help his parents. Tobias was never able to explain the motives for his friendliness, because at the time of the investigation he had caused Terlinden considerable trouble. The man seemed not to have held it against him; on the contrary, he had immediately engaged one of the best criminal lawyers in Frankfurt to defend Tobias. But even he was unable to forestall the maximum sentence.

"I don't want to bother you two for long, I just came to make you an offer," said Claudius Terlinden, sitting back down on the kitchen chair. He had changed hardly at all in the intervening years. Slim and suntanned even now in November, with his slightly graying hair combed back, although his formerly sharply chiseled features had turned a bit puffy. "Once you've settled down here, if you can't find a job, you could come work for me. What do you say to that?"

He gazed expectantly at Tobias over the rims of his reading glasses. He was not an impressive man in terms of either physical size or good looks, but he did radiate the calm self-confidence of a successful entrepreneur. He also possessed an innate authority, which made other people behave courteously, even obsequiously, in his presence. Tobias did not sit down but remained leaning on the door frame with his arms crossed. Not that he could see many alternatives to Terlinden's offer, but something about it made Tobias suspicious. In his expensive suit, his dark cashmere coat, and with his shoes polished to a high sheen, Claudius Terlinden was like a foreign presence in the shabby kitchen. Tobias felt a growing sense of powerlessness. He didn't want to become indebted to this man. His eyes shifted to his father, who sat there with his shoulders hunched, mutely staring at his clasped hands like a devoted serf before the lord of the manor. This image did not please Tobias in the least. His father shouldn't have to bow to anyone, especially not Claudius Terlinden. Half the village felt indebted to him because of his smug generosity, since no one was ever able to reciprocate. But Terlinden had always held the advantage. Almost all the young people from Altenhain had worked for him at one time or profited from his help in some way. In return Terlinden expected only gratitude. Since half the people in Altenhain were employed by him anyway, he enjoyed a godlike status in this one-horse town. The silence turned awkward.

"Well, then." Terlinden stood up, and Hartmut Sartorius instantly jumped to his feet. "You know where to find me. Let me know what you decide."

Tobias merely nodded and watched him leave. He stayed in the kitchen as his father showed their guest to the door.

When his father returned two minutes later, he said, "He means well."

"I don't want to be dependent on his benevolence," Tobias replied fiercely. "The way he walks in here, like . . . like a king bestowing the favor of his presence on his subjects. As if he's better than us!"

Sartorius sighed. He filled the kettle and put it on the stove.

"He's helped us a lot," he said softly. "We had never saved up anything, always put it into the farm and the restaurant. The lawyer cost a lot of money, and then people stopped coming here to eat. Eventually I couldn't make the mortgage payments to the bank. They threatened to foreclose on the property. Claudius took care of our debts to the bank."

Tobias stared at his father in disbelief.

"You mean, the whole farm actually belongs . . . to *him*?"

"Strictly speaking, yes. But we have a contract. I can buy back the farm at any time and have the right to live here until I die."

Tobias needed to digest this news. He declined the tea that his father offered him.

"How much do you owe him?"

Hartmut Sartorius hesitated a moment. He knew his son's fiery temper well. "Three hundred and fifty thousand euros. That's how much I owe the bank."

"The land alone is worth at least twice that!" said Tobias, making an effort to control himself. "He exploited your situation and got an unbelievable bargain."

"Beggars can't be choosers." Hartmut Sartorius shrugged. "There was no alternative. Otherwise the bank would have auctioned off the farm, and we would have been out on the street."

Something suddenly occurred to Tobias. "What about the Schilling land?" he asked.

His father looked away, staring at the teapot.

"Dad!"

"Good Lord." Hartmut Sartorius looked up. "It was just a meadow!"

Tobias was beginning to understand. The pieces were snapping into place in his mind. His father had sold the Schilling land to Claudius Terlinden, and that's why Mother had left him! It was not merely a meadow, but the dowry that she had brought into the marriage. The Schilling land had been an apple orchard with little true value. But after the change in the land-use plan in 1992 it had become probably the most valuable piece of land in the Altenhain district, because it comprised almost fifteen-hundred square meters in the very center of the planned industrial park. Terlinden had had his eye on the property for years.

"How much did he pay you for it?" asked Tobias in a low voice.

"Ten thousand euros," his father admitted, hanging his head. A lot that big in the middle of the industrial park was worth fifty times that amount. "Claudius needed it urgently, for his new construction project. After everything he'd done for us, I couldn't refuse. I had to let him have it."

Tobias's jaw tightened as he clenched his fists in helpless fury. He couldn't reproach his father, because he was the one to blame for the regrettable situation into which his parents had fallen. He suddenly had the feeling that he might suffocate in this house, in this damned village. Still he would stay—for as long as it took him to find out what had really happened eleven years ago.

Amelie left the Black Horse shortly before eleven, going out the back way through the kitchen. She would have liked to stay longer tonight so she could hear more about the topic of the day. But Jenny Jagielski strictly adhered to the labor regulations for minors, since Amelie was only seventeen and she didn't want to risk any hassle with the authorities. Amelie didn't care; she was happy to have the waitress job and earn her own keep. Her father had turned out to be a skinflint, just as her mother had always described him, and denied her the money to buy a new laptop. He told her that the old one was good enough.

The first three months in this miserable village had been dreadful. But now that the end of her involuntary sojourn in Altenhain was in sight, she had decided to make the best of the next five months until her eighteenth birthday. By April 21, 2009, she would be on the first train back to Berlin anyway. Then nobody could stop her.

Amelie lit a cigarette and looked around in the dark for Thies, who waited for her every night to walk her home. Their close friendship was like raw meat for the village gossips. The wildest rumors made the rounds, but Amelie couldn't care less. At the age of thirty Thies Terlinden still lived with his parents, because he wasn't quite right in the head, as people in the village surreptitiously whispered. Amelie shouldered her knapsack and headed off. Thies was standing under the streetlight by the church, his hands thrust deep in his jacket pockets, his gaze fixed on the ground, but he fell in beside her as she passed.

"What a commotion there was tonight," said Amelie. Then she told Thies about what had happened at the Black Horse and what she had learned about Tobias Sartorius. She had gotten used to almost never getting an answer out of Thies. People said he was stupid and couldn't talk; they called him the village idiot. But that wasn't true. Thies wasn't stupid at all, he was just . . . different. Amelie was different too. Her father didn't like the fact that she spent time with Thies, but there was nothing he could do about it. With cynical amusement, Amelie sometimes thought that her bourgeois father probably bitterly regretted having rescued his wacky daughter from his brief first marriage. He'd only done it at her stepmother Barbara's insistence. In Amelie's eyes her father was nothing more than a gray, shapeless blob with no corners, edges, or spine, a man who cautiously proceeded through his humdrum bookkeeper life, always at pains not to rock the boat. It had to be sheer horror for him to have an ex-con seventeen-year-old daughter with behavioral problems, whose face was decorated with half a pound of metal, and who wore only black clothes. As far as her hair and makeup were concerned, she could have been the model for Bill Kaulitz from the band Tokio Hotel.

Arne Fröhlich undoubtedly had excellent reasons for objecting to

Amelie's friendship with Thies, although he had never issued an ultimatum. Not that it would have done any good. Amelie had spent her whole life disregarding other people's opinions. She thought the real reason her father tacitly tolerated their friendship was that Thies was the son of his boss. She flicked her cigarette butt into a storm drain and continued thinking out loud about Manfred Wagner, Tobias Sartorius, and the dead girl.

Instead of walking down the well-lighted main street she had turned into the narrow, gloomy lane that led from the church through the village, past the cemetery and the back yards of the houses all the way to the edge of the woods. After walking for ten minutes she and Thies reached Waldstrasse, where only three houses stood a bit above the rest of the village on large plots of land. In the middle was the house where Amelie lived with her father, her stepmother, and her two younger half siblings; to the right of it stood the Lauterbachs' bungalow; and a bit off to the left, surrounded by parklike grounds, was the big old villa belonging to the Terlinden family, right at the edge of the forest. Only a few yards from the wrought-iron gate of the Terlindens' estate was the rear entrance to the Sartorius farm, which stretched all the way down the hill to the main road. In the old days it had been a real farm, with cows and pigs. Today the whole place was one big pigsty, as Amelie's father was fond of saying disparagingly. An eyesore.

Amelie stopped at the foot of the steps. Usually she and Thies parted here, and he would then keep walking without saying a word. But today he broke his silence when Amelie was about to go up the stairs.

"This is where the Schneebergers used to live," he said in his monotone voice. Amelie turned around in astonishment. For the first time this evening she looked directly at her friend, but as usual he averted his eyes.

"Really?" she asked in disbelief. "One of the girls that Tobias Sartorius killed lived in *our* house?"

Thies nodded without looking at her.

"Yes. This is where Snow White lived."

Friday, November 7, 2008

Tobias opened his eyes and for a moment felt utterly bewildered. Instead of the whitewashed ceiling of his cell, he saw Pamela Anderson beaming at him from a poster. Only then did he realize that he was no longer in the slammer, but in his old room in his parents' house. Without moving, he lay there listening to the sounds coming through the window that was open a crack. The church bell tolled six times, announcing the early hour; somewhere a dog barked, another joined in, then both fell silent. The room was unchanged: the desk and the bookcase of cheap veneer, the wardrobe with the crooked door. The posters of the Eintracht Frankfurt soccer team, Pamela Anderson, and the Williams-Renault with Damon Hill, who had won the 1996 Formula 1 world championship. The little stereo that his parents had given him in March 1997. The red couch where . . .

Tobias sat up and shook his head. In prison he had kept his thoughts under better control. Now the agonizing memories caught up with him: What would have happened if Stefanie hadn't broken up with him that night? Would she still be alive today? He knew what he had done. They had explained it to him a hundred times, after all—first the police, then his lawyer, the prosecutor, and the judge. The findings had been conclusive. There was circumstantial evidence, there were witnesses, there was the blood in his room, on his clothes, in his car. And yet two full hours had vanished from his memory. To this day it was nothing but a black hole.

He remembered quite clearly the sixth of September 1997. The planned parade at the village fair had been canceled as a sign of respect, because in London late that morning Princess Diana had been laid to rest. Half the world had been glued to their TV sets as the coffin with England's mortally wounded rose was conveyed through the streets of Britain's capital. Still, in Altenhain they hadn't wanted to cancel the whole village fair. It would have been better if everyone had stayed home that evening.

Tobias sighed and turned over on his side. It was so quiet that he could hear his heart beating. For a moment he succumbed to the illusion that he was twenty years old again and nothing had happened. His place at the university was waiting for him in Munich. With his top grades he had been admitted easily. Now painful memories began merging with happier times. The boisterous graduation party was held in the back yard of the home of a friend from his class in Schneidhain. There he had kissed Stefanie for the first time. Laura had almost burst in fury and before his eyes had thrown herself at Lars to make him jealous. But how could he think about Laura when he was holding Stefanie in his arms? She was the first girl he had actually made an effort to pursue; usually girls ran after him in droves, to the great annoyance of his pals. For weeks he had wooed Stefanie until she finally gave in.

The next four weeks had been the happiest in his life—until the disillusionment of September sixth. Stefanie had been chosen Queen of the Fair, a silly title that had been Laura's for years. But this time Stefanie had won instead. Tobias had been working with Nathalie and a few others at the bar inside the big tent, and he had watched as Stefanie flirted with other guys until she suddenly disappeared. Maybe he had already drunk more than was good for him. Nathalie had noticed how much he was suffering and told him, "Go and look for her." He had dashed out of the tent, but he didn't have to search for long. When he found her, jealousy had exploded like a bomb inside him. How could she do this to him? Making a fool of him right in front of everyone? All because of a stupid leading role in an even stupider play?

At this point Tobias threw off the covers and jumped out of bed. He had to do something—work or find some other way to distract his mind from these tormenting memories.

Amelie was walking with her head down through the fine drizzle. As she did every morning, she had turned down her stepmother's offer to drive her to the bus stop, but now she had to hurry if she didn't want to miss the school bus. November was showing its most unpleasant side, with fog and rain, but Amelie didn't really mind the dismal dreariness of the month. She liked her solitary walk through the sleeping village. In the earbuds of her iPod the music of the Schattenkinder roared loud enough to shred her eardrums; they were one of her favorite Dark Wave groups. She had lain awake half the night thinking about Tobias Sartorius and the murdered girls. At the time Laura Wagner and Stefanie Schneeberger had been seventeen years old, the same age she was now. And she lived in the same house where one of the victims purportedly had lived. She absolutely had to find out more about the girl that Thies had called Snow White. What had happened in Altenhain back then?

A car came to a stop next to Amelie. Probably her stepmother, who could practically drive her mad with her enervating kindness. But then Amelie recognized Claudius Terlinden, her father's boss. He had rolled down the window on the passenger side and was motioning for her to come closer. She turned off the music.

"Would you like a ride?" he asked. "You're getting soaked."

The rain really didn't bother Amelie, but she had no objection to riding with Terlinden. She liked the big black Mercedes with the light-colored leather seats; it smelled brand new, and she was fascinated by the technological advancements that Claudius Terlinden was only too happy to demonstrate for her. She inexplicably liked her neighbor, although with his expensive suits, big cars, and ostentatious villa he was actually the prototype of the decadent moneybags that she and her pals back home in Berlin had hated with all their hearts. But there was something else. Lately Amelie had been asking herself whether she was entirely normal, because every time any male was somewhat friendly, her thoughts would immediately turn to sex. How would Mr. Terlinden react, she wondered, if she put her hand on his thigh and made him an unambiguous offer? Just thinking about it made a hysterical giggle rise inside her and she had to make an effort to subdue it.

"Well, come on then!" he called, motioning her to get in. "Climb in."

Amelie stuffed her earbuds in her jacket pocket, opened the door, and dropped into the passenger seat. The heavy door of the luxury car closed with a satisfying thunk. Terlinden headed off down Waldstrasse and smiled at Amelie.

"What's eating you?" he asked. "You look like you're brooding about something."

Amelie hesitated a moment, then said, "Can I ask you a question?"

"Of course. Shoot."

"Those two girls who disappeared. Did you know them?"

Terlinden cast a quick glance at her. He wasn't smiling anymore. "Why do you want to know that?"

"I'm just curious. There's been so much talk since that man came back. I think it's kind of exciting."

"Hmm. It was a sad story back then. And it still is," he said. "Naturally I knew both of the girls. Stefanie was our neighbors' daughter. And I had known Laura since she was a kid. It's just horrible for the parents that the girls were never found."

"Hmm," Amelie said pensively. "Did they have nicknames?"

"Who do you mean?" Terlinden seemed astonished by this question.

"Stefanie and Laura."

"I don't know. Why . . . oh yeah, Stefanie did. The other kids called her Snow White."

"Why is that?"

"Maybe because of her last name. Schneeberger." Terlinden frowned and slowed down. The school bus was already at the bus stop with its blinkers on, waiting for the few pupils who were going to Königstein.

"No, that's not right," Terlinden said, remembering now. "I think it had something to do with a play that was going to be put on at the school. Stefanie had been given the leading role. She was supposed to play Snow White."

"Supposed to?" Amelie asked. "Didn't she play the part?"

"No. Before that she . . . um . . . she disappeared."

The bread slices popped up from the toaster with a clack. Pia spread salted butter on both pieces, then a good layer of Nutella, and slapped the two halves together. She was virtually addicted to this unconventional combination of salty and sweet, and she enjoyed every bite, licking the melted butter and Nutella mixture off her fingers before it dripped onto the newspaper lying open before her. Yesterday's discovery of a skeleton at the site of the old airfield was mentioned in a five-line filler, while the *Frankfurter Neue Presse* devoted four columns in their local section to the eleventh day of the trial of Vera Kaltensee. Today at nine Pia had to go before the district court and make her statement about the incidents in Poland last summer.

Her thoughts wandered involuntarily to Henning. Yesterday the one cup of coffee they were going to have together had become three. He had talked to her more openly than he ever had during their sixteen years of marriage, but Pia had no advice on how to solve his current dilemma. Since the episode in Poland he had been together with Pia's best friend Miriam Horowitz. Yet he had let himself be enticed—under circumstances he didn't explain, to Pia's regret—into climbing into bed with his ardent admirer, the prosecutor Valerie Löblich. Definitely a slipup, as Henning had insisted, but with dire consequences, because the Löblich woman was now pregnant. He was overwhelmed by the situation and toyed with the idea of fleeing to the United States. For years the University of Tennessee had been tempting him with the offer of a very lucrative position of great interest to a physician. As Pia pondered Henning's problems and at the same time contemplated whether she should follow the first caloric overload with a second helping, Christoph emerged from the bathroom and sat down at the kitchen table across from her. His hair was still damp, and he smelled of aftershave.

"Do you think you could manage to come tonight?" he asked, pouring himself a cup of coffee. "Annika would love to see you."

"If nothing comes up, it should be no problem." Pia gave in to temptation and made herself another piece of toast. "I have to give a statement in court around nine, but otherwise we don't have anything urgent."

Christoph grinned in amusement at the Nutella and butter combination and bit into his sensible and healthy black bread with cottage cheese. The mere sight of him still caused a warm tingle in Pia's belly. Those dark-brown caramel-candy eyes of his had captivated her on their first encounter and had never lost their attraction. Christoph Sander was an impressive man who felt no need to flaunt his strong points. Although he didn't possess the uncompromising good looks of Pia's boss, his features had something remarkable about them that made people take another look. Above all it was his smile, which started in his eyes and then spread across his whole face, that always triggered in Pia the almost irrepressible desire to throw herself into his arms.

She and Christoph had met two years earlier, when the investigation of a murder case had taken Pia to the Opel Zoo in Kronberg. Christoph, the director of the zoo, had fallen for her on the spot—the first man for whom she'd felt any attraction since breaking up with Henning. The feeling had been mutual. Unfortunately Oliver von Bodenstein had considered Christoph a prime suspect for quite a while. After the case was finally solved and Christoph absolved of all suspicion, their relationship had developed rapidly. From passionate infatuation love had eventually evolved, and they had been a couple for a good two years now. They had kept their separate residences, of course, but that was going to change soon because Christoph's three daughters, whom he had raised by himself after the sudden death of his wife seventeen years ago, were about to leave the nest. Andrea, the eldest, had been working in Hamburg since the spring; Antonia, the youngest, was more or less living with her boyfriend, Lukas; and now Annika wanted to move in with her child's father in Australia. Tonight was her farewell party at their father's house, and tomorrow she would leave for Sydney.

Pia knew that Christoph was anything but happy about this. He didn't trust Jared, the young man who had gotten Annika pregnant four years ago. In his defense, however, Annika hadn't told him she was pregnant and instead had broken up with him. But in the long run everything had worked out. In the meantime Jared Gordon had earned a doctorate in marine biology and was working at a research station on an island in the Great Barrier Reef. So he was something of a professional colleague, and Christoph had given his daughter and her boyfriend his blessing, although reluctantly.

Since it was out of the question for Pia to give up Birkenhof, Christoph had rented out his house in Bad Soden as of January first. Annika's farewell party this evening was also Christoph's farewell to the house where he had lived for many years. His bags were already packed, and the movers would be coming for the furniture next Monday. Until the Frankfurt zoning department gave the green light for the planned remodeling and expansion of Pia's little house, the larger pieces of furniture had to be put in storage temporarily. Yes, Pia was quite happy with the latest developments in her personal life.

Tobias had raised all the window shades and inspected the dismal state of the interior of the house by daylight. His father had gone out shopping, so he had started by cleaning the windows. Just as he was doing the window in the dining room, his father returned and walked past him, head down, into the kitchen. Tobias climbed down from the stepladder and followed him.

"What happened?" His gaze fell on the empty shopping basket.

"They wouldn't wait on me," Hartmut Sartorius replied softly. "It's not that bad. I'll go over to the supermarket in Bad Soden."

"But you shopped at Richter's yesterday, didn't you?" Tobias asked. His father gave a feeble nod. Instantly making up his mind, Tobias took his jacket from the wardrobe, grabbed the basket with his father's wallet in it, and left the house. He was shaking with anger. The Richters used to be good friends with his parents, but today the scrawny old crone had thrown his father out of the store. He wasn't going to put up with that.

As Tobias was about to cross the street, out of the corner of his eye he noticed something red on the façade of his father's former restaurant and turned around. Someone had scrawled HERE LIVES A RUTHLESS KILLER in red spray paint on the wall of the building. For a few seconds Tobias stared mutely at the ugly graffiti, which had to be evident to every passerby. His heart was hammering against his ribcage, and the knot in his stomach clenched even tighter. Those bastards! What was the point of this? Were they trying to drive him out of his parents' house? What were they going to do next, set it on fire? He counted to ten, then turned around and walked straight across the street to the Richters' grocery store.

The assembled gossip mafia had seen him coming through the big plate-glass windows. When the bell on the door jingled they were all standing there as if in some tableau: Margot Richter standing like a queen behind the cash register, wiry and malevolent, with her spine ramrod straight, as always. Her burly husband had planted himself behind her, taking cover rather than exuding any sort of menace. With one glance Tobias took the measure of each of the other people present. He knew them all, the mothers of his childhood friends. In front stood Inge Dombrowski, the hairdresser and uncrowned queen of slanderous innuendo. Behind her Gerda Pietsch with her bulldog face, twice as fat as she used to be, and probably with a tongue twice as spiteful. Next to her Nadia's mother Agnes Unger, careworn and now gray-haired. Unbelievable that she could have produced such a beautiful daughter.

"Good morning," he said. An icy silence confronted him. But they didn't try to stop him from approaching the shelves. The refrigerator motors were humming loudly in the tense silence. Tobias loaded everything into his basket that his father had jotted down on his shopping list. When he neared the checkout counter, everyone was still standing as if frozen in place. Showing no sign of emotion, Tobias set all the goods on the conveyor belt, but Margot Richter had her arms crossed over her chest and made no move to begin the checkout process. The bell on the door jingled again, and a delivery driver who had no idea what was going on came in. He noticed the tense mood and stopped in his tracks. Tobias didn't budge an inch. It was a test of will, not only between him and Margot Richter, but between him and all of Altenhain.

"Let him pay." Lutz Richter relented after a couple of minutes. Her teeth clenched, his wife obeyed and mutely punched Tobias's purchases into the cash register.

"Forty-two seventy."

Tobias gave her a fifty-euro bill, and she reluctantly handed him his change without uttering a word. The look she gave him could have frozen the Mediterranean, but it didn't bother Tobias. In the joint he had fought other power struggles and had come through the victor often enough.

"I've served my time and now I'm back." He looked around him at the embarrassed faces and downcast eyes. "Whether you like it or not."

Around eleven thirty Pia arrived at the police station in Hofheim, after giving her testimony in the trial of Vera Kaltensee in the Frankfurt district court. For the past few weeks no one had felt the desire to depart this life in a dubious manner, so there was relatively little to do at K-11, the police crime division. The skeleton from the underground tank at the airfield in Eschborn was the only current case. The results from the medical examiner were still not in, so Detective Inspector Kai Ostermann was going through the missing persons cases from the past year with no particular urgency. He was on his own. On Monday his colleague Frank Behnke had called in sick and would be out all week. When he fell off his bicycle he had reportedly suffered numerous facial injuries and bruises. The fact that DI Andreas Hasse was also sick surprised nobody. For years he had taken sick leave for weeks and months at a time. In K-11 they had gotten used to getting along without him, and nobody missed him. Pia ran into her youngest colleague, Kathrin Fachinger, at the coffee vending machine in the lobby, where she was having a chat with the secretary of Commissioner Nicola Engel. The days when Kathrin used to run around wearing frilly blouses and plaid pants were long gone. She had replaced her round owl glasses with a modern rectangular-style frame, and lately she'd taken to wearing skintight jeans, high-heeled boots, and a tight-fitting pullover that perfectly accentuated her enviably slim figure. Pia didn't know the reason for this change, and once again she was astounded by how little she knew about the private lives of her colleagues. In any case the youngest member on the force had clearly gained self-confidence.

"Pia! Wait up!" Kathrin called, and Pia stopped.

"What's up?"

Kathrin glanced conspiratorially around the lobby.

"Last night I was in Sachsenhausen with a few friends," she said in a low voice. "You won't believe who I saw over there."

"Not Johnny Depp?" Pia teased her. Everyone in K-11 knew that Kathrin was a big fan.

"No, I saw Frank," she went on, unfazed. "He's working as a bartender at the Klapperkahn restaurant, and he's not sick at all."

"You're kidding!"

"And now I don't know what to do. I should really tell the boss, don't you think?"

Pia frowned. If a police officer wanted to take a job on the side, he had to submit an application and wait for authorization. A job in a bar with a less than stellar reputation was definitely not something that would receive approval. If Kathrin was right, then Behnke risked a reprimand, a fine, or even disciplinary action.

"Maybe he was just filling in for one of his pals." Pia wasn't particularly fond of her colleague Frank Behnke, but she didn't feel good about the consequences that might result from an official condemnation.

"No, he wasn't," said Kathrin with a shake of her head. "He spotted me and went right for my jugular. He accused me of spying on him. What a load of crap! And then the asshole had the nerve to say I'd be in big trouble if I reported him."

Understandably, Kathrin was both deeply upset and furious. Pia didn't doubt her account for a second. That sounded just like her colleague. Behnke was about as diplomatic as a pit bull.

"Did you say anything to Schneider yet?" Pia quizzed her.

"No," Kathrin said, shaking her head. "Although I really wanted to. I'm so pissed off."

"That's understandable. Frank has a real talent for getting someone's goat. Let me talk to the boss. Maybe we can resolve this matter discreetly."

"Why bother?" Kathrin replied, infuriated. "Why does everyone stick up for that shithead? He always gets away with everything, venting his foul mood on the rest of us, and never having to pay for it."

She was saying exactly what Pia felt. For some reason Frank Behnke possessed a fool's license to do whatever he wanted. At that moment Bodenstein, their boss, entered the lobby.

Pia looked at Kathrin. "Make sure you know what you're doing," she said.

"I do," replied Kathrin, walking determinedly over to Bodenstein. "I need to have a short talk with you, boss. In private."

Amelie had decided that research into the girls' murders in Altenhain clearly took priority over school, so after third period she told the teacher she was sick. Now she was sitting at her desk at home in front of her laptop, entering the name of her neighbor's son in Google. She got literally hundreds of hits. With increasing fascination she read the press accounts of events in the summer of 1997 and the course of the trial, at which Tobias Sartorius had been sentenced to ten years in prison. The prosecution's case had been completely based on circumstantial evidence because the girls' bodies were never found. That fact had been considered particularly damning, and Tobias's silence had had a deleterious effect on the severity of the sentence.

Amelie looked at the photos, which showed a dark-haired youth with still unfinished facial features, giving a hint of the man he would someday become. Today Tobias Sartorius must be pretty good-looking. In the photos he was wearing handcuffs, but he didn't cover his face under a jacket or behind a file folder. He looked straight into the cameras. They had called him an "ice-cold killer," arrogant, emotionless, and cruel.

> The parents of the murdered girls are appearing as joint plaintiffs in the trial of Tobias S., the son of an innkeeper from the small village in the lower Taunus region. However, the desperate pleas of the mothers, Andrea W. and Beate S., left the A student unmoved. When asked what he had done with the bodies of the two girls, S. remained silent. In a psychological report his intelligence was certified as being above average. Tactics or arrogance? Even when Judge S. made the offer to change the charge of first-degree murder in the death of Stefanie S. to manslaughter, the young man remained steadfastly silent. The utter lack of empathy astounded even experienced legal observers. The district attorney's office has no doubt of his guilt, since there were no gaps in the chain of circumstantial evidence and the reconstruction of the sequence of events. It is true that S. earlier attempted to prove his innocence through numerous slanderous statements regarding other alleged memory lapses, but the court was not swayed. Tobias S. received the pronouncement of sentence with no external show of emotion, and the court refused to consider an appeal.

Amelie scanned other similar reports of the trial until she at last found an article that dealt with the preceding events. Laura Wagner and Stefanie Schneeberger had disappeared without a trace on the night of September 6, 1997. The annual fair was going on in Altenhain, and the whole village was in attendance. Tobias Sartorius quickly became the prime suspect in the investigation because neighbors had seen the two girls enter his parents' house that evening but never come out. Tobias and his former girlfriend Laura Wagner had carried on a serious and violent argument at the front door. They had both consumed a large quantity of alcohol at the fair. A little later Stefanie Schneeberger, Tobias's current girlfriend, had arrived. He stated later that she had broken up with him that evening, and in despair he had drunk almost a whole bottle of vodka in his room. The next day, police dogs had discovered traces of blood on the Sartorius property; the trunk of Tobias's car had been found to be stained with blood; and blood and skin scrapings that were traceable to the two girls were found on his clothing and in his house. Witnesses said they had seen Tobias driving his car later that night as he headed down the main street. Finally, Stefanie Schneeberger's backpack had been stowed in his room, and he had put Laura Wagner's necklace in the milk room under a washbasin.

A love triangle was presumed to have triggered the events: Tobias had left Laura for Stefanie, then Stefanie had broken up with him. All of which resulted in the bloody deeds. The overconsumption of alcohol could have acted as a catalyst on Tobias. Up to the last day of the trial he had denied having anything to do with the girls' disappearance, but the court had refused to accept his alleged memory lapses, nor had any witnesses turned up to give him an alibi. On the contrary. His friends had stated to the court that Tobias was a hothead with a violent temper, used to having girls worship him. It was possible that out of frustration he had overreacted to being dumped by Stefanie. He was left without a hope in the world.

That only served to further ignite Amelie's curiosity, since she hated nothing more than injustice, after being so often the victim of unfair accusations. She could understand how Tobias must have felt if his protestations of innocence were actually true. She was going to conduct more inquiries into the matter—although she didn't know exactly how. First she had to get to know Tobias Sartorius.

Twenty past five. He had to hang out here on the train platform for another half hour before the other guys showed up; maybe they would take him along to the youth center for rehearsals. Nico Bender had made a point of skipping soccer practice so he wouldn't miss the S-Bahn from Schwalbach at five to six. Although he was crazy about playing soccer, the guys and their band were much more important. They used to be friends, but since his parents had forced him to go to school in Königstein instead of Schwalbach, he didn't really belong anymore. He was way cooler than Mark or Kevin, because he could play really good drums. Nico sighed and looked at the bearded man in the baseball cap who had been standing motionless at the other end of the platform for half an hour. In spite of the rain the man hadn't come to join him in the covered waiting area. He didn't seem to care if he got wet.

The S-Bahn from Frankfurt arrived. Eight cars on the commuter train. Would he be able to see the guys from where he stood? If they were in the first car, he might miss them. The doors slid open and people got out, putting up umbrellas and running with their heads down to the pedestrian bridge or past him to the underpass. His pals weren't on the train. Nico stood up and walked slowly along the platform. Then he saw the man in the baseball cap again. He followed a woman in the direction of the bridge and spoke to her. She stopped but then seemed to be frightened, because she dropped her shopping bag and ran off. The man sprinted after her and grabbed her by the arm. She flailed at him with her other arm. Nico stood there as if mesmerized. It was like something out of a movie! The platform was empty again, the doors of the train slid shut, and the S-Bahn pulled out of the station. Then he saw the man and woman up on the pedestrian bridge. It looked like they were going to fight. All of a sudden the woman disappeared. Nico heard brakes squeal, then a thud, followed by the crash of metal and a splintering sound. The endless row of bright headlights on the other side of the tracks came to a stop. Stunned, Nico realized that he had just witnessed a crime. The man had pushed the woman over the railing of the bridge and onto the heavily trafficked Limesspange expressway! And now he was running right at Nico, head down, the woman's purse in his hand. Nico's heart was in his throat; he was terrified. If the guy knew that he'd been watching him, he wasn't going to mess around. In panic Nico took off. Like a rabbit he raced into the underpass, running as fast as he could until he reached his bicycle, which he had left on the Bad Soden side of the tracks. He didn't care about the guys in the band now, or the youth center. He jumped onto his bike and stomped on the pedals, puffing, panting as the man came up the stairs to the street and yelled something after him. Nico risked a glance over his shoulder and saw with relief that the guy wasn't following him. Then he raced at top speed along the forested area of the Eichwald until he was safe at home.

The intersection at the Sulzbach North S-Bahn station was a picture of devastation. There had been a seven-car collision, and firemen were trying to extricate people from the twisted mass of metal using acetylene torches and heavy equipment and strewing sand in the pools of spilled gasoline. Several ambulances were lined up to take care of the injured. Despite the cold and the rain, rubberneckers had gathered behind the police cordon, watching the horrendous spectacle with ghoulish fascination. Bodenstein and Kirchhoff made their way through the uniforms over to Chief Detective Superintendent Hendrik Koch from the Eschborn district, who was one of the first on the scene of the accident.

"I've seen a lot of accidents in my day, but this is one of the worst." Horror was written all over the face of the experienced police officer. He explained the situation to Bodenstein and Kirchhoff. A woman had fallen from the pedestrian bridge at 5:26 P.M., landing on the windshield of a BMW coming from the direction of Schwalbach. Without braking, the driver pulled sharply to the left and sped into the opposite lanes head-on. Multiple collisions on both sides of the highway had resulted. One driver, who had stopped at the red light in Sulzbach, said he had seen someone push the woman over the railing onto the road below.

"What happened to the woman?" Kirchhoff asked.

"She's alive," replied Superintendent Koch and added, "for the time being. The EMT is working on her over there in one of the ambulances."

"We got a report of one death."

"The driver of the BMW suffered a fatal heart attack. Probably from fright. Attempts to resuscitate him failed." Koch nodded toward the middle of the intersection. A body lay next to the completely demolished BMW. A pair of shoes stuck out from under a rain-spattered blanket. Over by the police cordon there was a sudden commotion. Two policemen were restraining a gray-haired woman who was trying to force her way inside the blocked-off area. Koch's radio crackled and a voice squawked.

"That's probably the wife of the BMW driver," he said to the detectives in a tense voice. "Excuse me."

He said something into his radio and set off across the battlefield. Pia didn't envy him the task before him. Informing loved ones of someone's death was one of the hardest parts of their job, and neither psychological training nor years of experience made it any easier.

"Don't worry about the woman," Bodenstein said. "I'll go talk to the witness."

Pia nodded and went over to the ambulance where the seriously injured were being treated. The rear door opened and the EMT stepped out. Pia recognized him from previous accident scenes.

"Ah, Ms. Kirchhoff," he greeted her. "We've stabilized her and will be taking her to the hospital in Bad Soden. Several broken bones, facial lacerations, and probably some internal injuries. You can't talk to her."

"Was she able to tell you who she is?"

"She had a car key in her—" The medic stopped and took a step back as the ambulance began to move off, the siren making all conversation impossible. Pia spoke with him a bit more, then thanked him and went over to her colleague. In the jacket pocket of the injured woman they had found only the car key, nothing else. The woman, who was about fifty, had not been carrying a purse. A search of the bridge and train platform turned up only a bag of groceries. In the meantime Bodenstein had spoken to the driver who witnessed the woman's fall from the bridge. He swore up and down that somebody had pushed the woman—a man, he was sure of that despite the darkness and the rain.

Bodenstein and Kirchhoff went up the stairs to the bridge.

"This is where she fell from." Pia looked at the spot marked on the bridge. "How high is it, do you think?"

"Hmm," Bodenstein said, looking over the railing, which came up to about his hip. "Fifteen or twenty feet, I'd say. I can hardly believe she survived the fall. The car she hit was going pretty fast."

From up there the view was almost surreal: the wrecked cars, the blue and orange flashing lights, the rescue crew wearing reflective vests. Rain was blowing obliquely through the light cast by the floodlights. What must have gone through that woman's mind as she lost her balance and knew that nothing could save her? Or did it happen so fast that she had no time to think at all?

"She had a guardian angel," Pia said with a shudder. "I hope he doesn't leave her in the lurch now."

She turned and headed over to the train platform, followed by Bodenstein.

Who was this woman? Where was she coming from and where was she headed? One moment she was sitting in the train, unsuspecting, and a few minutes later she was lying with shattered bones in an ambulance. That's how fast it could happen. One false step, one wrong move with the wrong person—and nothing would ever be the same. What had the man wanted from her? Was he a robber? It almost looked that way; Bodenstein found it odd that she hadn't been carrying a purse.

"Every woman carries a purse," he said to Pia. "She had just gone shopping, so she needed money, a wallet or something."

"Do you really think that the man was trying to rob her on a crowded train platform at five thirty in the afternoon?" Pia scanned up and down the tracks.

"Maybe it was a crime of opportunity. In this weather everyone would want to get home fast. Maybe he followed her on the S-Bahn because he saw her taking money out of an ATM."

"Hmm." Pia pointed to the camera monitoring the platform. "Let's take a look at the surveillance video. With a little luck the lens may have been wide-angle enough for us to see the bridge."

Bodenstein nodded pensively. Would two families have to deal with bad news tonight just because some stranger tried to snatch a woman's purse? Not that it would have changed anything about the tragic occurrence, yet to Bodenstein it seemed appalling that death and mutilation should result from such a random and ridiculous act. Two officers emerged from the underpass. They had found a red Honda Civic in the parking lot next to the rail embankment, and the key from the woman's pocket fit. When they ran the plates they discovered that the owner lived in Neuenhain. Her name was Rita Cramer.

Bodenstein steered his BMW easily into a parking space in front of the ugly high-rise in the Neuenhain district of Bad Soden. Kirchhoff had to search for a while to find Rita Cramer's name among the fifty listed next to the entrance intercom. She pressed the button, but no one answered. So Pia rang other residents until someone finally buzzed her in. The building, despite its ugly outward appearance, was very well maintained inside. On the fifth floor

Bodenstein and Kirchhoff were met by an elderly woman who perused their IDs with a mixture of suspicion and curiosity. Pia glanced impatiently at her watch. Almost nine! She had promised Christoph that she would come to Annika's party, and it was anybody's guess how long all this would take. She was actually supposed to have the evening off. She silently cursed Hasse and Behnke for calling in sick.

The neighbor knew Rita Cramer and had a key to her apartment, which she got out without any fuss after the detectives had identified themselves and told her about the accident. Unfortunately the neighbor didn't know whether Cramer had any relatives. She never had visitors, at any rate.

The apartment was certainly depressing. Spotlessly clean and recently tidied up, but only sparsely furnished. Nowhere was there any indication of Rita Cramer's personality, no photos of loved ones, and the walls were decorated with pictures that you could buy for a couple of euros in home remodeling stores. Bodenstein and Kirchhoff went through the apartment, opening cabinet doors and drawers in the hope of finding a relative's name or some reason for the assault. Nothing.

"As anonymous as a hotel room," was Bodenstein's assessment. "There's not a thing to go on."

Pia went into the kitchen. Her eyes fell on the blinking answering machine. She pressed the REWIND button. Unfortunately the caller had not left a message on the tape but simply hung up. Pia jotted down the number displayed on the phone. A prefix in Königstein. She took out her cell phone and punched in the number. After the third ring an answering machine picked up.

"A doctor's office," she said. "They're closed."

"Are there any other messages?" Bodenstein asked. Kirchhoff pressed REWIND again, then shook her head.

"Odd that somebody can live like this." She replaced the phone and looked through the kitchen calendar, which was still showing the month of May. There was not a single thing written on it. On a corkboard hung a flyer from a pizza delivery service and the faded blue copy of a parking ticket from April. None of it signified a happy, contented life.

"Tomorrow we'll call this doctor's office," Bodenstein decided. "There's

nothing else we can do today. I'll drive by the hospital and check on Rita
Cramer's condition."

They left the apartment and returned the key to the neighbor.

"Could you drop me at Christoph's before you go to the hospital?" Pia
asked as they took the elevator down. "It's on the way."

"Oh, right, the party."

"How do you know about that?" She shoved open the glass door so vigorously that she almost struck a man in the back as he bent over to study the
name labels.

"Excuse me," she said. "I didn't see you."

Pia caught a fleeting glimpse of his face as she smiled her apology.

"No harm done," said the man, and they went on.

Bodenstein turned up the collar of his coat. "I like to be well informed
about my colleagues. But you know that."

Pia remembered her conversation with Kathrin Fachinger that morning. This seemed the ideal opportunity.

"Well, then you also must know that our colleague Behnke is doing some
moonlighting that would definitely not meet with official approval."

Oliver frowned and gave her a quick look.

"No, until this morning I wasn't aware of that," he admitted. "Were you?"

"I'm probably the last person Behnke would confide in," Pia replied with
a snort of contempt. "He always makes such a secret of his private life, as if he
were still in the Special Assignment Unit."

Oliver studied Pia in the pallid glow of the streetlight.

"He has some fairly major problems," he said. "His wife left him a year
ago. He couldn't keep up with the mortgage payments and ended up losing
the house."

Pia stopped and stared at him speechless for a moment. So that was the
reason for Behnke's behavior, for his constant irritability, his foul moods, his
aggressiveness. And yet she felt no sympathy for him, only annoyance.

"You're going to take his side again, aren't you? What is it between you
two? Why do you always make allowances for him?"

"I'm not making allowances for him," Oliver countered.

"And how come he gets to keep making mistakes and neglect his job without suffering any consequences?"

"I suppose I hoped he'd manage to straighten out his life somehow if I didn't pressure him too much." Bodenstein shrugged. "But if he really is moonlighting in an unauthorized job, then I can't do anything more for him."

"So you're going to report it to Dr. Engel?"

"I'm afraid I have to." He sighed and started walking again. "But I'll have a talk with Frank first."

Saturday, November 8, 2008

"Oh my God." Dr. Daniela Lauterbach reacted with genuine horror when Bodenstein told her how he happened to get her telephone number. She turned pale beneath her suntan. "Rita is a good friend of mine. We were neighbors until she got divorced last year."

"A witness said he saw someone push Mrs. Cramer over the railing of the pedestrian bridge," said Bodenstein. "That's why we're investigating the case as a possible attempted murder."

"That's appalling! Poor Rita! How is she doing?"

"Not well. She's in critical condition."

Dr. Lauterbach clasped her hands as if in prayer and shook her head in dismay. Bodenstein estimated that she was about his age, late forties or early fifties. She had a very feminine figure and her shiny dark hair was pulled back in a simple bun. With her warm brown eyes that were surrounded by laugh lines she radiated good humor and a motherly concern. She was obviously a doctor who took enough time for her patients and their troubles. Her extensive practice was located on the pedestrian street in Königstein above a jewelry store: big bright rooms with high ceilings and parquet floors.

"Let's step into my office," the doctor suggested. Bodenstein followed her into a very large room dominated by a massive, old-fashioned desk. On the walls were large expressionist paintings in somber colors that presented an unusual but intriguing contrast to the otherwise pleasant decor.

"May I offer you some coffee?"

"Oh yes, please," said Bodenstein with a smile and a nod. "I haven't had time for any today."

"You're certainly on the job early." Dr. Lauterbach set a cup under the automatic espresso machine sitting on a sideboard next to all sorts of medical literature and pressed a button. The coffee grinder started up, and the appetizing aroma of freshly ground coffee filled the room.

"So are you," Bodenstein replied. "And on a Saturday too."

Late the night before he had left a message on the office answering machine, and she had called back at eight thirty this morning.

"I make house calls on Saturday mornings." She handed him a cup of coffee, and he declined milk and sugar. "And then I usually try to catch up on paperwork. It just keeps piling up these days. I'd rather spend the time with my patients."

She motioned him toward her desk, and Bodenstein sat down in one of the visitors' chairs. The window behind her desk offered a wonderful view across the grounds of the nearby spa to the ruins of Königstein Castle on the hilltop.

"So, how can I help you?" Dr. Lauterbach asked after taking a sip of her coffee.

"In Mrs. Cramer's apartment we found not a single reference to any relatives," Bodenstein replied. "But there must be someone we should inform about the accident."

"Rita still has a good relationship with her ex-husband," said the doctor. "I'm sure that he would like to know." Again she shook her head in concern. "Who could have done this?" She fixed her brown eyes on Bodenstein, giving him a pensive look.

"That's what we want to know too. Does she have any enemies?"

"Rita? Good God, no! She's such a sweet person and she's had to put up with a lot in her life. But she has never been bitter."

"Put up with what? What are you referring to?" Bodenstein studied the doctor attentively. Daniela Lauterbach, with her calm, steady demeanor, seemed extremely personable. His own family doctor processed his patients as if on a conveyor belt. Every time Bodenstein had to pay him a visit, the pace of the examination was so frenetic that it made him nervous.

"Her son had to go to jail," said Dr. Lauterbach with a sigh. "That was very hard for Rita. It's probably the reason her marriage broke up."

Bodenstein, who had been about to take a sip of coffee, stopped short.

"Mrs. Cramer's son is in jail? What for?"

"He *was* in jail, but he was released two days ago. Ten years ago he murdered two girls."

Bodenstein searched his memory, but he couldn't recall any juvenile double murderer named Cramer.

"After her divorce Rita took her maiden name again, so that she wouldn't be instantly associated with that horrible case," Dr. Lauterbach explained, as if reading Bodenstein's mind. "Her married name was Sartorius."

Pia could hardly believe her eyes. She scanned the document written in sober officialese and printed on gray recycled paper. Her heart had leaped when she discovered the long-awaited letter from the zoning commission for the city of Frankfurt in her mailbox. But what she now read was totally unexpected. Since she and Christoph had decided to live together at Birkenhof, they'd been planning to remodel the house, which was a bit too small for two people, not to mention having room for guests. An architect friend had drawn up plans for the remodeling and a preliminary inquiry for construction. Pia had been waiting impatiently for a reply, because she really wanted to get started on the project. She read through the letter a second and third time, then put it aside, got up from the kitchen table, and went to take a quick shower. Afterward she wrapped a towel around her and sullenly looked at herself in the mirror. It was three thirty by the time she left the party, yet Pia had gotten up at seven to let the dogs out and feed the other animals. Then she had enjoyed a brief break in the rain to exercise the two young horses and muck out their stalls. She just couldn't cope with late-night partying anymore. At forty-one it was harder to recover from all-nighters than it had been at twenty-one. Absently she brushed her shoulder-length blond hair and plaited it into two braids. Going back to sleep was unthinkable after getting such bad news anyway. She went through the kitchen, removing the unpleasant letter from the table, and continued into the bedroom.

"Hey, sweetie," murmured Christoph, blinking away sleep in the bright light. "What time is it?"

"Quarter to ten."

He sat up and massaged his temples with a groan. Contrary to habit he had heavily indulged in alcohol last night. "So when does Annika's plane leave?"

"Around two. We still have plenty of time."

"What's that you have there?" he asked when he spied the letter in Pia's hand.

"A catastrophe," she said morosely. "The zoning office answered."

"And?" Christoph was trying hard to wake up.

"It's a demolition order!"

"What?"

"The previous owner built this house without a permit—imagine! And now our inquiry has awakened sleeping dogs. All that's approved is a garden hut and a horse stall. I don't get it."

She sat down on the edge of the bed, shaking her head. "I've been registered at this address for a few years now; the garbagemen pick up the trash, I pay the water and sewer bills. Did they really think I've been living in a garden hut?"

"Let me see." Christoph scratched his head as he read the official letter. "We'll lodge a protest. It's just not right. The next-door neighbor is building a huge house, and you can't even remodel your little bungalow!"

The cell phone on the nightstand rang. Pia, who was on call that day, reluctantly picked it up. She listened for a few moments in silence.

"All right, I'll be there," she said, punched off the call, and tossed the cell on the bed. "Damn."

"You have to go?"

"Yes, sorry. A young man in Niederhöchstadt who was on the train platform yesterday reported that he saw a man push a woman over the railing."

Christoph put his arm around her shoulders and pulled her close. Pia gave a deep sigh. He kissed first her cheek, then her lips. Why couldn't this youth have waited until this afternoon to report the incident? Pia simply didn't feel like working right now. Actually, it was Behnke's turn to be on call this weekend. But he was "sick," after all. And Hasse was "sick" too. To hell with those idiots! Pia leaned back and cuddled up to Christoph's body, warm with sleep. His hand slid under the bath towel and caressed her belly.

"Now stop worrying about this piece of paper," he whispered, kissing her again. "We'll figure it out. They're not going to tear the house down to-morrow."

"Nothing but problems, day in and day out," Pia murmured, deciding that the kid could wait a while longer at the station in Niederhöchstadt.

Bodenstein sat in his car across from the hospital in Bad Soden and waited for his colleague to show up. Dr. Lauterbach had given him the address of Rita Cramer's ex-husband in Altenhain, but before he could give the man the bad news he had wanted to stop by the hospital and get an update on her condition. She had survived the first night; after an operation she now lay in an induced coma in the ICU. It was eleven thirty when Kirchhoff pulled up next to him, got out, and made her way around the puddles to his car.

"The kid gave us a pretty good description of the man." She plopped into the passenger seat and fastened her seatbelt. "If Kai can manage to get a decent photo off the surveillance video, we'll have a picture to give to the press."

"Excellent." Bodenstein started the engine. He had asked Pia to ride with him to visit Rita Cramer's ex-husband. On the short drive to Altenhain he told her about his conversation with Dr. Daniela Lauterbach. Pia had a hard time concentrating. She was still worried about the letter from the zoning office. Demolition order! That was the last thing she had expected. What if the city was serious and forced her to have the house torn down? Where would she and Christoph live then?

"Are you listening to me at all?" asked Oliver.

"Sure," said Pia. "Sartorius. Neighbor. Altenhain. I'm sorry, but we didn't get home till four in the morning."

She yawned and closed her eyes. She was dead tired. Unfortunately she didn't possess Oliver's iron constitution. He never seemed the least bit tired even after all-night stakeouts and exhausting investigations. Had she ever seen him yawn?

"The case was all over the headlines eleven years ago," she could hear her boss saying. "Tobias Sartorius got a maximum sentence for one count of murder and one count of manslaughter after a trial based solely on circumstantial evidence."

"Ah yes," she murmured. "Now I remember. Double homicide with no bodies. Is the guy still in prison?"

"No. Tobias Sartorius was released last Thursday. And he's back in Altenhain, staying with his father."

Pia thought about this for a few seconds, then opened her eyes.

"You mean there could be a connection between his release and the attack on his mother?"

Bodenstein cast an amused glance at her. "Unbelievable," he said.

"What?"

"Your shrewd insight never fails even when you're half asleep."

"I'm wide awake," said Pia, fighting off another yawn.

They passed the sign at the town limits of Altenhain and found the address on the main street that Dr. Lauterbach had written down. Bodenstein turned into the unpaved parking area in front of the former restaurant. A man was busy applying white paint to cover up some bright red graffiti on the façade. It said HERE LIVES A RUTHLESS KILLER. The red letters still shimmered through the white paint. On the sidewalk near the driveway stood three middle-aged women.

"You murderer!" Bodenstein and Kirchhoff heard one of them yell as they opened the car doors to climb out. "Get out of this town, you piece of crap! Or you'll be in for it!"

She spat on the ground.

"What's going on here?" Bodenstein asked, but the three women paid no attention to him and simply walked away. The man had totally ignored the taunts. Bodenstein greeted him politely and introduced himself and Kirchhoff.

"Why were those women yelling at you?" Pia asked with curiosity.

"You'd better ask them," the man said brusquely. He gave her an indifferent look and went on with his work. Despite the cold he wore only a long-sleeved gray T-shirt, jeans, and work boots.

"We'd like to speak with Mr. Sartorius."

Then the man turned around, and Pia thought she recognized him.

"Weren't you at Mrs. Cramer's apartment building in Neuenhain yesterday?" she asked. If the man was surprised, he didn't show it. He stared at her with his extraordinary sea-blue eyes, without smiling, and she felt suddenly flushed.

"Yes, that's right. Is there something wrong with that?"

"No, of course not. But what were you doing there?"

"Visiting my mother. We had agreed to meet at a certain time, but she never showed up. I was worried."

"Oh, so you must be Tobias Sartorius."

He raised his eyebrows and his lips twitched derisively.

"Yes, that's me. The killer of young girls."

He was quite attractive in an unsettling way. The narrow white scar that ran from his left ear to his chin made a well-chiseled face more interesting instead of disfiguring it. Something in the way he looked at her prompted a strange feeling in Pia, and she wondered what might be the cause.

"Your mother had a serious accident yesterday afternoon," Bodenstein said. "She was operated on last night and is now in intensive care. She's in critical condition."

Pia saw how Tobias Sartorius's nostrils flared for a moment, and he pressed his lips together to a tight line. Then he carelessly tossed the paint roller into the paint can and went to the gate of the farmyard. The detectives exchanged a brief glance and followed him. The yard looked like a rubbish heap. Suddenly Oliver uttered a suppressed cry and abruptly stopped. Pia turned to her boss.

"What is it?" she asked in astonishment.

"A rat!" Oliver gasped. He had turned white as chalk. "The thing ran right over my foot!"

"No wonder, with all the filth in here." Pia shrugged and wanted to keep going, but Oliver stood there like a pillar of salt.

"I hate rats more than anything," he said, his voice quavering.

"But you grew up on a farm," Pia countered. "There must have been an occasional rat there."

"That's exactly why."

Pia shook her head in disbelief. She never would have thought her boss would have such a phobia.

"Come on," she said. "They'll run away when they see us. Garbage rats are shy. My girlfriend used to have two tame rats. But that was different. We used to—"

"I don't want to hear it!" Oliver took a deep breath. "You go first."

"Okay, okay, no problem." Pia smirked as Oliver followed on her heels. Ready to flee at any moment, he suspiciously eyed the heaps of trash on both sides of the narrow path that led to the house.

"Yikes, there's another one! And a fat one at that," said Pia, stopping short. Oliver ran into her and looked around in a panic. His usual composure was gone.

"Just kidding," Pia said with a grin, but Oliver didn't see anything to laugh about.

"You do that again and you'll be walking home," he threatened. "You almost gave me a heart attack!"

They moved on. Tobias Sartorius had gone inside, but the front door was standing open. Oliver caught up with Pia at the stairs and climbed the three steps to the door like a hiker relieved to have solid ground underfoot after slogging through a swamp. An elderly man with stooped shoulders appeared in the doorway. He was wearing worn-out slippers, stained gray pants, and a threadbare knit cardigan that hung loose around his skinny body.

"Are you Hartmut Sartorius?" asked Pia, and the man nodded. He seemed just as run-down as his farm. Deep furrows were etched into his long, narrow face, and the only similarity with Tobias was his unusually blue eyes, although they had lost all brightness.

"My son tells me it's about my ex-wife." His voice was feeble.

"Yes," said Pia with a nod. "She had a serious accident yesterday."

"Please come in." He led them down a narrow, dim hall into a kitchen that could have been cozy if it weren't so dirty. Tobias stood by the window with his arms crossed.

"Dr. Lauterbach gave us your address," Bodenstein began. He had rapidly regained his composure. "According to witnesses, late yesterday afternoon your ex-wife was shoved over the railing of the pedestrian bridge at the Sulzbach North S-Bahn station, directly into the path of an oncoming car."

"Good Lord." All color drained out of the older man's gaunt face, and he grabbed for the back of a chair. "But . . . but who would do such a thing?"

"That's what we want to find out," said Bodenstein. "Do you have any idea who might have done this? Did your ex-wife have any enemies?"

"My mother didn't," said Tobias Sartorius from the background. "But I do. Just about everybody in this damned town hates me."

His voice sounded bitter.

"Do you have anyone particular in mind?" asked Kirchhoff.

"No," Hartmut Sartorius replied quickly. "No, I don't believe anyone would be capable of something so terrible."

Pia's gaze fell on Tobias Sartorius, who was still standing by the window. With the backlight she couldn't really see his expression, but from the way his eyebrows raised and his mouth twisted she could tell that he disagreed with his father. Pia could almost feel the angry vibes that seemed to emanate from his tense body. In his eyes blazed a long-suppressed fury like a tiny, dangerous flame that was waiting for a reason to flare up into a brushfire. Tobias Sartorius was definitely a ticking time bomb. His father, on the other hand, seemed tired and powerless like a very old man. The condition of the house and the farm spoke for itself. The man's zest for living was extinguished, and he had barricaded himself behind the ruins of his life. Being the parent of a murderer was always horrible. But it must have been even worse for Hartmut Sartorius and his ex-wife, living in a village as small as Altenhain, with each day bringing a new gauntlet to run. Mrs. Sartorius hadn't been able to take it anymore. She had left her husband behind, although undoubtedly with a guilty conscience. She hadn't succeeded in getting a new start; the loveless void of her apartment clearly demonstrated that.

Pia looked over at Tobias Sartorius. He was gnawing absentmindedly on the knuckle of his thumb, staring into space. What was he plotting behind that blank expression of his? Was he upset about what he had done to his parents? Bodenstein handed Hartmut Sartorius his card, which the man glanced at and then put in the pocket of his cardigan.

"Maybe you and your son should go see your ex-wife. She's really not doing very well."

"Of course. We'll drive over to the hospital right away."

"And if you have any idea who might have done this, don't hesitate to give me a call."

Sartorius senior nodded, but his son didn't react. Pia had a bad feeling. She hoped that Tobias Sartorius would not take it upon himself to search for the man who had attacked his mother.

Hartmut Sartorius drove his car into the garage. The visit with Rita had been dreadful. The doctor he spoke to refused to offer any sort of prognosis. She'd been lucky, he said, that her spinal column was virtually unscathed, but of the 206 bones in the human body about half of hers were broken. She had also suffered severe internal injuries when she fell onto the moving car. On the drive back home Tobias hadn't uttered a word, merely stared glumly into space. When they walked through the gate and approached the house, Tobias stopped by the steps to the front door and turned up the collar of his jacket.

"Where are you going?" Hartmut asked his son.

"I'm just going to get some fresh air."

"Now? It's almost eleven thirty. And the rain is coming down in buckets. You'll get soaked in this terrible weather."

"For the past ten years I haven't had any weather at all," said Tobias. "It doesn't bother me to get wet. And at this time of night at least nobody will notice me."

Hartmut hesitated, but then he put his hand on his son's arm.

"Don't do anything foolish, Tobi. Promise me that."

"Of course not. Don't worry about me." He gave a brief smile, even though he didn't feel like smiling at all, and waited until his father went inside. With his head down he walked through the darkness, past the empty stables and the barn. The sight of his mother lying in the ICU with her bones crushed, attached to all those tubes and other apparatus, had hit him harder than he'd expected. Was this attack on her somehow related to his release from prison? If she died, which the doctors had not ruled out as a possibility, then whoever had pushed her off the bridge would have a murder on his conscience.

Tobias stopped when he reached the rear gate to the farm. It was closed, overgrown with ivy and weeds. It probably hadn't been opened at all in recent years. Tomorrow morning he would start cleaning up. After ten years he had a tremendous longing to breathe fresh air and do his own work.

After only three weeks in the joint he could tell that he'd turn into a zombie if he didn't make an effort to use his mind. His lawyer had informed him that he had no chance for early release; an appeal had been denied. So Tobias had begun taking correspondence courses from Hagen University, studying to become a locksmith. Every day he had worked for eight hours; after an hour for exercise, he sat up half the night over his books, in order to distract himself and make the monotony of the days more bearable. Over the years he had become accustomed to the strict regulations, and the sudden lack of structure to his life now seemed threatening to him. Not that he was homesick for the joint, but it was going to take a while before he got used to freedom again.

Tobias vaulted over the gate and stopped underneath the cherry laurel, which had become a huge tree. He turned left and walked past the driveway of the Terlinden estate. The double wrought-iron gate was closed; the camera on top of one of the gateposts was new. Right behind the house the woods began. After about fifty yards Tobias turned down the narrow footpath, called the Gouge by the locals, which wound through the village to the cemetery, past the rear gardens and backyards of the houses built so close together. He knew every angle, every set of steps, and every fence—nothing had changed. As a boy he and his pals had often run along this path, on the way to church, to play soccer, or to visit a friend.

He stuck his hands in his jacket pockets. To the left old Maria Kettels had lived in a tiny cottage. She would have been his only defense witness, because she had seen Stefanie late that evening, but her testimony was not heard by the court. Everybody in Altenhain knew that Maria suffered from dementia and was also half blind. Back then she must have been at least eighty, and he was sure she must be in the graveyard by now.

Next to her property was that of the Paschkes. It bordered directly on the Sartorius land and was as neatly kept as always. Old man Paschke was in the habit of instantly spraying chemicals on any weed that poked up its head. He used to work for the city of Frankfurt and had access to the city supply depot. His neighbors who had worked for chemical giant Hoechst AG also had no qualms about using company materials to build and renovate their houses and yards. The Paschkes were the parents of Gerda Pietsch, the mother of Tobias's friend Felix. Everyone in the village was related to someone who lived only a couple of blocks away, and everyone knew the family histories of everyone else. They also knew the darkest secrets, and liked to gossip about the transgressions, failures, and illnesses of their neighbors. Because of its geographically unfavorable location in a narrow valley, the village of Altenhain had been largely spared new construction. Hardly anyone ever moved there, so the village community had remained more or less the same for the past hundred years.

Tobias had reached the cemetery and pushed with his shoulder against the small wooden gate, which opened with a tormented screech. The naked branches of the mighty trees standing among the graves whipped back and forth in the wind, which was blowing up a storm. He walked slowly along the rows of graves. Cemeteries had never given him the creeps. He thought there was something peaceful about them. Tobias approached the church as the clock in the tower struck twelve times for midnight. He stopped, tilted his head back, and for a moment looked up at the squat tower built of gray quartzite.

Wouldn't it be better if he accepted Nadia's offer and moved in with her until he could get back on his feet? People didn't want him in Altenhain, that was obvious. But he couldn't just leave his father in the lurch. He was deeply indebted to his parents, who had never turned their backs on him, even when he was convicted of killing those two girls.

Tobias walked around the church and entered the vestibule. He gave a start when he noticed a movement to his right. In the weak glow of the streetlight he recognized a dark-haired girl, who was sitting on the arm of a wooden bench next to the entry portal and smoking a cigarette. His heart skipped a beat and he could hardly believe his eyes. Before him sat Stefanie Schneeberger.

• • •

Amelie was no less startled when a man suddenly entered the church. His jacket was wet and shiny, and his dark hair hung dripping wet into his face. She had never seen him before, but she knew at once who he was.

"Good evening," she said, taking her iPod buds out of her ears. The voice of Adrian Hates, the leader of her absolute favorite band Diary of Dreams, squawked from the earbuds until she shut off the iPod. There was total silence except for the sound of the rain. A car drove by on the street below the church. For a split second the beams of its headlights flitted across the man's face. Without a doubt, this was Tobias Sartorius. Amelie had seen enough photos of him online to recognize him. He actually looked rather nice. Attractive even. Not at all like the other guys in this dump of a town. And not at all like a murderer.

"Hello," he answered at last, scrutinizing her with a peculiar expression. "What are you doing here so late?"

"Listening to music. Having a smoke. It's raining too hard to walk home right now."

"I see."

"I'm Amelie Fröhlich," she said. "And you're Tobias Sartorius, aren't you?"

"Yes I am. How do you know that?"

"I've heard a lot about you."

"That's no surprise, if you live in Altenhain." His voice had a cynical ring to it. He seemed to be considering how to categorize her.

"I've lived here since May," Amelie explained. "Actually I'm from Berlin. But I didn't get along with my mother's new boyfriend, so she sent me here to stay with my father and stepmother."

"And they let you just run around like this at night?" Tobias leaned against the wall and looked her over carefully. "When a murderer has just come back to town?"

Amelie grinned. "I don't think they've heard anything about that yet. But I have. I work evenings right over there." She nodded in the direction of the restaurant located on the other side of the parking lot next to the church. "For the past two days you've been the main topic of conversation."

"Where?"

"At the Black Horse."

"Oh, right. That wasn't here when I left."

Amelie remembered that when the murders took place in Altenhain, Tobias Sartorius's father ran the only restaurant in the village, the Golden Rooster.

"So what are you doing here this time of night?" Amelie dug a pack of cigarettes out of her backpack and held it out to him. He hesitated a moment and then took a cigarette and lit it with her lighter.

"I'm just walking around." He braced his foot against the wall. "I was in the joint for ten years, where I couldn't exactly do that."

They smoked for a while in silence. Across the parking lot a couple of late customers were leaving the Black Horse. They heard voices and then the sound of car doors slamming. The sound of the engines moved off down the road.

"Aren't you afraid at night, in the dark?"

"No." Amelie shook her head. "I'm from Berlin. Sometimes I've squatted with a few pals in abandoned buildings slated for demolition, and we'd have trouble with the squatters who were already living there. Or with the law."

Tobias exhaled the cigarette smoke through his nose.

"Where do you live?"

"In the house next to the Terlindens."

"Oh yeah?"

"Yeah, I know. Thies told me about it. That's where Snow White used to live."

Tobias froze.

"Now you're lying," he said after a while, his voice sounding different.

"No I'm not," Amelie countered.

"Sure you are. Thies doesn't talk. Ever."

"He does with me. Every so often. He's a friend of mine."

Tobias took a drag on his cigarette. The light from the glowing tip lit up his face, and Amelie saw him raise his eyebrows.

"Not a boyfriend, if that's what you're thinking," she was quick to add. "Thies is my best friend. My only friend."

Sunday, November 9, 2008

The party for Countess Leonora von Bodenstein's seventieth birthday was not held at the elegant Schlosshotel but in the indoor equestrian arena, although Bodenstein's sister-in-law had protested vehemently. But the countess didn't want anyone to make a big fuss over her, as she put it. Modest nature-lover that she was, she had expressly wished for a small celebration in the stables or the arena, so Marie-Louise von Bodenstein had acquiesced. She had handled all the arrangements for the "event" in her typical energetic and professional way, and the result was breathtaking.

Oliver and Cosima arrived at the Bodenstein estate with Sophia shortly after eleven, finding a parking spot only with difficulty. In the historic interior courtyard of the riding stable with the cobblestones and its carefully renovated half-timbered buildings there was not a straw to be seen, and the big stable door was standing wide open.

"My God," Cosima remarked in amusement. "Marie-Louise must have coerced Quentin into putting in a night shift."

The tall old stables, built around 1850, formed one side of the noble stable building of the count's castle. Over the years it had accumulated a venerable patina of spiderwebs, dust, and swallow droppings—but all that had vanished. The horse stalls, the walls, and the high ceilings shone with fresh radiance; the mullioned windows had been polished to a sheen, and even the colors in the frescoes depicting scenes from the hunt had been freshened up. The horses, who were curiously watching the commotion in the wide stable aisle over the doors of their stalls, had had their manes braided in celebration of the day. In the entrance hall, lovingly decorated as if for a harvest thanksgiving feast, the waiters from the Schlosshotel were pouring champagne.

Oliver grinned. His younger brother Quentin was one of those comfortable sorts of people. He was a landowner who ran the estate and riding stables, and it didn't bother him in the least if the tooth of time left its mark. He had increasingly turned over to his wife the responsibility for the restaurant up in the castle, and in recent years Marie-Louise had transformed it into a first-class Michelin-starred establishment, whose excellent reputation extended far beyond the local area.

They found the birthday girl amid the circle of family and well-wishers in the vestibule of the arena, which was also wonderfully decorated. Oliver was just about to wish his mother many happy returns when the hunting horn corps of the congenial Kelkheim Riding Club opened the program in the riding arena. The presentations were a surprise by the horse owners and riding students for their countess. Oliver exchanged a few words with his son Lorenz, who was filming the occasion with camera in hand. His girlfriend Thordis was responsible for the success of the dressage quadrille, the performance by the trick riding group, and she would later ride in the jumping quadrille. In the crowd Oliver ran into his sister Theresa, who had come especially for the celebration. They hadn't seen each other in a long time and had much to talk about. Cosima had taken a seat with Sophia next to her mother, Countess Rothkirch, in the grandstand on one side of the riding arena and was following the dressage quadrille with interest.

"Cosima looks ten years younger," said Oliver's sister, sipping on her champagne. "I might get jealous."

"A baby and a good husband work wonders," Oliver replied with a grin.

"Self-righteous as always, little brother," Theresa teased him back. "As if you men have anything to do with why a woman looks good!"

She was two years older than Oliver and was bubbling over with energy, as usual. Her elegantly proportioned face was striking rather than beautiful, and the first gray strands mixed in with her dark hair did nothing to diminish her radiance. She had worked hard for each wrinkle and gray hair, she once said. Her husband had been taken from her too soon, struck down by a heart attack, leaving her with an ailing coffee-roasting business in Hamburg, a family castle in Schleswig-Holstein that needed a lot of work, and several properties mortgaged to the hilt in Hamburg's best neighborhoods. Promoted to administrator of the company after her husband's death, and despite raising three children and facing a dim outlook for the future, she had energetically taken the reins and fearlessly dived into the fray against creditors and the banks. Now, after ten years of hard work and shrewd dealings, both the firm and private property had been saved and restored. Not one employee's position had been lost, and Theresa enjoyed the utmost respect from her staff and business partners.

"Apropos men," Quentin put in. "How's it going with you, Esa? Any news?"

She smiled. "A lady takes her pleasure and keeps her mouth shut."

"Why didn't you bring him along?"

"Because I knew that you would pounce on the poor guy and dissect him mercilessly." She then nodded in the direction of her parents and the rest of the relatives, who were spellbound as they watched the action in the arena. "And the whole clan too."

"So there is somebody," Quentin persisted. "At least tell us something about him."

"No." She held out her empty glass to her younger brother. "Why don't you see about getting us a refill?"

"Why is it always me?" Quentin complained, but obeyed out of long habit and left.

"Are you and Cosima having problems?" Theresa asked, turning to Oliver. He gave his sister a startled look.

"No. Why would you think that?"

She shrugged but didn't take her eyes off her sister-in-law. "Something is different between the two of you."

Oliver knew his sister's infallible intuition. There was no point in lying that he and Cosima were not getting along.

"Well, last summer after our silver anniversary we had a small crisis," he admitted. "Cosima had rented a finca on Mallorca and wanted to spend three weeks there with the whole family. After a week I had to leave, because a difficult case came up. She took offense at that."

"Aha."

"She accused me of leaving her all alone with Sophia, even though that wasn't the original plan. But what could I do? I can't just switch gears to be a full-time parent and play the househusband!"

"But you should be able to manage three weeks of vacation," Theresa replied. "I don't want to meddle, but you *are* an official. In your absence wouldn't there be someone to cover for you?"

"Do I hear a hint of contempt for my profession in your voice?"

"Don't be so touchy, dear," his sister tried to mollify him. "But I can understand why Cosima was angry. She has a job too, and doesn't really fit the traditional kids-kitchen-church role, in which you, the old macho man, would prefer to cast her. Maybe you're even happy that she doesn't go off on expeditions anymore and you have her completely under your thumb."

"That's not true at all," Oliver countered, looking upset. "I have always supported her in her work. I think what she's doing is very admirable."

Theresa looked at him, and a mocking smile spread across her face. "Nonsense. You can say that to everyone else, but not to me. I've known you too long."

Feeling caught, Oliver said nothing. His eyes wandered over to Cosima. As usual, his big sister had effortlessly succeeded in putting her finger on the sore point. She was right this time too. He was actually relieved that since Sophia was born, Cosima was no longer going off for weeks at a time to travel all over the world . But he didn't like hearing it from his sister.

Quentin returned with three glasses of champagne, and their conversation drifted to other, less charged topics. After the riding demonstrations were over, Marie-Louise opened the buffet that her coworkers had set up in the anteroom of the stables. People began moving toward the inviting-looking cocktail tables, the long rows of tables with white tablecloths and benches with comfortable cushions, and the arrangements of fall flowers. Oliver ran into relatives and old acquaintances he hadn't seen in a long time; there was plenty to talk and laugh about. The mood was relaxed. He saw Cosima talking with Theresa and hoped that his sister wasn't inciting her against him with some of her feminist slogans. Next year Sophia would be starting daycare, and then Cosima would have more time to herself. She was working on a new film project that took up a lot of her time. In a sudden urge of goodwill Oliver resolved to start coming home earlier and to keep weekends free to give Cosima a respite from all the childcare. Maybe then the tension would ease that had existed between them ever since the big fight on Mallorca.

"Dad." Rosalie tapped him on the shoulder and he turned to see his older daughter. She was studying to be a chef at the Schlosshotel with Jean-Yves St. Clair, the star French chef. Today she was in charge of the buffet. She was

holding Sophia by the hand. The child was smeared with a brownish sub-
stance from top to toe, and Oliver hoped it wasn't what it looked like.

"I can't find Mom," Rosalie said, agitated. "Maybe you could change the
little princess. Mama must have some spare clothes for her in the car."

"What's that all over her face and hands?" Oliver managed to free his
long legs from under the table.

"Don't worry, it's only chocolate mousse," said Rosalie. "I have to get
back to work."

"Okay, come over here, little piggie." Oliver grabbed his younger daughter and took her in his arms. "Look what a mess you are."

Sophia braced her little hands against his chest and started thrashing
about. She couldn't stand having her freedom of movement restricted. With
her little peach cheeks, soft dark hair, and cornflower-blue eyes she looked
good enough to eat, but it was all an illusion. Sophia had inherited Cosima's
temperament and knew how to get her way. Oliver carried her out the stable
door and crossed the courtyard. He happened to glance to the left through
the open door to the smithy and to his astonishment saw Cosima pacing back
and forth with her cell phone to her ear. The way she was running her hand
through her hair, cocking her head and laughing, surprised him. Why did
she have to go outside to make a call? Before she could catch sight of him he
hurried on, but a faint feeling of suspicion remained deep inside him like
a tiny barb.

As on every Sunday after church the usual suspects had gathered in the Black
Horse. Drinking early in the day was a man's prerogative; the women had to
stay home and tend to the Sunday roast. This was one of the reasons that
Amelie found Sundays in Altenhain to be the epitome of stuffy bourgeois
life. Today even the boss was there in person. During the week Andreas Jagielski took care of his two high-end restaurants in Frankfurt and left the running of the Black Horse to his wife and brother-in-law; he only showed up
himself on Sundays. Amelie didn't particularly like him. Jagielski was a massive man with bulbous frog eyes and bulging lips. After the Wall came down
he was one of the first former East Germans to move to Altenhain; Amelie
had learned that from Roswitha. He had worked as a cook at the Golden

Rooster but had scornfully deserted his employer at the first sign of the inn's impending collapse, only to start up business across the street as a competitor with the Black Horse. Offering the exact same menu as Hartmut Sartorius, but with much more favorable prices and the luxury of a big parking lot, Jagielski had pulled the rug out from under his former boss and significantly contributed to the final demise of the Golden Rooster. Roswitha had loyally stuck it out with Sartorius to the very end and only reluctantly accepted the job with Jagielski.

In the morning Amelie got ready with great care, removing all her piercings, fixing her hair in two braids, and putting on less dramatic makeup. From her stepmother's wardrobe she had borrowed a white blouse that was actually too small for her, and in her own wardrobe she had found a sexy plaid miniskirt. Black tights and calf-high Doc Martens completed the outfit. Standing in front of the mirror she had unbuttoned the blouse far enough so that the black bra and the swell of her breasts were visible. Jenny Jagielski had refrained from comment, merely giving Amelie a fleeting glance, but her husband had taken a good long look deep into her décolletage and then gave her a wink.

Now he was sitting at the round table fully occupied by the regulars in the middle of the room, in between Lutz Richter and Claudius Terlinden. The latter was a rarely seen guest at the Black Horse, but today he seemed affable and approachable. Even at the bar the men were sitting elbow to elbow, with Jenny and her brother drawing beers in tandem. Manfred Wagner had recovered, and he even seemed to have been to the barber, because his scraggly beard was gone and he looked reasonably civilized. As Amelie approached the table with another round of beer, she caught the name of Tobias Sartorius and pricked up her ears.

". . . bold and arrogant just like before," proclaimed Lutz Richter. "He's got some nerve showing up here again."

There was a murmur of agreement; only Terlinden and Jagielski kept quiet.

"If he keeps on like that, there'll be trouble sooner or later," someone else said.

"He won't stay here for long," said a third man. "We'll make sure of that."

It was Udo Pietsch, the roofer, who had said that, and the other men nodded and murmured in approval.

"Come on, boys, none of you is going to make sure of anything," Claudius Terlinden intervened. "He has served his time, and now he can live here with his father as long as he doesn't cause any trouble."

Everyone at the table fell silent; no one dared contradict him, but Amelie saw some of the men exchanging furtive glances. Claudius Terlinden was mistaken if he thought he could put an end to a discussion about the collective animosity that people in Altenhain felt toward Tobias Sartorius.

"Eight beers for the gentlemen," Amelie spoke up, finding the tray a bit heavy by now.

"Oh yes, thank you, Amelie." Terlinden nodded to her benevolently, but his expression suddenly froze for a fraction of a second. He recovered at once and gave a rather forced smile. Amelie could tell that her altered appearance was the cause of his astonishment. She smiled back, cocked her head coquettishly and held his glance a bit longer than decent girls should, then she turned to clear off the neighboring table. She could feel him following her every movement with his eyes, and she couldn't resist wiggling her hips a little as she walked back to the kitchen with the tray of dirty glasses. She hoped the men were really thirsty; she was dying to eavesdrop some more. Until now her interest in the whole story had arisen from the fact that there was an actual connection between herself and one of the murder victims. But after her encounter with Tobias Sartorius yesterday, there was a new motivation for her interest. She liked him.

Tobias Sartorius was speechless. When Nadia told him that she lived on Karpfenweg by the West Harbor in Frankfurt, he had envisioned a renovated old building in the Gutleut district, but what he now saw was something completely different. In the huge area of the former West Harbor a few blocks south of the main train station, a new and exclusive part of the city had sprouted with modern office buildings on the land side and twelve seven-story apartment blocks on the former pier, which had been given the name Karpfenweg. He parked his car at the side of the road and walked in amazement across the bridge over the former harbor basin carrying a bouquet of flowers. A few yachts were bobbing up and down in the black water by the boat docks. Late that afternoon Nadia had called and invited him to her place for dinner. Tobias hadn't felt much desire to drive all the way into the city, but he owed Nadia something for the steadfast loyalty she had shown him over the past ten years. He had showered and left in his father's car at seven thirty, with no idea what changes awaited him. It started with a brand-new traffic circle at Tengelmann supermarket in Bad Soden; the Main-Taunus shopping center had also grown. And in Frankfurt he couldn't find his way at all. For someone who wasn't used to driving, the city was a true nightmare. He was forty-five minutes late when he finally located the building with the right number.

"Take the elevator to the eighth floor," Nadia's cheerful voice told him over the intercom. The buzzer sounded and Tobias entered the foyer of the building, which was extravagantly adorned with granite and glass. The glass-enclosed elevator whisked him in seconds all the way to the top, with a fantastic view of the Frankfurt skyline across the water. The city had certainly changed in recent years. There were many new skyscrapers.

"There you are!" Nadia welcomed him radiantly as he stepped out of the elevator on the eighth floor. He clumsily handed her the bouquet wrapped in cellophane, which he had bought at a gas station.

"Oh, you didn't have to do that." She took the bouquet, grabbed his hand, and led him into the apartment, which took his breath away. The penthouse was gigantic. Huge picture windows all the way to the shiny parquet floor offered spectacular views in all directions. A fire crackled in the fireplace, the warm voice of Leonard Cohen filtered from invisible loudspeakers, and discreet lighting and burning candles lent the already spacious rooms even more depth. For a moment Tobias was tempted to turn on his heel and run away. He was not an envious person, but the sight of this dream apartment made him feel even more like a pathetic failure and tied his throat in knots. He and Nadia were worlds apart. What the hell did she want from him? She was famous, she was rich, she was beautiful—surely she could spend her evenings with other prosperous, amusing, and stimulating people instead of with an embittered ex-con like him.

"Let me have your jacket," she said. He took it off and instantly felt ashamed of the cheap, shabby thing. Nadia proudly led him into the big kitchen that opened onto the living room. A butcher's block stood in the middle, granite and stainless steel predominated, and the stylish appliances were by Gaggenau. There was a tantalizing aroma of roast meat, and Tobias could feel his stomach growling. He had spent the whole day slaving away at the farm sorting trash, hardly taking time for a break. Nadia took a bottle of Moët & Chandon out of the gleaming stainless steel refrigerator as she told him that she had acquired the apartment only as a pied-à-terre for the times when she stayed overnight in Frankfurt—she couldn't stand hotels. But for now it was her main residence. She poured champagne into two crystal flutes and handed him one.

"I'm happy you could come," she said with a smile.

"And I thank you for the invitation," replied Tobias, who had recovered from the initial shock and was able to return her smile.

"To you," Nadia said, clinking her glass softly against his.

"No, to you," Tobias answered seriously. "Thanks for everything."

How lovely she was. In the past her almost androgynous face with the sweet freckles had always seemed a bit angular, but now it had softened and her bright eyes sparkled. She had pulled back her honey-blond hair into a knot, but a few strands had come loose, hanging in tendrils against her lightly tanned neck. She was slender, but not too thin. Her teeth between the full lips were white and regular, the result of those hated braces from her teen years.

They smiled at each other and took another sip of champagne, but all at once the face of another woman appeared in front of Nadia's. This was precisely how he had wanted to live with Stefanie, after they finished medical school, when he was making a good living as a doctor. He had been convinced that she was the love of his life; he had dreamed of their future together, of children . . .

"What is it?" Nadia asked. Tobias met her concerned gaze.

"Nothing. What do you mean?"

"You suddenly looked so upset."

"Do you know how long it's been since I had champagne?" He forced himself to grin, but the memory of Stefanie had cut him to the quick. After all these years, he still couldn't stop thinking about her. The dream of complete happiness had lasted only a brief four weeks, and it had ended in catastrophe.

He banished the unwelcome thoughts and sat down at the table in the kitchen, which Nadia had set so beautifully. There was tortelloni filled with ricotta and spinach, a perfectly cooked beef filet with a Barolo sauce, arugula salad with shaved Parmesan cheese, and a wonderful bottle of 1992 Pomerol.

Tobias discovered that, contrary to what he had feared, he found it easy to talk with Nadia. She told him about her work, including some funny episodes and odd encounters—and in an amusing way, without mentioning how successful she was. After the third glass of red wine Tobias started to feel its effects. They left the kitchen and took seats on the leather couch in the living room, she in one corner, he in the other. Like old friends. Over the fireplace hung a framed movie poster from Nadia's first feature film—the only reminder of her great success as an actress.

"It's incredible what you've achieved," said Tobias pensively. "I'm really proud of you."

"Thank you very much." She smiled and tucked one leg under her. "It's strange—who would have thought it possible when we were kids: Ugly duckling Nathalie becomes a big movie star."

"But you were never ugly," countered Tobias, astounded that she had ever viewed herself that way.

"Well, you never considered me attractive."

For the first time that evening their conversation was approaching the delicate topic that they had both been carefully avoiding.

"But you were always my best friend," said Tobias. "All the other girls were jealous because I spent so much time with you."

"But you never tried to kiss me . . ."

She said this in a teasing tone of voice, but suddenly Tobias realized that it must have hurt her feelings back then. No girl wanted to be the best friend of a cute boy, even though in his eyes it signified how much he respected her. Tobias tried to remember why he'd never fallen in love with Nadia. Maybe because she had always been more like a little sister. They had literally played in the same sandbox and had gone to the same kindergarten and elementary school. He'd always taken for granted that she was in his life. But now something had changed. Nadia had changed. This was no longer Nathalie, the dependable, honest, reliable companion of his childhood. Next to him sat an extremely attractive, beautiful woman, who was sending him quite unequivocal signals, as he now realized. Could she actually want more from him than friendship?

"Why haven't you ever married?" he asked her suddenly. His voice had turned husky.

"Because I've never met the right man." Nadia shrugged and leaned forward to top off their glasses with more red wine. "My career is an absolute relationship killer. Anyway, most men can't tolerate having a successful wife. And I certainly don't want to marry some vain, narcissistic fellow actor. That would never work. I'm fine with the way things are."

"I've been following your career. In the joint you have plenty of time to read and watch TV."

"Which of my movies did you like best?"

"I don't know." Tobias smiled. "They're all good."

"You're flattering me." She tilted her head to one side. A loose strand of hair fell into her eyes. "You really haven't changed at all."

She lit a cigarette, took a drag, and then stuck it between Tobias's lips the way she had so often done before. Their faces were very close. Tobias raised his hand and touched her cheek. He felt her breath warm on his face, then her lips on his mouth. They both hesitated for a moment.

"It would be bad for your reputation if someone found out that you know an ex-con," Tobias whispered.

"What if I told you that my reputation has never mattered to me?" she replied in a hoarse voice. She took his cigarette from his hand and dropped it casually in the ashtray behind her. Her cheeks glowed and her eyes shone. He felt her desire echoing his own yearning and pulled her on top of him. His hands slid up her thighs and grasped her hips. His heart was pounding and a wave of lust surged through his body as her tongue penetrated his mouth. When was the last time he had slept with a woman? He could scarcely remember. *Stefanie . . . the red sofa . . .* Nadia's kiss turned passionate. Without stopping they tore off their clothes and made love full of desire, mute and gasping and with no trace of tenderness. There would be time enough for that later.

Monday, November 10, 2008

Claudius Terlinden drank his coffee standing up and gazed out the kitchen window down at the house next door. If he hurried he could give the girl at the bus stop a ride again. A couple of months ago when the secretary of his company, Arne Fröhlich, had introduced his almost grown daughter from his first marriage, the thought hadn't occurred to Terlinden. The piercings, the crazy hairdo, and the weird black clothes had irritated him as much as her sullen expression and cold demeanor. But yesterday at the Black Horse, when she had smiled at him, the realization had struck him like a bolt of lightning. The girl bore an almost spooky resemblance to Stefanie Schneeberger. The same finely etched and alabaster-pale facial features, the voluptuous mouth, the dark, knowing eyes—simply incredible.

"Snow White," he murmured. Last night he had dreamed about her, a strange, sinister dream in which the present and the past became entangled in a bewildering way. When he awoke in the middle of the night bathed in sweat, it had taken him a moment to realize that it was only a dream.

He heard footsteps behind him and turned around. His wife appeared in the kitchen doorway, her hair perfect despite the early hour.

"You're up early." He went to the sink and ran hot water in the cup. "Have you got something planned?"

"I have an appointment with Verena downtown at ten."

"Oh." How his wife spent her day didn't interest him in the least.

"Things are starting to happen again," she said then. "Just when grass was beginning to grow over the whole episode."

"What do you mean?" Terlinden cast an annoyed glance at her.

"It might have been better if the Sartoriuses had moved away from here."

"Where would they go? A story like that would follow them everywhere."

"Whatever. There are going to be problems. People in town are already sharpening their knives."

"That's what I was afraid of." Claudius Terlinden put his coffee cup in the dishwasher. "By the way, Rita was seriously injured in an accident Friday afternoon. They say somebody pushed her off a bridge into the path of an oncoming car."

"What?" Christine Terlinden's eyes widened in shock. "Where did you hear that?"

"I spoke to Tobias briefly last night."

"You what? Why didn't you tell me?" She gave her husband an incredulous look. Christine Terlinden was still a remarkably beautiful woman at the age of fifty-one. She wore her natural blond hair in a fashionable page boy. She was petite and delicate, and managed to look elegant even in a dressing gown.

"Because I didn't see you afterwards."

"You talk to the boy, visit him in prison, help out his parents—have you forgotten how he dragged you into this whole mess?"

"No, I haven't," Claudius Terlinden replied. His eyes fell on the kitchen clock on the wall. Quarter past seven. In ten minutes Amelie would be leaving her house. "All Tobias told the police back then was what he'd heard. And actually it was better that way, than if—" He broke off. "Just be glad it all worked out. Otherwise Lars would definitely not be in the position he's in today."

Terlinden dutifully brushed his wife's proffered cheek with a kiss.

"I've got to go. I might be late getting home tonight."

Christine Terlinden waited until she heard the front door close. She took a cup from the table, set it under the espresso machine, and pressed the button for a double. With cup in hand she went over to the window and watched her husband's dark Mercedes slowly roll down the driveway.

A moment later she saw him stop in front of the Fröhlichs' house, his red taillights glowing in the dim early morning light. The neighbor girl seemed to be waiting for him and climbed into the car. Christine Terlinden inhaled with a little gasp and her fingers tightened around the handle of her cup. She had seen it coming ever since she first met Amelie Fröhlich. She had noticed the fateful likeness at once. She didn't care for the fact that the girl was cultivating a friendship with Thies. Even back then it had been difficult to keep her mentally handicapped son out of the whole thing. Was everything now going to repeat itself? The almost forgotten feeling of helpless despair spread through her veins.

"Oh no, dear God," she murmured. "Please, please, not again."

The photo that Ostermann had copied from the surveillance video of the train station platform was only in black and white, and pretty grainy, but the man's face in the baseball cap was easy to see. Unfortunately the angle of the camera prevented a clear view of what happened on the bridge, but the credible testimony of fourteen-year-old Niklas Bender was enough to detain the man if he were found. Bodenstein and Kirchhoff had driven to Altenhain to show the photo to Hartmut Sartorius and his son. But even after they rang several times, no one opened the door.

"Let's go over to the grocery store and show the picture around," Pia suggested. "Somehow I have a feeling that this attack had something to do with Tobias."

Oliver nodded. Pia's intuition was as good as his sister's, and her hunches were often correct. He had thought about the conversation with Theresa all last evening and waited in vain for Cosima to tell him who she had been talking to on her cell outside the riding hall. Oliver had convinced himself that it was probably completely trivial, and that was why Cosima had already forgotten about it. She made a lot of calls and her colleagues also phoned her a lot, even on Sundays. This morning at breakfast he had decided not to attach much importance to the matter, especially since Cosima had behaved completely normally. She had been in a good mood and had cheerfully told him about her plans for the day: to work on the film in the cutting room, meet the voice-over guy, and have lunch with the team in Mainz. All quite normal. She had kissed him good-bye, as she had almost every morning for the past twenty-five years. He was obviously worrying for no reason.

The doorbell of the little grocery store jingled as they entered the shop. In one aisle a group of women with shopping baskets had their heads together, probably exchanging the latest village gossip.

"Your call, boss," Pia said softly to Oliver, who usually had no problem wrapping most women around his little finger with his outrageous good looks and Cary Grant charm. But today Bodenstein didn't seem up to par.

"No, you'd better do it," he replied. Through an open door they could see into the courtyard, where a powerful-looking gray-haired man was unloading crates of fruit and vegetables from a delivery truck. Pia shrugged and headed straight for the group of women.

"Good morning." She flashed her badge. "Hofheim Criminal Police." Suspicious and curious looks.

"On Friday afternoon the ex-wife of Hartmut Sartorius was the victim of a malicious attack." Pia chose her words carefully, going for added drama. "I assume that you all know Rita Cramer?"

They nodded.

"We have here a photo of the man who pushed her off a bridge directly into the path of an oncoming vehicle."

The lack of shocked reactions led her to believe that news of the accident had already made the rounds in the village. Pia took out the photo and held it out to the woman in the white smock, apparently the owner of the store.

"Do you recognize this man?"

The woman glanced at the photo, squinting her eyes, then looked up and shook her head.

"No," she said, feigning regret. "I'm sorry. I've never seen him before."

The other three women, at a loss, also shook their heads, but Pia didn't miss the quick glance that one of them exchanged with the store owner.

"Are you quite sure? Take another look. The quality isn't very good."

"We don't know this man." The store owner handed the photo back to Pia and returned her gaze without batting an eyelash. She was lying. It was obvious.

"Too bad." Pia smiled. "May I ask your name?"

"Richter. Margot Richter."

At that moment the man from the back courtyard came stomping into the store carrying three crates of fruit and noisily set them down.

"Lutz, they're from the criminal police," Margot Richter told him, before Pia could even open her mouth. Her husband came closer. He was tall and corpulent, with a cheerful face, his nose swollen and red from the cold and exertion. The look he gave his wife betrayed the fact that he was totally under her thumb and wouldn't have much to say. He grabbed the photo with his big paw, but before he could look at it, his wife plucked it out of his hand.

"My husband doesn't know this guy either."

Pia felt sorry for the husband, who must not have much to laugh about.

"Allow me." She took the picture from Mrs. Richter and held it out to her husband before she could protest again. "Have you ever seen this man? On Friday he pushed your former neighbor in front of an oncoming car. Since then Rita Cramer has been in intensive care in an induced coma, and we still don't know whether she's going to survive."

Richter hesitated briefly, seeming to weigh his answer. He wasn't a good liar, but he was an obedient spouse. For an instant he glanced uncertainly at his wife.

"No," he said at last. "I don't know him."

"All right then. Thank you very much." Pia forced a smile. "Have a nice day."

She left the store, followed by Bodenstein.

"They all knew him."

"No doubt about it." Bodenstein looked down the main street. "Over there is a beauty shop. Let's try there."

They walked the few yards along the narrow sidewalk, but when they entered the small, old-fashioned salon the hairdresser was just hanging up the phone with a guilty look on her face.

"Good morning," said Pia, nodding toward the telephone. "I'm sure that Mrs. Richter has already told you why we're here. So I can probably skip the question."

The woman gave them a clueless look, her gaze shifting from Pia to Oliver and stopping there. If Bodenstein had been feeling more himself today, the hairdresser wouldn't have had a chance.

"What is it with you?" Pia asked Oliver, slightly miffed, when they were out on the sidewalk a minute later. "All you had to do was flash that hairdresser a smile and she would have melted and probably given us the name, address, and telephone number of our suspect."

"I'm sorry," Oliver said lamely. "I'm just not really with it today."

A car rushed by down the narrow street, then a second one, then a truck. They had to step back against the wall of the building so as not to be hit by a side mirror.

"At any rate, this afternoon I'm going to requisition all the old files on the Sartorius case," said Pia. "I swear, this is all connected."

An inquiry in the florist's shop was just as fruitless as those at the kindergarten and the office of the elementary school. Margot Richter had already disseminated her instructions. The whole community had closed ranks and was practicing a real Sicilian code of silence in order to protect one of their own.

Amelie was lying in the hammock that Thies had specially arranged for her between two potted palms. She was swaying from side to side. Outside the mullioned windows the rain was pouring down, drumming on the roof of the orangerie, which was hidden behind a large weeping willow on the spacious grounds of the Terlinden villa. In here it was warm and cozy. It smelled of oil paints and turpentine, because Thies used the long building as a studio as well as the winter refuge for the delicate Mediterranean plants from the park. Hundreds of painted canvases were lined up along the walls, arranged precisely by size. Dozens of brushes stood in old jam jars. In everything he did, Thies was compulsively orderly. All the potted plants—oleanders, palms, lantana, and dwarf lemon and orange trees—stood in rows, also arranged by size. Nothing was arbitrarily placed. The tools and equipment that Thies used in the summertime to take care of the large park hung on the wall or stood in rank and file on the floor. Sometimes Amelie would intentionally move something or leave a cigarette butt somewhere just to tease Thies. Each time he would correct this intolerable disturbance without delay. He also saw immediately if any of the plants had been moved.

"I think it's totally exciting," said Amelie. "I would love to find out more, but I don't know how."

She didn't expect an answer, but still cast a quick glance at Thies. He was standing in front of his easel painting with great concentration. His pictures were largely abstract and done in somber colors—not the best choice for the home of anyone who was depressed, Amelie thought. At first sight Thies looked completely normal. If his expression weren't so stony he would have been a rather handsome man, with that oval face, the narrow, straight nose, and the soft, full lips. It was easy to see the resemblance to his beautiful mother. He had inherited her dazzling blond hair, and big Nordic blue eyes, and thick, dark eyelashes. But what Amelie liked the most were his hands. Thies had the sensitive, delicate hands of a pianist, and gardening work had not damaged them at all. When he was excited they would flutter here and there like startled birds in a cage. But right now he was quite calm, as he almost always was when he was painting.

"I keep asking myself," Amelie went on with her musing, "what could Tobias have done with those two girls? Why didn't he ever tell anyone? Then maybe he wouldn't have had to stay in prison for so long. It's weird. But for some reason I like him. He's so different from the other guys in this dump."

She clasped her hands behind her head, closed her eyes, and contentedly continued her morbid pondering. "Did he chop them up? Maybe he even encased them in concrete and buried them somewhere on his farm."

Thies kept working, unfazed, mixing a dark green with a ruby red on his palette, then rejected the result after a brief scrutiny and added a little white to it. Amelie stopped the hammock from swaying.

"Do you think I look better when I take out my piercings?"

Thies said nothing. Amelie climbed carefully out of the swinging hammock and went over to him. She peered over his shoulder at the canvas. Her mouth fell open when she recognized what he'd been painting for the past two hours.

"Whoa," she said, simultaneously impressed and astonished. "That's so cool."

Fourteen well-worn file folders had been borrowed from the archives of Frankfurt police headquarters and were now in boxes next to Pia Kirchhoff's desk. In 1997 the Division of Violent Crimes in the Main-Taunus region didn't exist yet. In cases of homicide, rape, and manslaughter, Division K-11 in Frankfurt had been in charge until the reform of the Hesse state police a few years ago. But studying the documents would have to wait. Dr. Nicola Engel had called one of the useless team meetings that she loved so much, set to begin at four o'clock.

It was hot and sticky in the conference room. Since there was nothing spectacular on the day's agenda, the mood of the participants ranged from sleepy to bored. Outside the windows the rain was pouring down from an overcast sky, and it was already getting dark.

"The surveillance photo of the unknown man is being released to the press today," said the commissioner. "Somebody is bound to recognize him and call in."

Andreas Hasse, who had shown up for work this morning, pale and taciturn, sneezed.

"Why don't you just stay home instead of spreading your cold to the rest of us?" said Kai Ostermann irritably. He was sitting right next to Hasse, who didn't answer.

"Is there anything else?" Dr. Nicola Engel's attentive gaze moved from one person to the next, but her subordinates wisely avoided direct eye contact. She always seemed able to look right into their heads. With her seismographic senses she had been noticing the subliminal tension in the air for some time, and now she was trying to pinpoint the cause.

"I've gotten hold of the documents in the Sartorius case," said Kirchhoff. "Somehow I have the feeling that the attack on Mrs. Cramer might be directly connected to the release of Tobias Sartorius. The people we talked to in Altenhain today recognized the man in the photo, but they all denied it. They're trying to protect him."

"Is that your view of things too?" asked Dr. Engel, turning to Bodenstein, who had been staring into space the whole time.

"That is entirely possible." He nodded. "Their reaction did seem odd."

"Good." Dr. Engel looked at Kirchhoff. "Look through the documents, but don't spend too much time on it. We're also expecting to get the results on the skeleton from forensics, and that case takes precedence."

"They hate Tobias Sartorius in Altenhain," said Kirchhoff. "They've painted graffiti on his father's house, and when we got there on Saturday to report the news of the accident, three women were standing across the street hurling curses at him."

"I met that guy once." Hasse cleared his throat a couple of times. "This Sartorius was a cold-blooded killer. An arrogant, smug pretty boy who wanted everybody to believe that he'd suffered a blackout and couldn't remember a thing. But the evidence was clear. He kept lying all the way to the slammer."

"But he's served his time. He has a right to rejoin society," Kirchhoff countered. "And the attitude of the townspeople makes me mad. Why are they lying? Who are they protecting?"

"You think you'll be able to figure that out from reading the old files?" Hasse shook his head. "The guy killed his girlfriend when she broke up with him, and because his former girlfriend witnessed it, she had to die too."

Pia wondered about this unusual display of fervor from her colleague, who was normally rather indifferent.

"That's possible," she said. "And he did ten years for it. But maybe the old records of the trial will tell me who pushed Rita Cramer off that bridge."

"Do you really want to—" Hasse began, but Dr. Engel put a firm stop to the discussion.

"Ms. Kirchhoff will look through the documents until we have the facts about the skeleton."

Since there was nothing else to discuss, the meeting was adjourned. Dr. Engel went back to her office, and the rest of K-11 dispersed.

"I have to go home," said Oliver out of the blue, after glancing at his watch. Pia decided to drive home too, taking some of the files with her. Nothing of any importance was going to be happening here.

"Shall I carry the suitcase into the house, Minister?" asked the chauffeur, but Gregor Lauterbach shook his head.

"Never mind, I'll get it." He smiled. "You'd better be getting home now, Forthuber. I'll need you at eight tomorrow morning."

"Very good, sir. Good night, then, Minister."

Lauterbach nodded and grabbed the small suitcase. He hadn't been home in three days. First he'd had appointments in Berlin, then the cultural ministers' conference in Stralsund where his colleagues from Baden-Württemberg and Nordrhein-Westfalen had squabbled fiercely about the establishment of guidelines to meet the need for teachers. He heard the telephone ring as he opened the front door and turned off the alarm with a flick of the wrist. The answering machine switched on, but the caller didn't take the trouble to leave a message. Gregor Lauterbach set down his suitcase in front of the stairs, turned on the light, and went into the kitchen. He glanced at the mail piled on the kitchen table, neatly divided into two stacks by the housekeeper. Daniela wasn't home yet. If he remembered correctly, tonight she was giving a speech at a physicians' congress in Marburg. Lauterbach went farther into the living room and studied the bottles on the sideboard for a while before he decided on a forty-two-year-old Black Bowmore scotch. A gift from somebody who was trying to butter him up. He opened the bottle and poured a double shot into a glass. Since he'd become cultural minister in Wiesbaden, he and Daniela saw each other only by chance or to coordinate their appointment calendars. They hadn't slept in the same bed for ten years. Lauterbach kept a secret apartment in Idstein, where he met a discreet lover once a week. He had made it crystal clear to her from the outset that he had no intention of ever divorcing Daniela, so the topic never came up when they were together. Whether Daniela had some sort of relationship going as well, he had no idea, and he wasn't going to ask her about it. He loosened his tie, removed his suit jacket and tossed it over the back of the sofa, taking a sip of the whisky. The telephone rang again. Three times, then the answering machine went on.

"Gregor." The male voice had an urgent tone. "If you're home, please pick up. It's extremely important!"

Lauterbach hesitated for a moment. He knew that voice. Everything seemed to be extremely important all the time. But finally he sighed and picked up the receiver. The caller wasted no time in pleasantries. As Lauterbach listened, he could feel the hairs on the back of his neck stand on end. He straightened up involuntarily. A feeling of foreboding attacked him as suddenly as a raptor.

"Thanks for calling," he said in a hoarse voice and hung up. He stood there as if paralyzed in the dim light. A skeleton in Eschborn. Tobias Sartorius back in Altenhain. His mother had been pushed off a bridge by an unknown assailant. And a zealous officer from K-11 in Hofheim was rummaging through old files. Damn. The expensive whisky took on a bitter taste. He carelessly put down the glass and hurried upstairs to his bedroom. It might not mean anything. It could all be a coincidence, he tried to reassure himself. But in vain.

Lauterbach sat down on the bed, took off his shoes, and fell back onto the covers. A torrent of unwelcome images rushed through his head. How could a single insignificant error in judgment have produced such catastrophic repercussions? He closed his eyes. Exhaustion crept through his body. His thoughts slipped from the present along tangled paths into the world of dreams and memories. *White as snow, red as blood, black as ebony . . .*

Tuesday, November 11, 2008

"The skeleton is that of a girl who at the time of death was between fifteen and eighteen years old." Dr. Henning Kirchhoff was in a hurry. He had to catch a plane to London, where he was expected to testify as an expert witness at a criminal trial. Bodenstein was sitting in a chair in front of the ME's desk, listening as Dr. Kirchhoff packed the necessary documents in his briefcase and held forth on fused basilar sutures, partially fused iliac crests, and other indicators of aging.

"How long has she been inside the tank?" Bodenstein interrupted him at last.

"Ten to fifteen years max." The medical examiner stepped over to the light box and tapped on one of the X-rays. "She once had a broken arm. You can clearly see a healed fracture here."

Bodenstein stared at the photo. The bones glowed white against the black background.

"Ah yes, and there's something else that's very interesting . . ." Dr. Kirchhoff wasn't the sort of person to blurt out the information. Even when pressed for time he was still able to make his report suspenseful. He looked through a few X-rays, holding them up against the light of the box, and then hung up the one he wanted next to the negative of the humerus. "The first bicuspids on the right and left side of the upper jaw had been extracted, probably because her jaw was too small."

"And what does that mean?"

"That we saved your people some work." Dr. Kirchhoff fixed Bodenstein with his gaze. "That is, when we correlated the dental chart data in the computer with the list of missing women, we got a match. The girl was reported missing in 1997. We also compared our X-rays with antemortem X-rays of the missing girl—and look here . . . ," he said, hanging another negative on the light box, "here we have the fracture when it was still relatively fresh."

Bodenstein was growing impatient, but it suddenly dawned on him who it was that the workman at the old airfield in Eschborn had happened to dig up. Ostermann had made up a list of girls and young women who had disappeared in the past fifteen years and were never found. At the top stood the names of the two girls that Tobias Sartorius had murdered.

"Since there are no other organic materials available," Dr. Kirchhoff went on, "sequencing was impossible, but we were able to extract the mitochondrial DNA and got a second hit. As far as the girl from the tank is concerned, she's . . ."

He stopped talking, went around his desk, and rummaged through one of the many mountains of documents.

"Laura Wagner or Stefanie Schneeberger," Bodenstein surmised. Dr. Kirchhoff looked up with a peeved smile.

"You're a spoilsport, Bodenstein," he said. "Just for jumping the gun like that and messing up my story, I ought to keep you in suspense until I get back from London. But since you're kind enough to drive me to the S-Bahn station in this awful weather, I'll tell you on the way which one the skeleton belongs to."

Pia Kirchhoff was sitting at her desk, brooding. She had stayed up late the night before studying the files and had stumbled upon several inconsistencies. The facts in the Tobias Sartorius case were clear, the evidence against him unambiguous at first glance. Yet when she read the transcripts of the interviews, Pia couldn't help thinking of questions to which she found no answers. Tobias Sartorius had been twenty years old when he was sentenced to the most severe punishment under juvenile criminal law for the manslaughter of then seventeen-year-old Stefanie Schneeberger and the murder of Laura Wagner, also seventeen. A neighbor had witnessed the two girls entering the house of the Sartorius family within a few minutes of each other late in the evening of September 6, 1997. Tobias and his ex-girlfriend Laura Wagner had already had a loud argument out on the street. Before that all three had been at the fair where, according to witnesses, they had consumed considerable quantities of alcohol. The court had found Tobias guilty of killing his girlfriend Stefanie Schneeberger in the heat of the moment with a tire iron. He had then killed his ex-girlfriend Laura, who had witnessed the crime. Judging by the amount of Laura's blood found everywhere in the house, on Tobias's clothes, and in the trunk of the car, the murder must have been committed with extreme brutality. Clear indications of a gruesome killing had then been concealed. In a search of the property, Stefanie's backpack was found in Tobias's room; Laura's necklace was in the milk room under the sink; and finally the murder weapon, the tire iron, was discovered in the cesspool behind the cow stalls. The defense argument that after the altercation Stefanie had forgotten her backpack in her boyfriend's room was dismissed as irrelevant. Later, shortly after 11:00 P.M., witnesses had seen Tobias driving out of Altenhain in his car. But around 11:45 his friends Jörg Richter and Felix Pietsch said they had spoken with him at his front door! They said he was covered in blood and refused to come back to the fair with them.

Pia had stumbled across this discrepancy in the chronology. The court had assumed that Tobias removed the bodies of the two girls in the trunk of his car. But what could he have done in a mere three-quarters of an hour? Pia took a swig of coffee and rested her chin in her hand, deep in thought. Her colleagues had been very thorough, interviewing almost every inhabitant of Altenhain in the course of their investigation. And yet she had a vague feeling that something had been overlooked.

The door opened and her colleague Hasse appeared in the doorway. His face was a ghastly white; only his nose glowed red and inflamed from constantly blowing it.

"So," said Pia. "Are you feeling better?"

In reply Hasse sneezed twice in rapid succession, then inhaled with a sniffle and shrugged his shoulders.

"Jeez, Andreas, go home." Pia shook her head. "Climb into bed and get well. There's nothing happening here anyway."

"How far have you gotten with that stuff?" He nodded suspiciously toward the files stacked on the floor next to Pia's desk. "Did you find anything?"

Again she wondered about his interest, but he was probably just afraid she was going to ask him for help.

"Depends on your point of view," she said. "At first glance everything seems to have been very carefully checked. But something doesn't quite jibe. Who led the investigation back then?"

"Detective Chief Superintendent Brecht from K-11 in Frankfurt," said Hasse. "But if you wanted to talk to him, you're a year too late. He died last winter. I went to the funeral."

"Oh."

"A year after he retired. That's the way the government likes it. You slave away until you're sixty-five, then step right into the coffin."

Pia ignored the bitterness in his voice. Hasse was in no danger of working himself to death.

After dropping off Dr. Kirchhoff at the S-Bahn station by the stadium, Bodenstein took the frontage road headed for the interchange at Frankfurter Kreuz. Today Laura Wagner's parents would finally learn the fate of their daughter. Maybe it would give them some solace to bury the mortal remains of the girl and say a final farewell after eleven years of not knowing what happened to her. Bodenstein was so lost in thought that it took him a few seconds before he recognized the license plate of the dark BMW X5 directly in front of him. What was Cosima doing here in Frankfurt? Hadn't she just this morning complained to him that she would probably have to spend the rest of the week at the TV station in Mainz because she wasn't making any progress with editing the rough footage? Bodenstein punched in her cell number. Despite the poor visibility because of the drizzle and road spray, he could see the woman driver in the car ahead of him put a cell phone to her ear. He smiled as he heard her familiar voice. *Look in your rearview mirror,* was what he had actually intended to say, but a sudden idea stopped him. His sister's words flashed through his mind. He would put Cosima to the test and let her prove to him that his suspicions were unjustified.

"What are you doing right now?" he asked instead. Her reply left him speechless.

"I'm still in Mainz. Nothing is working out today," she said in a tone of voice that normally wouldn't have made him doubt her statement. The lie gave him such a shock that he began to shake. His hands gripped the steering wheel tighter, he took his foot off the gas, dropping back and letting another car pass him. She was lying! She just kept on lying! As she put on her blinker and turned right onto the A5, she told him that she'd rearranged the whole storyboard and hadn't been able to finish up the editing on time.

"We only had access to the cutting room until twelve," she said. The blood was rushing in his ears. The realization that Cosima, his Cosima, was telling him a bald-faced lie, ice cold and insolently, was more than Bodenstein could stand. He would have preferred to yell at her, shouting *Please, please, don't lie to me. I'm driving right behind you!* But he couldn't say a thing. He just muttered a few words and then ended the call. As if in a trance he drove the rest of the way to headquarters. At the police parking lot he turned off the engine and remained sitting in his car. The rain was drumming on the roof of the BMW and running down the windows. His world was falling apart. Why the hell was Cosima lying to him? The only explanation was that she had done something she didn't want him to know about. And he didn't want to know what it might be. This sort of thing happened to other people, but not to him! It took him fifteen minutes before he was able to get out of the car and walk over to the building.

In the steady drizzle Tobias loaded up the trailer of the tractor to haul everything to the containers that had been positioned next to the drained cesspool. Wood, bulky refuse, and trash. The guy from the waste disposal company had told him several times that it would be expensive if he didn't sort everything properly. The scrap dealer had come to the farm to pick up the scrap metal around noon. The dollar signs had flashed in his eyes when he saw what a goldmine lay before him. With two helpers he had loaded it all up, starting with the rusty chains that the cows used to be tethered with, to the big items from the stables and barn. The dealer had counted out 450 euros to Tobias, promising to come back the following week to pick up whatever was left. Tobias was aware that his every movement was being watched by his neighbor Paschke with the Argus eyes. The old man was hiding behind the curtain, but now and then he would peek out through a crack. Tobias paid no attention to him. When his father returned from work at four thirty, there was nothing left of the heaps of junk in the lower courtyard.

"But the chairs," Hartmut Sartorius objected, sounding distraught. "They were still good. And the tables. We could have repainted them . . ."

Tobias persuaded his father to go inside, then lit a cigarette and enjoyed his first well-deserved break since morning. He sat down on the top step and cast a satisfied glance at the now immaculate yard, with only the old chestnut tree standing in the middle. Nadia. For the first time he permitted his thoughts to stray back to the night before last. He might be thirty years old, but as far as sex was concerned, he was an absolute beginner. Compared to what he and Nadia had done, his experiences from before were downright childish. Over the years, for lack of comparison, he had pictured them as something magnificent and extraordinary. But now he was able to see them in the proper context. Childish hugs, the embarrassed in and out, lying on the stuffy childhood bed, the jeans and underwear around the knees, and always on the alert—half expecting parents to burst in because there was no lock on the door.

"Ah," he sighed pensively. It might sound pompous, but there was no doubt that Nadia was the one who made him a man. After the first hurried union on the sofa they had moved to the bed, and he had assumed that was all there was to it. They had held and caressed each other as they talked, and Nadia had confessed that she had always loved him. She hadn't realized it until he vanished from her life. And all those years she had unconsciously measured every man she met against him. He was annoyed by this admission from the lips of the beautiful stranger that he no longer was able to connect with the friend from his childhood, and yet it also made him deeply happy.

She had then succeeded in motivating him to his best sexual performance, making him sweat and doing things he would never have thought he was capable of. He imagined he could still smell her, taste her, feel her. Simply wonderful. Fantastic. Awesome. Tobias was so deep in thought that he didn't hear the soft footsteps and gave a start when a figure came unexpectedly around the corner of the house.

"Thies?" he asked in surprise. He stood up but made no attempt to approach the neighbor's son or even give him a hug. Thies Terlinden had never appreciated such familiarities. Now he didn't look Tobias in the eye, just stood there in silence, his arms clamped firmly to his sides. Today, as before, it was impossible to see his disability. That's how Lars must look now too, thought Tobias. Lars, the younger twin by two minutes, had been automatically elevated to the position of crown prince of the Terlinden dynasty because of his brother's illness. Tobias had never seen his best friend again after that fateful day in September 1997. Only now did it occur to him that he had never talked about Lars with Nadia, although the three of them had once been like siblings.

Suddenly Thies took a step toward Tobias and astonishingly held out his hand, palm up. In amazement Tobias understood what Thies was waiting for: They had always greeted each other that way, with a triple high-five. At first it had been their secret gang sign, later a joke that they had kept up. A brief smile appeared on Thies's handsome face when Tobias gave him the high-five.

"Hello, Tobi," he said in his odd voice that lacked any intonation. "Great to have you back."

Amelie wiped off the long counter at the bar. The dining room at the Black Horse was still empty at five thirty, too early for the evening crowd. To her own surprise it wasn't hard for her to abandon her usual outfit. Was her mother going to turn out to be right again? Was her Goth persona not a statement about life as she claimed, but nothing more than a rebellious phase of puberty? In Berlin she had felt good wearing the baggy black clothes, with all the piercings, heavy makeup, and flamboyant hairdo. Her friends all looked the same way, and nobody turned around to stare at them when they roamed the streets like a swarm of black ravens, kicking lampposts with their Doc Martens and occasionally playing soccer with garbage cans. She didn't give a shit what the teachers and other bourgeois people said. They were just bothersome creatures who moved their lips and spouted nonsense. But suddenly everything had changed. The appreciative glances of the men on Sunday, which were undoubtedly due to her feminine figure and revealing décolletage, had pleased her. More than that. She felt like she was walking on air when she realized that every man in the Black Horse was staring at her ass, including Claudius Terlinden and Gregor Lauterbach. She still felt high from it. Jenny Jagielski came waddling out of the kitchen, the crepe soles on her shoes squeaking. At the sight of Amelie her eyebrows went up.

"From scarecrow to vamp," she said sharply. "So, who's the new look for?"

Then she cast a critical eye at the work Amelie had done, running her finger along the counter. She found it satisfactory.

"You can go wash the glasses," she said. "My brother probably forgot to do it."

A dozen used glasses from the noon rush stood next to the sink. Amelie didn't care what the task was. The main thing was that she got paid every night. Jenny climbed onto a bar stool and lit a cigarette despite the smoking ban. She did that often when she was alone and in a placid mood, like today. Amelie seized the opportunity to ask about Tobias Sartorius.

"Of course I know him from before," Jenny replied. "Tobi was a good pal of my brother's, and he came over to our house a lot." She sighed and shook her head. "But it would have been better if he'd never come back here."

"Why?"

"Well, just think how it must be for Manfred and Andrea to see their daughter's murderer walking down the street!"

Amelie began drying the wet glasses, polishing them carefully.

"What happened anyway?" she asked casually, but her boss needed no urging, since she was in a mood to gab.

"Tobi was going steady with Laura first, then with Stefanie. They were both new in Altenhain. It was the day of the village fair when they disappeared. The whole town had gathered in the big tent. I was fourteen then and thought it was great that I was allowed to stay out all evening. Honestly, I didn't even notice what happened. Not until the next morning when the police showed up with dogs and a helicopter and everything else. That's when I realized that Laura and Stefanie had disappeared."

"I never would have thought something that exciting could happen in a dump like Altenhain," said Amelie.

"It was exciting, all right," said Jenny, staring pensively at the cigarette smoldering between her sausage-like fingers. "But afterwards nothing was ever the same in this town. Everything came to an end. Tobi's father ran the Golden Rooster. There was something going on there every night, much more than here. They still had a gigantic hall, and at carnival it got pretty wild. The Black Horse didn't even exist back then. My husband used to work as a cook at the Golden Rooster."

She fell silent, abandoning herself to her memories. Amelie shoved over an ashtray.

"I do know that the police questioned Jörg and his friends for hours," Jenny suddenly went on. "Nobody knew a thing. And then someone said that Tobi had killed the two girls. The cops had found Laura's blood in Tobi's car and Stefanie's things under his bed. And the tire iron that Stefanie had been beaten with was found in Sartorius's cesspool."

"How awful. Did you know Laura and Stefanie?"

"I knew Laura. She was in the clique with my brother Felix, Micha, Tobi, Nathalie, and Lars."

"Nathalie? Lars?"

"Lars Terlinden. And Nathalie Unger has become a famous actress. Today they call her Nadia von Bredow. Maybe you've seen her on TV." Jenny stared into the distance. "They both turned out to be successful. Lars must have a super job at some bank by now. Nobody knows what exactly he does. He left Altenhain. Yes, I've always dreamed of the big wide world. But usually things don't turn out the way you expect . . ."

It was hard for Amelie to imagine her chronically ill-tempered fat boss as a happy fourteen-year-old girl. Was that why she was often so mean? Because she'd had to stay in this dump of a town, with three eternally moaning little kids and a husband who contemptuously called her "Micheline" in front of everybody, referring to her rotund shape?

"And Stefanie?" asked Amelie, as Jenny threatened to sink back into her memories. "What was she like?"

"Hmm." Jenny stared contemplatively into space. "She was beautiful. White as snow, red as blood, black as ebony."

She looked at Amelie. Her bright eyes with the blond lashes looked like a pig's.

"You look a little bit like her." It didn't sound like a compliment.

"Really?" Amelie stopped what she was doing.

"Stefanie was of a whole different caliber from the other girls in the village," Jenny went on. "When she moved here with her parents, Tobi fell for her right away and broke up with Laura." Jenny gave a scornful snort. "So my brother saw his chance. The boys were all crazy about Laura. She was really pretty. But really bitchy too. She got mad as hell when Stefanie was chosen Queen of the Fair and not her."

"So why did the Schneebergers move away?"

"Would you stay in a town where something so awful happened to your child? They stayed here for about three months, then one day they were gone."

"Hmm. And Tobi? What kind of boy was he?"

"Oh, all the girls were in love with him. Me too." Jenny smiled sadly at the memories of those days, when she was still young and full of dreams. "He was handsome and simply... cool. And yet not conceited like the other guys. If they were going to the swimming pool, he didn't mind if I tagged along. The others would all moan about what a little nuisance I was, telling me to stay home. No, Tobi was really sweet. And smart too. Everybody thought he would do something great someday. Yep. And then this. But alcohol changes people. When Tobi had something to drink, he wasn't himself anymore..."

The door opened and two men came in. Jenny quickly put out her cigarette. Amelie cleared away the washed glasses and then went over to the customers and handed them menus. On the way back she grabbed the daily paper off one of the tables. It was open to the local section and she quickly scanned the page. The police were searching for the man who had pushed Tobias's mother off the bridge.

"Oh shit," Amelie muttered, and her eyes grew wide. Even though the photo was of poor quality, she recognized the man at once.

Bodenstein had been dreading the moment when he would have to face Cosima. He sat in his office and pondered the dilemma until it couldn't be put off any longer. She was upstairs in the bathroom when he came home, lying in the tub, to judge by the splashing he heard. Feeling at a loss, he was standing in the kitchen when he noticed her purse hanging over the back of a chair. Never in his life had Bodenstein searched through his wife's purse. Nor would he consider snooping through her desk—because he had always trusted her and assumed that she wouldn't try to hide anything from him. But now things were different.

He struggled with himself for a moment, then grabbed her purse and rooted around in it until he found her cell phone. His heart was pounding in his throat when he flipped open the phone. She hadn't turned it off. Bodenstein knew that he was committing a real breach of trust, but he couldn't help himself. In the menu he called up the message file and clicked through the text messages. Last night at 9:48 she had received a brief text from an unknown sender. *Tomorrow, 9:30? Same place?* And she had answered it only a minute later. Where had he been at that moment? Why hadn't he noticed Cosima texting her reply? *All set, can't wait!!!* With three exclamation points.

A queasy feeling spread through the pit of his stomach. The fears that he'd been carrying around all day seemed to be well founded. With those three exclamation points the more harmless possibilities like a doctor or hairdresser fell away. She would never be looking forward to such appointments with so much enthusiasm—especially not at ten to ten on a Monday night. Bodenstein listened with one ear cocked upward as he searched through the cell phone for other treacherous messages. But Cosima must have cleared the cache recently, because he found nothing else. He pulled out his own cell and saved the number of the unknown person who was going to

be meeting his wife apparently for the second time at nine thirty on a Tues-
day morning. Bodenstein flipped his cell shut and put it back in his pocket.
He felt terrible. The thought that Cosima was going behind his back and
lying to him was simply intolerable. He had never lied to her, not in over
twenty-five years of marriage. It was not always advantageous to be honest
and straightforward, but lies and false promises conflicted deeply with his
character and his strict upbringing. Should he explode and confront her
with his suspicions? Ask her why she had lied to him? Bodenstein ran both
hands through his thick, dark hair and took a deep breath. No, he decided,
he wouldn't say anything. He would preserve the appearance and illusion of
an intact relationship for a while yet. It might be cowardly, but he simply
didn't feel capable of grabbing hold of his life and smashing it to bits. There
was still a tiny hope that things weren't as they seemed.

They arrived in pairs or in small groups and were let in through the back entrance of the church after they had said the password. The invitation had
been given verbally, and the password was important because he wanted to
make sure that only the right people were there. It was eleven years ago that
he had called a secret meeting like this, preventing an even greater disaster.
Now it was high time to take renewed measures before the situation escalated.
He stood next to the organ in the gallery, hidden behind one of the wooden
beams, and watched with growing nervousness as the pews below him filled
up. The flickering of the few candles in the chancel cast grotesque shadows
on the ceiling and walls of the vaulted nave. Electric light might have attracted
unwanted attention, for even the dense fog that had settled outside wouldn't
have been able to conceal brightly lit church windows. He cleared his throat,
rubbing his moist palms together. A glance at his watch told him that it was
almost time.

They had all arrived. Slowly he felt his way down the wooden spiral staircase to the bottom, the steps creaking under his weight. When he emerged
from the darkness into the dim candlelight, the whispered conversations
died away. The bell in the church tower struck eleven—perfect choreography. He stepped in front of the first row of pews into the center aisle, looking

at the familiar faces; what he saw was encouraging. All eyes were directed at him, and he recognized in them the same determination as they'd had before. They all understood what was at stake.

"Thank you for coming here this evening," he began his speech, which he had long been polishing in his mind. Although he spoke softly, his voice carried to the farthest corners. The acoustics of the church were perfect; he knew that from choir practice. "The situation has become untenable now that *he* is here again, and I have asked you here today so that we can decide what to do about it."

He was not a practiced speaker; he was trembling inside with the nervousness he always felt whenever he had to speak to an audience. And yet in a few words he succeeded in expressing the concerns of himself and the village. None of those present had to be told what was at risk this evening, so no one batted an eye when he announced his decision. For a moment there was a deathly silence. Somebody coughed softly. He could feel the sweat running down his back. Even though he was absolutely convinced of the necessity of his plan, he was still aware that he was standing in a church and had just incited these people to murder. His gaze swept over the faces of the thirty-four people before him. He had known every one of them since he was a kid. None of them would ever breathe a word of what was discussed here. Back then, eleven years ago, it had been no different. He waited, tensely.

"I'm in," came a voice finally from the third row.

There was silence. One more volunteer was needed. There had to be at least three.

"I'll come along too," somebody said at last. A deep sigh went through the gathering.

"Good." He was relieved. For a moment he'd been afraid that they would back down. "It will serve as a warning. If he doesn't leave town voluntarily after that, we'll really have to get serious."

Wednesday, November 12, 2008

Dr. Nicola Engel regarded her decimated K-11 team with displeasure. There were only four present at the morning meeting; besides Behnke, Kathrin Fachinger was missing too. While Ostermann reported on the less than satisfactory response to their public appeal for help, Oliver von Bodenstein stirred his coffee with an absentminded expression on his face. Pia Kirchhoff thought he looked bleary eyed, as though he hadn't gotten enough sleep. What the heck was going on with him? For the past couple of days he'd given the impression of being one step removed from himself. Kirchhoff suspected family trouble. In May of last year he'd been acting so strangely, and it turned out that he was worried about Cosima's health. His concerns had proved to be groundless—he hadn't had a clue that she was pregnant.

"So." Dr. Engel took the floor, since Bodenstein failed to do so. "The skeleton from the airplane hangar turned out to be Laura Wagner from Altenhain, who has been missing since September 1997. The DNA was a match, and the healed fracture of her upper arm matches the X-ray taken before she died."

Kirchhoff and Ostermann already knew the contents of the forensic report, but they listened patiently until their chief finished her lecture. Was Dr. Engel bored with her job? Was that why she kept interfering with the work of K-11? Her predecessor, Dr. Nierhoff, had put in an appearance only once in a blue moon, primarily when an especially important case needed to be solved.

"I just wonder," said Pia when Dr. Engel had finished, "how Tobias Sartorius could have driven from Altenhain to Eschborn, broken into a secure, locked military site, and managed to get the body into an underground tank, all within forty-five minutes."

There was silence around the table. Everybody looked at Bodenstein.

"Sartorius allegedly murdered the two girls in his parents' house," Kirchhoff clarified. "He was seen by the neighbor when he first entered the house with Laura Wagner and later, when he opened the door for Stefanie

Schneeberger. The next time he was seen was around midnight when his friends came to pick him up."

"What are you getting at?" Dr. Engel wanted to know.

"It's possible that Tobias Sartorius was not the perpetrator."

"Of course he was," Hasse countered at once. "Did you forget that he was convicted?"

"In a trial based purely on circumstantial evidence. And I ran across several inconsistencies when I studied the documents. At a quarter to eleven the neighbor saw Stefanie Schneeberger being let into the house by Tobias Sartorius, and half an hour later his car was seen by two witnesses in Altenhain."

"So?" said Hasse. "He murdered the girls, put them in his car, and took the two bodies away. They reconstructed it."

"At that time it was assumed that he had disposed of the bodies somewhere nearby. Now we know that this was not the case. And how did he get onto the closed military site?"

"The young people have always gone out there to party. They must have known about some secret entrance."

"That's ridiculous." Kirchhoff shook her head. "How could a man who'd been drinking heavily accomplish all that? And what did he do with the second body? We didn't find that one in the tank! I tell you, the time frame is much too tight!"

"Ms. Kirchhoff," Dr. Engel chided. "We're not doing an investigation here. The perpetrator was caught, convicted, sentenced, and has served his time. Now I want you to go see the parents of this girl and tell them that the mortal remains of their daughter have been found. And that's the end of it."

"And that's the end of it!" Kirchhoff mimicked her boss. "I have no intention of letting this matter rest. It's obvious that a sloppy investigation was done at the time, and the conclusions were totally arbitrary. I'm asking myself why."

Bodenstein, who had let her drive, didn't reply. He had folded his long legs into the uncomfortably cramped Opel, closed his eyes, and said not a word during the whole trip.

"Tell me, Oliver, what's going on with you?" Pia asked at last, slightly miffed. "I don't feel like driving around all day with somebody who's as talk-ative as a corpse."

Oliver opened one eye and sighed. "Cosima lied to me yesterday."

Aha. A family problem. As expected.

"And? Who hasn't lied occasionally?"

"Me." Oliver opened his other eye. "I have never lied to Cosima. I even told her about the Kaltensee case."

He cleared his throat and then told Pia what had happened the day be-fore. She listened with growing discomfort. It certainly sounded serious. Yet even in this situation Oliver's noble sense of honor gave him a guilty con-science, because he had snooped for evidence in his wife's cell phone.

"There's probably a completely innocent explanation for all of this," said Pia, although she didn't believe it. Cosima von Bodenstein was a beautiful, temperamental woman who was financially independent because of her job as a movie producer. Lately there had been some friction between her and Oliver—Pia had noticed that—but her boss hadn't seemed to take it seriously. How typical that he was now dumbfounded. He lived in an ivory tower. It was even more astonishing considering how fascinated he was by the abysses he witnessed in other people's relationships every day. Unlike Pia, he seldom let himself get emotionally involved in a case. He seemed able to maintain a distance that she found rather self-righteous. Did he think that something like this couldn't happen to him? That he was somehow above such mundane matters as marital problems? Did he really think that Cosima was satisfied just sitting around the house with a small child, waiting for him to come home? She was used to a whole different kind of life.

"But she's going out to meet somebody and telling me she was somewhere else entirely," he argued. "That sounds suspicious to me. What am I supposed to do?"

Pia didn't answer right away. In his situation she would have done every-thing to find out the truth. She probably would have confronted her husband at once, creating a scene with yelling and tears and accusations. It would be impossible for her to act as if nothing had happened.

"Just ask her," she suggested. "She's not going to lie to your face."

"No," he replied firmly. Pia sighed. Oliver von Bodenstein was not like other people. He might even accept a potential rival and suffer in silence, simply to preserve appearances and protect his family. In the area of self-control he had already earned top marks.

"Did you write down the cell phone number?"

"Yes."

"Give it to me. I'll make a call. With caller ID suppressed."

"No, I'd rather you didn't."

"Don't you want to find out the truth?"

Oliver hesitated.

"Listen here," said Pia. "It'll eat you up inside if you don't find out where you stand."

"Damn it!" he burst out. "I wish I'd never seen her in Frankfurt! I wish I'd never called her."

"But you did. And she lied."

Oliver took a deep breath and ran his hand through his hair. Pia had seldom seen her boss look so helpless. The present dilemma seemed to be making him feel worse than ever before.

"What am I going to do if I find out that she . . . that she's cheating on me?"

"You've jumped to the wrong conclusions about her behavior before," Pia reminded him, wanting to calm him down.

"This time it's different," he said. "Would you want to know the truth if you suspected you were being cheated on?"

"One hundred percent."

"And what if—" He broke off. Pia kept quiet. They had arrived at the cabinet shop of Manfred Wagner in the Altenhain industrial park. *Men,* she thought. *They're all the same. No problem making a decision on the job. But as soon as it's about a relationship and emotions come into play, they're all a bunch of damn cowards.*

Amelie waited until her stepmother had left the house. Barbara had believed her without question when she said that her first class of the day had been canceled. Amelie smirked. This woman was so gullible that it was almost boring telling lies to her. Entirely different from her own highly suspicious mother. She basically never believed a word Amelie said, so it had become a habit to lie to her. Her mother often swallowed the lies more easily than the truth.

Amelie waited until Barbara had driven off with the two toddlers in her red Mini, then she slipped out the front door and ran over to the Sartorius farm. It was still dark and no one was on the street; even Thies was nowhere to be seen. Her heart was pounding as she sneaked across the dismal yard, past the barn and the long stall building where no animals had lived for ages. She kept close to the wall, turned the corner, and almost had a heart attack when two masked figures suddenly appeared in front of her.

Before she could cry out, one of them grabbed her and pressed his hand over her mouth. He brutally twisted one of her arms behind her back and shoved her against the wall. The pain was so intense that she practically stopped breathing. What the hell was the matter with this guy, hurting her like this? And why were these characters waiting for her at seven thirty in the morning? Amelie had dealt with many threatening situations in her life, so after the first shock, her fear turned to fury. She doggedly struggled against the iron grip, kicking and flailing her free arm, trying to yank off the attacker's mask with the eye slits. With the strength of desperation she managed to get her mouth free when she saw a patch of bare skin right before her eyes, a spot between glove and sleeve. She bit down as hard as she could. The man uttered a muted cry of pain and shoved Amelie to the ground. Neither he nor his pal had reckoned on such ferocious resistance, and they were panting with exertion and anger. Finally the second man gave Amelie a kick in the ribs that took her breath away. Then he punched her in the face with his fist. Amelie saw stars, and all her instincts screamed at her to stay down and keep her trap shut. She heard footsteps hurrying off and then it was completely still except for her own labored breathing.

"Shit," she cursed, trying with an effort to get up. Her clothes were soaking wet and muddy. Blood ran down her chin and dripped onto her hands. Those shitheads had really hurt her.

The Wagner cabinet shop and the attached residence gave the impression that the owner had run out of money in the midst of construction. Unplastered walls, the front yard only partially paved, the rest covered with asphalt and full of potholes. It was actually just as depressing as the Sartorius place. Stacked up everywhere were boards and planks, some of them covered with moss, looking like they'd been lying there for years. Doors shrink-wrapped in plastic leaned against the wall of the workshop, and everything was filthy.

Kirchhoff first rang the bell of the residence, then at the door marked OF-FICE, but there was no answer. Inside the workshop the lights were on, so she pushed the metal gate open and went in. Bodenstein followed her. It smelled of fresh wood.

"Hello?" she called. She walked through the shop, which was a terrible mess, and found behind a stack of boards a young man wearing earbuds and nodding in time to the music. He was busy varnishing something with one hand and had a cigarette hanging out of his mouth. When Bodenstein tapped him on the shoulder he spun around. He tore the earbuds out of his ears, looking guilty.

"Put out your cigarette," Kirchhoff said to him, and he obeyed at once. "We're looking for Mr. or Mrs. Wagner. Are they here somewhere?"

"In the office over there," said the youth. "At least I think so."

"Thanks." Pia refrained from mentioning the fire code and set off to look for the boss, who obviously didn't care about much of anything. She found Manfred Wagner in a tiny, windowless office so cramped that three of them would hardly fit inside. The man had lifted the receiver off the phone and was reading the *BILD* tabloid. Apparently nobody cared much about customers. When Bodenstein knocked on the open door to announce his presence, the man reluctantly looked up from his paper.

"Yeah?" He was somewhere in his mid-fifties and smelled of alcohol despite the early hour. His brown coverall looked as if it hadn't seen the inside of a washing machine in weeks.

"Mr. Wagner?" Kirchhoff took over. "We're with the Hofheim Criminal Police and we'd like to talk with you and your wife."

Wagner turned pale as a ghost, staring at her with his red-rimmed, watery eyes like a bunny at a snake. At that moment a vehicle pulled up outside and then a car door slammed.

"That's . . . that's my wife," Wagner stammered. Andrea Wagner came into the workshop, her heels clacking on the concrete floor. She had short blond hair and was very thin. She must have been pretty once, but now she looked merely careworn. Grief, bitterness, and uncertainty about the fate of her daughter had etched deep furrows in her face.

"We've come to inform you that the mortal remains of your daughter Laura have been found," said Bodenstein after he introduced himself to Andrea Wagner. For a moment there was complete silence. Manfred Wagner let out a sob. A tear ran down his unshaven cheek, and he hid his face in his hands. His wife remained calm and composed.

"Where?" was all she asked.

"On the grounds of the old military airfield in Eschborn."

Andrea Wagner heaved a big sigh. "Finally."

There was so much relief in this word, more than she could have expressed in ten sentences. How many days and nights of vain hope and utter despair had these two people endured? How must it feel to be constantly haunted by the ghosts of the past? The parents of the other girl had moved away, but the Wagners had not been able to give up their business, which was their livelihood. They were forced to stay, while their hope for the return of their daughter grew ever fainter. Eleven years of uncertainty must have been hell. Maybe it would help now that they could bury her and say good-bye.

"No, leave it," Amelie insisted. "It's no big deal. Just a bruise, that's all."

She was certainly not going to undress and show Tobias the spot where one of those jerks had kicked her. It was embarrassing enough to be sitting here, looking so filthy and ugly.

"But the cut might need stitches."

"Bullshit. It'll heal just fine the way it is."

Tobias had stared at her as if she were a ghost when, shortly after seven thirty, she stood at his front door, dirty and smeared with blood. She told him that she'd just been attacked by two masked men in his yard. He made her sit down on a kitchen chair and carefully dabbed the blood from her face. Her nose had stopped bleeding, but the cut over her eyebrow, which he had stuck together in a makeshift way with two Band-Aids, might soon start bleeding again.

"You do that really well." Amelie gave him a crooked smile and took a drag on her cigarette. She felt shaky and her heart was pounding, but this reaction had nothing to do with the attack. It was because of Tobias. Up close and in the daylight he looked a lot better than she had first thought. The touch of his hands was like electric sparks, and the way he kept looking at her with his incredibly blue eyes, so anxious and thoughtful—that was almost too much for her nerves. No wonder all the girls in Altenhain had been after him in the old days.

"I'm wondering what they wanted," she said as Tobias busied himself with the coffee machine. She looked around with curiosity. So it was in this house that the two girls were murdered, Snow White and Laura.

"They were probably waiting for me, and you happened to run into them," he said. He set two cups on the table, along with the sugar bowl, and got some milk out of the fridge.

"You say that so matter-of-factly. Aren't you the least bit afraid?"

Tobias leaned against the counter and crossed his arms. He looked at her, his head tilted. "What am I supposed to do? Go into hiding? Run away? I won't give them the satisfaction."

"Do you know who they might have been?"

"I'm not a hundred percent sure. But I can guess."

Amelie could feel herself blushing under his gaze. What was going on? Nothing like this had ever happened to her before. She hardly dared look him in the eye, and he could probably tell what kind of emotional chaos he was unleashing inside her. The coffee machine was making alarming noises and sending out clouds of steam.

"It probably needs decalcifying," she diagnosed the problem. A sudden smile brightened her gloomy face, making her look totally different. Amelie stared at Tobias. She felt a crazy need to protect him, to help him.

"The coffeemaker really isn't a top priority," he said with a grin. "First I have to finish cleaning up outside."

At that moment the doorbell rang shrilly. Tobias went to the window, and the smile vanished from his face.

"It's the cops again," he said, looking tense. "You'd better go. I don't want anyone to see you here."

She nodded and got up. He led her down the hall to a door.

"This leads through the pantry to the stables. Can you make it on your own?"

"Sure. I'm not scared. Now that it's light out those guys aren't going to be hanging around anymore," she replied, determined to sound tough. They looked at each other and Amelie lowered her eyes.

"Thanks," said Tobias softly. "You're a brave girl."

Amelie made a dismissive gesture and turned to go. Then something occurred to Tobias.

"Wait a minute," he said, stopping her.

"Yes?"

"Why were you actually out in the yard?"

"From the picture in the paper I recognized the man who pushed your mother off the bridge," Amelie said after a brief hesitation. "It was Manfred Wagner. Laura's father."

"You again." Tobias Sartorius made no bones that the police were not particularly welcome. "I don't have much time. What is it now?"

Kirchhoff sniffed at the air, smelling the aroma of freshly brewed coffee.

"Do you have company?" she asked. Bodenstein thought he'd seen another person through the kitchen window, a woman with dark hair.

"No, I don't." Tobias remained standing in the doorway with his arms folded. He didn't invite them in, although it had started to rain. Fine with him.

"You must have been working like a maniac," said Pia with a friendly smile. "The place looks fantastic."

Her attempt at friendliness fell flat. Tobias Sartorius remained aloof, his body language radiating disapproval.

"We just wanted to tell you that the remains of Laura Wagner have been found," Bodenstein said then.

"Where?"

"You ought to know that better than we do," Bodenstein countered coolly. "After all, you did transport Laura's body there on the evening of September 6, 1997, in the trunk of your car."

"No, I did not." Tobias frowned, but his voice remained calm. "I never saw Laura again after she ran off. But I've already told the police that a hundred times, haven't I?"

"Laura's skeleton was discovered by construction workers at the old military airfield in Eschborn," said Kirchhoff. "In an underground tank."

Tobias looked at her and swallowed. There was a look of utter incomprehension in his eyes.

"At the airfield?" he murmured quietly. "I would never have gone there."

All his animosity seemed to drop away at once; he appeared dismayed and distraught. Kirchhoff reminded herself that he'd had eleven years to prepare himself for this moment of being confronted with what he'd done. He must have reckoned that someone would find the girl's corpse one day. Maybe he had practiced his reaction, planning in detail how he could make his look of surprise believable. On the other hand—why would he do that? He had served his time, and it shouldn't matter to him if the bodies were found now. She thought about how her colleague Hasse had characterized this man: arrogant, overbearing, ice cold. Was that true?

"We'd be interested to know whether Laura was already dead when you threw her in the tank," said Bodenstein. Kirchhoff kept her eyes fixed on Tobias. He was very pale and his mouth was quivering as though he were about to break out in tears.

"I can't answer that question," he replied tonelessly.

"Then who can?" asked Kirchhoff.

"That's something that has occupied my mind day and night for eleven years." His voice sounded like he was struggling to maintain control. "I don't care whether you believe me or not. I have long since gotten used to being considered the villain."

"Things would have gone much better for your mother if you'd said back then what you did with the girl," Bodenstein remarked. Tobias shoved his hands in the pockets of his jeans.

"Does that mean you found out who the bastard was that pushed my mother off the bridge?"

"No, we haven't yet," Bodenstein conceded. "But for the time being we're assuming it was someone from the village."

Tobias laughed. A brief, cheerless snort.

"Congratulations on your incredibly astute observation," he said mockingly. "I could help you out, because I happen to know who it was. But why should I?"

"Because that person committed a crime," replied Bodenstein. "You have to tell us what you know."

"I don't have to do shit." Tobias Sartorius shook his head. "Maybe you're better than your colleagues were eleven years ago. Things would have *gone considerably better* for my mother, my father, and me if the police had done their work properly and caught the real killer."

Kirchhoff wanted to say something to placate him, but Bodenstein spoke before she had a chance. "Naturally"—his voice was sarcastic—"you're innocent, of course. We know that. Our prisons are full of innocent people."

Tobias looked at him stonefaced. Fury suppressed with difficulty flickered in his eyes. "You cops are all the same—arrogant and full of yourselves," he hissed contemptuously. "You don't have a clue what's going on here. Now get out and leave me in peace!"

Before Kirchhoff or Bodenstein could say a word, he slammed the door in their faces.

"You shouldn't have said that," Pia said reproachfully as they walked back to the car. "Now you've really turned him against us, and we still don't know anything more."

"But I was right!" Oliver stopped short. "Did you see his eyes? The guy is capable of anything, and if he really does know who pushed his mother off the bridge, then that man is in danger."

"You're biased," Pia chided him. "He comes home after ten years in the joint—possibly having been sentenced unjustly—and finds out that everything here has changed. His mother is attacked and seriously injured, unknown vandals spray graffiti on his parents' house. Is it any wonder he's pissed off?"

"Give me a break, Pia! You can't seriously believe that they convicted the wrong guy for a double murder!"

"I don't believe anything. But I've found discrepancies in the old case files, so I have my doubts."

"The man is ice cold. And as far as how the villagers have reacted, I can perfectly understand it."

"Don't tell me you condone somebody scrawling insults on the walls and the whole village conspiring to cover up the identity of the real killer!" Pia shook her head in disbelief.

"I'm not saying that I condone it," said Oliver. They were standing underneath the arch of the village gate and squabbling like an old married couple, so they didn't notice when Tobias Sartorius left his house and headed across the yard in back.

Andrea Wagner couldn't sleep. They had found Laura's body, or rather, what was left of it. Finally, finally, all the uncertainty was over. They had given up hoping for a miracle long ago. At first they had felt nothing but boundless relief, but now the grief had set in. For eleven long years she had forbidden herself tears and sadness, displaying great strength and supporting her husband, who had abandoned himself to brooding about their missing child. But she couldn't afford to break down. She had to keep the company going so that they could pay their debts at the bank. And there were the younger children, who deserved their mother's attention. Nothing was the same as it once had been. Manfred had lost all his energy and joie de vivre, acting as if a millstone were attached to his leg, succumbing to his whiny self-pity and too much drinking. Sometimes she despised him. It was so easy for him to slip into hating Tobias's family, and to her that seemed like a cop-out.

Andrea opened the door to Laura's room, where nothing had been changed for the past eleven years. Manfred had insisted on it, and she had acquiesced. She turned on the light, taking the photo of Laura from the desk and sitting down on the bed. She waited in vain for the tears to come. Her thoughts strayed to that moment eleven years ago, when the police had stood at the front door and informed her that after evaluating the evidence they had arrested Tobias Sartorius for the murder of their daughter.

Why Tobias? she had thought in bewilderment. Offhand she could think of ten other boys who had more reasons to take revenge on Laura than Tobias did. Andrea had known what people in the village were whispering about her daughter. They had called her a slut, a calculating little bitch with big ambitions. While Manfred loved and idolized his oldest daughter unconditionally and always found excuses for her bad behavior, Andrea had seen Laura's weaknesses and hoped she would eventually grow out of them. But the girl hadn't had the chance. It was odd, really, that she had such a hard time remembering anything positive when she thought of Laura. Memories of the unpleasant things were more vivid, and there had been plenty of those. Laura had always had a low opinion of her father and was ashamed of him. She would have preferred a father like Claudius Terlinden, who had style and power—it was something she never hesitated to tell Manfred to his face at every suitable or unsuitable opportunity. Manfred had swallowed these insults without batting an eye, and they did no damage to the love he felt for his beautiful daughter. Andrea, on the other hand, was shocked to realize how little she knew her daughter, and blamed herself for failing to bring her up better. At the same time she was scared. What if Laura found out that she was having an affair with Claudius, her boss?

Night after night she had lain awake worrying about her daughter. During Laura's teenage years Andrea had probably had even more reasons for concern. Laura was getting wild with the boys in town—until she finally starting going steady with Tobias. All of a sudden she seemed changed: content and happy. Tobias was doing her good. Undoubtedly he was something special; he was good-looking, he excelled in school and at sports, and the other boys listened to him. He was exactly what Laura had always wanted, and his popularity also rubbed off on her, his girlfriend. For half a year everything went well—until Stefanie Schneeberger came to Altenhain. Laura had instantly recognized her as competition and quickly made friends with her, but it did no good. Tobias fell for Stefanie and broke up with Laura, who clearly couldn't cope with this setback. Her mother had no idea what exactly had transpired between the two young people that summer, but she knew that Laura was playing with fire when she urged her friends to turn against Stefanie. Andrea had discovered Laura at the photocopier in her office with a big stack of copies she had made. Laura blew her top when her mother tried to take a look at what was printed on them. They got into a fierce argument, and in her fury Laura ended up leaving the original in the copier. There was only one sentence in bold type on the white page: **SNOW WHITE MUST DIE**.

Andrea had folded up the sheet of paper and kept it, but she never showed it to her husband or the police. The idea that *her* child would wish the death of another human being was simply intolerable. Had Laura become the victim of her own intrigue? Andrea had kept her mouth shut and let things run their course. And every night she'd listened to Manfred glorifying their daughter.

"Laura," she murmured, caressing the photo with her forefinger. "What did you do?"

Suddenly a tear ran down her cheek, then another. She blinked, wiping her hand over her face. It wasn't grief that brought tears to her eyes, but the feeling of guilt that she hadn't loved her daughter.

It was half past one before he stood in front of her house. For three hours he had driven around the area aimlessly. So much had bombarded him today that he simply couldn't stand staying at home. First Amelie, who had suddenly appeared covered in blood. The shock at the sight of her. It wasn't the blood on her face that had made his adrenaline level shoot up to the heights of Mount Everest, but her incredible likeness to Stefanie. Yet she was completely different. Not the vain little beauty queen who had bewitched him, seduced him, and duped him, only to dump him with such ice-cold indifference. Amelie was an impressive girl. And she seemed to have no fears of being touched.

Then the cops showed up. They had found Laura's body. Because it was raining so hard, he'd had to leave off cleaning up the yard and instead turned his anger to cleaning out his room. He ripped down the stupid posters from the walls and summarily stuffed the contents of the cabinets and all the drawers into blue trash bags. Just get rid of all that crap! Suddenly he was holding a CD in his hand. *Time to Say Goodbye* by Sarah Brightman and Andrea Bocelli. Stefanie had given him the CD because she had kissed him for the first time to this song in June, at the graduation party. He put the CD on, not understanding the empty feeling that abruptly seized him with the first chord, refusing to let him go. He had never before felt so alone and abandoned, not even in prison. There at least he could hope for better days, but now he knew that they would never come. His life was over.

It took a moment before Nadia opened the door and let him in. He'd been afraid that she wasn't home. He hadn't come to sleep with her, he hadn't been thinking of that at all, but when she stood before him, blinking at the bright light, her blond hair loose on her shoulders, so sweet and warm, a flash of sexual desire shot through him with a power he wouldn't have thought possible.

"What—" she began, but Tobias muffled the rest of her question with a kiss, pulling her close, almost expecting her to resist and push him away. But the opposite happened. She slipped his wet leather jacket from his shoulders, unbuttoned his shirt, and shoved up his T-shirt. The next instant they were lying on the floor and he entered her impetuously, felt her tongue in his mouth and her hands on his ass, inciting him to plunge harder and faster. Much too soon he felt the tidal wave roaring, the heat that made him sweat from every pore. Then it broke over him, so glorious and such a relief that he moaned—a moan that turned to a muted cry. With his heart pounding he lay on top of her for a few seconds and could hardly believe what he had done. He rolled off, lying on his back with his eyes closed, gasping for air like a fish out of water. Her soft laughter made him open his eyes.

"What is it?" he asked in confusion.

"I think we need a little more practice," she said. With a nimble movement she got to her feet and held out her hand to him. He took it, got up with a groan, and followed her into the bedroom after getting rid of his shoes and jeans. The spirits of the past had vanished. At least for the moment.

Thursday, November 13, 2008

"The police came by my house yesterday." Tobias blew on the hot coffee that Nadia had poured for him. Last night he hadn't wanted to bring up that topic, but now he had to tell her about it. "They found Laura's skeleton at the old airfield in Eschborn. In an underground tank."

"What?" Nadia, who was just about to take a sip from her cup, stopped short. They were sitting at the gray granite table in the kitchen, where they had sat together last night. It was a little past seven, and it was still pitch dark outside the panoramic window. Nadia had to catch a flight to Hamburg at eight o'clock, where the exterior shots were being filmed for a new episode of the series in which she played the detective superintendent.

"When . . ." She set down her cup. "I mean . . . How do they know it's Laura?"

"No idea." Tobias shook his head. "They didn't say much. At first they didn't want to tell me where they found the skeleton. The cop in charge just said I must know where it was."

"Oh my God," Nadia gasped.

"Nadia." He leaned over and put his hand on hers. "Please tell me if you want me to leave."

"Why would you think that?"

"I can see that you're scared of me."

"What nonsense."

He let go of her hand, stood up, and turned his back to her. For a moment he struggled with himself. Half the night he had lain awake, listening to her steady breathing and asking himself when she might find him superfluous. He was already apprehensive about the day she would get rid of him with embarrassed excuses, then avoid him, pretending that she wasn't home. That day was bound to come. He wasn't the right man for her. He could never fit in with her world, her life.

"It's not easy to ignore the topic," he said at last in a hoarse voice. "I was convicted of murder and did ten years in the joint. We can't simply act as if that never happened and we're still twenty years old."

He turned around. "I have no idea who killed Laura and Stefanie. I can't rule out that it could have been me, but why can't I remember? And so far I can't. There's only this . . . this black hole. The psychologist at the trial said that the human brain sometimes reacts with a sort of amnesia, like after a bad shock. But don't you think I would remember something, at least? Like putting Laura in the trunk and driving somewhere? But it's all a blank. The last thing I remember is Stefanie telling me that she . . . that she . . . didn't love me anymore. And then Felix and Jörg came to the door at some point, and I had drunk so much vodka that I was feeling terrible. Then suddenly the cops were standing there and claiming that I'd killed Laura and Stefanie!"

Nadia sat there studying him with her big jade-green eyes.

"Don't you see, Nadia?" His tone was pleading. The pain inside him was back, stronger than ever before. Too much was at stake. He didn't want to get into a relationship with Nadia when he knew that she would only end up disappointed again. "It torments me not to know what really happened. Did I kill them? Or didn't I?"

"Tobi," Nadia said softly. "I love you. And have for as long as I can remember. It doesn't matter to me, even if you did do it."

Tobias grimaced in despair. She simply didn't want to understand. He urgently needed someone to believe him. To believe in him. He couldn't handle living as an outcast; it would destroy him.

"But it matters to me," he insisted. "I've lost ten years of my life. I no longer have a future. Somebody has destroyed me. And I can't just act like it's all in the past now."

"So what do you plan to do?"

"I want to know the truth. Even if it means finding out that I really did do it."

Nadia pushed back her chair. She came over to him, threw her arms around him, and looked into his eyes.

"I believe you," she said softly. "And if you want, I'll help you with everything. Just don't go back to Altenhain. Please."

"Where am I supposed to go?"

"Stay here. Or in my house in Ticino in Switzerland. Or in Hamburg." She smiled, warming to the idea. "That's it! Come with me now! You'll like the house. It's right on the water."

Tobias hesitated. "I can't just leave my father alone like that. And my mother needs me too. As soon as she's feeling better, then maybe."

"From here you can drive to see your father in Altenhain in fifteen minutes." Nadia's big green eyes were close to his. He could smell the scent of her skin, the fragrance of her shampoo. Half the men in Germany dreamed of being asked to move in with Nadia von Bredow. What was stopping him?

"Tobi, please!" She put her hand on his cheek. "I'm worried about you. I don't want anything bad to happen to you. When I think what might have happened if those guys caught you instead of that girl . . ."

Amelie. He'd forgotten all about her. She was in Altenhain, and somewhere in that village the truth about those terrible events was hiding.

"I'll be careful," he reassured her. "Don't worry."

"I love you, Tobi."

"I love you too," he replied, and took her in his arms.

"Boss?" Kai Ostermann was standing in the doorway of his office, holding two sheets of paper in his hand.

Bodenstein stopped in his tracks. "What's up?"

"We just got this fax." Ostermann handed him the pages and scrutinized Bodenstein's face; since it revealed nothing, Ostermann refrained from commenting.

"Thanks" was all Bodenstein said, going into his office with his heart pounding. It was the GPS track of Cosima's cell phone over the past two weeks, which he had ordered the day before yesterday from the phone company. For the first time he had used his professional clout to find out something of a personal nature. The urge to know was stronger than his guilty conscience about an action that a malicious officer might interpret as abuse of his position. He sat down at his desk and took a moment to prepare himself. What he read robbed him of any illusion. She had indeed been in Mainz on two different days, and only for about an hour each time. But she had spent the mornings of eight days in Frankfurt. Bodenstein leaned his elbows on the desk, rested his chin on his fists, and paused to think. Then he grabbed the phone and punched in the number of Cosima's office. Kira Gasthuber, Cosima's production assistant and jill-of-all-trades, picked up after two rings. Cosima was out of the office for a short time. Why didn't he try her cell?

So that she won't lie to me, you nitwit, thought Bodenstein. He was about to hang up when he heard the bright voice of his youngest daughter in the background. All at once an alarm went off in his head. Cosima normally took Sophia everywhere with her. Why had she left the girl at the office today? To his question Kira replied that Cosima hadn't been out for long, and Sophia was amusing herself as best she could with her and René.

When he hung up, Bodenstein sat for a while at his desk. His thoughts were churning. Five times Cosima's phone had been tracked to the cellular zone located in the north end of Frankfurt between Glauburgstrasse, Oeder Weg, the Eckenheimer highway, and Eschersheimer Park. On the city map it might look small, but that area contained hundreds of buildings with thousands of apartments. Damn. Where was she? And most importantly, with whom? How would he react if it turned out that she was actually cheating on him? And how come he thought she had a need to cheat on him? Sure, their sex life was no longer as lively as before Sophia was born; the presence of a small child took care of that. But it wasn't as if Cosima was missing out on anything. Or was she? To his dismay he could no longer remember the last time he had slept with his wife. He thought back. He did remember! It was the night she came home a little tipsy and in a good mood from her friend's birthday party. Bodenstein got out his day planner and searched for that date. A strange feeling came sneaking up on him that got stronger the farther back he paged. Had he totally forgotten to enter Bernhard's birthday? No, he hadn't. Bernhard had celebrated his fiftieth on September 20 at Schloss Johannisberg in the Rheingau. That couldn't be right! He counted and realized that he hadn't slept with Cosima in eight weeks. Was he the one to blame if she was unfaithful? There was a knock on the door and Nicola Engel stepped in.

"What's up?" he asked.

With a frosty expression on her face, she asked, "When were you planning on telling me that Detective Inspector Behnke has been moonlighting against regulations at a bar in Sachsenhausen?"

Damn. It had totally slipped his mind, he was so wrapped up in his own problems. He didn't ask where she had heard about it, and made no attempt to offer excuses.

"I wanted to talk with him first," was all he said. "I haven't had a chance to do that yet."

"Tonight at six thirty you will. I've ordered Behnke to come in, sick or not. See about fixing this situation."

•   •   •

His cell phone rang as he was heading for the exit at the customs checkpoint. Lars Terlinden switched his briefcase to the other hand and took the call. All day long he'd been at the beck and call of the board of directors in Zürich. A couple of months ago they'd been celebrating him like the Savior Himself for this very same deal, and now they wanted to crucify him. Damn it, he was no prophet. How was he to know that Dr. Markus Schönhausen's real name was Matthias Mutzler, that he wasn't from Potsdam, but from some village in the hills of southern Germany, and a con man of the worst sort? Ultimately it wasn't Lars's problem if the legal department of his bank didn't do their homework. Heads had rolled, and his would be next if he couldn't figure out a way to make up the loss, which totaled in the hundreds of millions.

"I'll be at the office in twenty minutes," he told his secretary as the milky glass pane slid open before him. He was exhausted, burned out; his nerves were shot and he was done with the world. All by the age of thirty. He could only sleep by taking pills, and eating was difficult, but drinking was okay. Lars Terlinden knew that he was well on the way to becoming an alcoholic, but he would worry about that problem later, when this crisis was over. Although there was no end in sight. The world economy was shaky, the biggest banks in the States were going broke. Lehman Brothers was just the beginning. His own employer, still one of the biggest Swiss banks, had let go five thousand workers worldwide in the past year. In the offices and corridors, naked fear about the future was the rule. His phone rang again, so he stuck it in his pocket and ignored it. The news of the collapse of Schönhausen's real estate empire six weeks ago had come out of the blue; just two days earlier he had met with Schönhausen at the Hotel Adlon in Berlin for dinner. By that time the man had known for a while that bankruptcy was looming, that slippery weasel. At this very moment he was being sought by Interpol because he'd skipped out. After much effort Lars Terlinden had at least succeeded in securitizing a large part of the credit portfolio and selling it to investors, but 350 million euros were gone.

A woman stepped into his path. In a hurry, he tried to go around her, but she resolutely stood her ground and spoke to him. Only then did he recognize his mother, whom he hadn't seen in eight years.

"Lars!" she implored. "Lars, please wait!"

She looked the same as always. Petite and immaculate, her golden blond hair cut in a perfect pageboy. Light makeup, a pearl necklace on her sun-tanned décolletage. She smiled meekly, and that instantly made him see red.

"What do you want?" he snapped. "Did your husband send you?"

He never deigned to say the words "my father."

"No, Lars. Could you stop for a moment? Please."

He rolled his eyes and did as she asked. As a boy he had adored his mother, even worshipped her. He always missed her terribly whenever she went on trips for a few days or several weeks and he and Thies were left in the housekeeper's care. He would have forgiven her everything in return for her love, but he never got more than a smile, lovely words, and promises. Only after a very long time did he realize that she could give him nothing more because she had nothing left to give. Christine Terlinden was an empty vessel, a shallow beauty with no personality to speak of, who had made it her life's work to be the ideal wife for the successful CEO Claudius Terlinden.

"You're looking good, son. A bit too thin perhaps." Even now she was true to herself. After all this time she could only come up with this hackneyed phrase. Lars Terlinden had begun to feel contempt for his mother when he realized that all his life she had deceived him.

"What do you want, Mother?" he repeated impatiently.

"Tobias is back from prison," she told him, lowering her voice. "And the police have found Laura's skeleton. At the old airfield in Eschborn."

He clenched his teeth. Suddenly his life raced backward at time-lapse speed. Here in the middle of the arrival hall at Frankfurt Airport he had the horrible feeling of shrinking to a pimply nineteen-year-old with naked fear breathing down his neck. Laura! He would never forget her face, her laugh, her carefree joy that had all come to such an abrupt end. He hadn't had a chance to speak to Tobias again. His father had made all the decisions for him so fast, banishing him at once to the farm of some acquaintance in deepest Oxfordshire. *Think about your future, boy! Stay out of this and keep your mouth shut. Then nothing will happen.* Of course he had listened to his father. Had stayed out of it and kept his mouth shut. It was too late by the time he heard about Tobi's conviction. For eleven years he had done everything he could to avoid thinking about any of it: that awful night, his horror, his fear. For eleven shitty years he had worked almost round the clock just so he could forget. And now his mother came sashaying up in her little fur coat and tore open the old wounds with her doll-like smile.

"I'm not interested in that anymore, Mother," he snapped. "It has nothing to do with me."

"But—" she began, but he didn't let her finish speaking.

"Leave me alone!" he snarled. "Don't you get it? I don't want you to contact me ever again! Just stay away from me, the way you've always done."

With that he turned on his heel and left her standing there. He strode to the escalator that led down to the S-Bahn commuter train station.

They stood in the garage drinking beer out of the bottle, just like before. Tobias felt uncomfortable, and all the others looked like they did too. Why in the world had he come here? Much to his surprise his old friend Jörg had called that afternoon and invited him over to have a beer along with Felix and a couple of other old pals. In their youth they had often met in the big garage that belonged to Jörg's uncle to tinker with their motor-assisted bicycles, later with their mopeds, and finally with their cars. Jörg was a gifted auto mechanic who had dreamed since he was a boy of becoming a race-car driver. The garage was just as Tobias remembered it, smelling of motor oil and lacquer, of leather and polish. They sat on the same old workbench, on turned-over beer crates, and on piles of car tires. Nothing around them had changed. Tobias stayed out of the conversation, which had an air of forced camaraderie, no doubt because of his presence. Each of the men had greeted him with a handshake, of course, but the joy of seeing each other again was somewhat constrained. After a while Tobias, Jörg, and Felix found themselves standing together. Felix had become a roofer with his father's company. Even as a teenager he was powerfully built, and the hard work combined with avid beer consumption over the years had turned him into a colossus. His jovial eyes almost vanished in a layer of fat when he laughed. Tobias was reminded of a raisin bun. Jörg, on the other hand, looked almost the same as he used to, except that his hairline had receded quite a ways.

"So what did Lars wind up doing?" Tobias asked.

"Not what his old man had hoped." Felix gave a malicious grin. "Even rich people have problems with their kids. In this case one of them is a moron and the other one told his father to fuck off."

"Lars has really made a cushy career for himself," said Jörg. "My mom told me, she heard it from a relative. Investment banking. Big-time money. He's married with two kids, and he bought a huge villa in Glashütten after he got back from England."

"I thought he always wanted to study theology and become a pastor," said Tobias. To his amazement it still hurt to think about his best friend who had disappeared from his life so suddenly.

"Well, I never wanted to be a roofer either." Felix popped another bottle of beer with the opener on his key chain. "But the army didn't want me and the police didn't either, and I gave up on the bakery apprenticeship shortly after . . . uh . . . you know . . ."

He broke off, lowering his eyes in embarrassment.

"And after my accident I could write off my career as a race-car driver," Jörg hastened to add before the silence got even more awkward. "So I didn't wind up in the Formula 1, but at the Black Horse instead. You know that my sister married Jagielski, don't you?"

Tobias nodded. "My father told me."

"Ah." Jörg took a swig from the beer bottle. "It seems like none of us got to do what we dreamed of doing."

"Nathalie did," Felix countered. "Man, did we ever laugh when she said she wanted to be a famous actress!"

"She always was ambitious," said Jörg. "The way she used to boss us around. But I never thought she'd turn into such a celebrity."

"Well, yeah." Tobias smiled wryly. "Just like I never dreamed I'd learn locksmithing in the joint or study economics."

His friends hesitated for a moment, embarrassed, but then they laughed. The alcohol was loosening them up. After the fifth bottle of beer Felix turned talkative.

"To this day I blame myself for telling the cops that we'd gone back to your place, man," he said to Tobias, dropping his hand on his shoulder.

"You guys just told the truth." Tobias shrugged. "Nobody had any idea what it would all lead to. But it doesn't matter now. I'm back, and I'm really glad that you guys don't cross the street when you see me, like most of the people here."

"Bullshit." Jörg slapped his other shoulder. "We're friends, man! Remember how we fixed up that old Opel that my uncle spent a thousand hours restoring? And how we drove the shit out of it? Man, those were the days!"

Tobias remembered, and Felix did too. So now they'd reached the *Remember when* phase. The party at the Terlindens when the girls got naked and ran around the house wearing Mrs. Terlinden's furs. Micha's birthday when the cops showed up. The tests of courage at the cemetery. The trip to Italy with the junior soccer club. The bonfire on St. Martin's Day that got out of hand because Felix had used a canister of gasoline to get it going. They couldn't stop laughing and recalling the old days. Jörg had to wipe away tears of laughter.

"Do you guys remember how my sister stole my old man's key ring and we raced around inside the old airplane hangar? Man, that was cool!"

Amelie sat at her desk surfing the Web when the doorbell rang. She closed her laptop and jumped up. It was a quarter to eleven. Damn. Had the old lady forgotten her front door key? In her stocking feet she rushed downstairs before the bell rang again and woke the kids up after she'd coaxed them into bed an hour ago. She cast a glance at the little monitor that was connected to cameras on both sides of the front door. The fuzzy black-and-white picture showed a man with blond hair. Amelie tore open the front door and was surprised to see Thies standing there. In all the time she'd known him, he'd never once come to her front door, and he certainly had never rung the bell. Her surprise turned to concern when she saw the condition her friend was in. She had never seen Thies so upset. His hands were fluttering here and there, his eyes were flickering, and he was twitching all over.

"What's the matter?" Amelie asked softly. "Did something happen?"

Instead of answering, Thies held out a roll of paper that was carefully tied with a wide ribbon. Amelie's feet were turning into blocks of ice on the cold steps, but she was truly worried about her friend.

"Wouldn't you like to come inside?"

Thies shook his head vigorously and kept glancing around, as if afraid that he'd been followed.

"You can't show these pictures to anybody," he said suddenly in his slightly hoarse-sounding voice. "You have to hide them."

"Got it," she said. "I will."

The headlights of a car crept up the street through the fog and caught them for a moment as the car turned into the Lauterbachs' driveway. The garage was located only five yards below the stairs Amelie was standing on—alone now, as she suddenly realized. Thies seemed to have been swallowed up by the earth. Daniela Lauterbach turned off the engine and climbed out.

"Hello, Amelie!" came her friendly greeting.

"Hello, Dr. Lauterbach," Amelie replied.

"Why are you standing there on the porch? Did you lock yourself out?"

"I just got home from work," Amelie said quickly, without quite knowing why she lied to her neighbor.

"All right then. Say hello to your parents. Good night." Dr. Lauterbach waved and opened the door of the two-car garage with the remote. She went inside and the garage door came down behind her.

"Thies?" Amelie hissed. "Where are you?"

She jumped when he came out from behind the big yew tree next to the front door.

"What's all this about?" she whispered. "Why—?"

The words stuck in her throat when she saw Thies's face. In his eyes she saw naked fear—what was he afraid of? Deeply worried, she reached out her hand and touched his arm to calm him. He flinched.

"You have to take good care of those pictures." The words came out in a stammer, and his eyes were shining feverishly. "Nobody can see those pictures. Not even you! You have to promise me!"

"Okay, okay, I promise. But what—"

Before she could finish her question, Thies had vanished into the foggy night. Amelie stared after him, shaking her head. She couldn't make any sense out of her friend's behavior. But that was no surprise—Thies wasn't like anyone else.

•   •   •

Cosima lay sound asleep on the couch in the living room; the dog had curled up behind her knees and didn't raise his head but just lazily wagged the tip of his tail when Bodenstein came in and stopped to take in the peaceful scene. Cosima was snoring quietly, her reading glasses had slipped down her nose, and the book she'd been reading lay on her chest. Normally he would have gone over to wake her with a kiss, cautiously, so as not to frighten her. But the invisible wall that suddenly stood between them held him back. To his astonishment, the usual feeling of tenderness that he felt whenever he saw his wife was now missing. It was high time they had an open confrontation, before the mistrust poisoned their marriage. What he really ought to do right now was grab her by the shoulder and shake her and then demand to know why she'd lied to him. But he was stopped by his cowardly craving for harmony and the fear of learning a truth that he wouldn't be able to bear. He turned away and went into the kitchen. The dog, driven by greedy hope, jumped off the couch to follow him, which woke up Cosima. She appeared in the kitchen with a sleepy look on her face, as he took a yogurt out of the fridge.

"Hello," he said.

"I guess I fell asleep," she replied. He ate the yogurt, watching her discreetly. All at once he saw the wrinkles in her face that he'd never noticed before, the skin starting to sag at her throat, and the puffiness under her tired eyes. She looked like a woman of forty-five. Had the soft-focus lens of his affection disappeared along with his trust?

"Why did you call me at the office and not on my cell?" she asked casually as she searched in the fridge for something.

"I don't remember," he lied, carefully scraping out the last of the yogurt from the container. "I must have hit the wrong speed-dial number. It wasn't important."

"Well, I was just down at the Main-Taunus Center shopping for a few things." Cosima closed the refrigerator door and yawned. "Kira took care of little Sophie for me. It's always a little faster if I don't have to take her along."

"Hmm, of course." He set the empty yogurt container down for the dog to lick. For a moment he pondered whether he ought to ask her what she bought, because he didn't believe a word she'd said. And suddenly it was clear to him that he never would again.

• • •

Amelie hid the roll of pictures in her chest of drawers and sat back down at her laptop. But she could no longer concentrate. It seemed that the pictures were calling softly to her: *Look at us! Come on! Take us out!*

She turned on her chair and stared at the dresser, wrangling with her conscience. Downstairs car doors slammed and the front door opened.

"We're back!" her father called. Amelie hurried downstairs to say hello to the people she lived with. Although Barbara and the little tykes had welcomed her kindly, she could never bring herself to think "my family," much less say it. Then she went back to her room and lay down on the bed. In the next room the toilet flushed. What could be in those pictures? Thies always painted such abstract stuff, except for that cool portrait of her that she'd seen yesterday. But why did he absolutely want to hide these pictures? It seemed to be damned important to him since he'd actually rung her doorbell and asked her not to show them to anybody. And that was really strange.

Amelie waited until peace and quiet returned to the house, then she went over to the chest of drawers and took out the roll. It was pretty heavy, so it must be more than only two or three pictures. And they didn't smell as strongly of paint as freshly painted ones did. Carefully she untied the many knots in the ribbon that Thies had wrapped around the roll. There were eight pictures in a relatively small format. And they were completely different, not at all Thies's usual painting style. Very representational and true to life with people that . . . Amelie froze and looked more closely at the first painting. She felt a tingle at the back of her neck and her heart started beating faster. In front of a big barn with a door wide open two boys were bending over a blond girl lying on the ground, her head in a pool of blood. Another boy with dark curly hair stood by, while a fourth was running with a panic-stricken expression straight toward the observer. And this fourth boy was—Thies! She feverishly began looking at the other paintings.

"Oh my God," she whispered. The barn with the open door, next to it a somewhat lower stable building, the same people. Thies sat next to the barn, the boy with the dark curls stood at the open door of the stable and watched what was happening inside the stall. One of the boys was raping the blond girl, and the other one was holding her down. Amelie swallowed and turned to the next one. Again the barn, another girl with long black hair and a tight, bright-blue dress, kissing a man. He had his hand on her breast and she had wound one leg around his thigh. The image looked incredibly lifelike. In the rear of the dark barn was the curly-haired boy from the other pictures. The pictures looked almost like photographs. Thies had caught every detail: the colors of the clothes, the necklace on the girl, the text on a T-shirt. Unbelievable! The pictures undoubtedly showed the Sartorius barnyard. And they depicted the events from September 1997. Amelie smoothed out the last picture with both hands and was stunned by what she saw. The house was so quiet that she could hear her pulse pounding in her ears. The picture showed the man who had kissed the black-haired girl, but from the front this time. She knew him. She definitely knew him.

Friday, November 14, 2008

"Good morning." Gregor Lauterbach nodded to his office manager Ines Schürmann-Liedtke and stepped into his big office in the Cultural Ministry of the state of Hessen on Luisenplatz in Wiesbaden. Today his calendar was totally booked up. For eight o'clock a discussion with his deputy minister was scheduled, and at ten he had to give a speech at the plenum in which he would present the budget proposal for the coming year. At noon an hour was reserved for a brief lunch with representatives of the teachers' delegation from Wisconsin, the U.S. sister state of Hessen. On his desk the mail lay sorted according to importance in different colored resubmission folders. On top was the folder with the correspondence he had to sign. Lauterbach unbuttoned his jacket and sat down at his desk to take care of the most pressing items. Twenty to eight. The deputy minister would be punctual, he always was.

"Your coffee, sir." Ines Schürmann-Liedtke came in and set down a cup of steaming coffee.

"Thank you," he said with a smile. The woman was not only an intelligent and highly efficient office manager, but also a real feast for the eyes: an amply

built brunette with big brown eyes and skin like milk and honey. She reminded him a bit of his wife, Daniela. Sometimes he permitted himself lusty
daydreams in which Ines played a leading role, but in reality his behavior toward her was always above reproach. He could have replaced the staff in his
office two years ago when he took over this position, but he had liked Ines
immediately, and she thanked him for saving her job with absolute loyalty
and unbelievable diligence.

"You're looking wonderful again today, Ines," he said, sipping his coffee.
"That shade of green looks magnificent on you."

"Thank you very much." She smiled at the compliment, but turned professional at once and read off the list of callers who had asked that he call them
back. Lauterbach listened with one ear as he signed the letters Ines had written, nodding or shaking his head. When she was done he handed her the
correspondence. She left the office and he devoted himself to the mail that
had already been sorted. There were four letters marked PERSONAL and ad-
dressed to him, and Ines had not opened those. He slit them open with the
letter opener, scanned the first two quickly and put them aside. When he
opened the third one, he caught his breath.

*If you keep your mouth shut, nothing will happen. If not, the police
will find out what you lost that time in the barn when you screwed
your underage pupil. Fond greetings from Snow White.*

His mouth was suddenly dry as dust. He looked at the second page, which
showed a photo of a key ring. Fear crept through his veins, and he broke out
in a cold sweat. This was no joke. His thoughts raced. Who had written this?
Who could have known about him and his slipup with that girl? And why
the hell was this letter arriving now? Gregor Lauterbach felt like his heart
was going to jump out of his chest. For eleven long years he'd succeeded in
repressing those fateful events. But now it had all come back, so vividly that
it seemed like only yesterday. He stood up and went to the window, staring
out at Luisenplatz, deserted in the gradually lifting darkness of this dreary
November morning. He breathed slowly in and out. *Just don't lose your nerve*

now! In a desk drawer he found the well-worn notebook in which he'd kept telephone numbers for years. When he picked up the receiver he noticed to his consternation that his hand was shaking.

The gnarled old oak stood in the front part of the large park, not twenty feet from the wall that surrounded the entire property. She had never noticed the treehouse before, perhaps because in the summertime it had been hidden by the thick foliage of the tree. It wasn't easy in a miniskirt and stockings to climb up the rickety-looking rungs of the ramshackle ladder, which was slippery from the rain of the past few days. She hoped Thies wouldn't choose this moment to come out of his studio. He would know at once what she was doing here. Finally she reached the treehouse and crawled into it on all fours. It was a solid box of wood, like the elevated blinds that hunters used in the woods. Amelie straightened up cautiously and looked around, then sat down on the bench and looked out the window in front. Bingo! She dug her iPod out of her jacket pocket and called up the photos she had taken last night. The perspective matched one hundred percent. From here there was a sweeping view over half the village; the upper part of the Sartorius farm with its barn and cowshed lay directly at her feet. Even with the naked eye every detail was crystal clear. If she assumed that the cherry laurel had been somewhat smaller eleven years ago, then whoever painted the pictures must have watched from this very spot.

Amelie lit a cigarette and braced her feet against the wooden wall. Who had been sitting here? It couldn't have been Thies, because he was visible in three of the pictures. Had somebody taken photos from up here that Thies had found and made paintings of later? Even more interesting was the question of who the other people in the pictures were. Laura Wagner and Stefanie "Snow White" Schneeberger, that was obvious. And the man who had done it in the barn with Snow White—she knew him too. But who were the three boys? Amelie pondered as she took a drag of her cigarette and considered what she should do with what she'd discovered. The police were out of the question. In the past she'd had nothing but bad experiences with cops; that was one of the reasons she'd been shipped off to her father's dump of a town, even though she'd heard nothing from him for twelve whole years except on birthdays and Christmas. Alternative two, telling her parents, who would also run to the cops, didn't make any sense.

A movement in the Sartorius barnyard caught her eye. Tobias went into the barn, and a little later the engine of the old tractor started up with a clatter. He was probably going to spend the somewhat dry day cleaning up some more. What if she showed *him* the pictures?

Even though Dr. Engel had expressly stated that there would be no new investigation into the two eleven-year-old murder cases, Pia kept on working with the sixteen files. Mostly to distract her thoughts from the threat behind the succinct words of the zoning department. In her mind she had already furnished the new house at Birkenhof and made it into the tasteful and cozy home she had always dreamed of owning. Much of Christoph's furniture fit wonderfully in her interior decoration dreams: the ancient, scratched refectorium table, where twelve people could sit comfortably, the well-worn leather sofa from his winter garden, the antique hutch, the charming recamier ... Pia sighed. Maybe everything would turn out all right and the building office would send the permit so she could finally get started.

She went back to focusing on the documents lying in front of her, scanned a report, and jotted down two names. Her last encounter with Tobias Sartorius had left her with a strange feeling. What if he'd been telling the truth all these years, and he really didn't kill those two girls? That would mean that the real killer was still running around loose, while the wrongful conviction had cost Sartorius ten years of his life and his father his livelihood. Next to her notes she drew a map of the village of Altenhain. Who lived where? Who was friends with whom? At first glance it seemed as though Tobias Sartorius and his parents had been respected and well-liked people in the village. But if you read between the lines, there was obvious envy underlying the words of the people questioned. Tobias Sartorius had been an extremely good-looking young man, intelligent, good at sports, and generous. He seemed to possess all the best qualifications for a brilliant future; nobody spoke ill of the star pupil, the sports ace, the heartthrob of every schoolgirl. Pia looked at some of the photos. What had it been like for Tobias's plain-looking friends with their pimply faces to be constantly compared with him? How must it have felt always to stand in his shadow, and never have first choice of the cutest girls? Weren't envy and jealousy preprogrammed? And then an opportunity had suddenly presented itself to take revenge for all the tiny defeats: "Yes, Tobias does have a violent temper sometimes," one of his best friends had stated. "Especially when he's been drinking. Then he can flip out completely."

A former teacher had characterized Tobias as a very good, ambitious pupil to whom everything came easily, but who could also apply himself to his studies with incredible discipline. Outspoken, self-confident to the point of arrogance, sometimes a hothead, and rather mature for his age. An only child who was practically worshipped by his parents. But also a boy who had a hard time dealing with competition and setbacks. Damn, where had she seen that? Pia leafed through the stacks of paper. She was looking for the transcript of the interview with Tobias's teacher, who was also the teacher of the two girls at the time of their disappearance, but it was no longer there. Pia stopped abruptly, then rummaged on her desk for her notes from last week, and compared her list to the one she had made today.

"Well, that's one thing," she said.

"What's going on?" Ostermann, eating a donut, looked over at her from his computer screen.

"The transcript from Gregor Lauterbach's interview in the case of Stefanie Schneeberger and Tobias Sartorius is missing," she replied, still shuffling paper. "How could that happen?"

"It must be in a different file." Ostermann turned back to his work and his donut. He loved to eat those deep-fried rings, and Pia had been wondering for years why her colleague hadn't become obese long ago. But Ostermann seemed to have a sensational metabolism since he could burn off the thousands of calories that he gobbled down each day. In his place she'd be literally rolling down the street by now.

"No," said Pia, shaking her head. "It's simply not here anymore!"

"Pia," Ostermann said in a patient tone of voice, "we're with the *police*. People can't just walk in here and snatch transcripts out of a case file."

"I know that. But the fact is, it's gone. I read it last week." Pia frowned. Who could be interested in that old case? Why would anyone want to steal unimportant interview transcripts? The telephone on her desk rang. She picked up and listened for a moment. In Wallau a delivery van had run off the road and burst into flames after rolling over several times. The driver was seriously injured, but in the wreckage of the vehicle the firemen had discovered at least two bodies burnt beyond recognition. With a sigh she closed the file and stowed her notes in a drawer. The prospect of crawling around in a muddy field didn't thrill her.

The wind howled around the barn, whistled through the roof beams and shook the barn door as if demanding entry. It didn't bother Tobias Sartorius. That afternoon he had spoken on the phone with a real estate agent and set up an appointment for him to look at the property next Wednesday. By then the barnyard, barn, and the old stables had to be in tiptop shape. He began flinging old tires one after another onto the bed of the trailer. They were stacked by the dozens in a corner of the barn; his father had used them to weigh down the tarps over the haystacks and rolls of straw out in the field. Now there were no more rolls of hay or straw, and car tires were nothing but rubbish.

All day long the shadow of a fleeting memory had been haunting him; it was driving Tobias crazy that he couldn't recall what it was. In the garage last night, one of his friends had said something that triggered a sudden association in him, but the memory was submerged somewhere in the depths of his consciousness and refused to be lured to the surface, no matter how hard he tried. Breathless, he stopped for a moment to wipe his forearm across his sweaty brow. He felt a cold breeze and turned around when he caught sight of something from the corner of his eye. He gave a start.

Three figures in dark clothes and wearing menacing masks had entered the barn. One of them slid shut the heavy iron bolt on the door. They stood there mute, fixing their gaze on him through the eye slits of their ski masks. The baseball bats in their gloved hands betrayed their intentions. Adrenaline shot through Tobias's body from the tips of his hair to his toes. He had no doubt that two of the men were the ones who had knocked down Amelie. They had come back to get their real target, which was him. He started backing away and thought feverishly how he could escape from the three men. There was no window in the barn, no back door. But there was a ladder that led up to the empty hayloft. It was his only chance. He forced himself not to look over at it, so as not to reveal his plan to the three men. Despite the panic rising inside him he managed to stay calm. He had to get to the ladder before they were on him.

They were still about twenty feet away when he took off. In seconds he was at the ladder, climbing as fast as he could. A blow from one of the bats struck his calf with full force. He felt no pain, but his left leg instantly went numb. With clenched teeth he kept climbing, but one of his pursuers was not much slower, grabbing his foot and pulling on it. Tobias held on to the rungs of the ladder and kicked at the man with his free foot. He heard a muffled cry of pain and felt the hand around his ankle let go. The ladder swayed and suddenly he grabbed at thin air and almost lost his hold. Three rungs were missing! He glanced down, feeling like a cat perched on a naked tree trunk with three bloodthirsty rottweilers at his heels. Somehow he reached the next rung and pulled himself up with all his might; the numb leg tingled and was no help at all. Finally he reached the hayloft. Two of the guys were climbing up after him, but the third had vanished.

Tobias looked around frantically in the dim light of the hayloft. The ladder was bolted to the wooden planks, so it was impossible to tip over. He hobbled as fast as he could to the lowest point of the roof and pressed his hand up against the roof tiles. One of them loosened, then a second one. He kept looking back over his shoulder. The head of his first pursuer appeared over the edge of the loft. Damn! The hole in the roof was much too small for him to squeeze through. When he had realized the senselessness of his efforts, he ran over to the hatch; the trailer full of car tires was parked underneath. With the courage of desperation he made the leap. One of the pursuers turned around on the ladder and climbed hurriedly back down like a big black spider. Tobias slid down to the ground, ducking into the shadows under the trailer. He tentatively felt his way along the ground, cursing his mania for cleaning up. There was nothing lying around that he could use as a weapon to defend himself. His heart hammered against his chest and he paused for a second, then bet everything on one card and took off running.

They caught up with him at the moment he grabbed the bolt of the door. Their blows rained down on his shoulders and arms and the small of his back. His knees buckled and he rolled up in a ball, using his arms to protect his head. They beat him and kicked him without saying a word. Finally they grabbed his arms, pulled them apart with raw force and tore his sweater and T-shirt over his head. Tobias clenched his teeth so he wouldn't moan or beg for his life. He saw one of the men tying a clothesline into a noose. No matter how hard he tried to defend himself, they had the superior strength. They bound his wrists and ankles together behind his back and put the noose around his neck. Tied up helpless as a package with his torso unprotected, he could offer no resistance as they dragged him roughly across the raw, icy ground to the rear wall, where they shoved a stinking rag into his mouth and blindfolded him. Panting he lay on the ground, his heart racing. The clothesline cut off his air if he moved even a millimeter. Tobias listened for sounds but heard only the storm that was still raging around the barn. Would the three be content with this? Did they intend to kill him? Were they gone? The tension eased off a bit, but his muscles were cramping. But his relief was premature. He heard a hiss and smelled paint. At the same instant a blow struck him in the face, and his nose broke with a crack that echoed through his skull like a shot. Tears sprang to his eyes and blood stopped up his nose. Through the gag in his mouth he could barely get enough air. The panic was back, a hundred times worse than before, because now he could no longer see his attackers. Kicks and blows rained down on him, and in these seconds that turned into hours, days, and weeks he became more and more convinced that they were going to kill him.

There wasn't much going on at the Black Horse. Not all the players were present at the usual game of poker at the regulars' table; even Jörg Richter was missing, which made his sister's mood sink to an all-time low for the year. Actually Jenny Jagielski was supposed to go to parents' night at the kindergarten this evening, but in the absence of her brother she couldn't bring herself to leave the Black Horse to her employees, especially since Roswitha was out sick and only Amelie was helping her out waiting tables. It was nine thirty when Jörg Richter and his pal Felix Pietsch showed up. They took off their wet jackets and sat down at a table. A little later two more men came in that Amelie had often seen with her boss's brother. Jenny headed over to her brother like an avenging angel, but he blew her off with a few curt words. She turned with her lips pressed tight and went back behind the bar. Angry red patches were visible on her throat.

"Bring us four beers and four Willi shots!" called Jörg Richter to Amelie. They could use a little schnapps with their beer.

"Nothing doing!" Jenny Jagielski retorted furiously. "What a scumbag!"

"But the others are paying customers," said Amelie innocently.

"Have they ever paid you?" Jenny snapped, and when Amelie shook her head, she said: "Customers my foot. They're nothing but freeloaders!"

It wasn't even two minutes before Jörg himself marched behind the bar and tapped four beers. His mood was just as foul as his sister's, and they wound up in a heated, whispered argument. Amelie wondered what was happening. A subtle sense of aggression filled the air like electricity. Fat Felix Pietsch was beet red in the face, and the other two men wore surly expressions. Amelie was distracted from her train of thought when the three missing poker players came barging in and called to her for orders of schnitzel with fried potatoes, rump steak, and wheat beer as they made their way to the round table. They hung up their wet jackets and coats and sat down. One of them, Lutz Richter, immediately began telling a story. The men put their heads together and listened attentively. Richter shut up when Amelie came over with their drinks; he waited to go on until she was out of earshot. Amelie didn't attach any importance to the men's strange behavior, because in her mind she was again thinking about Thies's paintings. Maybe it would be best to do what Thies had told her, and keep silent.

He came up to the front door and took off his soaking-wet jacket and filthy shoes on the porch. In the mirror next to the wardrobe he saw how he looked and lowered his head. It wasn't right, what they had done. Absolutely not right. If Terlinden found out, then he'd be in for it—and the other two as well. He went into the kitchen, found another bottle of beer in the door of the fridge. His muscles ached, and tomorrow he would surely have bruises on his arms and legs, the guy had fought back hard. But in vain. The three of them together were much stronger than he was. He heard footsteps approaching.

"So?" the curious voice of his wife sounded behind him. "How'd it go?"

"As planned." He didn't turn around but took a bottle opener out of the drawer. With a hiss and a soft plop the cap popped off the bottle. He shuddered. That was the same sound he'd heard when the nasal bone of Tobias Sartorius broke under his fist.

"Is he . . . ?" She left the sentence unfinished. Then he turned around and looked at her.

"Probably," he said. The rickety kitchen chair groaned under his weight when he sat down. He took a gulp of beer. It tasted flat. The others would have let the guy suffocate, but he had quickly removed the gag from the unconscious man's mouth without them seeing. "At any rate we gave him something serious to think about."

His wife raised her eyebrows, and he averted his eyes.

"Something to think about. That's just great," she said with contempt.

He thought about how Tobias had looked at them, the naked fear of death on his face. Not until they had blindfolded him was he able to join in the punching and kicking. Out of annoyance at his own weakness he had then put all his strength into the assault. Now he was ashamed. No, it hadn't been the right thing to do.

"You weaklings," his wife spat out. With an effort he suppressed his rising rage. What the hell did she expect from him? That he would kill a man? A neighbor? The last thing they needed now was cops sniffing around all over town and asking stupid questions. There were too many secrets that were better left alone.

It was just after midnight when Hartmut Sartorius woke up. The TV was still on—some sort of slasher movie in which screaming teenagers with eyes wide in fear fled from a masked psychopath who came after them one by one and slaughtered them with an axe and a chainsaw. In a daze Sartorius felt for the remote and turned off the TV. His knee hurt when he stood up. In the kitchen a light was on; the uncovered pan with the schnitzel and fried potatoes stood untouched on the stove. A glance at the kitchen clock told him how late it was. Tobias's jacket wasn't hanging in the wardrobe, but the car key lay on the shelf under the mirror, so he hadn't driven off somewhere. The boy was really overdoing it with his manic cleaning. He wanted to be able to present the property next week to the real estate agent in the best possible condition. Hartmut had agreed with every suggestion Tobias made, but he knew that he would definitely have to talk to Claudius with regard to the agent. Claudius Terlinden was still the sole owner of the whole estate, even if Tobias didn't like it. Hartmut went to take a pee, then he smoked a cigarette at the kitchen table. By then it was twenty minutes to one.

With a sigh he got to his feet and went into the hallway. He pulled on his old cardigan before he opened the front door and went out in the cold pouring rain. To his astonishment the floodlight at the corner of the house was out, although Tobias had installed a motion detector there only three days ago. He walked across the barnyard and saw that it was also dark in the stable and barn, but the car and tractor were there. Was Tobias out with his friends? A peculiar feeling crept up on him when he flicked the light switch at the door of the cowshed. It clicked, but the light didn't go on. He hoped that nothing had happened to Tobias while he was sleeping comfortably in the house in front of the TV.

Hartmut went into the milk room and over to the circuit breakers. Here the light worked, because this room was connected to the house circuit. Three breakers had tripped. He switched them back on, and at once the glaring floodlights came on above the doors of the stable and barn. Hartmut crossed the barnyard and uttered a low curse when he stepped in a puddle with his felt slipper.

"Tobias?" He stopped and listened. Nothing. The stable was empty, no sign of his son anywhere. He continued on. The wind tore at his hair, penetrating the mesh of his cardigan. He was freezing. The storm had scattered the heavy cloud cover, and scraps of cloud scudded rapidly past the half moon. In this pale light the three big containers that stood next to each other farther up the yard looked like enemy tanks. The feeling that something wasn't right grew stronger when he saw that one side of the barn door was swinging back and forth in the wind. He tried to grab the door but it was torn away by a new gust, as if it had a life of its own. With all his strength Hartmut pulled it shut behind him. The floodlight went off only seconds later, but he knew his way around the farm in the dark and went straight to the light switch.

"Tobias!"

The fluorescent tubes hummed and flickered on, and at the same moment he saw the red graffiti on the wall. WHOEVER WONT LISSEN MUST PAY! He noticed the misspelling, then he discovered the crumpled form on the ground. The shock registered in his limbs so strongly that he started to shake. He stumbled across the barn, dropped to his knees, and saw with horror what had happened. Tears welled up in his eyes. They had tied Tobias hand and foot, and the cord around his neck was so tight that it had cut deep into his flesh. His eyes were blindfolded, his face and his naked torso showed clear signs of cruel abuse. It must have happened hours ago, because the blood had already congealed.

"Oh God, oh God, Tobi!" With trembling fingers Hartmut set about untying the cords. They had sprayed one word: MURDERER! in red paint on Tobias's naked back. Hartmut touched his son's shoulder and gave a start. His skin was ice cold.

Saturday, November 15, 2008

Gregor Lauterbach was pacing restlessly in his living room. He'd already drunk three glasses of scotch, but the calming effect of the alcohol failed to materialize. All day long he'd been able to push aside the threatening contents of the anonymous letter, but as soon as he got home he was overcome by fear. Daniela was already in bed, and he hadn't wanted to disturb her. For a moment he had thought of calling his lover and asking her to meet him at his apartment, as a form of distraction, but he quickly dismissed the idea. This time he had to deal with things by himself. He had also taken a sleeping pill and gotten into bed. But the ringing of the phone yanked him out of sleep at one in the morning. Calls at that time of night were never good news. He had lain in bed shivering in a cold sweat, as if unhinged by fear. Daniela had taken the call in her room, and a little later she came down the hall softly so as not to wake him. Not until the front door closed behind her did he get up and go downstairs. Sometimes she had to go out at night to visit a patient. He didn't have her on-call schedule memorized. By this time it was a little after three, and he was getting close to a nervous breakdown.

Who could have sent him the letter? Who knew about Snow White and him and the lost key ring? Good God! His career was on the line, his reputation, his whole life! If this letter or one like it fell into the wrong hands, it was all over. The press was just waiting for a nice juicy scandal. Gregor Lauterbach wiped his sweaty palms on his bathrobe. He poured himself another scotch, a triple this time, and sat down on the sofa. Only the light in the entry hall was on, in the living room it was dark. He couldn't tell Daniela about the letter. Even back then he should have kept his mouth shut. She was the one who had built this house and paid for it seventeen years ago. With his small civil servant's salary he never could have afforded a villa like this. It had amused her to take him, the humble high school teacher, under her wing and introduce him to the right social and political circles. Daniela was a very good doctor; in Königstein and the surrounding area she had plenty of very wealthy and extremely influential private patients who recognized and nurtured her husband's political talent. Gregor Lauterbach owed everything to his wife. He'd been forced to make that painful admission when she had very nearly withdrawn her favor and support. His relief when she forgave him had been boundless. At the age of fifty-eight she still looked dazzling—a fact that kept causing him problems. Even though since that time they no longer slept together, he did love Daniela with all his heart. The other women who had flitted through his life and shared his bed were unimportant, offering no more than physical satisfaction. He didn't want to lose Daniela. No, he *couldn't* lose her! Under no circumstance. She knew too much about him, she knew his weaknesses, his inferiority complexes, and the excruciating attacks of fear of failure, which he managed to keep under control for the most part. Lauterbach gave a start when the key turned in the front door. He got up and dragged himself into the hall.

"You're still up," his wife said in astonishment. She looked calm and composed, as always, and he felt like a sailor on a rough sea who gratefully catches sight of the lighthouse in the distance.

She scrutinized him and sniffed. "You've been drinking. Has something happened?"

How well she knew him. He'd never been able to put anything past her. He sat down on the bottom step.

"I can't sleep," was all he said, omitting any explanation. All of a sudden and with a vehemence that shocked him, he longed for her motherly love, for her embrace, her consolation.

"I'll give you a lorazepam," she said.

"No!" Gregor Lauterbach stood up, staggered a bit, and reached out his hand to her. "I don't want any pills. I want . . ."

He broke off when he saw her look of surprise. All at once he felt wretched and pathetic.

"What do you want?" she asked softly.

"I just want to sleep in the same bed with you tonight, Dani," he whispered hoarsely. "Please."

Pia Kirchhoff looked at the woman sitting across from her at the kitchen table. She had informed Andrea Wagner that forensics had released the mortal remains of her daughter Laura. Since the mother of the dead girl had seemed composed, Pia asked her a few questions about Laura and her relationship with Tobias Sartorius.

"Why do you want to know about that?" Mrs. Wagner asked suspiciously.

"For the past few days I've been examining the old documents in detail," Kirchhoff replied. "And somehow I have the feeling that something was overlooked. When we told Tobias Sartorius that Laura had been found, I got the impression that he really didn't know a thing about it. Don't get me wrong; I'm not trying to say that I consider him innocent."

Andrea Wagner looked at her with a dull expression. For a while she said not a word.

"I've stopped thinking about all that," she said then. "It's hard enough to keep going with the entire village watching. My other two children had to grow up in the shadow of their dead sister, and I did everything in my power to make sure they had a fairly normal childhood. But it's not easy with a father who drinks himself into a stupor every night at the Black Horse because he won't accept what happened."

She didn't sound bitter; it was merely a statement of fact.

"I refuse to let that topic get to me anymore. Otherwise our whole life here would have fallen apart long ago." She motioned toward a stack of paper on the table. "Unpaid bills, dunning notices. I work in the supermarket in Bad Soden so that the house and the cabinet shop won't go into foreclosure. Then we'd wind up in the same situation as Hartmut Sartorius. Somehow things must go on. I can't afford to live in the past the way my husband does."

Kirchhoff said nothing. This wasn't the first time she'd seen how a terrible event could throw the life of a whole family off the track and destroy it forever. How strong people like Andrea Wagner must be to get up morning after morning and keep on, with no hope of improvement. Was there anything at all in the life of this woman that made her happy?

"I've known Tobias since he was born," Andrea Wagner went on. "We were friends with the family, as we were with everyone here in the village. My husband was in charge of the volunteer fire department and youth trainer at the sports club. Tobias was his best forward. Manfred was always very proud of him." A smile flitted across her pale, careworn face, but vanished at once. She sighed. "No one would have believed Tobias was capable of such a thing, and I didn't either at first. But you can't tell what's going on in a person's head by looking them in the face, can you?"

"No, you're quite right about that." Kirchhoff nodded in agreement. The Wagner family had gone through enough bad times, God knows, and she didn't want to open old wounds. Actually she had no basis for asking questions about a case that had been cleared up long ago. She simply had this vague feeling that bothered her.

She said good-bye to Mrs. Wagner, left the house, and walked across the neglected yard toward her car. From inside the workshop the screeching sound of a saw assaulted her ears. Pia stopped, then turned around and went over to open the door of the cabinet shop. It was only fair to tell Manfred Wagner that he would soon be able to lay his daughter to rest and finally put an end to a terrible chapter in his life. Maybe then he would somehow be able to regain his footing. He stood with his back to her at a workbench, pushing a board through a band saw. When he shut off the machine, Pia announced her presence. The man wasn't wearing ear protection, only a slovenly baseball cap, and from the corner of his mouth drooped an extinguished cigarillo. He cast an unfriendly look in her direction before leaning forward to concentrate on another board. His baggy pants slipped down and Pia was faced with the unsightly view of the top of his hairy behind.

"What do you want?" he muttered. "I'm busy."

He hadn't shaved since their last meeting, and his clothes exuded the sharp smell of old sweat. Pia shuddered and took an involuntary step back. What must it be like to have to live day in and day out with such a slovenly man? Her empathy with Andrea Wagner grew stronger.

"Mr. Wagner, I was just speaking with your wife, but I also wanted to tell you in person," Pia began.

Wagner straightened up and turned to face her.

"Forensics has . . ." Pia stopped short. The baseball cap! The beard! There was no doubt. Before her stood the man she'd been looking for from the still photo taken from the surveillance camera footage.

"What?" He stared at her with a mixture of aggression and indifference, but then he went pale, as if he'd read Pia's mind. He shrank back, and his guilty conscience was written all over his face.

"It . . . it was an accident," he stammered, raising his hands helplessly. "I swear to you, I didn't want it to happen. I . . . I only wanted to talk to her, really!"

Pia took a deep breath. So she had been right to assume there was a connection between the attack on Rita Cramer and the events of September 1997.

"But . . . but . . . when I heard that this . . . this filthy murderer got out of the joint and was back here in Altenhain, then . . . then all at once the memories came rushing back over me. I thought about Rita, I know her well. We were friends before. I only wanted to talk to her so that she'd make sure that son of hers got out of town . . . but then she ran away . . . and she took a swing at me and hit me . . . and all at once . . . all at once I got so mad . . ."

He broke off.

"Did your wife know about this?" Pia wanted to know. Wagner shook his head mutely. His shoulders slumped.

"Not at first. But then she saw the photo."

Naturally Andrea Wagner had recognized her husband, just as everyone else in Altenhain had. She had kept quiet to protect him. He was one of their own, a man who had lost his daughter in a most gruesome way. Maybe they even considered the misfortune he had dealt the Sartorius family as some sort of poetic justice.

"Did you think you'd get away with it because the whole village covered up what you'd done?" Any empathy Pia had felt for Manfred Wagner had been swept away.

"No," he whispered. "I . . . I wanted to go to the police."

Suddenly worry and anger overcame him. He slammed his fist onto the workbench. "That lousy murderer has done his time, but my Laura is dead forever! When Rita refused to listen to me, I saw red all of a sudden. And the railing was so low."

Andrea Wagner stood in the courtyard with her arms crossed and watched as two police officers led her husband away. The look she gave him spoke volumes. There was no remnant of affection between them, much less love. The children had to be the only thing that kept them together, or maybe it was the duties of daily life, or the sheer impossibility of imagining a separation, but not much more. Andrea Wagner despised her husband, who chose to drown his sorrows and problems in alcohol instead of standing up and dealing with them. Pia felt real empathy with the sorely afflicted woman. The future of the Wagner family didn't look any rosier than their past. She waited until the patrol car left the property. Bodenstein had already been notified and would talk to Wagner at the station later.

Pia got into her car, fastened her seatbelt, and turned the car around. She drove through the small industrial park, which consisted mainly of the Terlinden firm. Behind a tall fence there were large workshops scattered among neat lawns and parking lots. To get to the main building, a big semicircular structure with a high glass façade, the road led through barriers and gatehouses. Several trucks waited for admission at one of the gates, and on the other side one truck was being inspected by guards. The truck behind it honked. Pia had already put on her left-turn blinker to turn onto the B19 toward Hofheim, but then she decided to pay a brief visit to the Sartorius family and turned right instead.

The early morning fog had lifted and given way to a dry, sunny day—a breath of late summer in the middle of November. Altenhain seemed deserted. Pia saw only a young woman walking two dogs, and an old man standing in the driveway of his farm, his arms resting on the low gate as he talked with an older woman. She drove past the Black Horse, its parking lot still empty, and the church, then followed the sharp right-hand curve and had to brake because a fat gray cat was crossing the narrow road at a dignified pace. In front of Hartmut Sartorius's former restaurant stood a silver Porsche Cayenne with Frankfurt plates. Pia parked next to it and entered the property through the wide-open gate. All the piles of rubbish and junk were gone, and even the rats seemed to have moved on to greener pastures. She went up the three steps to the front door of the residence and rang the bell. Hartmut Sartorius came to the door. Behind him stood a blond woman. Pia could hardly believe her eyes when she recognized Nadia von Bredow, the actress. Her face was well known all over Germany because of her popular role as Detective Inspector Stein from *Scene of the Crime,* set in Hamburg. What was she doing here?

"I'll track him down," she was saying to Hartmut Sartorius, who seemed more careworn than ever next to this tall, elegant figure. "Thank you. I'll see you later."

She barely glanced at Pia and walked past her without saying hello or even nodding. Pia watched her go, then turned to Tobias's father.

"Nathalie is the daughter of our neighbor," he explained before she asked, because he probably noticed the amazement in Pia's face. "She and Tobias played together in the sandbox as kids, and she kept in touch with him through his whole prison term. The only person who did."

"Aha.' Pia nodded. Even a famous actress had to grow up somewhere, so why not in Altenhain?

"What can I do for you?"

"Is your son here?"

"No. He went for a walk. But please come in."

Pia followed him through the house into the kitchen, which like the grounds now looked considerably cleaner than on her last visit. Why did people always take the police into their kitchen?

•   •   •

Deep in thought, Amelie walked along the edge of the woods, hands in her jacket pockets. The heavy rain the night before had been followed by a calm, mild day. Thin veils of mist hovered over the orchards; the sun found its way through the gray clouds, making the fall colors of the forest glow. On the branches of the deciduous trees the last leaves shone red, yellow, and brown. She noticed the scent of acorns and damp earth, of a fire that someone had lit in one of the meadows. Amelie, child of the big city, inhaled the fresh, clear air deep into her lungs. She felt more alive than she could remember, and she had to admit that life in the country definitely had its pleasant sides. Below in the valley lay the village. How peaceful it looked from a distance. A car crawled like a red ladybug along the street and vanished in the maze of tightly packed houses. On the wooden bench by the old crossroads sat a man. As Amelie approached she recognized to her amazement that it was Tobias.

"Hey," she said, stopping in front of him. He raised his head. Her astonishment then turned to horror when she saw his face. Dark purple bruises covered the whole left side of his face, one eye was swollen shut, and his nose had grown to the size of a potato. A cut on his eyebrow had been taped shut.

"Hey," he replied. They looked at each other for a moment. His beautiful blue eyes were glassy and he was in a lot of pain, that was obvious. "They ambushed me. Last night, in the barn."

"Oh great." Amelie sat down beside him. For a while neither of them said a word.

"You really ought to go to the cops," she said hesitantly, not entirely convinced. He snorted in derision.

"Not on your life. Do you happen to have a cigarette?"

Amelie dug in her backpack and came up with a crumpled cigarette pack and a lighter. She lit two cigarettes and handed him one.

"Last night Jenny Jagielski's brother showed up pretty late with his pal, fat Felix, at the Black Horse. They sat around in a corner with two other guys and were laughing about something," Amelie said without looking at Tobias. "And at the usual game of poker at the regulars' table, old Pietsch was missing, along with Richter from the store, and Traugott Dombrowski. They didn't show up until quarter to ten."

"Hmm," Tobias said, taking a drag on his cigarette.

"Maybe it was some of them."

"Probably so," said Tobias indifferently.

"Yeah, but . . . if you know who might have done it . . ." Amelie turned her head and met his gaze. She looked away quickly. It was much easier to talk to him if she didn't look him in the eye.

"So why are you on my side?" he asked suddenly. "I did ten years in the slammer because I killed two girls."

His voice didn't sound bitter, only tired and resigned.

"I did three weeks in juvie because I lied for a friend and claimed that the dope the cops found was mine," said Amelie.

"What are you trying to say?"

"That I don't believe you killed those two girls."

"Nice of you." Tobias bent over and his face contorted. "I have to remind you that there was a trial with a pile of evidence that all pointed to me."

"I know." Amelie shrugged. She took another drag on her cigarette, then flicked the butt into the meadow on the other side of the gravel road. She had to tell him about those paintings. But how to begin? She decided on a round-about way.

"Did the Lauterbachs live here back then?" she asked.

"Yes," Tobias said in surprise. "Why do you ask?"

"There's a picture," said Amelie. "Actually several of them. I've seen them, and I think Lauterbach is in three of them."

Tobias gave her a look that was both interested and puzzled.

"So, I think there's somebody who witnessed what really happened back then," Amelie added after a brief pause. "Thies gave me pictures that . . ."

She fell silent. A car was coming up the narrow road at high speed, a silver station wagon. The gravel crunched under the wide tires when the Porsche Cayenne stopped right in front of them. A beautiful blonde climbed out. Amelie jumped up and shouldered her backpack.

"Wait!" Tobias stretched out his arm to her imploringly and stood up with a pained expression. "What kind of pictures? What's going on with Thies? Nadia is my best friend. You can tell her too."

"No, I'd rather not." Amelie gave the woman a skeptical look. She was very slim and made an elegant impression with her tight jeans, the turtleneck sweater, and the beige down vest with the prominent logo of an expensive designer label. Her smooth blond hair was pulled back in a knot, and she had a concerned look on her elegantly proportioned face.

"Hello!" the woman called, coming closer. She scrutinized Amelie briefly, giving her a suspicious look, then turned her undivided attention to Tobias.

"Oh my God, sweetheart!" She put her hand softly on his cheek. At the sight of this intimate gesture Amelie felt a pang in her heart, and she took an immediate dislike to Nadia.

"I'll see you later," she said curtly and left them to each other.

For the second time today Pia had taken a seat at a kitchen table and politely turned down a cup of coffee. Then she had informed Hartmut Sartorius about Manfred Wagner's confession and arrest.

"How's your ex-wife doing?" she asked.

"Her condition is unchanged," said Sartorius. "The doctors just give me the runaround and refuse to say anything definite."

Pia studied the gaunt, exhausted face of Tobias's father. The man hadn't suffered any less than the Wagners—on the contrary. While the parents of the victim were shown sympathy and solidarity, the parents of the perpetrator had been ostracized and punished for the actions of their son. The silence turned uncomfortable. Pia didn't really know why she'd come. What was she actually looking for here?

"So are people pretty much leaving you and your son alone?" she asked at last. Hartmut Sartorius emitted a curt, bitter laugh. He opened a drawer and pulled out a crumpled piece of paper, which he handed to Pia.

"This was in the mailbox today. Tobias threw it out, but I retrieved it from the garbage can."

You murdering bastards, Pia read. *Get out of here before another accident happens.*

"A threatening letter," she said. "Anonymous?"

"Of course." Sartorius shrugged and sat back down at the table. "Yesterday they attacked him in the barn and beat him up." His voice faltered and he had to fight for control as tears shone in his eyes.

"Who?" Pia wanted to know.

"All of them." Sartorius made a helpless gesture. "They were wearing masks and had baseball bats. When I . . . when I found Tobias in the barn . . . I thought at first he was . . . he was dead."

He bit his lip and lowered his eyes.

"Why didn't you call the police?"

"It wouldn't do any good. This is never going to stop." The man shook his head with a mixture of resignation and despair. "Tobias is doing his best to get the farm back in shape and hopes we can find a buyer."

"Mr. Sartorius." Pia was still holding the letter. "I've read all the documents in your son's case. And I noticed some inconsistencies. Actually it amazes me that Tobias's lawyer didn't file an appeal."

"He wanted to, but the court refused to consider any appeal. The circumstantial evidence, the eyewitnesses—there was no room for any doubt." Sartorius rubbed his hand over his face. Everything about him radiated discouragement.

"But now Laura's remains have been found," Pia insisted. "And I've been asking myself how your son could possibly have gotten the dead girl out of the house and into the trunk of his car, taken her to Eschborn to the restricted site of a former military airfield and thrown her into an old underground tank, and then driven back here, all in under forty-five minutes."

Sartorius raised his head and looked at her. A tiny spark of hope gleamed in his watery blue eyes, but it vanished just as quickly.

"It won't do any good. There's no new evidence. And even if there was, to the people here he's a murderer and that's what he'll always be."

"Maybe your son should leave Altenhain for a while," Pia suggested. "At least until after the girl is buried, when feelings here have died down a bit."

"Where is he supposed to go? We don't have any money. Tobias won't be able to find a job any time soon. Who's going to hire an ex-con, even if he has a diploma?"

"He could move into his mother's apartment temporarily," Pia suggested, but Sartorius only shook his head.

"Tobias is thirty years old," he said. "I know you mean well, but I can't order him to do anything."

•   •   •

"I just had a déjà-vu moment when I saw the two of you sitting on the bench."
Nadia shook her head. Tobias had sat back down and was cautiously feeling his
nose. The memory of his fear of death from last night had settled like a dark
shadow over the sunny day. When the men finally stopped beating him and
disappeared, he had silently said good-bye to life. If one of them hadn't come
back to take the rag out of his mouth he would have suffocated. They had really
been serious about it. Tobias shuddered at the thought of how close to death he
had come. The injuries he had suffered were painful and looked dramatic, sure,
but they weren't life-threatening. His father had called Dr. Lauterbach last
night and she came over at once to patch him up. She had taped closed the cut
on his eyebrow and left some painkillers for him. She didn't seem to hold it
against him that he had dragged her husband into the whole mess in 1997.

"Don't you think so?" Nadia's voice interrupted his train of thought.

"What did you say?" he asked. She was so beautiful and looked so anxious. She was actually expected on the set in Hamburg, but apparently he
was more important. After he called she must have left at once. That was the
sign of a true friend.

"I was just saying how strange it is for that girl to look so much like Stefanie. Unbelievable!" said Nadia and took his hand. She caressed the balls of
his thumbs, a tender touch that under other circumstances might have pleased
him. But right now it didn't.

"Yes, Amelie really is incredible," he replied thoughtfully. "Incredibly
brave and fearless."

He thought about how she had recovered so quickly from the attack in
the barnyard. Any other girl would have dissolved in tears and run home or
to the police, but not Amelie. What was it she'd wanted to tell him? What
had Thies said to her?

"Do you like her?" Nadia wanted to know. If he hadn't been so deep in
his thoughts, he might have some other, more diplomatic response.

"Yes," he said. "I like her. She's so . . . different."

"Different from whom? Me?"

Then Tobias looked up. He met her scandalized gaze and wanted to
smile, but the smile turned into a grimace.

"Different from the people here, I meant." He squeezed her hand. "Amelie is only seventeen. She's like a little sister."

"All right, then be careful that you don't turn little sister's head with those blue eyes of yours." Nadia pulled her hand away and crossed her legs. She looked at him with her head cocked. "I don't think you have the slightest idea what sort of effect you have on women, do you?"

Her words reminded him of his younger days. How come he'd never noticed that Nadia's critical remarks about other girls had always hidden a spark of jealousy?

"Aw, come on now," he said with a dismissive gesture. "Amelie works at the Black Horse and overheard something there. For one thing, she recognized Manfred Wagner in the photo the police made public. He was the one who shoved my mother off the bridge."

"What?"

"Yes, he did. And she also thinks that Pietsch, Richter, and Dombrowski were the ones who beat me up last night. They showed up unusually late for their card game."

Nadia stared at him incredulously. "You're kidding!"

"Nope. Amelie is also firmly convinced that somebody saw something back then that might exonerate me. Just as you drove up she was about to tell me something about Thies, about Lauterbach, and about some pictures."

"That would be . . . that would be really incredible!" Nadia jumped up and took a few steps toward her car. She turned around and gave Tobias an outraged look. "But why didn't that person ever say anything?"

"Yeah, if I only knew." Tobias leaned back and tentatively stretched out his legs. Every movement of his battered body hurt, in spite of the painkillers. "In any case, Amelie must have found out something. Stefanie once told me that she'd gotten it on with Lauterbach. You remember him, don't you?"

"Of course." Nadia nodded, staring at him.

"At first I thought she was just saying that to make herself seem important, but then I saw the two of them together behind the tent, at the fair. That's the reason I made a beeline for home. I was . . ." He broke off, searching for the right words to describe the tumult of emotions that had been running wild inside him. It would have been impossible to slip a piece of paper between them, they were standing so close, and Lauterbach had his hand on her ass. The abrupt realization that Stefanie was messing around with other men had thrown him into a churning maelstrom.

". . . furious," Nadia finished his sentence.

"No," Tobias countered. "I was *not* furious. I was . . . hurt and sad. I really did love Stefanie."

"Just imagine if that piece of information got out." Nadia gave a soft and slightly nasty laugh. "What do you think the headlines would say? Our cultural minister the child molester!"

"So you think they had a real relationship?"

Nadia stopped laughing. In her eyes he saw a peculiar expression that he couldn't interpret. She shrugged.

"I would have believed it of him, at any rate. He was crazy about his Snow White. He even gave her the leading role although she had almost no talent. Whenever she came around the corner his tongue would be hanging out of his mouth."

Suddenly they were in the midst of the topic they had avoided so assiduously until now. At the time Tobias hadn't been surprised that Stefanie got the leading role in the Christmas pageant put on by the drama club. In terms of appearance she was perfect for the role of Snow White. He had vivid memories of the evening when that first occurred to him. Stefanie had climbed into his car, wearing a white summer dress and red lipstick, her dark hair blowing in the wind as they drove. *White as snow, red as blood, black as ebony*— she had said those words herself and then laughed. Where did they drive to that night? All of a sudden he knew, as if struck by a bolt of lightning. There it was again, the thought that had been nagging at him for days. *Do you guys remember how my sister stole my old man's key ring and we raced around inside the old airplane hangar?* That's what Jörg had said on Thursday night in the garage. Of course he remembered! That evening they had headed over there, and Stefanie had dared him to drive faster because they were alone in the car. Jörg's father, Karl-Heinz Richter, had been at the telephone exchange, and in the seventies and eighties he had worked on the grounds of the old military airfield. As kids he, Jörg, and the others had been allowed to go with him and play at the deserted site. Later, when they were older, they had organized secret car races and parties. And now Laura's skeleton had been found at that very location. Could it be a coincidence?

He stood before her as if he'd shot up out of the ground, just as she had turned around again to take a last look at Tobias and this blond bitch driving that luxury ride.

"Jeez, Thies!" Amelie gasped in shock, surreptitiously wiping the tears from her cheek. "Do you have to scare me like that, damn it?"

Sometimes it was really spooky the way Thies could just appear and vanish without making a sound. Only now did she notice that he looked sick. His eyes were sunk deep in their sockets and had a feverish gleam to them. He was trembling all over, with his arms wrapped tight around his upper body. The thought shot through her mind that he really looked like a crazy person. Then she felt ashamed for thinking such a thing.

"What's wrong? Don't you feel good?" she asked.

He didn't react, just looked around nervously. His breathing was fast and irregular, as if he'd been running. Suddenly he uncrossed his arms and grabbed Amelie's hand, much to her surprise. He had never done that before. She knew that he didn't like being touched.

"I couldn't protect Snow White," he said in a hoarse, tense voice. "But I'll take better care of you."

His eyes shifted restlessly, and he kept looking toward the edge of the woods as if he expected some sort of danger to emerge from that direction. Amelie shuddered. All at once the pieces of the puzzle fell into place.

"You saw what happened, didn't you?" she whispered. Thies turned abruptly and pulled her along with him, holding her hand tight. Amelie stumbled after him through a muddy ditch and thick undergrowth. When they reached the protection of the woods, Thies slowed down a bit, but he was still walking too fast for Amelie, who smoked too much and never exercised. He held her hand in an iron grip; when she stumbled and fell he would immediately pull her to her feet. They were climbing a hill. Dry branches crackled under their feet, magpies scolded from the tops of the fir trees. Without warning he stopped. Amelie looked around, panting and through the trees she spied the bright-red roof tiles of the Terlinden villa a little ways down the slope. Sweat ran down her face and she coughed. Why had Thies taken her around the entire perimeter of the property? The road through the park would have been far less trouble. He let go of her hand and began fiddling with a rusty, narrow gate, which opened with a reluctant screech. Amelie followed him through the gate and saw that she was now right behind the orangerie. Thies wanted to grab her hand again, but she pulled away.

"Why are you running all over the place like a madman?" She tried to quell the uneasiness that suddenly filled her, but there was something definitely wrong with Thies. The almost lethargic calm that he usually displayed had vanished, and when he looked at her now, straight in the eye and without averting his gaze, his expression scared her.

"If you promise not to tell anybody," he said softly, "I'll show you my secret. Come on!"

He opened the door to the orangerie with the key that was under the doormat. She deliberated briefly whether to simply walk away. But Thies was her friend, he trusted her. So she decided to trust him too, and followed him into the room that she knew so well. He closed the door softly and looked around.

"Could you please tell me what's going on?" Amelie asked. "Has something happened?"

Thies didn't answer. At the back of the large room he moved a big potted palm aside and picked up the board on which it had stood, propping it against the wall. Amelie stepped forward with curiosity and looked in amazement at a trap door set into the floor. Thies opened the hatch and turned to her. "Come on," he urged her.

Amelie stepped onto the steep, rusty iron stairs that led down into the darkness. Thies closed the trap door above them, and a second later a faint lightbulb went on. He squeezed past her and opened a massive iron door. A flood of warm dry air rushed toward them, and Amelie was flabbergasted when she entered a large cellar room. A bright carpet, walls painted a happy orange. A shelf full of books on one side, a comfortable-looking sofa on the other. The back half of the room was separated off with a folding screen. Amelie's heart was in her throat. Thies had never given any indication that he wanted anything from her, and even now she didn't think he would pounce on her and try to rape her. Anyway, in an emergency it was only a few steps to the stairs and then out into the park.

"Come on," Thies said again. He pushed the screen aside, and Amelie saw an old-fashioned bed with a high wooden headboard. On the wall photographs were hung neatly in rows and columns, as was Thies's habit.

"Come over here. I've told Snow White so much about you."

She moved closer, and suddenly she couldn't breathe. With a mixture of horror and fascination she looked into the face of a mummy.

"What is it?" Nadia squatted down in front of him, putting her hand gently on his thigh, but he pushed her away impatiently and stood up. He hobbled forward a few yards and then stopped. What he was thinking was monstrous!

"Laura's body lay in an underground tank on the grounds of the old military airfield in Eschborn," said Tobias in a hoarse voice. "You must remember how we used to have parties out there. Because Jörg's father had the key to the gate."

"What do you mean?" Nadia came after him and looked at him blankly.

"It wasn't me who threw Laura in that tank," Tobias replied vehemently, grinding his teeth. "Damn it, damn it, damn it." He balled up his hands into fists. "I want to know what really happened! My parents were ruined, I sat in prison for ten years, and then Laura's father pushes my mother off a bridge! I can't stand it anymore!" he yelled, as Nadia stood mutely in front of him.

"Come stay with me, Tobi. Please."

"No!" he snapped. "Don't you get it? That's exactly what they wanted to achieve, those assholes!"

"Yesterday all they did was beat you up. What if they come back and they're serious this time?"

"Kill me, you mean?" Tobias looked at Nadia. Her lower lip was trembling slightly, her big green eyes were swimming in tears. Nadia didn't deserve to be yelled at. She was the only one who had stood by him all this time. She would have even visited him in prison, but he hadn't wanted her to. Suddenly his fury subsided and he felt only guilt.

"Please forgive me," he said softly, reaching out his arms. "I didn't mean to shout at you. Come here."

She leaned against him, snuggling her face against his chest, and he wrapped his arms around her.

"Maybe you're right," he whispered into her hair. "We can't turn back time."

She raised her head and looked at him. There was deep anxiety in her eyes. "I'm afraid for you, Tobi." Her voice quavered a little. "I don't want to lose you again, now that I finally have you back."

Tobias grimaced. He closed his eyes and put his cheek on hers. If he only knew whether things could ever work out for them. He didn't want to be disappointed, not again. He'd rather live the rest of his life alone.

Manfred Wagner looked like a heap of misery as he sat at the table in the interview room. With an effort he raised his head when Kirchhoff and Bodenstein came in. He stared at them with the red-rimmed, watery eyes of an alcoholic.

"You have been charged with multiple felony counts," Bodenstein began sternly after he had turned on the tape recorder and stated the requisite formalities for the transcript. "Grievous bodily harm, dangerous disruption of traffic, and—depending on what the district attorney decides—negligent manslaughter or even homicide."

Manfred Wagner turned another shade paler. His gaze shifted to Kirchhoff and back to Bodenstein. He swallowed.

"But . . . but . . . Rita is still alive," he stammered.

"That's true," said Bodenstein. "But the man whose windshield she fell onto suffered a heart attack at the scene of the accident. Not to mention the property damage to the other vehicles that were involved in the pileup. This matter will have serious consequences for you, and it doesn't help that you didn't turn yourself in to the police."

"I was meaning to," Wagner protested in a whiny voice. "But . . . but they all advised me not to."

"Who do you mean by 'they'?" Kirchhoff asked. Any sympathy she'd had for this man was gone. He had suffered a terrible loss, but that didn't justify his assault on Tobias's mother.

Wagner shrugged but didn't look at her.

"All of them," he repeated, as vague as Hartmut Sartorius had been a few hours earlier, when Kirchhoff asked him who was behind the anonymous threatening letters and the attack on his son.

"I see. Do you always do what 'all of them' say?" It came out sharper than she intended, but had an effect.

"You have no idea!" Wagner flared up. "My Laura was someone really special. She could have amounted to something. And she was so beautiful. Sometimes I could hardly believe that she was really my daughter. And then she had to die. Just tossed aside like a piece of garbage. We were a happy family. We'd just built a house out in the new industrial park, and my cabinet shop was doing well. There was a good sense of community in the village, everyone was friends with everyone else. And then . . . Laura and her girlfriend disappeared. Tobias murdered them, that ice-cold bastard! I begged him to tell me why he killed them and what he did with her body. But he never said a word."

He doubled up and sobbed without restraint. Bodenstein wanted to turn off the tape recorder, but Kirchhoff stopped him. Was Wagner really crying out of sorrow for his lost daughter or because he was feeling sorry for himself?

"Cut out the playacting," she said.

Wagner's head flew up and he stared at her as dumbfounded as if she'd kicked him in the ass. "I lost my child," he began in a quivering voice.

"I know that," Kirchhoff cut him off. "And for that you have my complete sympathy. But you still have two children and a wife who need you. Didn't you think at all about what it would mean for your family if you did something to hurt Rita Cramer?"

Wagner fell silent, but suddenly his face contorted with fury.

"You have no idea what I've been through for the past eleven years!" he cried.

"But I do know what your wife has been through," Kirchhoff replied coolly. "She has not only lost a child, but also a husband, who goes out every night drinking out of sheer self-pity, leaving her in the lurch. Your wife is fighting to survive. What are you doing?"

Wagner's eyes began to flash in anger. Kirchhoff had obviously hit a sore spot.

"What the hell business is that of yours?"

"Who advised you not to turn yourself in to the police?"

"My friends."

"Probably the same friends who stand idly by as you get tanked up at the Black Horse every night and take your life in your hands. Am I right?"

Wagner opened his mouth to reply but changed his mind. His hostile expression turned unsure, and he looked at Bodenstein.

"I'm not going to let you get to me." His voice shook. "I'm not saying another word without a lawyer present."

He crossed his arms and lowered his chin to his chest like a recalcitrant child. Kirchhoff looked at her boss and raised her eyebrows. Bodenstein pressed the STOP button on the tape recorder.

"You'd better go home," he said.

"You mean I'm ... I'm not ... under arrest?" Wagner croaked in astonishment.

"No." Bodenstein stood up. "We know where to find you. The DA will bring an indictment against you. So you are going to need a lawyer."

He opened the door. Wagner staggered past him, accompanied by the uniformed officer who had been present in the room. Bodenstein watched him go.

"The guy's so pitiful that I almost feel sorry for him," Pia said next to him. "But only almost."

"Why did you come down on him so hard?" Oliver wanted to know.

"Because I have a hunch that there's a lot more hidden behind all of this than we can see at the moment," Pia said. "There's something going on in that dump of a village. And it's been going on for the past eleven years. I'm absolutely sure of it."

Sunday, November 16, 2008

Bodenstein was not in the mood for another family celebration, but since it would be held at his home with a small group, he accepted his fate and served as the sommelier. His son Lorenz was turning twenty-five. The night before, Lorenz had partied into the wee hours with his huge circle of friends at a disco whose proprietor he knew from his DJ days, but he wanted to spend Sunday afternoon with his family to celebrate his birthday in a calmer setting. Cosima's mother had come from Bad Homburg, Oliver's parents and Quentin arrived with his three daughters—Marie-Louise couldn't get away from her Schlosshotel—and the mother of Lorenz's girlfriend Thordis, the veterinarian Inka Hansen, completed the guest list. They were all seated around the dining room table, with its white place settings and decorations in lovely autumn colors. Chef St. Clair had given his best cook, Rosalie, the day off, so from early morning she was to be found, with red cheeks and on the verge of a nervous breakdown, dashing about in the kitchen, which she had banned everyone from entering. The result was fantastic. The roast goose liver with almond crème and lemon followed a watercress mousse soup with marinated shellfish and quail eggs. For the main course Rosalie had really outdone herself: the saddle of venison with mélange of petits pois, crispy cannelloni and carrot-ginger purée couldn't have been prepared better by the master chef himself. The guests applauded the young chef enthusiastically, and Oliver gave his eldest daughter a hug. She was utterly exhausted from all the work and the burden of responsibility.

"I think we'll keep you," he joked, kissing her on the top of her head.

"Thank you, Dad," she replied wearily. "Now I need a schnapps!"

"In honor of the day you shall have one," he said with a smile. "We'd like another . . ."

"We'd rather have more champagne," Lorenz butted in, motioning to his sister. She remembered something they'd prearranged and vanished like lightning back to the kitchen, followed by Lorenz and Thordis. Oliver sat down and exchanged a glance with Cosima. He'd been watching her unobtrusively all morning. At around ten o'clock Rosalie had ordered them out of the house, so he and Cosima had driven out to the Taunus to take a walk around Glaskopf Hill in the beautifully warm Indian summer weather. Cosima had acted completely normal; there was nothing unusual about her behavior, and she had even taken his hand during their walk. His suspicions began to weaken, and yet he hadn't dared bring up the topic with her.

Rosalie, Lorenz, and Thordis came back to the dining room, balancing full glasses of champagne on a tray, and served one to each guest, even the three young teenage nieces, who giggled gleefully. In the absence of their strict mother, Quentin decided not to object.

"Dear family," Lorenz then announced solemnly. "Thordis and I wanted to take this opportunity to announce in the presence of the whole family, that we are engaged to be married."

He put his arm around Thordis's shoulder, and the two smiled at each other happily.

"Don't worry, Dad," said Lorenz with a grin as he looked at his father. "We don't *have to* get married—we just want to."

"Time for a toast," said Quentin. Chairs were pushed back and everyone rose to congratulate the two. Even Oliver hugged his son and future daughter-in-law. The announcement of their engagement didn't really surprise him, but he was astounded that Lorenz had kept the secret so well. He caught Cosima's eye and went over to her. She wiped away a tear of emotion.

"You see," she said with a smile. "Even our eldest son has turned bourgeois and is going to marry."

"He's certainly been keeping us in suspense long enough with his adventurous life," said Oliver. Since he graduated Lorenz had spent an alarmingly long time as a DJ and in all sorts of temp jobs in radio and television. Oliver would have liked to exert his authority over his son, but Cosima had remained calm, firmly convinced that someday Lorenz would find his true calling. By now he was successfully moderating a daily three-hour show for a large private radio station. And on the side he made a surprisingly good living as the MC of galas, sporting events, and other functions all over Germany.

Everyone took their seats, and the mood was happy and relaxed. Even Rosalie had left her kitchen and was drinking champagne.

"Oliver." His mother leaned over to him. "Could you get me a glass of water?"

"Yes, of course." He pushed back his chair, stood up and walked through the kitchen, which his hardworking daughter had almost finished cleaning up. In the pantry he took two bottles of mineral water from a case. At that instant a cell phone rang in one of the jackets hanging on hooks next to the door to the garage. A special ringtone. Oliver knew the sound. It was Cosima's cell. He struggled with himself, but this time his suspicions won out. He quickly stuck one bottle of water under his arm so he could search the pocket of the jacket she'd been wearing earlier in the day. He found the phone in the inside pocket, flipped it open, and pressed the message symbol.

MY DARLING, I THINK OF YOU ALL DAY LONG! LUNCH TOMORROW? SAME TIME, SAME PLACE? I LOOK FORWARD TO IT!

The letters on the display blurred before his eyes and his knees felt weak. Disappointment hit him in the stomach like a fist. How could she pretend like that? Smiling and walking hand in hand with him around Glaskopf Hill? Cosima would notice that someone had read the text message, because the message symbol was now grayed out. He almost wished she would talk to him about it. He stuck the phone back in her jacket, waited until his heart slowed to normal, and went back into the dining room. Cosima sat there with Sophia on her lap, laughing and joking as if everything was fine. He felt like calling her out in front of everyone and telling her that there was a text message from her lover on her cell, but then his eyes fell on Lorenz, Thordis, and Rosalie. It would be selfish and irresponsible to spoil this lovely day for them with his unconfirmed suspicion. He had no choice but to grin and bear it.

With an effort Tobias opened his eyes and groaned. His head was roaring and the slightest movement made him feel terrible. He leaned over the edge of the bed and threw up into the bucket someone had put beside his bed. The vomit stank terribly. He fell back and wiped his mouth. His tongue was furry, and the carousel in his head wouldn't stop. What had happened? How did he get home? Images raced through his foggy brain. He remembered Jörg and Felix and other old pals, the garage, the vodka mixed with Red Bull. There had been a couple of girls there too, and they kept giving him conspicuously curious glances, whispering and giggling with each other. He had felt like an animal in the zoo. When did all that happen? What time was it now?

With great effort he managed to sit up and lift his legs over the edge of the bed. The room spun before his eyes. Amelie had also been there—or was he mixing things up? Tobias got to his feet, braced himself against the slanted ceiling, stumbled to the door, opened it, and felt his way along the hall. He'd never had such a bad hangover in his life. In the bathroom he had to sit down to pee or he would have fallen over. His T-shirt reeked of cigarette smoke, sweat, and puke. Disgusting. He got up from the toilet and was shocked when he saw his face in the mirror. The hematomas around his eyes had spread down and formed purple and yellow spots on his pale, unshaven cheeks. He looked like a zombie, and he felt like one too. Footsteps in the hallway, a knock on the door.

"Tobias?" his father called.

"Yeah, come in." He turned on the faucet and cupped his hands under the cold water, drinking a few swallows. It tasted terrible. The door opened and his father looked him up and down with concern.

"How are you feeling?"

Tobias sat back down on the toilet seat. "Like shit." It took a huge effort to raise his head, which felt like lead. He tried to look at his father, but his eyes kept sliding away. At first everything looked very close, then far away. "What time is it?"

"Three thirty. Sunday afternoon."

"Oh God." Tobias scratched his head. "I really can't take much more of this."

His memory came back, at least in part: Nadia had been with him up by the edge of the woods, talking to him. Afterward she drove him home because she had to get to the airport in a hurry. But what had he done then? Jörg. Felix. The garage. Lots of alcohol. Lots of girls. He hadn't been feeling well. Why not? Why did he go there in the first place?

"Amelie Fröhlich's father just called," said his father. Amelie. There was something he needed to remember about her. Oh yeah, she'd wanted to tell him something important, but then Nadia showed up and Amelie ran off.

"She didn't come home last night." The urgent tone of his father's voice made him pay attention. "Her parents are worried and are thinking of calling the police."

Tobias stared at his father. It took a moment before he understood. Amelie hadn't come home. And he'd had a lot to drink. Just like eleven years ago. Ice settled over his heart clenched.

"You . . . you don't think I had anything to—" he broke off and gulped.

"Dr. Lauterbach found you last night at the bus stop in front of the church on her way back from an emergency call. It was half past one. She drove you home. We had a hell of a time getting you out of the car and up to your room. And you were talking about Amelie the whole time . . ."

Tobias closed his eyes and dropped his face in his hands. He tried in vain to remember. But there was—nothing. His friends in the garage, the giggling, whispering girls. Had Amelie been there too? No. Or was she? No. Please no. Please, please no.

Monday, November 17, 2008

The entire K-11 team had gathered in the conference room around the big table; except for Hasse they were all present, even Behnke, who looked grumpier than usual.

"Sorry I'm late," said Pia Kirchhoff, heading for the last vacant chair. She took off her jacket. Nicola Engel glanced demonstratively at her watch.

"It's twenty past eight," she noted sharply. "We're not the *Rosenheim Cops* on TV, after all. In the future please organize your farm work so that it doesn't interfere with your work schedule."

Pia could feel the heat rush to her face. *Stupid cow!*

"I was at the pharmacy getting some cold pills," she replied, equally caustic. "Or would you rather I took a sick day?"

The two women stared each other down for a moment.

"All right. I see that everyone is present now," said the commissioner without apologizing for her unjustified insinuation. "We have a missing girl. Our colleagues from Eschborn informed us this morning."

Pia scanned the group. Behnke was leaning back in his chair with his legs spread, vigorously chewing gum. He kept shooting fierce glances over at Kathrin, who responded with a hostile expression and her lips pressed tight. Pia recalled that at the insistence of Dr. Engel, Oliver had talked to Behnke last week. What had come of that? In any case Behnke seemed to know that Kathrin had reported seeing him working in the bar in Sachsenhausen. The tension between the two could not be ignored. Bodenstein sat at the head of the table staring down at the tabletop. His face was stony, but the shadows under his eyes and the vertical furrow between his eyebrows revealed that something was bothering him. Even Ostermann made an unusually sullen impression. He seemed caught in the middle. Behnke was an old friend, and Ostermann had always protected him, covering his mistakes. But he'd finally become fed up with Behnke taking advantage of his friendship. And Ostermann usually agreed with Kathrin Fachinger—so whose side was he on?

"Has the Wallau case been cleared up?" Dr. Engel asked. It took Pia a moment to realize the question was directed at her.

"Yes," she replied, frowning at the memory of the large-scale operation by the evidence team and forensic medical examiners at the accident scene. "They did find two bodies, but we probably won't have much to do with them."

"Why is that?"

"They were two roasted suckling pigs that were supposed to be delivered to a party," Pia explained. "The van was completely destroyed in the accident because the party service driver had a couple of butane bottles in the cargo area that blew up in the fire."

Dr. Engel frowned. "All the better. And the Rita Cramer case is in the hands of the DA." She turned to Bodenstein. "So you can take over the case of the missing girl. She'll probably turn up somewhere soon. Ninety-eight percent of cases with missing teenagers are cleared up within a few hours or after a couple of days."

Bodenstein cleared his throat. "But two percent aren't," he said.

"Talk to the parents and the girl's friends," Dr. Engel advised. "I have an appointment now with the National Criminal Police. Keep me informed."

She stood up, nodded to the team, and left.

"What have we got?" Bodenstein asked Ostermann when the door closed behind her.

"Amelie Fröhlich, seventeen years old, from Bad Soden. Her parents reported her missing yesterday. They saw her last on Saturday morning. But because she's run away from home before, they waited until now to report it."

"Good." Bodenstein nodded. "Pia and I will go talk to the parents. Frank, you and Fachinger will drive—"

"No," Kathrin interrupted her boss, who gave her a startled look. "I'm definitely not riding with Behnke anywhere."

"I can ride with Frank," Ostermann offered hastily. For a moment there was utter silence. Behnke chewed on his gum and grinned contentedly to himself.

"Do I have to take personal disagreements into consideration?" Bodenstein asked. The furrow between his eyebrows had deepened. He looked really angry, which was rare for him. Kathrin was pouting. It was a clear instance of insubordination.

"Be careful, people." Bodenstein's voice sounded dangerously calm. "I don't give a *shit* who has problems with whom at the moment. We have work to do, and I expect all of you to comply with instructions. Perhaps I've been a bit too lax in the past, but I'm nobody's fool. Ms. Fachinger and Mr. Behnke will drive to the girl's school and talk to her teachers and classmates. When they're finished with that, they'll start on the girl's neighbors. Is that clear?"

The answer was stubborn silence. And suddenly Bodenstein did something he'd never done before. He slammed his fist down on the table.

"I asked if that was clear!" he roared.

"Yes," replied Kathrin Fachinger icily. She got up, grabbing her jacket and bag. Behnke also got up. The two left the room, and then Ostermann also retreated to his office.

Oliver took a deep breath and looked at Pia.

"Oh, man." He exhaled and gave her a crooked grin. "That felt good."

• • •

"Altenhain?" Pia asked in surprise. "But Ostermann said something about Bad Soden."

"Waldstrasse 22." Oliver pointed to the GPS in his BMW, which he tended to follow blindly, although in the past it had sometimes gotten him lost. "It's in Altenhain. But it belongs to Bad Soden."

A sense of foreboding crept over Pia. Altenhain. Tobias Sartorius. She would never admit it, but she felt a certain sympathy for the young man. Now another girl had gone missing, and she could only hope that he'd had nothing to do with it. But she didn't doubt for a second how the villagers would react, and it didn't matter if he had an alibi or not. Her bad feeling grew when they reached the residence of Arne and Barbara Fröhlich. The house stood only a few yards from the rear exit of the Sartorius property. They stopped in front of the handsome brick house with a deep hipped roof and several dormer windows. The parents were waiting for them.

Arne Fröhlich, despite his cheerful surname, was a serious man of about forty-five with a receding hairline, thin sandy hair, and steel-rimmed glasses. His face was distinguished by the lack of any striking features. He was neither fat nor thin, of medium height, and looked so ordinary that it was almost uncanny. His wife, in her early thirties, was the complete opposite. Extremely attractive, with medium blond hair, expressive eyes, regular features, a wide mouth, and a slight snub nose. What did she possibly see in her husband?

They were both worried but very composed, with no trace of the hysteria usually displayed by the parents of missing children. Barbara Fröhlich gave Pia a photo. Amelie was obviously a striking girl, but not in the way her mother was: her big brown eyes were heavily made up with kohl and eyeliner, and she had several piercings in her eyebrows, lower lip, and chin. She had teased her hair and styled it so it stood out like a shelf from her head. Beneath the dramatic façade Amelie was a good-looking girl.

"She has run away several times before," her father replied to Bodenstein's question of why they had delayed in reporting their daughter missing. "Amelie is my daughter from my first marriage and somewhat ... hmm ... difficult. We took her in six months ago; before that she'd been living with my ex in Berlin, and there she also had big problems with ... the police."

"What sort of problems?" asked Bodenstein. The answer was clearly unpleasant for Arne Fröhlich.

"Shoplifting, drugs, trespassing, and vagrancy," he enumerated. "Sometimes she'd be gone for a week. My ex-wife was feeling completely overwhelmed and asked me to take Amelie in. That's why we called around first and waited for her to show up."

"But then it occurred to me that she didn't take any clothes with her," Barbara Fröhlich added. "Not even the money she'd earned waitressing. I thought that was odd. And she also left her driver's license here."

"Was Amelie fighting with anyone? Did she have problems at school or with her friends?" Bodenstein went through the usual questions.

"No, on the contrary," said the stepmother. "I even had the impression that she had changed for the better recently. She didn't wear her hair quite as wild, and she started borrowing clothes from me. Normally she wears nothing but black, but suddenly she put on a skirt and blouse . . ." She fell silent.

"Do you think there's a boy behind this change?" Pia ventured. "She may have met someone online and left to go see him."

Arne and Barbara Fröhlich exchanged a baffled look and shrugged.

"We gave her plenty of freedom," the father offered. "Lately Amelie has been quite dependable. My boss, Mr. Terlinden, arranged a job for her waiting tables at the Black Horse so she could earn her own money."

"Any problems at school?"

"She doesn't have many girlfriends," said Barbara. "She likes to be alone. She hasn't talked much about school, but she's only been there since September. The only one she hangs out with regularly is Thies Terlinden, our neighbor's son."

For a moment Arne Fröhlich pressed his lips together. It was obvious that he didn't approve of this friendship.

"What do you mean by that?" asked Pia, digging deeper. "Are they a couple?"

"Oh no," said Barbara, shaking her head. "Thies is . . . well . . . different. He's autistic, lives with his parents, and takes care of their garden."

At Bodenstein's request Barbara showed them Amelie's room. It was large and cheerful, with two windows, one facing the street. The walls were bare; the posters of pop stars that other girls Amelie's age liked to put up would have been totally wrong. Barbara explained it by saying that Amelie felt that she was only "passing through."

"On her eighteenth birthday next year she wants to go straight back to Berlin," she said, and they could hear the regret in her voice.

"How do you get along with your stepdaughter?" Pia walked over and opened the desk drawers.

"We get along fine. I try to be lenient when it comes to rules. Amelie reacts to restrictions by retreating into herself rather than protesting loudly. I think she's gradually coming to trust me. She's often gruff with her half sisters, but both of them are very attached to her. When I'm not around she'll play with them for hours with their Playmobil figures or read them a story."

Pia nodded. "Our colleagues will need to take her computer along. Does Amelie keep a diary?"

She picked up the laptop and saw something that confirmed her worst suspicions. On the desk blotter there was a drawing of a heart. And inside was a name in curlicue letters: Tobias.

"I'm worried about Thies," Christine Terlinden replied to the angry question from her husband about what could be so urgent that she would ask him to come home in the middle of a special board meeting. "He's . . . completely distraught."

Claudius Terlinden shook his head and went downstairs to the basement. When he opened the door to Thies's room, he could see at once that his wife's use of the word "distraught" was a vast understatement. With a vacant stare Thies was kneeling on the floor stark naked in the middle of the room in a carefully arranged circle of toys, and he kept hitting himself in the face with his fist. Blood was running from his nose down his chin, and there was a sharp stench of urine. The sight was a shock and a painful reminder to Terlinden of episodes in the past. For a long time he had categorically refused to accept that his eldest son was mentally ill. He hadn't wanted to hear the diagnosis of autism, even though the signs were all there in Thies's alarming behavior. Worse still was the boy's repellent habit of ripping everything to bits and smearing it with feces and urine. He and Christine had faced this problem in utter helplessness, deciding the only solution was to lock up the boy and keep him away from other people—especially his brother Lars. But as Thies grew older and turned more and more maniacal and aggressive, they could no longer close their eyes to the truth. Reluctantly Claudius Terlinden had taken a good look at his son's syndrome and learned in conversations with doctors and therapists that there was no outlook for a cure. Daniela Lauterbach, their neighbor, had finally explained what Thies needed to be able to cope with his illness reasonably well. Familiar surroundings were important, in which nothing was ever changed and the unexpected rarely occurred. It was equally important for Thies to have his own strictly ritualized world into which he could retreat. For a while all went well, until the twelfth birthday of the twin brothers. Something happened on that day that completely derailed Thies. Something snapped in him so violently that he almost killed his brother and seriously injured himself.

That was the last straw for Claudius Terlinden, and the boy was taken raging and yelling to the locked psychiatric children's ward, where he remained for three years. There they treated him with calming medications, and his situation improved. Tests had shown that Thies was of above-average intelligence. Unfortunately he had no idea what to do with this intelligence, because he lived as a captive in his own world, completely isolated from his surroundings and his fellow human beings.

Three years later Thies had been allowed to leave the facility in which he lived for a visit at home. He was calm and peaceful but had seemed in a virtual stupor. At home he immediately went down to the basement and began to set out his toys from long ago. He did that for hours, a disconcerting sight. Under the influence of the medications he didn't suffer a single outburst. Thies even opened up a little. He helped the gardener, and he began painting. Although he still ate his meals using his childhood utensils from his teddy bear plate, by and large he ate, drank, and behaved normally. The doctors were quite pleased with this development and advised the parents to bring the boy home. Since then, now over fifteen years later, there had been no incident. Thies moved about freely in the village but spent most of his time in the garden, which he had single-handedly transformed into a symmetrically designed park with boxwood hedges, flowerbeds, and lots of Mediterranean plants.

And he painted, often until he was exhausted. The large-format pictures were impressive works: unconventional, disturbingly somber, oppressive messages from the hidden depths of his autistic inner life. Thies had nothing against exhibiting his work, and twice he had even accompanied his parents to openings. Nor did it bother him when he had to part with the paintings, as Claudius Terlinden had feared at first. So Thies continued to paint and tend to the garden, and everything was fine. By now Thies was even able to handle contact with the public without reverting to disturbing behavior. Now and then he even spoke a few words. He seemed to be on the right path to opening a tiny crack in the door to his inner self. And now this. What a setback! Without a word and deeply disturbed, Claudius Terlinden regarded his son. The sight of him pained him to his soul.

"Thies!" he called in a soft voice, then a bit more sternly: "Thies!"

"He hasn't been taking his medication," Christine Terlinden whispered behind him. "Imelda found it in the toilet."

Claudius Terlinden went into the room and knelt down outside the circle. "Thies," he said softly. "What have you got there?"

"Whathaveyougotthere," repeated Thies tonelessly and rhythmically hit himself in the face like clockwork. "Whathaveyougotthere . . . whathaveyougotthere . . . whathaveyougotthere . . ."

Terlinden saw that he was holding something in his fist. When he tried to grab his son's arm, Thies jumped up suddenly and fell upon his father, pounding and kicking him. Claudius Terlinden was surprised by the attack and instinctively defended himself, but Thies was no longer a little boy. He was a grown man with muscles steeled by gardening work. His eyes were wild, spittle and blood dripped from his chin. Panting, Claudius Terlinden fended off his son and as if through a fog he heard his wife screaming hysterically. Finally he managed to force open Thies's fist and take away what he was holding. Then he crawled on all fours to the door. Thies didn't pursue him but emitted a ghastly howl and curled up on the floor.

"Amelie," he babbled. "Amelie Amelie Amelie Amelie. Whathaveyou-

gotthere . . . Whathaveyougotthere . . . Whathaveyougotthere . . . Daddy . . .
Daddy . . . Daddy . . ."

Breathing hard, Claudius Terlinden got to his feet. He was trembling all
over. His wife stared at him, her hands clapped over her mouth, her eyes full
of tears. Terlinden unfolded the paper and almost had a stroke. From the
crumpled photo Stefanie Schneeberger was laughing up at him.

Arne and Barbara Fröhlich had gone to see friends in the Rheingau on Saturday morning with their two younger children and didn't return home until
late. Amelie had worked the evening shift at the Black Horse. When she
wasn't home by midnight, her father had called the restaurant and learned
from the incensed boss that Amelie had left shortly after ten, although they
were at their wits' end, they were so busy. After that the Fröhlichs had called
around to all their daughter's classmates and friends whose numbers they
could find. No luck. Nobody had seen Amelie or talked to her.

Oliver and Pia questioned Jenny Jagielski, the proprietor of the Black
Horse, who told them what Arne Fröhlich had said before. Amelie had been
acting strangely distant all evening and kept trying to make a phone call
from the kitchen. At ten o'clock she got a call and just took off. And on Sunday
she didn't turn up as usual to serve the early drinks crowd. No, Jenny didn't
know who had made the phone call that sent Amelie rushing off in such a
hurry. The rest of the staff had no idea either. That evening all hell broke
loose in the restaurant.

"Stop for a moment at the store," Pia said to Oliver as they drove back
down the main street. "It can't hurt to ask around one more time."

It turned out that they had come at a good time with regard to making inquiries. On this Monday morning Margot Richter's small store was obviously
the central meeting place for the female inhabitants of Altenhain. This time the
ladies proved much more communicative than they were at their last visit.

"And this is exactly how it all started back then," said Inge Dombrowski
the hairdresser, and the other women present nodded in agreement. "I don't
want to imply anything, but Willi Paschke told me he saw Amelie over at the
Sartorius place."

"I also saw her go into their house recently," another woman piped up, adding that she lived kitty-corner from Hartmut's house and had an excellent view.

"She's also bosom buddies with our village idiot," a fat woman commented from the produce counter.

"Yes, that's right," three or four other women eagerly confirmed.

"With whom?" Pia inquired.

"With that Thies Terlinden," the hairdresser explained. "He's a few cards short of a deck, and prowls around at night through the village and the woods. I wouldn't be surprised if he'd done something to that girl."

The other women nodded in agreement. In Altenhain there were always plenty of suspicions to go around. Neither Oliver nor Pia said anything to that, but simply let the women talk. They were clearly enjoying whetting their knives and sharing their lust for scandal. They seem to have forgotten the police were present.

"The Terlindens should have locked that son up in a home long ago," one woman insisted. "But in this town nobody dares say a word to the old man."

"Right, because then they'd have to worry about losing their job."

"The last person who said something against the Terlindens was Albert Schneeberger. Then his daughter disappeared, and soon he was gone too."

"It's strange how Terlinden helped out Sartorius. Maybe the two boys did have something to do with it."

"That Lars sure left Altenhain in a hurry afterwards."

"And now I hear Terlinden has even offered the murderer a job. Unbelievable! Instead of making sure he gets lost."

For a moment silence descended over the store; everyone seemed to be pondering the possible meaning of these words. Then they all started jabbering at once. Pia decided to play dumb.

"Excuse me!" she shouted, trying to make herself heard. "Just who is this Terlinden you keep talking about?"

Abruptly the women realized that they weren't alone. One after the other hurried to leave the store under some pretext, most of them with empty baskets. Margot Richter remained behind at her cash register. Until now she had kept out of the discussion. As befitted a good shop owner, she kept her ears open but preserved her neutrality.

"That's not the result we had in mind," said Pia apologetically, but the shop owner was unperturbed.

"They'll be back soon enough," she said. "Claudius Terlinden is the owner of the Terlinden company up there in the industrial park. The family and the company have been here in Altenhain for more than a hundred years. And without them not much would happen here at all."

"How do you mean?"

"The Terlindens are very generous. They support the associations, the church, the elementary school, the district library. With them it's a family tradition. And half the village works at the plant. The one son, Thies, that Christa called 'the village idiot,' is a very peaceful guy. He wouldn't harm a fly. I can't imagine he could have done anything to hurt the girl."

"By the way—do you know Amelie Fröhlich?"

"Yes, of course." She gave a slightly disapproving smile. "You can't miss her, the way she dresses! Besides, she works with my daughter at the Black Horse."

Pia nodded and jotted down a note. Once again her boss was leaving her totally in the lurch, standing next to her absentmindedly and not saying a word.

"So what do you think could have happened to the girl?"

Margot Richter hesitated a moment, but her eyes twitched to the right, and Pia knew immediately who she suspected, because from her spot behind the cash register she had a clear view of the Golden Rooster. The gossip about Terlinden's son was only a smoke screen. In reality everyone in town suspected Tobias Sartorius, who had done something like this before, after all.

"I have no idea what could have happened," Margot Richter said evasively. "Maybe she'll turn up."

"Tobias Sartorius is in great danger of being lynched," Pia said, seriously troubled, when they got back to K-11. "Last Friday night he was attacked and beaten up in his barn, and his father is still getting anonymous threatening letters, not to mention the graffiti smeared on the wall of his house."

Ostermann had already confiscated Amelie's laptop and diary, which to his dismay was written in a secret code that he couldn't decipher. Kathrin Fachinger and Frank Behnke had met with Bodenstein and Kirchhoff at the same time and had nothing really helpful to report. Amelie had no close girlfriends. She kept to herself and on the school bus talked only with the two girls in her class who also lived in Altenhain. The two girls did say that Amelie had been showing a lot of interest in Tobias Sartorius and the horrible events of eleven years ago. She kept asking questions about it. And yes, she had probably even talked to *that guy* more than once.

Ostermann came into the conference room with a fax in his hand. "We got the call list from Amelie's cell phone," he announced. "The last call was on Sunday evening at 10:11. She called a landline number in Altenhain, and I already checked it out."

"Sartorius?" Bodenstein guessed.

"Right. The call lasted only seven seconds, and apparently no words were spoken. Earlier she had dialed this number twelve times and hung up immediately. After 10:11 p.m. her cell phone was turned off, so her movements can't be tracked, because the phone's signal was captured by the only cell tower in Altenhain, which has a radius of about five kilometers."

"But incoming calls were captured, weren't they?" Bodenstein asked, and Ostermann shook his head.

"What did you get from the computer?"

"I haven't cracked the password yet." Ostermann frowned. "But I looked through the diary, at least the parts that I could decipher. Tobias Sartorius, someone named 'Thies,' and 'Claudius' were mentioned often."

"In what context?"

"She seemed to be interested in Sartorius and this Claudius. I don't know yet what sort of interest she had."

"Good work." Bodenstein looked at the other team members, and his old decisiveness had returned. "At present the girl has been missing for less than forty hours. I want the whole program: at least two hundred people to do a ground search, dogs, and a chopper with an infrared camera. Behnke, you organize a special team; I want every available officer to canvass every resident in the village. Fachinger, check out the bus connections and taxi companies. The time period in question is between ten p.m. Saturday till two a.m. Sunday morning. Any questions?"

"We should talk to this Thies and his father," said Kirchhoff. "And to Tobias Sartorius."

"Right. The two of us will do that right away." Bodenstein looked around the room. "Oh yes, Ostermann. Press, radio, TV, and the usual entry in the missing persons list. We'll meet here again at six p.m."

An hour later Altenhain was swarming with police. A canine unit with specially trained "man-trackers" was on the way; these dogs could pick up and follow a scent up to four weeks old. One hundred riot police were systematically combing the meadows and edges of the woods surrounding the village, mapped out in quadrants. A helicopter with an infrared camera flew low over the treetops, and the criminal police officers from the "Amelie" special team rang the doorbell at every house and apartment in Altenhain. Everyone involved was motivated and full of hope that the girl would be found quickly and unharmed. Each of them was also aware that the pressure to produce rapid results was enormous. Oliver's phone rang off the hook. He had turned over the driving to Pia and was concentrating on coordinating the entire effort. Roadblocks on the street in front of the Fröhlichs' house were set up to keep away the press and curious neighbors. The canine units would begin their search at the last place Amelie had been seen, the Black Horse. Yes, a friend was allowed to visit the Fröhlichs, and the pastor too. Yes, the surveillance footage from the police camera at the entrance to the village would be checked. No, civilians were not allowed to help in the search. Just as they pulled up to the Golden Rooster, Dr. Engel called and wanted to know the state of things.

"As soon as there is something to report, you'll be the first to know, of course," said Bodenstein curtly, ending the call.

Hartmut Sartorius opened the front door but peeked out with the safety chain on.

"We'd like to speak with your son, Mr. Sartorius," said Bodenstein. "Please let us in."

"Do you suspect him every time some girl comes home too late?" The words sounded gruff, almost aggressive.

"You've already heard?"

"Yes, of course. Word gets around quickly here."

"Tobias is not a suspect." Bodenstein remained quite calm because he could see how nervous Sartorius was. "But Amelie did call your home number thirteen times the night she disappeared."

The door closed, the safety chain was unhooked, and Sartorius let them in. He straightened his shoulders and was obviously preparing himself for this visit by the authorities. His son, though, looked terrible. He sat slumped on the sofa in the living room; his face was disfigured by bruises and he nodded weakly to Bodenstein and Kirchhoff when they came in.

"Where were you on Saturday night between ten p.m. and early Sunday morning?" Bodenstein wanted to know.

"Come on now!" Sartorius exclaimed. "My son was home all evening. On Friday night he was attacked in the barn and beaten half to death!"

Bodenstein didn't let himself be thrown off track. "On Saturday night at 10:11 p.m. Amelie called your number. The call was picked up, but it was so short that probably no words were exchanged. Before that she had already tried to call twelve times."

"We have an answering machine that switches on immediately," said Sartorius. "Because of all the anonymous and abusive calls we get."

Pia looked at Tobias. He was staring into space and seemed not to be following the conversation at all. Surely he had some idea about what was brewing in the village.

"Why would Amelie have tried to call you?" she asked him directly. He shrugged.

"Mr. Sartorius," she said insistently, "a girl from the neighborhood who had contact with you is missing. Whether you like it or not, people are going to link you to her disappearance. We just want to help you."

"Oh right," retorted Hartmut Sartorius bitterly. "That's exactly what your colleagues said back then. We just want to help you, boy. All you have to do is tell us what you did with the girls! And then nobody believed my son. Now go. Tobias was here at home all Saturday night."

"That's enough, Papa," Tobias finally said. He grimaced as he laboriously got to his feet. "I know you mean well."

He looked at Kirchhoff. His eyes were red.

"I ran into Amelie on Saturday around noon. Up the hill by the woods. She wanted to tell me something urgently. Apparently she found out something about the old case. But then Nadia came by and Amelie left. That's why she probably tried to call me later. I don't have a cell phone, so she would have tried the house."

Kirchhoff recalled her meeting with Nadia von Bredow last Saturday, and the silver Cayenne. It could be true.

"What did she tell you?" Bodenstein wanted to know.

"Unfortunately not very much," Tobias replied. "She said there was someone who saw everything that happened. She mentioned Thies and some paintings. And Lauterbach was in them too."

"Who?"

"Gregor Lauterbach."

"The cultural minister?"

"Yes, precisely. He lives right behind Amelie's father's house. He used to be Laura and Stefanie's teacher."

"And yours too, wasn't he?" Pia remembered the transcript she had read, the one that then disappeared from the folder.

"Yes," Tobias confirmed with a nod. "He was my German teacher when I was a senior."

"What did Amelie find out about him?"

"No idea. As I said, Nadia showed up, and Amelie wouldn't say any more. All she said was that she'd tell me everything later."

"What did you do after Amelie left?"

"Nadia and I talked for a while, then we drove here and sat in the kitchen for about half an hour. Until she had to leave to catch the plane to Hamburg." Tobias grimaced and ran his hand through his uncombed hair. "Then I went to see a friend. We ended up drinking with some other friends. Quite a bit."

He looked up. His expression was blank. "Unfortunately I can't remember when or how I got home. I have a twenty-four-hour blank spot in my memory."

Hartmut Sartorius shook his head in despair. He looked like he wanted to burst into tears. The buzz of Bodenstein's cell, which he'd set on vibrate, sounded loud in the sudden silence. He took the call, listened, and said thanks. His eyes sought Kirchhoff's.

"What time did your son come home, Mr. Sartorius?" he asked, turning to Tobias's father. Sartorius hesitated.

"Tell him the truth, Papa." Tobias's voice sounded tired.

"About one thirty Sunday morning," his father said at last. "Dr. Lauterbach, our doctor, drove him home. She found him as she was coming back from a late emergency call."

"Where?"

"At the bus stop in front of the church."

"Did you drive anywhere yesterday?" Bodenstein asked Tobias.

"No, I walked."

"What are the names of your friends that you spent Saturday night with?" Pia pulled out her ballpoint and wrote down the names that Tobias mentioned.

"We'll be talking to them," Bodenstein said somberly. "But I have to ask you to remain available."

The leader of the search party had reported finding Amelie's backpack. It was lying in some bushes between the parking lot of the Black Horse and the church—not far from the bus stop where Dr. Lauterbach had picked up Tobias Sartorius on Saturday night.

"It was the same thing eleven years ago," said Pia pensively as she drove the few yards over to where the backpack was found. "Tobias had been drinking and blacked out. The prosecutors and the court didn't believe him."

"Do you believe him?" asked Oliver. Pia thought about it. Tobias Sartorius acted like he was telling the truth. He liked the neighbor girl. But hadn't he also liked the two girls he murdered ten years ago? Back then jealousy was involved, and wounded vanity. As far as Amelie was concerned, that wasn't the case. Had the girl actually found out something that was directly connected to the old crime, or had Tobias Sartorius made that up?

"I can't judge findings in the old case," she replied. "But today, I don't think Tobias was lying to us. He really doesn't remember."

Oliver refrained from commenting. He had learned to appreciate his colleague's intuition over the years, since it had often put them on the right track. His gut feelings, on the other hand, had more often led them hopelessly astray. But he didn't believe that Tobias Sartorius was innocent—either of the two homicides, or the events of today.

The backpack contained Amelie's wallet, her iPod, makeup kit, and all sorts of junk, but no cell phone. One thing was for sure: She hadn't run away from home. Something must have happened to her. The sniffer dogs had lost the scent at the parking lot and were now waiting impatiently with their handler for the next deployment, which for them was an exciting game. Pia, who had the layout of the village clear in her mind thanks to the map she'd drawn, spoke with the officers who were gradually assembling at the parking lot. The door-to-door questioning had turned up nothing helpful.

"The dog found some traces at the edge of the woods, everywhere on the street where the girl lives, at the neighbors' house, and at their garden house," the search leader reported.

"Which neighbors?"

"The Terlindens," said the officer. "The woman told us that Amelie came often to visit her son. So it may be a cold trail." He seemed disappointed. Nothing was as discouraging as a search with no result.

Kai Ostermann succeeded in cracking the password to Amelie's computer. He took a look at the browsing history of the Web sites Amelie had visited lately. Contrary to his expectations she was seldom active in popular social sites like Facebook and MySpace. She did have user profiles all over the place, but she didn't update them and didn't have very many contacts. But she had done extensive research on the old murder cases from 1997 and the sentencing of Tobias Sartorius. In addition, she was interested in the residents of Altenhain and had entered names in various search engines. She seemed to have a particularly strong interest in the Terlinden family. Ostermann was disappointed. He had hoped to come across some chat partner or some other suspicious Internet acquaintance, something that would have led to a concrete lead.

The meeting called on short notice by Bodenstein, at which twenty-five people squeezed into the conference room of K-11, turned out to yield very little. The search had been halted at nightfall without result. Thanks to the infrared camera in the chopper they had discovered a pair of lovers in a car in a hidden woodland parking spot, and a deer in a death struggle that had escaped a hunter after a bad shot, but no sign of Amelie. They had spoken with the driver of the 803 bus from Bad Soden to Königstein, who had made a stop by the church in Altenhain, as well as with his colleague, who had passed by going the other way a short time later. Neither of the two men had noticed a dark-haired girl. None of the taxi companies in the area had had a lone girl as a fare in that time period. One of the colleagues from K 23 had located a man who'd been walking his dog late Saturday night and saw a man sitting on the bench at the bus stop, sometime around twelve thirty.

"We ought to search the Sartorius house and property," Behnke suggested.

"What for? There's no reason to do that," Kirchhoff countered at once, although she knew that wasn't completely true. Unfortunately, things didn't look good for Tobias Sartorius. His friends had confirmed that he showed up at the garage around seven o'clock. Jörg Richter had called him late that afternoon to invite him over. Tobias had a few drinks, but not enough to make him black out. Around ten he had left the garage, quite suddenly. At first they thought he just went outside to take a leak, but he never came back.

"A seventeen-year-old girl has disappeared, and she's been proven to have had contact with a man convicted of killing two girls," Behnke sputtered. "I have a daughter that age, so I can understand what must be going through the parents' minds!"

"Do you think somebody has to have kids to understand what her parents must be feeling?" Pia snapped back. "And as long as you're proposing searches, why don't you have Terlinden's house searched too? The dogs found tons of traces there."

"That's true, actually," Bodenstein put in, before things between the two wound up in an argument in front of the whole team. "But Amelie's stepmother said that the girl often spent time at the neighbors' house. So it's questionable whether the traces we found have any relevance to the case."

Pia said nothing. Tobias had asked his father to tell the truth, although he must have known that it might tend to incriminate him. He should have kept quiet or used his father as an alibi as Hartmut had first tried to do. Had he refused to lie because it hadn't worked the first time?

"I think Amelie discovered something that has a direct connection to the old case," she said after a moment. "And I also believe that several people have an invested interest in making sure certain secrets don't come out."

"Nonsense." Behnke shook his head emphatically. "This guy obviously loses control when he drinks. He left the party, Amelie happened to run into him, and he bumped her off."

Pia raised her eyebrows. As usual, Behnke tended to reduce everything to the lowest common denominator.

"And what did he do with her body? He didn't have a car."

"So he claims." Behnke nodded toward the whiteboard. "Take a look at the girl."

Everyone automatically turned to look at the photo of Amelie that was tacked up on the bulletin board.

"She looks a lot like the kid that he killed in 1997. The guy is sick."

"All right then," Bodenstein decided. "Fachinger, you take care of the search warrants for the Sartorius house, car, and property. Kai, you keep working on the diary. The rest of you please remain available. We'll resume the search tomorrow morning at eight and expand the radius."

With a scraping of chairs the team adjourned. The mood was still one of muted optimism. The majority of the officers were in agreement with Behnke and hoped for results from the search of the Sartorius house. Pia waited until her colleagues had left the conference room, but before she could speak to her boss and present her reservations, Dr. Nicola Engel entered the room with two men in suits and ties.

"Just a moment," she said to Behnke, who was about to leave. Pia caught the eye of Kathrin Fachinger and they left the room together.

"Ms. Fachinger? Please wait outside for me." With that Dr. Engel closed the door behind them.

"Well," said Kathrin in the lobby. "Now I can't wait to see what happens."

"Who was that?" Pia asked, astounded.

"Internal Affairs." Kathrin actually seemed pleased. "I hope they tear that shithead a new asshole."

Only then did Pia recall the incident with Behnke working in the bar, and Kathrin's unsuccessful refusal to be his partner in the investigation.

"So how did he act toward you today?" she asked.

Kathrin only raised her eyebrows. "I probably shouldn't tell you any-thing," she replied. "He was absolutely disgusting. He chewed me out in front of everybody like some stupid girl. I kept my mouth shut. I've got only one thing to say: If he gets away with it this time, I'm going to ask for a transfer. I won't put up with any more crap from that jerk."

Pia nodded. She knew where Kathrin was coming from. But she had a hunch that this time Frank Behnke wasn't going to get off lightly. Dr. Engel seemed to hold some sort of grudge against him from the time they'd worked together at K-11 in Frankfurt. Things didn't look good for their colleague Mr. Asshole, and she wasn't sorry about that at all.

Tuesday, November 18, 2008

The newspaper lay open before him on the desktop. Another girl had disap-peared in Altenhain, shortly after the skeleton of Laura Wagner was found. Lars Terlinden was well aware that sitting in his glass office he was highly visible from the trading room and his outer office, so he resisted the impulse to bury his face in his hands. If only he had never returned to Germany! In his greed for more money he had left his high-salary job as a derivatives bro-ker in London and had taken a position in management for a large Swiss bank in Frankfurt. That had caused quite a stir in the banking profession, because he was only twenty-eight years old. But everything led to success for the "German Wunderkind," as *The Wall Street Journal* called him—and he was under the illusion that he was the biggest and best. But he'd been jolted back to reality, and from now on he would have to look his past in the eye and acknowledge what he had done out of cowardice.

Lars Terlinden uttered a deep sigh. His only mistake of any lasting con-sequence had been to secretly follow them home from the fair, driven by the insane need to confess his love to Laura. If only he had let it be! If only he had . . . He shook his head vehemently, folded up the paper, and tossed it in the wastebasket. It was no use brooding over the past. He needed to put all his attention on the problems confronting him at the moment. There was too much at stake for him to be distracted by all this old stuff. He had a family to think of and loads of financial obligations that he could only meet with great difficulty in these times of economic crisis. The gigantic villa in the Taunus had not been paid off, or the vacation home on Mallorca, and the lease payments for his Ferrari and his wife's station wagon were due every month. He felt caught in a spiral again, just like back then. And he could feel more and more clearly that this current spiral was hurling him downward at breathtaking speed. To hell with Altenhain!

For the past three hours Tobias had been sitting in front of the building on Karpfenweg and staring into the water of the harbor basin. He wasn't bothered by the unpleasant cold or by the skeptical looks of the residents of the building who suspiciously scrutinized his battered face as they passed by. He couldn't stand being at home anymore, and he couldn't think of anyone to talk to but Nadia. And he had to talk or he was going to explode. Amelie had disappeared. In Altenhain the police were turning over every rock in a huge search effort, just as they'd done before. And once again, he thought he was innocent, but doubt gnawed at him with sharp little teeth. The damned alcohol! He was never going to touch a drop again. He heard heels clicking behind him. Tobias raised his head and recognized Nadia coming toward him with rapid steps, her cell phone at her ear. All of a sudden he asked himself whether he would even be welcome. Her stylish appearance merely amplified the oppressive feeling of inadequacy that came over him every time he was with her. He felt like a bum in his worn, cheap leather jacket and with his beat-up face. Maybe it would be better to get out of here and never come back.

"Tobi!" Nadia put away her phone and hurried to him with a horrified expression. "What are you doing out here in the cold?"

"Amelie is missing," he said. "The police have already been to my house." With effort he stood up. His legs felt like ice and his back hurt.

"Why?"

He rubbed his hands and blew on them.

"Once a killer of girls, always a killer of girls, you know. Besides, I have no alibi for the time when Amelie disappeared."

Nadia stared at him. "Let's go inside." She pulled out her key and opened the street door. He followed her, walking stiffly.

"Where were you?" he asked as they rode up to the penthouse in the glass elevator. "I've been waiting a couple of hours outside."

"I was in Hamburg. You know that." She shook her head and laid her hand on his, concerned. "You really ought to get yourself a cell phone."

He finally remembered that Nadia had flown to Hamburg on Saturday for a film shoot. She helped him out of his jacket and shoved him toward the kitchen.

"Sit down," she said. "First I'll make you some coffee to warm up with. My goodness!"

She tossed her coat over the back of a chair. Her cell rang with a polyphonic ringtone, but she ignored it and kept on fiddling with the espresso machine.

"I'm really worried about Amelie," Tobias said. "I have no idea what she really found out about the old case or who she may have talked to about it. If anything has happened to her, it will be all my fault."

"You didn't force her to sniff around in the past," Nadia replied. She set two cups of coffee on the table, got some milk from the fridge, and sat down facing him. Without makeup, the violet shadows under her eyes made her look exhausted.

"Come on now." She put her hand on his. "Drink your coffee. And then you're getting in the bath to thaw out."

Why didn't she understand what was going on inside him? He didn't want to drink any shitty coffee or take a shitty bath! He wanted to hear from her lips that she believed he was innocent, and then get her help to figure out what could have happened to Amelie. Instead she was talking about coffee and warming him up, as if it made any difference.

Nadia's cell rang again, then a little later, the landline. With a sigh she got up and took the call. Tobias stared into space. Although the detective had obviously not believed him, he was more worried about Amelie than about himself. Nadia came back, stepped behind him, and flung her arms around his neck. She kissed his ear and his unshaven cheek. Tobias had to stop himself from trying to pull free. He was in no mood for affection. Couldn't she tell? He got goose bumps when she ran her finger along the mark on his throat that the clothesline had left. To make her stop, he grabbed her wrist, shoved his chair back, and pulled her onto his lap.

"On Saturday night I was with Jörg and Felix and a couple of other guys at Jörg's uncle's garage," he whispered urgently. "First we drank some beer, then this Red Bull stuff with vodka in it. That really knocked me for a loop. When I woke up Sunday morning, I had a gigantic hangover and couldn't remember a thing."

Her eyes were very close to his, and she gazed at him intently.

"Hmm," was all she said. He thought he knew what she was thinking.

"You don't believe me," he reproached her and shoved her off his lap. "You think that I . . . killed Amelie, like I did Laura and Stefanie back then! Am I right?"

"No! No, I don't!" Nadia protested. "Why would you want to hurt Amelie? She wanted to help you."

"That's right. She did. I don't understand it either." He got up, leaned against the fridge, and ran his hand through his hair. "The fact is, I don't remember anything between nine thirty in the evening and four o'clock Sunday afternoon. In theory I could have done it, and that's what the cops think too. Plus, Amelie tried to call me umpteen times. And my father says I was brought home at one thirty in the morning by Dr. Lauterbach. She found me drunk at the bus stop in front of the church."

"Shit," said Nadia and sat down.

"You said it." Tobias relaxed a little, reached for the cigarettes on the table, and lit one for himself. "The cops told me to stay available."

"But why?"

"Because I'm a suspect, pure and simple."

"But . . . but they can't do that," Nadia began.

"They can," Tobias interrupted her. "They've done it before. And it cost me ten years of my life."

He inhaled the smoke of the cigarette, staring past Nadia into the dim gray fog outside. The brief period of good weather was over, and November was showing its most unpleasant side. Heavy rain was pouring down the windowpanes from low-hanging black clouds. The Friedensbrücke spanning the Main river could only be seen as a silhouette.

"There must be somebody who knows the truth," Tobias ruminated, reaching for his coffee cup.

"What are you talking about?" Nadia asked.

Tobias looked up. It irritated him that she seemed so calm and collected. "About Amelie," he repeated, noticing that she briefly raised her eyebrows. "I'm sure that she found out something dangerous. Thies must have given her some pictures, but she didn't tell me what they showed. I think somebody felt threatened by her."

The tall gate with the gilded spikes on top in front of the Terlinden estate was closed, and no one opened it even after she rang several times. But the tiny camera with the blinking red light followed every move she made. Pia shrugged, signaling the results of her efforts to her boss, who was still in the car talking on the phone. She had already tried in vain to speak with Claudius Terlinden at his company. He wasn't in his office because of personal problems, his secretary had informed her with regret.

"Let's head over to the Sartorius place." Oliver started the engine and backed up a ways to make a U-turn. "Terlinden isn't going anywhere."

They drove past the rear entrance to the Sartorius farm, which was swarming with officers. The search warrant had been approved without difficulty. Kathrin Fachinger had called Pia late last night to let her know. But the real reason for the call was to report on how things had gone with Internal Affairs. The leniency that Behnke had previously enjoyed was now over; even Bodenstein's attempt at an intervention wouldn't have changed matters. Since Behnke had not obtained authorization for his second job, he now had to expect disciplinary action, a reprimand in his personal file, and most probably a demotion. In addition, Dr. Engel had bluntly told him to his face that she would have him immediately suspended if he ever behaved inappropriately toward Kathrin Fachinger or threatened her in any way. Pia would never have filed an official complaint against Behnke. Was that a sign of cowardice or of loyalty to others on the force? Quite frankly, she admired her younger female colleague for having the courage to report a male colleague to the supervisory board. All of them had obviously underestimated Kathrin.

The usually deserted parking area in front of the Golden Rooster was now full of police vehicles. On the sidewalk across the street curious onlookers had gathered despite the rain. Six or seven older people who had nothing better to do. Bodenstein and Kirchhoff got out of the car. Using a scrub brush, Hartmut Sartorius was busy removing new graffiti from the façade of the former restaurant. A hopeless undertaking. ATTENTION, it said, HERE LIVES A KILLER OF GIRLS!

"You're not going to get that off with soap," Bodenstein told him. The man turned around. There were tears in his eyes. He was a picture of misery with his wet hair and soaked blue smock.

"Why won't they leave us alone?" he asked in despair. "We were always good neighbors before. Our children played together. And now it's nothing but hate!"

"Let's go inside," Pia suggested. "We'll send over somebody to remove it."

Sartorius dropped the scrub brush into the bucket. "Your people are turning everything in the place upside down." His voice sounded accusatory. "The whole village has started talking again. What do you want with my son?"

"Is he home?"

"No." He shrugged. "I don't know where he went. I don't know anything anymore."

His gaze wandered past Kirchhoff and Bodenstein. All of a sudden, with a fury that surprised both of them, he grabbed the bucket and ran across the parking lot. Before their eyes he seemed to grow and became for a moment the man he once must have been.

"Get the hell out of here, you damned assholes!" he roared, and tossed the bucketful of hot soap suds across the street at the people who had gathered there. "Piss off, why don't you? Leave us alone!"

His voice cracked; he was about to attack the rubberneckers when Bodenstein managed to grab his arm. The spurt of angry energy vanished as fast as it had appeared. Sartorius collapsed like a hot-air balloon that has opened its parachute valve and released all the air.

"I'm sorry," he said softly. A shaky smile flitted across his face. "But I should have done that long ago."

When the evidence techs had finished searching the house, Hartmut Sartorius closed the rear entrance of the former restaurant and led Kirchhoff and Bodenstein into the big, rustically furnished dining hall, in which everything looked like it had simply been shut down for the midday break. There were chairs on the tables, not a speck of dust on the floor, and menus bound in fake leather were stacked neatly next to the cash register. The bar had been polished to a high gloss, the draft beer dispenser gleamed, and the bar stools were neatly lined up. Pia looked around and shivered. Time seemed to have stood still inside this place.

"I'm here every day," said Sartorius. "My parents and grandparents ran both the farm and the Golden Rooster. I just can't bring myself to change anything."

He brought the chairs from a round table near the bar and motioned Bodenstein and Kirchhoff to take a seat.

"Would you like something to drink? Maybe a cup of coffee?"

"Yes, that would be nice," Bodenstein said with a smile. Sartorius busied himself behind the bar, taking cups from the cupboard, putting coffee beans in the machine. Familiar movements he'd done a thousand times, which gave him a sense of security. As he worked he kept up a lively account of the old days, when he did the butchering and cooking, and pressed his own cider.

"People used to come here from Frankfurt," he said with unmistakable pride in his voice. "Just to have our cider. And you wouldn't believe how many people would show up! Upstairs, in the big hall, there were parties every week. Earlier, when my parents were alive, there were movies and boxing matches and God knows what all. People back then didn't have cars and didn't go to a different town to eat."

Bodenstein and Kirchhoff exchanged a silent glance. Here, in his domain, Hartmut Sartorius was again the owner who had the welfare of his guests at heart, and who was incensed by the graffiti on the façade. He was no longer the stooped, humiliated shadow he had become due to circumstances. Only now did Pia comprehend the full scope of the loss that this man had suffered, and she felt a deep sympathy. She had wanted to ask him why he never moved away from Altenhain after those terrible events, but now this question seemed superfluous. Hartmut Sartorius was so solidly rooted in this village where his family had lived for generations, as solidly as the chestnut tree standing outside.

"You cleaned out the farmyard," Bodenstein began the conversation. "That must have taken a lot of work."

"Tobias did that. He wants me to sell everything. Actually he's right, because we'll never be able to make a go of it here. But the problem is, the property no longer belongs to me."

"Who does it belong to?"

"We had to borrow a lot of money to pay Tobias's legal bills," Sartorius volunteered. "It was more than we could handle, especially since we had already gone into debt to put a new kitchen in the restaurant and pay for the tractor and other things. For three years I was still able to pay my bills, but then . . . people stopped coming. I had to close the place. If it hadn't been for Claudius, we'd be out on the street today."

"Claudius Terlinden?" Pia asked, pulling out her notebook. Suddenly she understood what Andrea Wagner had meant the other day when she said that she didn't want to wind up like Sartorius. She would rather get a job than be dependent on Claudius Terlinden.

"Yes. Claudius was the only one who stood by us. He got us the lawyer and later he regularly visited Tobias in prison."

"Aha."

"The Terlinden family has lived in Altenhain as long as our family has. Claudius's great-grandfather was the blacksmith in the village until he came up with an invention, which he used to set up a metalworking shop. Claudius's grandfather expanded the family business and built that villa over by the woods," Sartorius told them. "The Terlindens have always been socially minded. They've done a great deal for the village, and for their employees and families. They don't have to keep doing that, but Claudius is always ready to listen. He's willing to help anyone who's in a jam. Without his support the organizations in the village wouldn't have a chance. A couple of years ago he gave the volunteer fire department a new fire engine; he's on the board of the local athletic club and sponsored the first- and second-string soccer teams. Yes, they can even thank him for the artificial turf."

Lost in thought, Sartorius stared into space for a moment, but Bodenstein and Kirchhoff took care not to interrupt. After a pause Sartorius continued.

"Claudius even offered Tobias a job with his firm. Just until he finds something else. Lars was Tobias's best friend. He used to come in and out of the house like a second son, and Tobias also felt completely at home at the Terlindens'."

"Lars," Pia said. "He's mentally handicapped, isn't he?"

"Oh no, not Lars." Sartorius shook his head emphatically. "You're thinking of Thies, the other brother. And he isn't mentally handicapped. He's autistic."

Oliver, who had been extensively briefed on the old case by Pia, said, "If I remember correctly, at the time there was some suspicion directed at Claudius Terlinden as well. Didn't your son tell you that Terlinden had something going on with Laura? If that's the case, Tobias is probably not his favorite person."

"I don't think there was anything between Claudius and the girl," Sartorius said after thinking it over. "Laura was pretty and a little wild. Her mother was the housekeeper at the Terlinden villa, so Laura went there often. She told Tobias that Claudius was pursuing her, probably to make him jealous. It hurt her feelings that he'd broken up with her. But Tobias was head over heels in love with Stefanie, so Laura no longer had a chance. Hmm, she was also of a whole different caliber, that Stefanie. Already a mature young woman, very beautiful and very self-assured."

"Snow White," said Pia.

"Yes, that's what they called her after she got the part."

"What part?"

"Oh, in a school play. The other girls were very jealous. After all, Stefanie was the new girl here, but she still got the coveted lead role in the drama club play."

"But Laura and Stefanie were friends, weren't they?" Pia asked.

"The two of them and Nathalie were all in the same class. They got along well and belonged to the same clique." Sartorius was clearly thinking back to more peaceful times.

"Who was in that clique?"

"Laura, Nathalie, and the boys: Tobias, Jörg, Felix, Michael—I can't remember the rest. When Stefanie came to Altenhain, she was quickly accepted into the group."

"And Tobias broke up with Laura because of her."

"Yes."

"But then Stefanie broke up with *him*. Why did she do that?"

"I don't know the exact reason," Sartorius said with a shrug. "Who knows what goes on among the young people? Supposedly she'd fallen for her teacher."

"For Gregor Lauterbach?"

"Yes." His expression darkened. "They turned that into a motive at the trial. Tobias was supposed to be jealous of the teacher so he . . . killed Stefanie. But that's utter nonsense."

"So who got the lead role after Stefanie couldn't play the part?"

"If I remember rightly, it was Nathalie."

Pia shot Oliver a glance.

"Nathalie—who is now Nadia," she said. "She always remained loyal to your son. Even to this day. Why?"

"The Ungers are our next-door neighbors," said Sartorius. "Nathalie was like a little sister to Tobias. Later she was his best friend. She was . . . a pal. Rather tomboyish but not bitchy at all. She was game for anything. Tobias and his friends always treated her like a boy because she did everything with them. When they were even younger, she rode a moped, climbed trees, and joined in their fights."

"To get back to Claudius Terlinden," Bodenstein began, but at that moment Behnke marched in, followed by two more officers. They came through the restaurant's back door, which was ajar. That morning Bodenstein had entrusted Behnke with leading the search of the house. He took up position in front of the table, his colleagues like two aides-de-camp on either side.

"We found something interesting in your son's room, Mr. Sartorius."

Kirchhoff noticed the triumphant gleam in Behnke's eyes, the arrogant twitch at the corners of his mouth. He enjoyed displaying the superiority he felt in situations like this, based on his authority as a police officer. A shabby character trait that Pia deeply resented.

As if touched by a magic wand, Sartorius again seemed to cave in.

"This," Behnke announced without taking his eyes off Sartorius, "was in the seat pocket of a pair of jeans in your son's room." He flared his nostrils, sure of victory. "Does this belong to your son? Hmm? I don't think so. There are initials on the back written in indelible ink. Take a look."

Bodenstein loudly cleared his throat and reached out his hand, gesturing to Behnke to hand over the item. Pia could have kissed her boss for that. She had to stop herself from breaking into a grin. Without a word Oliver had put Behnke in his place—and he did it in front of his colleagues from the evidence team. Behnke's furious gnashing of teeth was almost audible as he reluctantly handed his boss the plastic bag with his discovery.

"Thank you," said Bodenstein without even looking at him. "You can all continue your work outside."

Behnke's lean face first turned pale, then red with anger at this rebuke. Woe to the poor devil who now crossed his path and made a mistake. He glanced at Kirchhoff, but she succeeded in maintaining a completely disinterested expression. Meanwhile, Bodenstein examined the find in the plastic bag and frowned.

"This seems to be a cell phone belonging to Amelie Fröhlich," he said gravely, after Behnke and the other two officers had gone. "How could it have wound up in your son's pants pocket?"

Hartmut Sartorius had turned pale, and he shook his head in bewilderment.

"I . . . I have no idea," he whispered. "I really don't."

Nadia's cell rang and vibrated, but she merely cast a quick glance at the display and put it down.

"Go ahead and take it." The melody was gradually getting on Tobias's nerves. "They aren't going to let up."

She grabbed the phone and took the call. "Hello, Hartmut," she said, looking at Tobias, who straightened up involuntarily. What did his father want with Nadia?

"Oh?...Aha...Yes, I understand." She listened without taking her eyes off Tobias. "No...I'm sorry. He isn't here...No, I don't know where he could be. I just got back from Hamburg myself...Yes, of course. If he calls me I'll tell him."

She hung up. For a moment it was quite still.

"You lied," Tobias said. "How come?"

Nadia didn't answer at once. She lowered her eyes and sighed. When she looked up she was struggling with tears.

"The police just searched your house," she said tensely. "They want to talk to you."

A search of the house? Why was that? Tobias got up abruptly. He couldn't possibly leave his father alone in this situation. He had long ago reached the limit of what he could tolerate.

"Please, Tobi," Nadia begged. "Don't go there. I...I...won't let them arrest you again."

"Who says they want to arrest me?" Tobias replied in astonishment. "They probably just have a few more questions."

"No!" She jumped up and the chair crashed to the granite floor. Her expression was desperate, and tears were pouring from her eyes.

"What's the matter?"

She flung her arms around his neck and hugged him. He couldn't figure out what was wrong. He stroked her back and held her close.

"They found Amelie's cell phone in the pocket of your jeans." Her voice sounded muffled against his neck. Tobias was speechless. Anxious now, he pulled away. There must be some mistake. How could Amelie's cell end up in his jeans?

"Don't go," Nadia begged him. "Let's go somewhere, somewhere far away, until all this is cleared up."

Tobias stared mutely into space. With an effort he tried to get his feeling of confusion under control. He clenched and unclenched his fists. What the hell had happened during the hours when he had blacked out?

"They're going to arrest you," said Nadia again, though now sounding more controlled. She wiped the tears from her cheeks with the back of her hand. "You know they will. And then you won't have a chance."

She was right, he knew that. Events were repeating themselves in a downright eerie way. Eleven years ago it was Laura's necklace that was found in the milk room and used as circumstantial evidence to prove his guilt. He felt panic prickling at his spine, and he sank down onto a kitchen chair. No doubt he was the ideal perpetrator. Based on the fact that Amelie's cell phone was found in his pants pocket they would tie a noose and put it around his neck as soon as he turned himself in. Suddenly the old wound burst open again; like poisonous pus the self-doubt crept through his veins, his body, through every convolution of his brain. *Murderer, murderer, murderer!* They had said it to him for so long, until he became convinced he had really done it. He looked at Nadia.

"Okay," he said in a hoarse whisper. "I won't go there. But . . . what if I really did do it?"

"Not a word to the press or anyone else about the cell phone," Bodenstein ordered. All the officers taking part in the house search had gathered under the entrance gate. The rain was pouring down and the temperature had dropped twenty degrees in the past twenty-four hours. The first snowflakes were mixed in with the rain.

"But why?" Behnke protested. "The guy goes and disappears and we stand here like a bunch of idiots!"

"I don't want to start a witch hunt," Bodenstein countered. "The mood in the village has been stirred up enough. I'm ordering a total information blackout until I've spoken with Tobias Sartorius. Is that clear?"

The men and women nodded; only Behnke crossed his arms in exasperation and shook his head. The humiliation from earlier smoldered inside him like a burning fuse, and Bodenstein knew that. On top of everything else, Behnke had understood exactly what his assignment to secure evidence meant: this degrading treatment was a punishment. Bodenstein had made it clear to him in private how bitterly disappointed he was by Behnke's breach of trust. In the past twelve years Bodenstein had always generously ironed out any problems that Behnke had provoked because of his explosive temperament. But now, he had explicitly told him, it had to stop. This violation of regulations could not be excused by family problems. Bodenstein hoped that Behnke would follow his orders; otherwise it would no longer be possible to protect him from the threat of suspension.

Oliver turned away and swiftly followed Pia to the car.

"Put out an APB on Tobias Sartorius." He turned on the engine but didn't drive off. "Damn, I was so sure that we wouldn't find any trace of the girl at their farm."

"You believe he did it, don't you?" Pia grabbed her phone and called Ostermann. The wipers scraped across the windshield, and the heater fan was on full blast. Bodenstein bit his lip pensively. To be honest, he wasn't really paying attention. Every time he tried to concentrate on the case, the image of a naked Cosima rolling in the sheets with a strange man leaped into his mind. Had she met the guy yesterday too? When he got home late at night she was already in bed asleep. He had taken the opportunity to check her cell phone, and found that all her call lists and text messages had been deleted. This time he hadn't felt a single pang of conscience, even when he went through her coat and purse. He had almost given up his suspicions when he discovered in her wallet, stuck between the credit cards, two condoms.

"Oliver!" Pia's voice startled him out of his reverie. "Kai found a passage in Amelie's diary where she writes that her neighbor has started waiting for her, to drive her to the bus stop."

"Yeah, so?"

"The neighbor is Claudius Terlinden."

Oliver didn't know where Pia was going with this. He couldn't think. His mind just couldn't seem to process the information.

"We have to talk to him," said Pia with a hint of impatience in her voice. "We don't know enough yet about the girl's circle of friends and acquaintances to establish Tobias Sartorius as the only possible perpetrator."

"Yes, you're right." He shifted into reverse and lurched into the street.

"Watch out for the bus!" Pia screamed, but too late. Brakes squealed, metal crashed into metal, and the car was shaken by a violent impact. Oliver's head was slammed hard against the side window.

"Oh great." Pia undid her seatbelt and climbed out. Dazed, Oliver looked back over his shoulder and saw through the rain-glazed window the contours of a large vehicle. Something warm was running down his face; he touched his cheek and stared in confusion at the blood on his hand. Only then did he realize what had happened. The thought of getting out in the rain and talking with an angry bus driver in the middle of the street made him sick. Everything made him sick. The door opened.

"Man, you're bleeding!" Pia's voice sounded at first shocked, but all of a sudden she burst out in snorting laughter. Behind her on the rainy street a crowd had gathered. Almost every one of their colleagues involved in the house search obviously wanted to inspect the damage to the BMW and the bus.

"What's there to laugh about?" Oliver gave her an offended look.

"Please forgive me." The tension that had been building inside her over the past few hours had given way to an almost hysterical laughing fit. "But somehow I thought your blood would be blue, not red."

It was almost dark by the time Pia steered the rather dented but still drivable BMW through the gate of the Terlinden estate; this time it stood wide open. Fortunately Dr. Lauterbach just happened to be in her "branch office," although normally she held consultations in her office in the old Altenhain courthouse on Wednesday afternoons. But she'd only stopped by to pick up a medical file for a visit to a patient when the accident occurred outside. She had quickly and expertly dressed the cut on Bodenstein's head and advised him to lie down for the rest of the day, because there was the chance of a concussion. But he had staunchly refused. Pia, who had rapidly brought her outburst of levity under control, had an idea what was bothering her boss, although he hadn't mentioned Cosima or his suspicions.

They were headed along the curving driveway, illuminated by low lamps, which led through a park with magnificent old trees, boxwood hedges, and flowerbeds bare in winter. Beyond a curve the house appeared out of the misty twilight. It was a big old villa in half-timbered style with oriels, towers, pointed gables, and invitingly lit windows. They drove into the inner courtyard and pulled up right in front of the three steps at the front door. Under the porch roof supported by massive wooden pillars an array of Halloween pumpkins grinned at them. Pia rang the doorbell, and at once a multivoiced barking arose inside the house. Through the old-fashioned milky glass panes of the front door she could dimly make out a whole pack of dogs jumping at the door; the highest jumper was a long-legged Jack Russell terrier, yapping like a maniac. A cold wind drove the fine rain, which was gradually changing to sharp little snow crystals, under the porch roof. Pia rang the bell again, and the barking of the dogs rose to an ear-splitting crescendo.

"I hope somebody hurries up," she grumbled, putting up the collar of her jean jacket.

"Sooner or later someone will open the door." Oliver leaned on the wooden railing and didn't bat an eye. Pia gave him a sullen look. His stoic patience was making her blood boil. Finally footsteps approached, the dogs fell silent and vanished as if by magic. The front door was opened, and in the doorway appeared a girlish, delicate blonde dressed in a fur-edged vest over a turtleneck sweater, a knee-length checked skirt, and fashionable high-heeled boots. At first glance Pia took the woman to be in her mid-twenties. She had an ageless, smooth face and big blue baby-doll eyes, with which she scrutinized first Pia, then Oliver with polite reserve.

"Mrs. Terlinden?" Pia searched in the pocket of her down vest, then in her jean jacket underneath for her badge, while Bodenstein remained mute as a fish. The woman nodded. "My name is Pia Kirchhoff, and this is my colleague Oliver von Bodenstein. We're from K-11 in Hofheim. Is your husband at home?"

"No, I'm sorry." With a friendly smile Mrs. Terlinden offered her hand, which betrayed her real age. She must have passed fifty a few years ago, and her youthful attire suddenly seemed like a disguise. "Can I help you?"

She made no move to invite them inside. Through the open door Pia nonetheless caught a glimpse of the interior and saw a wide flight of stairs whose steps were covered with a Bordeaux-red carpet, an entry hall with a marble floor in a chessboard pattern, and dark framed oil paintings on high walls papered in saffron yellow.

"As you probably know, your neighbors' daughter has been missing since Saturday night," Pia began. "Yesterday the tracking dogs kept barking in the vicinity of your house, and we've asked ourselves why."

"I'm not surprised. Amelie visits us often." Mrs. Terlinden's voice sounded like a bird chirping. Her eyes shifted from Pia to Oliver and back again. "She's friends with our son Thies."

With a gesture that seemed unconscious she reached up to smooth her hair, perfectly coiffed in a pageboy style. Then she glanced, a bit irritated, over at Bodenstein, who remained quiet in the background. The white bandage on his forehead glowed brightly in the dim light.

"Friends? Is Amelie your son's girlfriend?"

"No, no, not at all. They just get along with each other," Mrs. Terlinden replied guardedly. "Amelie doesn't judge him or make him feel that he's . . . different."

Although Pia was steering the conversation, Mrs. Terlinden kept glancing over at Oliver, as if seeking his support. Pia knew this type of woman, this masterly rehearsed mixture of feminine helplessness and *coquetry* that awakened the protective instinct in almost every man. Few women were actually that weak; most of them had discovered over time this role was an effective method of manipulation.

"We would very much like to speak with your son," she said. "Perhaps he can tell us something about Amelie."

"I'm afraid that won't be possible." Christine Terlinden pulled up the fur collar of her vest, again stroking her immaculate blond coiffure. "Thies is not well. Yesterday he had an attack, and we had to call the doctor."

"What sort of attack?" Pia persisted. If Mrs. Terlinden was hoping that the police would be satisfied with vague hints, she now saw she was mistaken. Kirchhoff's question seemed to annoy her.

"Well, Thies is very sensitive. Even small changes in his surroundings can sometimes throw him into a tailspin."

It sounded like a response she had committed to memory. The lack of any empathy in her words was remarkable. Obviously Mrs. Terlinden had little interest in what had happened to the neighbor girl. She hadn't even asked about her out of politeness. That was odd. Pia remembered the conjectures of the women in the grocery store who considered it entirely possible that Thies might have done something to the girl when he was prowling through the streets at night.

"What does your son do all day?" Pia asked. "Does he have a job?"

"No. Strangers expect too much of him," said Christine Terlinden. "He takes care of our garden and those of a few neighbors. He's a very good gardener."

Involuntarily Pia thought of an old mystery novel cliché: The murderer is always the gardener. Was it that simple? Did the Terlindens know more? Were they hiding their handicapped son in order to protect him?

The rain had finally turned to snow. A fine white layer had formed on the asphalt of the street, and Pia took great pains to bring the heavy BMW with its summer-tread tires to a gentle stop at the main entrance to the grounds of the Terlinden company.

"You should have your tires changed," she told her boss. "Winter tires from O to E."

"What?" Oliver frowned in annoyance. He was lost in thought, but clearly it had nothing to do with their work. His cell buzzed.

"Hello, Dr. Engel," he answered after glancing at the display.

"October to Easter," Pia murmured. She rolled down the window and showed the gate guard her ID. "Mr. Terlinden is expecting us."

That wasn't exactly true, but the man merely nodded, hurried back into his warm hut, and raised the barrier. Pia accelerated slowly so as not to skid and steered the car across empty parking spaces near the glass façade of the main building. Right in front stood a black Mercedes S-Class. Pia stopped behind it and climbed out. Why couldn't Oliver cut short his conversation with Engel? Her feet were blocks of ice because the short drive through Altenhain was barely enough to get the car heater going. The snow was coming down faster. How was she going to drive the BMW all the way back to Hofheim in the snow later on without ending up in a ditch? Her gaze fell on an ugly dent on the left rear fender of the black Mercedes, and she took a closer look. The damage couldn't be very old or rust would have formed.

She heard a car door slam behind her and turned around. Bodenstein held the front door open for her, and they entered the lobby. Behind a counter of polished walnut sat a young man; on the white wall behind him was only the name TERLINDEN in gold letters. Simple yet imposing. Pia told him their business, and after a brief phone call he accompanied them to an elevator in the rear of the lobby. They rode in silence to the fifth floor, where a stylish middle-aged woman awaited them. She was apparently on her way out the door since she was wearing a coat and scarf, with her bag over her shoulder, but she dutifully escorted them to her boss's office.

After everything Pia had heard about Claudius Terlinden, she'd expected a jovial patriarch and was at first a bit disappointed when she saw the rather average-looking man in suit and tie sitting behind a completely overloaded desk. He got up when they entered, buttoned his jacket, and came forward to greet them.

"Good afternoon, Mr. Terlinden." Bodenstein had woken up from his daze. "Please excuse us for bothering you so late in the day, but we've been trying to reach you for hours."

"Good afternoon," said Claudius Terlinden with a smile. "My secretary gave me your message. I was planning to call you early tomorrow morning."

He was somewhere in his mid- to late fifties, and his thick dark hair was graying at the temples. Seen close up he looked anything but average, Pia ascertained. Claudius Terlinden was not a handsome man: his nose was too big, his chin too angular, his lips a bit too full for a man, and yet he radiated a presence that fascinated her.

"Good Lord, your hands are freezing!" he said with concern when he offered his warm dry hand, and put his other hand on hers briefly. Pia gave a start; it felt like he'd given her an electric shock. A fleeting expression of astonishment flitted across Terlinden's face.

"Shall I get you some coffee or hot chocolate so you can thaw out a bit?"

"No, no, we're fine," said Pia, disconcerted by the intensity of his gaze, which had made her blush. They looked at each other a bit longer than necessary. What had just happened here? Was it a simple case of static electricity explainable by physics or something altogether different?

Before she or Bodenstein could ask their first question, Terlinden asked about Amelie.

"I'm extremely worried," he said gravely. "Amelie is the daughter of my legal advisor. I know her well."

Pia dimly recalled that her plan had been to go after him hard and insinuate that he was hot for the girl. But this plan had suddenly been quashed.

"Unfortunately we have no new information," said Bodenstein. Then he got straight to the point. "We've been told that you visited Tobias Sartorius several times in prison. What was your reason for doing so? And why did you pay off his parents' debts?"

Pia shoved her hands in her vest pockets and tried to remember what she'd been intending to ask Terlinden so urgently. But her mind was suddenly as blank as a freshly formatted computer hard drive.

"Everyone in the village treated Hartmut and Rita like lepers after that terrible tragedy," Claudius Terlinden replied. "I don't believe in blaming a whole family for the crimes of one member. Whatever their son may have done, there was nothing they could have done to prevent it."

"But Tobias suspected you of having had something to do with the disappearance of both girls. That claim must have caused you a lot of trouble."

Terlinden nodded. He stuck his hands in his pants pockets and tilted his head. It didn't seem to adversely affect his self-confidence that Bodenstein was a head taller than he was, forcing him to look up at the detective.

"I didn't hold that against Tobias. He was under tremendous pressure and simply wanted to defend himself by all available means. And it was true, as a matter of fact, that Laura had twice gotten me into extremely compromising situations. As the daughter of our housekeeper she was in the house often, and she imagined that she was in love with me."

"What kind of situations?" Bodenstein asked.

"One time she climbed into my bed while I was in the bath," replied Terlinden in an unemotional voice. "The second time she undressed in front of me in the living room. My wife was away, and Laura knew it. She told me straight out that she wanted to sleep with me."

For some incomprehensible reason his words annoyed Pia. She avoided looking at him and instead looked at the furnishings in his office. The huge desk of massive wood with imposing carvings on the sides rested on four gigantic lion's paws. Presumably it was very old and valuable, but Pia had seldom seen anything so ugly. Next to the desk stood an antique globe, and on the walls hung dark expressionistic paintings in simple dark frames, similar to those she had spied over Mrs. Terlinden's shoulder in their home.

"So what happened?" Bodenstein inquired.

"When I declined, she broke into tears and ran off. Just at that moment my son came in."

Pia cleared her throat. She had herself under control again.

"You often gave Amelie Fröhlich a ride in your car," she said. "She mentions it in her diary. She had the impression that you were deliberately waiting for her."

"I didn't wait for her," Claudius Terlinden said with a smile, "but I did give her a ride a few times if I happened to see her on the road to the bus stop or walking up the hill from the village."

His voice was calm and composed and gave no indication that he had a guilty conscience.

"You arranged the waitress job for her at the Black Horse. Why?"

"Amelie wanted to earn some money, and the proprietor of the Black Horse was looking for a waitress." He shrugged. "I know everybody here in the village, and if I can help I do it gladly."

Pia scrutinized the man. His searching gaze met hers, and she stood firm. She asked questions and he answered. At the same time something completely different was going on between them, but what was it? What was this strange magnestism that this man exerted over her? Was it his brown eyes? His pleasant, sonorous voice? The aura of calm self-confidence that surrounded him? No wonder he had impressed a young girl like Amelie, if he was able to cast his spell on a grown woman.

"When was the last time you saw Amelie?" Bodenstein asked.

"I don't know exactly."

"Then do you know where you were on Saturday night? We are particularly interested in the hours between ten p.m. and two a.m."

Claudius Terlinden took his hands out of his pockets and crossed his arms. Across the back of his left hand was a nasty scratch that looked fresh.

"That evening I went to dinner with my wife in Frankfurt," he said, after thinking a moment. "Because Christine had a bad headache, I dropped her off at the house first, then I drove over here and put her jewelry in the safe."

"When did you get back from Frankfurt?"

"About ten thirty."

"So you drove past the Black Horse twice," Pia noted.

"Yes." Terlinden looked at her with the concentration of a contestant on a quiz show when the host asks the decisive final question; he had answered Bodenstein's questions almost nonchalantly. This attention was starting to irritate Pia, and now Oliver also seemed aware of it.

"And you didn't notice anything unusual?" he asked. "Did you see anyone on the street? Someone out for a late-night walk, perhaps?"

"No, I didn't notice anything," Claudius Terlinden answered. "But I drive by there several times a day and don't pay much attention to my surroundings."

"Where did you get the scratch on your hand?" asked Pia.

Terlinden's face darkened. He was no longer smiling. "I had an argument with my son."

Thies—of course! Pia had almost forgotten what had led her here in the first place. Even Oliver seemed not to have thought about it again, but he smoothly adapted to the change in topic.

"Right," he said. "Your wife just told us that your son Thies suffered some sort of attack last night."

Claudius Terlinden hesitated briefly, then nodded.

"What sort of attack was it? Is he an epileptic?"

"No. Thies is autistic. He lives in his own world and feels threatened by any change in his normal surroundings. He reacts with autoaggressive behavior." Terlinden sighed. "I'm afraid that Amelie's disappearance was the catalyst for his attack."

"In the village there's a rumor that Thies might have had something to do with her disappearance," said Pia.

"That's nonsense," Terlinden contradicted her without any rancor. He sounded almost indifferent, as though this sort of talk was all too familiar to him. "Thies likes the girl a lot. But some people in the village think he belongs in an institution. Naturally they won't say that to my face, but I know it."

"We'd really like to talk to him."

"At the moment I'm afraid that's not possible." Terlinden shook his head regretfully. "We had to take him to the psychiatric ward."

"What will happen to him there?" Pia instantly conjured up ghastly images in her head of people in chains being maltreated with electroshock.

"They'll try to calm him down."

"How long will it take before we can talk to him?"

Claudius Terlinden shrugged. "I don't know. He hasn't had such a violent attack in years. I'm afraid that this event may have really set him back in his development. That would be a disaster. For us and for him."

He promised to inform Kirchhoff and Bodenstein as soon as the doctors gave the green light so they could have a talk with Thies. As Terlinden accompanied them to the elevator and held out his hand in parting, he smiled again.

"Very pleased to meet you," he said. This time his touch didn't give Pia an electric shock, yet she felt strangely dazed as the elevator door finally closed behind them. On the ride down she tried to overcome her confusion.

"Well, he really seemed to go for you," Oliver noted. "And you for him too." There was gentle mockery in his voice.

"Very funny," Pia retorted, zipping up her jacket to her chin. "I was just trying to scope him out."

"And? What was the outcome?"

"I think he was sincere."

"Really? I think just the opposite."

"Why? He answered all our questions without hesitating, even the unpleasant ones. For example, he didn't have to tell us that Laura had twice put him in an embarrassing position."

"That's exactly what I think is his trick," Oliver countered. "Isn't it a peculiar coincidence that Terlinden's son was removed from the line of fire at the very moment the girl disappeared?"

The elevator stopped at the ground floor and the doors opened.

"We haven't made any progress at all," said Pia, feeling suddenly discouraged. "Nobody wants to admit they saw Amelie."

"Or maybe it's just that no one wants to tell us," said Oliver. They crossed the lobby, nodded to the young man behind the reception counter, and stepped outside into the icy blast. Pia pressed the remote on her car key and the doors of the BMW unlocked.

"We have to talk to Mrs. Terlinden one more time." Oliver stopped by the passenger door and looked at Pia over the roof.

"So you suspect Thies and his father."

"Possibly. Maybe Thies did something to the girl and his father wants to cover it up, so he puts his son in the psych ward."

They got in, and Pia started the engine and drove out from under the protective roof. Snow covered the windshield at once, and thanks to fine sensors the wipers started moving.

"I want to know which doctor treated Thies," Bodenstein said pensively. "And whether the Terlindens really did go out to eat in Frankfurt on Saturday night."

Pia just nodded. The encounter with Claudius Terlinden had left her with an ambiguous feeling. Normally she didn't let herself be blinded so quickly by anyone, but the man had made a deep impression on her, and she wanted to figure out why.

Only the guard station was still manned when Pia entered police headquarters at nine thirty. By the time they'd reached Kelkheim the snow had turned to rain again, and despite his head wound Bodenstein had insisted on driving home by himself. Pia would have also preferred to call it a day. Christoph was no doubt already waiting for her, but she couldn't get the meeting with Claudius Terlinden out of her mind. Besides, Christoph understood that she had to work late occasionally.

She walked through the empty corridors and stairwells to her office, switched on the light, and sat down at her desk. Christine Terlinden had given them the name of the doctor who'd been treating Thies for years. It was no surprise that it was Dr. Daniela Lauterbach; she was a longtime neighbor of the Terlindens and could be on the spot quickly in a crisis situation.

Pia typed in her password. Ever since she left Claudius Terlinden's office she'd been going over and over the conversation in her mind, trying to recall every word, every sentence, all the subtle signals. Why was Oliver so convinced that Terlinden was mixed up in Amelie's disappearance, while she wasn't at all? Had the attraction that he'd exerted on her clouded her objectivity?

She entered Terlinden's name in a search engine and got thousands of hits. In the next half hour she learned a good deal about his company and his family, as well as about Claudius Terlinden's manifold social and philanthropic commitments. He was actively involved with dozens of foundations and supervisory boards and various associations and organizations. He had also funded scholarships for gifted young people from disadvantaged families. Terlinden did a lot for young people. Why? Officially he stated that as a person who had been particularly favored by fate he wanted to give something back to society. Definitely a noble sentiment, and one could find fault with that. But could there be something else behind it?

He claimed he had rejected Laura Wagner twice, when she had made explicit advances. Was that true? Pia clicked on the photos the search engine had found of him and studied the man who had aroused such strong feelings in her. Did his wife know that her husband was into young girls, and that's why he dressed so youthfully? Had he done something to Amelie because she resisted his advances? Pia chewed on her lower lip. She simply didn't want to believe it. Finally she logged off the Internet and entered his name in POLAS, the police computer search system. Nothing. He had no criminal record, had never been in trouble with the law. Suddenly her eyes fell on a link inserted at the lower right corner. She straightened up. On Sunday, November 16, 2008, at 1:15 A.M. someone had reported Claudius Terlinden to the police. Pia pulled up the file on her screen. Her heart began to pound as she read it.

"Well, what do you know," she murmured.

Wednesday, November 19, 2008

The alarm clock rang as it did every morning at exactly six-thirty, but for the past few days he hadn't really needed to set the alarm. Gregor Lauterbach had been awake for a long time. The fear of Daniela's questions had made it impossible for him to go back to sleep. Lauterbach sat up and swung his legs over the edge of the bed. He was soaked with sweat and felt like he'd spent the night on a torture rack. He dreaded facing the countless appointments scheduled for the day. How was he supposed to concentrate while in the back of his mind this threat kept ticking like an insidious time bomb? Yesterday another anonymous letter had arrived in the office mail, the contents even more distressing than the first one:

I wonder if your fingerprints could possibly still be identified on the tire iron that you tossed in the cesspool? The police will find out the truth and then you're in for it!

Who knew these details? Who was writing him these letters? And why now, after eleven years? Gregor Lauterbach got up and dragged himself into the bathroom. Bracing his hands on the washbasin, he stared at his unshaven, bleary-eyed face in the mirror. Should he call in sick? Make himself scarce until the storm gathering on the horizon blew over? No, impossible. He had to keep living as he always did. Under no circumstances could he let his resolve waver. His career ambitions didn't need to end with the position of cultural minister; politically he could still achieve a lot more if he didn't let himself be intimidated by shadows from the past. He couldn't permit a single mistake, which in any case happened eleven years ago, to destroy his life. Lauterbach straightened his shoulders and gave his mirror image a determined look. Because of his job, means and opportunities that he'd never dared dream of were now at his disposal. And he was going to use them.

It was still dark when Pia rang the bell at the closed gate of the Terlinden estate. Despite the early hour it didn't take long before the voice of Mrs. Terlinden spoke from the intercom. In a moment the gate opened as if by magic. Pia got back into the passenger seat of the plainclothes police car; Oliver was at the wheel. Followed by a patrol car and a tow truck they drove over the still virgin snow covering the winding drive. Christine Terlinden awaited them with a friendly smile at the front door, which under the circumstances was as misplaced as the polite greeting that Pia offered. At least for Mr. Terlinden it was not going to be a good morning.

"We'd like to speak with your husband."

"I've already told him you were coming. He'll be down shortly. Please come in."

Pia merely nodded, while Oliver said nothing. She had phoned him yesterday and then spent another half hour talking with the acting district attorney, who refused to give her an arrest warrant, but approved a search warrant for Terlinden's car and filed an application with the court. Now they stood in the imposing entry hall and waited. The lady of the house had vanished, and somewhere in a distant wing the dogs were barking.

"Good morning!"

Bodenstein and Kirchhoff looked up as Claudius Terlinden came down the stairs from the upper floor, impeccably dressed in suit and tie. This time the sight of him left Pia cold.

"You're certainly the early birds." He stood smiling before them without offering his hand.

"Where did the dent in the fender of your Mercedes come from?" asked Pia without any preamble.

"Excuse me?" Astonished, he raised his eyebrows. "I don't know what you mean."

"Then I'll have to refresh your memory." Pia didn't take her eyes off him. "On Sunday a resident of Feldstrasse reported a hit and run, because someone had bashed into his car the night before. He had parked it in front of his house at ten minutes to midnight and happened to be standing on his balcony at 12:33 a.m. smoking a cigarette when he heard a crash. He could see the car belonging to the person who caused the crash and even the license plate: MTK-T 801."

Terlinden didn't say a word. His smile had vanished. Crimson was climbing up his throat and spreading over his face.

"The next morning the man got a phone call." Pia explained that she had met the man, and then continued mercilessly. "A call from you. You offered to settle the whole matter with no bureaucracy, and consequently the man withdrew his complaint. Unfortunately, it was not deleted from the police computer."

Claudius Terlinden stared at Pia with a stony expression.

"What do you want from me?" he asked, making an effort to control himself.

"You lied to us yesterday," she replied with a charming smile. "Since I probably don't need to tell you where Feldstrasse is, I will ask you once again: Did you drive past the Black Horse on your way back from your firm, or did you take the short cut across the field and along Feldstrasse?"

"What's the meaning of all this?" Terlinden turned to Bodenstein, but he was silent. "What are you trying to imply?"

"That was the night Amelie Fröhlich disappeared," Kirchhoff answered for Bodenstein. "She was last seen at the Black Horse about the time you drove by there on the way to your office, about ten thirty. Two hours later, around twelve thirty, you came back to Altenhain, and from a different direction—not the way you claimed."

He stuck out his lower lip, squinting at her. "And from this you deduce that I waylaid the daughter of an employee, dragged her into my car, and murdered her?"

"Was that a confession?" Pia asked coolly.

To her annoyance Terlinden gave her an almost amused smile.

"By no means."

"Then tell us what you did between ten thirty and twelve thirty. Or was it perhaps not ten thirty, but a quarter past ten?"

"It was ten thirty. I was in my office."

"It took you two hours to put your wife's jewelry in the safe?" Pia shook her head. "Do you think we're stupid or what?"

The situation had shifted by a hundred and eighty degrees. Claudius Terlinden was in a jam, and he knew it. But he still kept his cool.

"Who did you have dinner with?" Pia asked. "And where?"

Silence. Then Pia remembered the cameras she had seen at the gate of the Terlinden company property, when she drove past on her way back from the Wagners.

"We could take a look at the footage from the surveillance cameras at the gate to your firm," she suggested. "That way you could prove to us that you're telling the truth about the timeline."

"You're very clever," said Terlinden appreciatively. "I like that. Unfortunately the surveillance system has been down for four weeks now."

"And the cameras at the entrance gate to your property?"

"They don't record."

"Well, then it looks pretty bad for you." Pia shook her head in feigned regret. "You have no alibi for the time when Amelie disappeared. Your hands are scratched as if you'd been fighting with someone."

"Aha." Claudius Terlinden remained calm, raising his eyebrows. "So what now? Are you going to arrest me because I took another way home?"

Pia kept her eyes steadfastly fixed on him. He was a liar, possibly also a criminal, who knew perfectly well that her assumptions were much too vague to justify an arrest.

"You're not under arrest, only temporarily detained." She managed a smile. "And not because you took another way home, but because you lied to us. As soon as you give us a plausible, verifiable alibi for the time period in question, you may go."

"Good." Claudius Terlinden shrugged his shoulders nonchalantly. "But please no handcuffs. I'm allergic to nickel."

"I assume you won't try to escape," Pia retorted dryly. "Anyway, our handcuffs are stainless steel."

The phone on his desk rang just as he was leaving the office. Lars Terlinden was expecting an urgent callback from the derivatives broker at the Credit Suisse. With the broker's help he had sold off a large part of the credit portfolio for this con man Mutzler before he appeared before a tribunal of the board of directors. He put down his briefcase and took the call.

"Lars, it's me," said his mother. He wished he could hang up.

"Please, Mother, leave me alone. I don't have time right now."

"The police arrested your father this morning."

Lars felt himself turn cold, then hot.

"Better late than never," he replied bitterly. "After all, he isn't God—he can't do whatever he likes in Altenhain just because he has more money than everybody else. Actually, he's been getting away with his little charade for far too long."

He went behind his desk and sat down in his armchair.

"How can you say that, Lars? Your father always wanted what was best for you."

"Wrong," said Lars coolly. "He only wanted what was best for him and for his firm. And back then he exploited the situation, the way he basically exploits every situation to his own advantage. He forced me into a job that I never wanted to do. Mother, believe me, I don't give a shit what's happening to him."

Suddenly everything was closing in again. Why did his father have to meddle in his life? Especially now, when he needed all his energy and concentration to save his career and his future. Anger was boiling over inside him. Why couldn't they just leave him alone? Images he had thought long forgotten were coming to his mind, unasked and unwanted, but he was powerless to stop the memories and the feelings that accompanied them. He knew that his father had been regularly fucking Laura's mother, who used to work in the villa as housekeeper. They would retreat to one of the attic guest rooms when his mother wasn't home. But that wasn't enough for him. He also had to get the daughters of his serfs, as his employees and the whole town used to call them, into bed—*ius primae noctis,* the same as a feudal lord in the Middle Ages.

While his mother was going on about something in a self-pitying voice, Lars thought about that evening. He had come home from training sessions at the firm and in the hall almost ran into Laura. Her face swollen from crying, she had stormed past him and out the door. He hadn't understood a thing back then, as he saw his father come out of the living room, stuffing his shirt back in his pants, his face flushed and his hair a mess. That swine!

At the time Laura had just turned fourteen. Only many years later did Lars accuse his father of sleeping with her, but he had denied everything. He said the girl had been in love with him, but he had rebuffed her overtures. And Lars had believed him. What seventeen-year-old wanted to think such things about his father? In retrospect he realized that he had doubted his father's protestations of innocence. He had lied to him far too many times.

"Lars?" his mother asked. "Are you still there?"

"I should have told the police the truth eleven years ago," he replied, making an effort to control his voice. "But my own father forced me to lie so that his name wouldn't be dragged through the mud. What happened now? Did he snatch the missing girl this time too?"

"How can you say such an outrageous thing?" His mother sounded shocked. Christine Terlinden was a master of self-deception. Whatever she didn't want to hear or see she simply ignored.

"My God, will you for once open your eyes, Mother!" Lars snapped. "I could say a lot more, but I won't. Because for me that chapter is closed, understand? It's over. Now I have to go. Please don't call me anymore."

The restaurant where Claudius Terlinden had spent that Saturday evening with his wife and friends was on Guiollettstrasse, across from the twin glass towers of the Deutsche Bank. That's what his wife had told Pia last night.

"Let me get out here, while you go find a parking spot," Oliver decided after Pia had driven around the block three times. Parking near the posh Ebony Club was impossible, and valets in English livery waited by the entrance to take the guests' cars and park them in the underground garage. Pia let Oliver out and he ran with head down through the pouring rain to the entrance. Nobody stopped him when he walked right past the PLEASE WAIT TO BE SEATED sign. The maître d' and half the staff were making a big fuss over some VIP with an entourage who didn't have a reservation. The restaurant was popular at midday, and apparently the financial crisis hadn't spoiled the appetite of the managers from the surrounding banks from enjoying an extravagant lunch. Bodenstein looked around inquisitively. He had heard a lot about the Ebony Club; the restaurant decorated in Indian colonial style was one of the most expensive and most talked about in the city.

His gaze fell on a couple at a table for two on the riser a bit farther back. He caught his breath. Cosima. As if entranced she was listening to a revoltingly good-looking man who seemed to be explaining something with expansive, spirited gestures. The way Cosima was sitting, leaning slightly forward, her elbows on the table and her chin resting on her clasped hands, set off alarm bells in his head. She brushed a lock of hair out of her face, laughing at something the guy had said, and then, to make matters worse, put her hand on his. Bodenstein stood petrified in the midst of the melee while the service staff ran busily past him; he may as well have been invisible.

That morning Cosima had told him in passing that she would be busy all day at the editing room in Mainz. Had she changed her plans on short notice, or had she knowingly lied to him again? How could she possibly guess that his investigation would bring him at this precise time to this precise restaurant out of the thousands in Frankfurt?

"May I help you?" A plump young woman had stopped in front of him and given him a rather impatient smile. His heart started pounding again with the force of a blacksmith's hammer. He was shaking all over, and he felt like he was going to throw up.

"No," he said without taking his eyes off Cosima and her companion. The waitress gave him an odd look, but he couldn't have cared less what she thought of him. Not twenty yards away his wife was sitting with the man whose company she looked forward to with three exclamation points. Bodenstein concentrated hard on breathing in and out. He wished he could simply go up to their table and punch the man in the face with no warning. But because he had been brought up with polite manners and self-control, he remained standing there and did nothing. The skilled observer in him automatically registered the obvious intimacy between the two, who were now putting their heads together and exchanging deep looks. Bodenstein saw out of the corner of his eye that the young waitress was informing the maître d', who in the meantime had found an acceptable table for his VIP. So he either had to go over to Cosima and her companion or leave at once. Since he didn't feel up to guilelessly pretending he was pleased to see them, he decided on the latter option. He turned on his heel and left the overcrowded restaurant. When he walked out the door he stared for a moment at the fence surrounding the construction site across the street before he turned down Guiollettstrasse in a daze. His pulse was racing, and his stomach was churning. The sight of Cosima and that guy had burned its way indelibly into his retinas. The very thing he had feared so much had happened: He was certain that Cosima was cheating on him.

Suddenly someone stepped into his path. He tried to move aside, but the woman with the umbrella took a step in the same direction, so he had to stop.

"Are you finished already?" The voice of Pia Kirchhoff penetrated the fog that surrounded him like a wall and dragged him abruptly back to reality. "Was Terlinden there on Saturday?"

Terlinden! He had completely forgotten.

"I . . . I didn't even ask," he admitted.

"Is everything all right?" Pia looked at him curiously. "You look like you've seen a ghost."

"Cosima is inside," he said tonelessly. "With another man. Even though she told me this morning . . ."

He couldn't go on, his throat seemed dry as sand. On unsteady legs he staggered to the next building and sat down on the step of the entrance, ignoring how wet it was. Pia looked at him, speechless and, it seemed to him, with sympathy. He lowered his eyes.

"Give me a cigarette," he demanded in a hoarse voice. Pia dug in her jacket pocket and handed him a pack and a lighter. He hadn't smoked in fifteen years and didn't miss it, but right now he had to admit that the craving for nicotine still slumbered deep inside him.

"The car is parked on Kettenhofweg, corner of Brentanostrasse." Pia held out the car key to him. "Go sit inside before you catch your death of cold."

He didn't take the key or give her an answer. He didn't give a damn whether he got wet or what the passersby thought as they stared at him idiotically. Nothing mattered. Although he had secretly long suspected it, he had desperately hoped for some harmless explanation for Cosima's lies and text messages. But he was not calm enough to confront her in the company of another man. He took a greedy drag on the cigarette, inhaling the smoke as deep as he could. It made him dizzy, as if he were smoking a joint and not a Marlboro. Gradually the kaleidoscope of thoughts tumbling through his mind slowed their furious pace and stopped. All that was left was a vast, empty silence. He was sitting on a step in the middle of Frankfurt, feeling profoundly alone.

Lars Terlinden had slammed down the receiver and sat for a couple of minutes without moving. Upstairs the board was waiting for him. The gentlemen had traveled from Zürich specifically to hear how he intended to recoup the 350 million euros he had blown. Unfortunately he had no solution to offer. They would hear him out and then tear him to pieces with a patronizing smile, those arrogant assholes; a year ago they had been slapping him on the back like the best of pals because of this same gigantic deal.

The phone rang again, this time the in-house line. Lars ignored it. He opened the top drawer and took out a sheet of letterhead and his Montblanc fountain pen, a gift from his boss in better days. He used it only for signing contracts. For a full minute he stared at the blank, cream-colored page, then he started to write. Without reading over what he had written, he folded the paper and stuck it in an envelope. He wrote an address on the envelope, stood up, grabbed his briefcase and coat, and left the office.

"This has to go out today," he told his secretary and dropped the envelope on her desk.

"Of course," she replied sharply. She had once been the executive assistant to the board, and she still felt it was beneath her dignity to be secretary to a division VP. "You do remember that you have an appointment, yes?"

"Of course." He left without looking at her again.

"You're already seven minutes late!"

He went outside to the hall. Twenty-four steps to the elevator, which seemed to be waiting impatiently for him with doors open. Upstairs on the twelfth floor the entire board had been sitting for seven minutes. His future was at stake, his reputation, yes, his entire life. Two female colleagues from the back office slipped into the elevator after him. He knew them by sight and nodded absently. They giggled and whispered, returning his nod of greeting. The doors closed silently. He was shocked when he saw the man in the mirror with the haggard face who returned his gaze with dull, dejected eyes. He was tired, infinitely tired and burned out.

"Where to?" asked the brunette with the big eyes politely. "Up or down?"

Her finger with the long fake nail paused expectantly over the button panel. Lars Terlinden couldn't tear his eyes away from the sight of his face in the mirror.

"Down," he replied. "All the way down."

• • •

Pia Kirchhoff walked into the Ebony Club, nodding in thanks to the door-man who had opened the door for her with a flourish. Only a short time ago she and Christoph had dined here with Henning and Miriam. Henning had shelled out five hundred euros for the meal, utterly excessive in her eyes. Pia didn't much care for trendy spots, cryptic menus, and wine lists in which the price for a single bottle could run into the four-figure bracket. Since she judged wines not by their labels but by her own personal taste, a bardolino or chianti at the pizzeria around the corner sufficed for a success-ful evening.

The maître d' slithered down from his high perch and steered toward her with a radiant smile. Without a word Pia held up her badge in front of his nose. His smile cooled at once by several degrees. A potential prospect for the maha-raja menu had suddenly transformed before his eyes into a toad that nobody would want to swallow. The criminal police were never welcomed anywhere, especially not in a posh restaurant in the midst of the noontime rush.

"May I inquire as to what this concerns?" murmured the maître d'.

"No, you may not," said Kirchhoff dryly. "Where's the manager?"

The smile vanished completely and with it the feigned courtesy.

"Wait here." The man left, and Pia looked around unobtrusively. There she was. There sat Cosima von Bodenstein having an intimate conversation with a man who was clearly ten years younger. He was wearing a rumpled busi-ness suit, and his shirt was open with no tie. His casual posture radiated self-importance. His tousled, dark blond hair reached to his shoulders. He had an angular face with an aggressively jutting chin, five-day beard, and a prom-inent aquiline nose. His skin was tanned from being outdoors—or the result of alcohol, Pia thought maliciously. Cosima von Bodenstein was animatedly going on about something, and he was looking at her with a smile, obviously fascinated. This was no business lunch, and no accidental meeting of old acquaintances—the erotic vibrations between the two were evident even to an impartial observer. They'd either come directly from bed or were pausing on the way there for a little lunch to pump up the anticipation. Pia felt genu-inely sorry for her boss, yet she also felt a certain sympathy for Cosima, who must be longing for an adventure after twenty-five years of marital routine.

The appearance of the restaurant's manager tore Pia away from her ruminations. He was in his mid-thirties, at most, but his sparse sandy hair and puffy face made him look older.

"I won't take up much of your time, Mr. . . ." Pia began, inspecting the huge man, who was so impolite that he hadn't offered her his hand or deigned to introduce himself.

"Jagielski," the man announced, peering down at her and dismissing his maître d' with an arrogant gesture. "What is it? We're in the middle of the noon rush."

Jagielski. The name triggered some vague association in Pia's mind.

"I see. Do you do the cooking?" she countered sarcastically.

"No." He was clearly annoyed, and his restless eyes kept flitting over the dining room. Suddenly he turned around, stopped a young waitress, and hissed a remark that made her blush.

"It's almost impossible to find properly trained help," he then explained to Pia without a hint of a smile. "These young things are a disaster. They just don't have the right attitude."

New customers arrived, and they were standing in the way. In that instant she recalled where she had heard the name Jagielski before. That was the name of the owner of the Black Horse in Altenhain. Her inquiry confirmed that it was no coincidence. Andreas Jagielski owned the Black Horse as well as the Ebony Club and another place in Frankfurt.

"So, what's the deal?" he asked. Politeness was not his strong suit. Neither was discretion. They were still standing in the middle of the foyer.

"I would like to know if a Mr. Claudius Terlinden had dinner here last Saturday evening with his wife."

He raised one eyebrow. "Why do the police want to know?"

"Because it's of interest to the police." His condescending arrogance was really getting on Pia's nerves. "Well?"

A tiny hesitation, then a curt nod. "Yes, he was here."

"Just with his wife?"

"I don't recall."

"Perhaps your maître d' would remember. You must keep a book of reservations."

Reluctantly Jagielski waved over the maître d' he had chased off earlier and told him to bring the reservation book. He held his hand out and waited silently while the maître d' again climbed onto his high perch and then scurried back. The manager licked his index finger and paged slowly through the leather-bound register.

"Ah, here it is," he said at last. "It was a party of four. Now I remember."

"Who was with them? Names?" Pia insisted. Several customers were trying to get their coats and leave. At last Jagielski led Kirchhoff in the direction of the bar.

"I don't see what business that is of yours," he said, lowering his voice.

"Listen here." Pia was impatient now. "I'm investigating the case of your missing waitress Amelie, who was last seen at the Black Horse on Saturday night. We're looking for witnesses who may have seen the girl after that."

Jagielski stared at her, thought it over for a moment, and probably decided that revealing the names would be harmless.

"Mr. and Mrs. Lauterbach were with them," he finally told her.

Pia was astonished. Why had Claudius Terlinden withheld the fact that he and his wife went out to eat with their neighbors? At his office yesterday he had expressly mentioned only his wife and himself. Odd.

Cosima von Bodenstein's companion was just paying the bill. The waitress beamed at him; apparently the tip was generous. He got up and went around the table to pull out Cosima's chair for her. Although he was the complete opposite of Bodenstein in appearance, at least he had similar good manners.

"Do you know the man with the red-haired lady over there?" Pia asked Jagielski all of a sudden. He didn't even have to raise his head to know who Pia was referring to. She turned around so that Cosima wouldn't recognize her as she went out.

"Yes, of course." His voice suddenly took on an almost incredulous tone, as if he couldn't believe that anyone wouldn't recognize the man. "That's Alexander Gavrilow. Does he have something to do with your investigation?"

"It's possible," Pia replied with a smile. "Thanks for your help."

•   •   •

Oliver was still sitting on the step smoking. At his feet lay four cigarette butts. For a moment Pia stood silently in front of her boss so she could take in this unusual sight.

"And?" He looked up. His face was pale.

"Imagine this: The Terlindens went out to eat with the Lauterbachs," Pia reported. "And the manager of the Ebony Club is also the owner of the Black Horse in Altenhain. Isn't that a coincidence?"

"I don't think so."

"What else do you want to know?" Pia was playing dumb.

"Did you . . . see them?"

"Yes, I did." She bent down to pick up the cigarette pack he had laid on the step beside him and put it in her pocket. "Come on. I don't feel like freezing my ass off."

Oliver got up stiffly, took one last drag on the cigarette, and flicked the butt into the wet street. As they walked Pia took a quick look at him in profile. Was he still hoping for an innocent explanation for this tête-à-tête between his wife and the attractive stranger?

"Alexander Gavrilow," she said, and stopped. "The polar explorer and mountain climber."

"Excuse me?" Oliver gave her a baffled look.

"That's the man Cosima was with," she explained, and then finished the sentence in her mind: . . . *and who is definitely fucking her.*

Oliver rubbed his hand over his face. "Of course." He was speaking more to himself than to Pia. "I thought that guy looked familiar. Cosima introduced him to me once, I think, at her last film premiere. They planned a film project together years ago, but nothing came of it."

"Maybe it was just a business lunch," Pia tried to reassure him in spite of her own opinions. "Maybe they were discussing a project you're not supposed to know about, and you're worrying about it for nothing."

Oliver looked at Pia, and for an instant a mocking glint flashed in his eyes but then vanished immediately.

"I have eyes," he said. "And I know what I saw. My wife is sleeping with that guy, and who knows how long it's been going on. Maybe it's good that I don't have to kid myself any longer."

He resolutely started walking, and Pia almost had to run to keep up
with him.

·   ·   ·

*Thies knows everything, and the police are getting curious. You ought
to make sure that you get hold of that item. Because you have everything to lose!*

The letters on the screen swam before his eyes. The e-mail had been sent
to his official address at the ministry. Good God, what if his secretary read
it? She usually printed his e-mails every morning and laid them out for him.
Only occasionally did he get to the office before she did. Gregor Lauterbach
bit his lip and clicked on the sender: SnowWhite1997@hotmail.com. Who
was hiding behind that address? Who, who, who? This question had dominated his thoughts since the first letter arrived; day and night he could hardly
think about anything else. Fear attacked him like a convulsive shudder.

There was a knock on the door before it opened. He jumped as if he'd had
a pail of boiling water dumped on him. At the sight of his face Ines
Schürmann-Liedtke found herself unable to utter the friendly morning greeting she had intended.

"Aren't you feeling well, sir?" she asked with concern.

"No," Lauterbach croaked, and let himself sink back into his chair. "I
think I'm coming down with the flu."

"Should I cancel your appointments for today?"

"Is there anything important?"

"No. Nothing really urgent. I'll call Forthuber so he can drive you home."

"Yes, Ines, please do that." Lauterbach nodded and coughed a little. She
went out. He stared at the e-mail. Snow White. His thoughts were racing.
Then he closed the message and blocked the sender with a right-click.

Barbara Fröhlich sat at the kitchen table, trying in vain to concentrate on a
crossword puzzle. After three days and nights of uncertainty her nerves were
shot. On Sunday she had taken the two younger kids to her parents in Hofheim, and Arne went to work on Monday although his boss told him to stay
home. But what was he going to do at home?

The days were dragging by at an excruciating pace. Amelie was still missing; there had been no sign of her. Her mother had called three times from Berlin, though probably more out of duty than concern. During the first two days women from the village had dropped by wanting to console and support her, but since she hardly knew these women they had merely sat awkwardly in the kitchen trying to make conversation. Last night she and Arne had had a terrible fight, the very first since they'd met. She had reproached him for his lack of interest in the fate of his eldest daughter, and angrily had even insinuated that he'd probably be glad if she never turned up. Strictly speaking it hadn't been a fight, because Arne had merely looked at her and said nothing. As usual.

"The police will find her," was all he said and vanished into the bathroom. She stayed in the kitchen, helpless, speechless, and alone. And all of a sudden she had seen her husband with new eyes. He had gutlessly retreated into his daily routine. Would he act any differently if it had been Tim or Jana who had disappeared? His only concern seemed to be that he might annoy people. They hadn't said another word, lying silently next to each other in bed. Ten minutes later he was already snoring, calmly and regularly, as if everything was just fine. Never in her life had she felt so abandoned as during that dreadful, endless night.

The doorbell rang, and Barbara flinched and stood up. She hoped it wasn't one of the village women again. She knew that they feigned sympathy for her so that later at the grocery store they could present an exclusive report on the situation. She opened the front door. Before her stood a stranger.

"Hello, Mrs. Fröhlich," said the woman. She had short dark hair, a pale, serious face with bluish smudges under her eyes, and she wore rectangular glasses. "Detective Superintendent Maren König from K-11 in Hofheim."

She showed her criminal police badge. "May I come in?"

"Yes, of course. Please do." Barbara Fröhlich's heart was pounding apprehensively. The woman looked so serious that she had to be bringing bad news. "Do you have any news about Amelie?"

"No, I'm afraid not. But my colleagues have learned that Amelie supposedly received some paintings from her friend Thies. Yet nothing of that sort was found in her room."

"I don't know about any paintings either." At a loss, she shook her head, disappointed that the detective couldn't tell her any news.

"Do you think we could take another look in Amelie's room?" Maren König asked. "The paintings, if they actually exist, could be extremely helpful."

"Of course. Come with me."

Barbara Fröhlich led her upstairs and opened the door to Amelie's room. She stood in the doorway and watched as the detective diligently searched the cupboards, then got down on her knees and looked under the bed and the desk. Finally she pulled the Biedermeier chest of drawers a bit out from the wall.

"A hidden door," the detective said, turning to Barbara Fröhlich. "May I open it?"

"Certainly. I didn't even know it was there."

"In many houses with sloping roofs there's a cubbyhole like this and it's used as a storage area," the police officer said with a little smile for the first time. "Especially if they don't have an attic."

She squatted down, pulled open the door, and crept into the tiny space between the wall and the roof insulation. A cold draft came into the bedroom. A moment later she emerged, holding a thick roll wrapped in paper and carefully tied with a red ribbon.

"My God," said Barbara Fröhlich. "You actually did find something."

Detective Superintendent Maren König straightened up and brushed the dust from her stockings. "I'll take the paintings with me. I can give you a receipt if you like."

"No, no, that's not necessary," Barbara Fröhlich hastened to assure her. "If the pictures can help you find Amelie, then please take them."

"Thank you." The detective put her hand on her arm. "And try not to worry too much. We're really doing everything humanly possible to find Amelie. I promise you that."

Her words were so kind that Barbara Fröhlich had to fight with all her might to quell the rising tears. Grateful, she merely nodded mutely. She briefly considered whether to call Arne and tell him about the paintings. But she was still deeply hurt by his behavior, so she didn't bother. Only later when she was making herself some tea did it occur to her that she had neglected to look at the pictures.

Tobias was restlessly pacing back and forth in the living room of Nadia's apartment. The big TV on the wall was on with the sound turned down. The police were searching for him "in connection with the disappearance of seventeen-year-old Amelie F.," he had just read on the crawl beneath the picture. He and Nadia had spent half the night discussing what he should do. She thought they should look for the paintings. She fell asleep around midnight, but he had lain awake, trying in vain to remember what happened. One thing was sure: If he turned himself in to the police, they would arrest him on the spot. He had no plausible explanation for how Amelie's cell phone could have wound up in his jeans pocket, and he still had not even the faintest memory of last Saturday night.

Amelie must have found out something about the events of 1997 in Altenhain, something that could be dangerous for someone. But who could that be? His thoughts kept leading him back to Claudius Terlinden. For eleven long years he had considered the man his only supporter on earth; in the joint he had looked forward to his visits and the long conversations with him. What a fool he'd been! Terlinden was only out for his own interests. Tobias didn't go so far as to blame him for the disappearance of Laura and Stefanie. But Terlinden had ruthlessly taken advantage of his parents' plight to get what he wanted: the Schilling land on which he had built the new administration building for his company.

Tobias lit a cigarette. The ashtray on the side table was already overflowing. He went to the window and looked out at the black water of the Main River. The minutes dragged by at an agonizing pace. How long had Nadia been gone? Three hours? Four? He hoped she found what they were looking for. Her plan was his only option. If the paintings actually existed, the ones that Amelie had mentioned on Saturday, then maybe he could use them to prove his innocence and at the same time find out who had kidnapped Amelie. Was she still alive? Was she . . . Tobias shook his head, but he couldn't get rid of the thought. What if it was true—what the psychologists, expert witnesses, and the court had all affirmed back then? Was it possible that under the influence of too much alcohol he actually turned into a monster, as he'd been portrayed by the media? In the past, he's always had a short fuse, and he had a hard time accepting defeats. He had expected to get what he wanted—good grades in school, girls, success in sports. He had seldom showed much consideration for others, and yet he'd been popular, the star of his group of friends. Or was that merely what he believed? Had his boundless conceit made him both blind and arrogant?

The reunion with Jörg, Felix, and the others had awakened vague memories in him, memories of long forgotten events that he had previously considered trivial. He had stolen Laura from Michael without feeling a hint of guilt toward his friend. Girls were nothing more than trophies that served his vanity. How often had he hurt someone's feelings with his thoughtlessness? How much anger and worry had he caused? He hadn't really understood until the moment when Stefanie broke up with him. He didn't want to accept what she told him. He had even knelt down and begged her, but she only laughed at him. What had he done then? What had he done with Amelie? How did her cell phone wind up in his pants pocket?

Tobias sank back on the sofa, pressed his palms against his temples, and tried desperately to put together the scraps of memory into a logical context. But the harder he tried, the less successful he was. It was driving him crazy.

Although her waiting room was full, Dr. Daniela Lauterbach did not make Bodenstein and Kirchhoff wait long.

"How's your head doing?" she asked with a smile.

"No problems." Bodenstein touched the bandage on his forehead. "A little headache, that's all."

"If you like I could take another look at it."

"That's not necessary. We don't want to take too much of your time."

"All right, then. You know where to find me."

Bodenstein nodded and smiled. Maybe he really ought to switch doctors. Daniela Lauterbach quickly signed three prescriptions that her nurses had placed on the reception counter, then led Bodenstein and Kirchhoff into her office. The parquet floor creaked underfoot. The doctor motioned them to the visitor's chairs.

"It's about Thies Terlinden." Bodenstein sat down, but Kirchhoff remained standing.

Dr. Lauterbach took a seat behind her desk and looked at him attentively. "What would you like to know about him?"

"His mother told us he'd had an attack and was now in the psychiatric ward."

"That's correct," said the doctor. "I can't tell you much more about it. Confidentiality, you understand. Thies is my patient."

"We've been told that Thies had been stalking Amelie," said Pia.

"He wasn't stalking her, he just kept her company," the doctor corrected. "Thies likes Amelie a lot, and that's his way of showing affection. Incidentally, from the start Amelie accepted the way he is. She's a very sensitive girl, in spite of her rather unusual appearance. That's fortunate for Thies."

"Thies's father has bloody scratches on his hands after an argument with Thies," said Pia. "Does Thies have a tendency toward violence?"

Dr. Lauterbach gave a somewhat worried smile. "Now we're approaching the area I can't discuss with you," she replied. "But I presume that you suspect Thies of hurting Amelie. I consider that out of the question. Thies is autistic and behaves differently from a 'normal' person. He is not capable of showing his feelings or even expressing them. Now and then he has these . . . outbreaks, but very, very seldom. His parents are tremendously concerned about him, and he does well on the medications, which he's been taking for years."

"Would you say that Thies is mentally handicapped?"

"Absolutely not!" Dr. Lauterbach shook her head vehemently. "Thies is highly intelligent and has an extraordinary gift for painting."

She pointed to the large-format abstract paintings that resembled those hanging on the walls in Terlinden's house and office.

"Thies painted those?" Pia looked at the pictures in astonishment. At first sight she hadn't discerned what they depicted, but now she could see it. She shuddered as she recognized human faces, distorted, desperate, the eyes of torment, fear, and terror. The intensity of these paintings was oppressive. How could anyone tolerate looking at these faces every day?

"Last summer my husband organized a show for him in Wiesbaden. It was a sensational success, and all forty-three paintings were sold."

She sounded proud. Dr. Lauterbach liked her neighbor's son, yet seemed to have enough professional distance to assess him and his behavior objectively.

"Claudius Terlinden supported the Sartorius family generously in the years following Tobias's conviction," Bodenstein now took over the conversation. "He hired a lawyer for Tobias, a very good one. Do you think it's possible that he did this because he had a guilty conscience?"

"Why would he?" Dr. Lauterbach was no longer smiling.

"Perhaps because he knew that Thies had something to do with the disappearance of the girls."

For a moment it was completely quiet, except for the incessant ringing of a telephone muted by the closed door.

The doctor frowned. "I've never looked at it that way," she conceded pensively. "The fact is that back then Thies was utterly infatuated with Stefanie Schneeberger. He spent a lot of time with that girl, the way he does with Amelie today . . ."

She broke off when she realized where Bodenstein was going with this. She gave him a concerned look. "Good God!" she said. "No, no, I can't believe that!"

"We really have to speak with Thies quite urgently," Pia said emphatically. "It could lead us to Amelie."

"I understand. But it's difficult. I was worried he might do some harm to himself in his current state, so I had no other option than to transfer him to the locked psychiatric ward." Dr. Lauterbach peered over her steepled hands and tapped her forefingers thoughtfully on her pursed lips. "I don't have the authority to arrange for Thies to talk with you."

"But if Thies has done something with Amelie, she could be in great danger," Pia replied. "Maybe he has locked her up somewhere and she can't get out."

The doctor looked at Pia. Her eyes were dark with worry.

"You're right," she said then. "I'll call the head psychiatric physician in Bad Soden."

"Oh, one more thing," Pia added, as if it had just occurred to her. "Tobias Sartorius told us that Amelie mentioned your husband in connection with the events of 1997. Apparently there was a rumor going around then that he had given the lead role in the play to Stefanie Schneeberger because he was especially fond of her."

Dr. Lauterbach had already reached out her hand for the phone but now drew it back.

"Tobias was accusing everyone back then," she replied. "He wanted to get his own neck out of the noose, which is perfectly understandable. But all suspicions lodged against third parties were completely cleared up in the course of the investigation. The fact is that my husband, who was the director of the drama club at the time, was absolutely taken by Stefanie's talent. Add to that her looks, which were perfect for the role of Snow White."

She put her hand again on the receiver.

"What time on Saturday did you leave the Ebony Club in Frankfurt?" Bodenstein now asked. "Can you remember?"

A surprised expression flitted across the doctor's face. "Yes, of course I remember," she said. "It was nine thirty."

"And you then rode back to Altenhain with Claudius Terlinden?"

"No. I was on call that evening, so I'd taken my own car. At nine thirty I was called to an emergency in Königstein."

"Aha. And the Terlindens and your husband? When did they leave?"

"Christine rode with me. She was worried about Thies, who was in bed with the flu. I dropped her off down by the bus stop and then continued on to Königstein. When I got back home at two a.m., my husband was already asleep."

Bodenstein and Kirchhoff exchanged a quick glance. Claudius Terlinden had really been lying about the course of events on that Saturday night. But why?

"When you returned from your emergency call, you didn't drive straight home, did you?" Bodenstein prodded. The question didn't surprise Dr. Lauterbach.

"No. It was a little past one when I left Königstein." She sighed. "I saw a man lying on the bench at the bus stop and stopped." She shook her head slowly, her brown eyes full of sympathy. "Tobias was dead drunk and already suffering from hypothermia. It took me ten minutes to get him into my car. Hartmut and I then got him up to his room and into bed."

"Did he say anything to you?" Kirchhoff wanted to know.

"No," said the doctor. "He wasn't responsive. First I considered calling the EMTs and having him taken to the hospital, but I knew he wouldn't have wanted that in any case."

"How come?"

"I'd treated him only a couple of days before that, after he'd been beaten up in the barn." She leaned forward and looked at Bodenstein so urgently that he felt uncomfortable. "I really can't help feeling sorry for him, no matter what he's done. The others may say that ten years in prison was too little. But I think that Tobias will be suffering for the rest of his life."

"There are indications that he may have had something to do with Amelie's disappearance," said Bodenstein. "You know him better than many other people. Do you think that's possible?"

Dr. Lauterbach leaned back in her chair and said nothing for a long moment, without taking her eyes off Bodenstein.

"I wish," she said at last, "I could say 'no' with full conviction. But unfortunately I can't."

She tore the short-haired wig off her head and dropped it carelessly on the floor. Her hands were shaking too much to untie the red ribbon that fastened the roll, so she impatiently grabbed some scissors and snipped through it. With heart pounding she unrolled the paintings on her desk. There were eight of them, and it took her breath away when she saw with horror what they depicted. That miserable shithead had captured on canvas the events of September 6, 1997, with true photographic precision; not the slightest detail had escaped him. Even the silly lettering and the stylized little pig on the dark green T-shirts were clearly visible. She bit her lips and the blood roared in her ears. Suddenly the memory came vividly alive. The humiliating feeling of defeat as well as the wild satisfaction at the sight of Laura, who finally got what she deserved. That damned arrogant slut! She looked at the other pictures, smoothing them out with both hands. Naked panic gripped her, just as it had then. Disbelief, bewilderment, cold rage. She straightened up and forced herself to take a deep breath. Three times, four. Be calm. Think it over. This was a disaster, it was the absolute maximum credible accident. It could completely destroy all her careful planning, and she couldn't let that happen. With trembling fingers she lit a cigarette. It was unthinkable what would have happened if the cops got hold of these pictures. It made her queasy. What should she do now? Were these really all the pictures, or had Thies painted more? She couldn't take the risk, there was too much at stake. Quickly she smoked the cigarette all the way down to the filter, and then she knew what to do. She'd already had to make all the decisions herself. With fierce determination she grabbed the scissors and cut the paintings, one after the other, into little pieces. Then she put them through the shredder, took out the sack of confetti, and grabbed her bag. This was no time to lose her nerve. Everything was going to be fine.

Detective Superintendent Kai Ostermann felt discouraged. He had to admit that the coded writing in Amelie's diary was an insoluble riddle to him. At first he'd thought it would be easy to decipher the hieroglyphics, but now he was about to give up. He simply couldn't see any system. Obviously she had used different symbols for the same letters, which made it almost impossible to crack the code. Behnke came in the door.

"Well?" Ostermann asked. Bodenstein had assigned Behnke to question Claudius Terlinden, who had been sitting in one of the detention cells since that morning.

"Refuses to say a word, that arrogant bastard." In frustration Behnke sat down heavily on the chair behind his desk and clasped his hands behind his head. "It's easy enough for the boss to say that I'm supposed to pin something on this guy—but what? I tried to provoke him, I was friendly, I threatened him—but he just sits there and smiles. What I'd really like to do is punch him in the mouth."

"That probably wouldn't do any good." Ostermann sent his colleague a quick look. That got Behnke's hackles up.

"You don't have to remind me that I'm up shit creek!" he yelled, pounding his fist so hard on the desk that the keyboard jumped. "I'm starting to think the old man wants to harass me so much that I'll quit!"

"That's bullshit. Besides, he didn't tell you to nail him. He just said to soften him up a little."

"Precisely. Then he'll waltz in here with his crown princess and make it look easy!" Behnke was red in the face with rage. "All I ever get to do is the shit work."

Ostermann almost felt sorry for Behnke. He'd known him since the police academy; they'd done patrols together and both had joined the Special Assignment Unit until Ostermann lost his lower leg during a deployment. Behnke had stayed in the SAU a couple more years, then he was transferred to the criminal police in Frankfurt and landed right in K-11, in the very top echelon of the police hierarchy. He was a good cop. Or had been. Later, when everything went south in his private life, his work also suffered. Behnke rested his head in his hands and fell into a listless brooding.

Then the door flew open. Kathrin Fachinger marched in, her cheeks glowing with anger.

"Tell me, have you completely lost it?" she snapped at her colleague. "You leave me alone with that guy and just take off! What's the deal here?"

"You always think you can do better than me, anyway!" Behnke said sarcastically. Ostermann was looking back and forth between the two combatants.

"We had a strategy," Fachinger reminded her colleagues. "And then you just roar off. But just imagine, he did talk to me." Her voice took on a triumphant undertone.

"Oh, that's just great! Why don't you run to the boss and tell him, you crazy bitch!"

"What did you say?" Fachinger loomed up before him, her hands on her hips.

"Crazy bitch is what I said!" Behnke repeated loudly. "And I'll make it even plainer: You're an ambushing, egotistical little bitch! You snitched on me, and I'm never going to forget it!"

"Frank!" Ostermann shouted, getting up.

"Are you threatening me?" Fachinger wasn't about to let herself be intimidated. She gave a contemptuous laugh. "I'm not afraid of you, you . . . you blowhard! All you know how to do is talk big and let everyone else do the work! No wonder your wife left you. Who'd want to be married to somebody like you?"

Behnke had turned beet red. He clenched his fists.

"People!" Ostermann admonished them anxiously. "Just cool it!"

It was too late. Behnke's long bottled up rage at his younger colleague went off like an explosion. He jumped up, knocked over his chair, and gave Fachinger a strong shove. She crashed against the cabinet, and her glasses flew onto the floor. Behnke deliberately stomped on them, crunching the shattered glass under the heel of his shoe. Kathrin got to her feet.

"Well," she said with a cold grin. "That's it for you, my dear colleague."

Behnke totally flipped out. Before Ostermann could stop him, he threw himself at Kathrin and punched her in the face. Reflexively her knee shot up and hit him in the balls. With a stifled moan of pain Behnke hit the floor. At that moment the door opened, and Bodenstein appeared in the doorway. His gaze shifted from Fachinger to Behnke.

"Can somebody please tell me what's going on here?" he asked, his voice carefully controlled.

"He attacked me and knocked my glasses off," said Kathrin Fachinger, pointing at the mangled glasses frames. "I was just defending myself."

"Is that true?" Bodenstein looked at Ostermann, who raised his hands helplessly and, after a brief glance at his colleague huddled on the floor, nodded.

"Okay," said Bodenstein. "I've had enough of this kindergarten. Behnke, get up."

Frank Behnke obeyed. His face was contorted with pain and hatred. He opened his mouth, but Bodenstein didn't let him speak.

"I thought you understood what Dr. Engel and I told you," he said icily. "You're suspended, effective immediately."

Behnke stared at him mutely, then went to his desk and grabbed his jacket hanging over the back of the chair.

"Leave your badge and service weapon here," Bodenstein commanded.

Behnke unfastened his weapon and tossed it and his badge carelessly on the desk.

"All of you can kiss my ass," he gasped, then squeezed past Bodenstein and left. For a moment there was complete silence.

"What did the interview with Terlinden turn up?" said Bodenstein to Fachinger, as if nothing had happened.

"He owns the Ebony Club in Frankfurt," she replied. "As well as the Black Horse and the other restaurant that Andreas Jagielski manages."

"What else?"

"That's all I could get out of him. But I think that explains a few things."

"You do? What?"

"Claudius Terlinden wouldn't have had to support Hartmut Sartorius financially if he hadn't personally destroyed the man's livelihood by opening the Black Horse," Fachinger replied. "In my opinion he is anything but a good Samaritan. First he ruined Sartorius, then he prevented him from losing the property and leaving Altenhain. I bet he has more people in the village under his thumb, like this Jagielski, who he put in charge of his restaurants. It reminds me a little of the mafia: He protects them, and in return they keep their mouths shut."

Bodenstein looked at his youngest colleague and frowned in thought. Then he nodded.

"Well done," he said. "Very good."

Tobias jumped up from the couch as if electrocuted when the front door opened. Nadia came in. She had a plastic bag in one hand and was trying to get her coat off with the other.

"So?" Tobias helped her off with her coat and hung it in the wardrobe. "Did you find anything?" After waiting tensely for hours he could hardly contain his curiosity.

Nadia went into the kitchen, put the bag on the table, and sat down.

"Not a thing." Tired, she shook her head, undid her ponytail, and ran her hand through her hair. "I searched the whole damn house. I'm beginning to think that Amelie made up these paintings."

Tobias stared at her. He was deeply disappointed.

"But that can't be!" he countered vehemently. "Why would she make up something like that?"

"No idea. Maybe she wanted to make herself seem important," said Nadia with a shrug. She looked exhausted, and there were dark shadows under her eyes. The whole situation seemed to be making her equally discouraged.

"Let's eat first," she said, reaching for the bag. "I brought home some Chinese."

Although Tobias hadn't eaten all day, the appetizing aroma coming from the paper boxes didn't tempt him. How could he think about eating? Amelie hadn't made up the story with the paintings—she would never do that. She wasn't the sort of girl who liked to show off. Nadia was totally wrong about that. He looked on silently as she opened one container, separated the chopsticks, and began to eat.

"The police are looking for me," he said.

"I know that," she said, her mouth full. "I'm doing everything I can to help you."

Tobias bit his lip. Damn it, he really couldn't blame Nadia for anything. But it was making him crazy to be consigned to doing nothing. Most of all he wanted to go out and look for Amelie on his own. But they would arrest him on the spot as soon as he set foot outside the door. There was nothing to do but be patient and trust Nadia.

Bodenstein parked across the street, turned off the engine, and remained sitting behind the wheel. From here he could watch Cosima through the brightly lit kitchen window busily moving about. He'd had another discussion with Dr. Engel because of Behnke. News of the incident had spread through the whole station like wildfire. Nicola Engel had approved the suspension of Behnke, but now Bodenstein had a serious problem on his hands. Not only Behnke, but Hasse was out too.

On the drive home Oliver had thought over how he should act toward Cosima. Silently pack his things and leave? No, he had to hear the truth from her lips. He felt no anger, only the utterly wretched feeling of boundless disappointment. After hesitating for several minutes, he got out and slowly crossed the rain-wet street. The house that he and Cosima had built together, in which he had lived for twenty happy years, in which he knew every nook and cranny, suddenly appeared foreign to him. Every evening he had been glad to come home. He had looked forward to seeing Cosima and the kids, to playing with the dog and doing the gardening in the summer, but now he dreaded opening the front door. How long had Cosima lain next to him in bed and longed secretly for another man? Someone else who would caress her and kiss her and make love to her? If only he hadn't seen Cosima together with that guy today. But he had, and now everything inside him was screaming, *Why? Since when? How? Where?*

He never would have believed that he would be in such a situation. His marriage was good, until . . . yes, until Sophia had come into the world. After that, Cosima changed. She had always been restless, but her expeditions in foreign lands had satisfied her longing for freedom and adventure so that she could tolerate daily life for the remaining months of the year. He had known that and accepted the traveling she did without complaint, although he'd always hated the long separations. After Sophia was born, hardly two years ago, Cosima had stayed at home. She had never let him sense that she was unhappy. But looking back he recognized the changes. Previously they had never argued, but now they often did. The fights were always over trivial things. They were quick to reproach each other and criticize individual quirks. Oliver stood with his key in his hand at the front door when suddenly and unexpectedly fury flared up inside him. For weeks she had concealed her pregnancy with Sophia from him. *She* had decided all by herself to have the child and present him with the fait accompli. In this instance she had to realize that having a baby with their gypsy lifestyle was out of the question, at least for a while.

He opened the door. The dog jumped out of his basket and greeted him effusively. When Cosima appeared in the kitchen doorway, Oliver's heart sank.

"Hello." She smiled. "You're kind of late today. Did you already eat?"

There she stood, in the same celadon green cashmere sweater that she'd been wearing at the Ebony Club at lunch, and looking the same as usual.

"No," he replied. "I'm not hungry."

"Just in case, I have meatballs and a noodle salad in the fridge."

She turned away, heading back to the kitchen.

"You weren't in Mainz today," he said. Cosima stopped and turned around. He didn't want her to lie to him, so he kept talking before she could say anything. "I saw you at the Ebony Club at lunch. With Alexander Gavrilow. Please don't try to deny it."

She crossed her arms and looked at him. Silence. The dog felt the sudden tension and crept soundlessly back to his basket.

"In recent weeks you've almost never been in Mainz," Oliver went on. "A few days ago I came out of the forensics lab and you happened to be driving right in front of me. I called you on your cell and saw you pick up the phone. And then you claimed you were in Mainz."

He stopped talking. He still hoped in a corner of his heart that she would laugh and give him a completely innocent explanation. But she didn't laugh or deny it. She just stood there with her arms crossed. Without a sign of guilty conscience.

"Please be honest with me, Cosima." His voice sounded pathetic in his ears. "Are you . . . are you having . . . an affair with Gavrilow?"

"Yes," she replied calmly.

His world collapsed, but Oliver managed to remain just as calm as Cosima.

"Why?" he asked, torturing himself.

"Oh, Oliver. What do you want me to say?"

"Preferably the truth."

"I met him this summer by chance at an opening in Wiesbaden. He has an office in Frankfurt, was planning a new project, and was looking for sponsors. We talked on the phone a few times. He had an idea that I could do a film about his expedition. I knew you wouldn't like it, so first I wanted to hear what sort of ideas he had in mind. That's why I didn't tell you that I met with him. And somehow it just . . . happened. I thought it was only a fling, but then . . ." She broke off, shaking her head.

Unbelievable. How could she meet another man and start an affair without him suspecting a thing? Was he too stupid, too trusting, or too self-involved? The lyrics of a song came to mind, a song that Rosalie in her worst phase of puberty had blasted constantly all over the house. *What does he have that I don't have? Tell me the truth, what it is. Now it's much too late, but what have you missed?* Such a dumb song—and now all of a sudden it contained so much truth. Oliver left Cosima standing there and went upstairs to the bedroom. In another minute he would have exploded, screamed in her face what he thought of adventurers like Gavrilow who started affairs with married mothers of small children. He had probably conducted his dalliances all over the world, that bastard! Oliver opened all of the clothes cabinets, yanked his suitcase down from one of the top shelves, and stuffed it with underwear, shirts, and ties, throwing in two suits on top. Then he went into the bathroom and packed his personal things in a toiletry bag. Ten minutes later he dragged the suitcase downstairs. Cosima was still standing in the same spot.

"Where are you going?" she asked softly.

"Away," he said without looking at her. Then he opened the front door and stepped out into the night.

Friday, November 21, 2008

At a quarter past six Bodenstein was torn out of a deep sleep by the ringing of his cell phone. In a daze he groped for the light switch until he remembered that he wasn't at home in his own bed. He had slept poorly and had crazy dreams. The mattress was too soft, the comforter too warm, so that he had alternated between sweating and freezing. His cell kept on ringing obstinately, stopped, and then began ringing again. Bodenstein rolled out of bed, felt around in the dark with no point of reference in the strange room and cursed when he stubbed his big toe on a table leg. Finally he found the light switch next to the door and then located his cell phone in the inside pocket of his jacket, which he had thrown over the chair last night.

A forest ranger had found a male corpse in a car at a forest parking lot below the Eichkopf mountain between Ruppertshain and Königstein. The evidence techs were already on their way. Could he drive out and stop by to take a brief look? Of course he would—what choice did he have? His face contorted in pain, he hobbled back to the bed and sat down on the edge. The events of the other day seemed like a bad dream. For almost an hour he had driven around until he almost by accident happened to pass the turnoff to his family's estate. Neither his father nor mother had asked him any questions when he showed up at the front door shortly before midnight and asked to stay for the night. His mother had made up a bed for him in one of the guest rooms on the top floor but hadn't pressed him for an explanation. She certainly must have seen from his face that he hadn't dropped by for fun. He was grateful for her discretion. There was no way he could have talked about Cosima and that guy.

With a sigh he got up, fished out his toiletry bag from his suitcase, and went across the hall to the bathroom. It was tiny and ice cold and reminded him unpleasantly of his childhood and youth, which had been devoid of any luxury. His parents had scrimped where they could, because money was always tight. Over there in the castle, where he had grown up, in the winter months only two rooms were heated; all the other rooms were only "lukewarm," as his mother used to call the barely 64-degree room temperature. Bodenstein sniffed at his T-shirt and wrinkled his nose. He couldn't avoid taking a shower. He thought nostalgically of the heated floors in his house, of the soft towels smelling of fabric softener. He showered in record time, drying himself with a rough, tattered hand towel, and then shaved with trembling fingers in the pale fluorescent light of the mirrored cabinet. Downstairs in the kitchen he encountered his father, who was drinking coffee at the scratched wooden table and reading the *Frankfurter Allgemeine Zeitung.*

"Good morning." He looked up and gave his son a friendly nod. "Coffee for you too?"

"Good morning. Yes, please." Bodenstein sat down. His father stood up, got a cup from the cupboard and poured his coffee. His father would never dream of asking him why he'd showed up in the middle of the night and slept in one of the guest rooms. His parents had always been frugal with words as well. And Oliver felt no desire to discuss his marital problems at a quarter to seven in the morning. So father and son drank their coffee in silent harmony. For as far back as he could remember they had always used the Meissen porcelain for all of their meals—out of thrift. The china service was a family heirloom, and there was no reason not to use it or to acquire a different set of dishes. It would have been of inestimable value except that almost every piece had been repaired multiple times over the years. Even Oliver's coffee cup had a crack and the handle had been glued back on. Finally he got up, put his cup in the sink, and said thank you. His father nodded and turned again to his newspaper, which he had politely put aside.

"Take a house key with you," he said in passing. "There's one on a red key ring hanging on the board next to the door."

"Thanks." Oliver took the key. "See you later."

His father obviously assumed that he would be back in the evening.

Headlights and flashing blue lights brightened the dark November morning as Bodenstein turned in at the forest parking lot directly beyond the Nepomuk curve. He parked his car next to the patrol car and set off down the path. The autumn smell of damp earth and decaying foliage penetrated his nostrils, and he recalled fragments of a Rainer Maria Rilke poem, one of the few he knew by heart. *Who is now alone will remain so for long, wandering restlessly among the avenues when the leaves are turning.* The feeling of loneliness pounced on him like a mad dog, and he had to force himself with all his might to go on, to do his job, although he would have preferred to creep away somewhere.

"Morning," he said to Christian Kröger, leader of the evidence team, who was unpacking his camera. "What's going on up there?"

"The news must have spread over the police band," said Kröger, shaking his head with a grin. "They're like little kids!"

"News of what?" Bodenstein still didn't understand and wondered at the crowd of people. In spite of the early hour, five police vehicles stood in the gravel parking lot, and a sixth was just turning in from the road. Bodenstein could already hear the murmur of voices from a long way off. All the officers, uniformed or in the white overalls of evidence techs, were talking excitedly.

"It's a Ferrari," one of the highway cops told him, eyes shining. "A 599 GTB Fiorano. I've only seen one once, at the International Auto Show in Frankfurt."

Bodenstein made his way through the crowd. There it was. At the very end of the lot gleamed a bright red Ferrari in the floodlight, reverently surrounded by about fifteen police officers, who were more interested in the cubic capacity of the engine, horsepower, tires, rims, torque, and acceleration of the noble sports car than in the dead man in the driver's seat. A hose stretched from one of the arm-thick, chromed exhaust pipes to the window, which had been carefully sealed on the inside with silver duct tape.

"That thing costs two hundred and fifty thousand euros," one of the younger officers said. "Crazy, don't you think?"

"The value probably dropped a bit overnight," said Bodenstein dryly.

"How so?"

"Maybe you didn't notice, but there's a dead body in the driver's seat." Bodenstein wasn't one of those men who flipped out at the sight of a red sports car. "Did anyone run the plates?"

"Yes," said a young female officer in the back of the crowd, who obviously didn't share the enthusiasm of her male colleagues. "The vehicle is registered to a bank in Frankfurt."

"Hmm." Bodenstein watched while Kröger shot his photos. Then he and a colleague opened the driver's side door.

"The economic crisis claims its first victim," somebody joked. Then a new discussion started about how much money you'd have to earn per month to be able to pay the lease on a Ferrari Fiorano. Bodenstein saw another patrol car roll into the parking lot, followed by two plainclothes cars.

"Cordon off a large area of the parking lot," he instructed the young female officer. "And please get rid of anyone who doesn't have a reason for being here."

The young woman nodded and energetically strode off to carry out her assignment. A few minutes later the parking lot was sealed off. Bodenstein squatted down next to the open driver's side door and examined the body. The blond man was still young, probably in his mid-thirties. He wore a suit and tie and had an expensive watch on his wrist. His head was tilted to one side, and at first glance he looked like he was asleep.

"Morning, Bodenstein," said a familiar voice behind him, prompting him to look back over his shoulder.

"Hello, Dr. Kirchhoff." He got up and nodded to the medical examiner. "Isn't Pia here?"

"No, today I'm on my own," Bodenstein replied. "Do you miss her?"

Dr. Kirchhoff put on a weary smile but didn't comment. For once he didn't seem in the mood for sarcastic remarks. Behind the lenses of his glasses his eyes were red-rimmed. He looked like he hadn't gotten much sleep last night either. Bodenstein made room for the ME and went over to Kröger, who was inspecting the briefcase that they'd found lying on the passenger seat of the Ferrari.

"Well?" he asked. Kröger handed him the dead man's briefcase. Bodenstein took out the ID and stared at it. He read the name a second time. Could it be a coincidence?

The head doctor of the psychiatric ward had informed Kirchhoff about Thies Terlinden's condition in as much detail as her oath of confidentiality allowed. Now Pia was even more curious to see the man. She knew that she shouldn't expect too much. The doctor had said that Thies probably wouldn't answer her questions at all. For quite a while Pia observed the patient through the window in the door. Thies Terlinden was an extremely good-looking young man with thick blond hair and a sensitive mouth. It was impossible to tell by looking at him what sort of demons he struggled with. Only his paintings revealed something of his internal torments. He was sitting at a table in a bright, cheery room, all of his attention focused on what he was drawing. Although he had calmed down under the influence of the medications, he wasn't allowed any sharp implements such as pencils or paintbrushes, so he had to settle for crayons, which didn't seem to bother him. He didn't look up when Pia entered the room, accompanied by the doctor and an orderly. The doctor introduced Pia and explained to him why she was here, saying that she wanted to talk with him. Thies bent farther over his picture, then leaned back abruptly and set the crayon on the table. The colorful crayons weren't lying helter-skelter; he had lined them up precisely like soldiers at roll call. Pia sat down on a chair across from him.

"I didn't do anything to Amelie," he said in a strange, monotone voice before Pia could say a word. "I swear. I didn't do anything, do anything."

"Nobody is saying that you did," Pia replied in a friendly voice.

Thies's hands were fluttering uncontrollably, and he was rocking his upper body back and forth. His gaze was fixed on the picture lying before him.

"You like Amelie a lot, and she visited you often, isn't that right?"

He nodded vehemently.

"I took care of her. Took care of her."

Pia exchanged a glance with the doctor, who had sat down a short distance away. Thies again grabbed a crayon, bent over the picture, and continued drawing. There was silence in the room. Pia thought about what question to ask next. The doctor had advised her to speak normally to Thies, not as if to a child. But that turned out not to be so easy.

"When did you see Amelie the last time?"

He didn't react, but kept drawing as if possessed, changing to a different crayon.

"What did you and Amelie talk about?"

This was completely different from a normal interview. Thies's face revealed nothing; his expression was as rigid as a marble statue. He didn't answer any questions, so Pia asked him no more. The minutes went by. Time meant nothing to autistic patients, the doctor had explained to Pia. They lived in their own world. Patience was required. But at eleven o'clock the funeral for Laura Wagner was being held at the cemetery in Altenhain, and she wanted to meet Bodenstein there. When she got up, disappointed, and was about to leave, Thies suddenly spoke.

"I saw her that evening, from the eagle's nest." He spoke in clear and distinct sentences that were grammatical and correct. Only the melody of the sentences was lacking, a result of his robotic delivery. "She was standing in the barnyard near the barn. I wanted to call out to her, but then . . . the man came. They talked and laughed and went into the barn so nobody could see what they were doing. But I saw it."

Pia cast a bewildered look at the doctor, who merely shrugged, uncomprehending. Barn? Eagle's nest? And what man had Thies seen?

"I can't talk about it," he went on, "or else they'll put me in a home. And I'll have to stay there till I die."

Suddenly he raised his head and looked at her with bright blue eyes, as desperate as a figure in the paintings in Dr. Lauterbach's office.

"I can't talk about it," he repeated. "Can't talk about it. Or they'll put me in a home." He pushed the picture he had drawn over to Pia. "Can't talk. Can't talk."

She looked at the picture and gave a shudder. A girl with long dark hair. A man running away. Another man bashing in the head of the dark-haired girl with a cross.

"That isn't Amelie, is it?" Pia asked softly.

"Can't talk," he whispered hoarsely. "Can't talk. Only draw."

Pia's heart beat faster as she grasped what Thies was trying to tell her. Somebody had forbidden him to talk about what he had seen. He wasn't talking about Amelie. And the picture didn't show Amelie either, but Stefanie Schneeberger and her murderer.

Thies had turned away from her again, grabbed a crayon, and was raptly drawing a new picture. It seemed as though he had withdrawn completely now. His features were still tense, but he had stopped rocking back and forth. Slowly Pia realized what this young man had been through in recent years. Someone had put pressure on him and threatened him so that he wouldn't tell anyone what he had seen eleven years ago. But who had done that? Suddenly she also realized what danger Thies Terlinden was in if that person found out what he had just told the police. To protect him she had to pretend, even to the doctor, that it was completely irrelevant.

"Oh well," she said. "Thanks a lot, at any rate." She got up, and the doctor and orderly did too.

"Snow White must die. That's what they said," Thies announced all of a sudden. "But nobody can do anything to her anymore. I'm watching out for her."

The fog and drizzle kept no one in Altenhain from accompanying the mortal remains of Laura Wagner on her last journey. The parking lot in front of the Black Horse couldn't hold all the cars. Pia simply parked up the street, climbed out of the car, and walked briskly toward the tolling bells of the church, where Oliver was waiting for her on the covered porch.

"Thies saw everything that happened in 1997," she blurted out the news. "He did paint pictures, just as Amelie told Tobias. Somebody put pressure on him, telling him that he'd be sent to a home if he ever told anyone what he saw."

"What did he say about Amelie?" Bodenstein was impatient, a sign that he too had found out something important.

"Nothing. Only that he didn't do anything to her. But he spoke about Stefanie and even drew a picture."

Pia fished the folded paper out of her purse and handed it to Oliver.

He glanced at it and frowned, then pointed at the cross. "That's the tire iron. The murder weapon."

Pia nodded excitedly. "Who could have threatened him? His father?"

"Maybe. He probably wouldn't have wanted his own son to get mixed up in such a crime."

"But Thies didn't do anything," Pia countered. "He was only a witness."

"I'm not talking about Thies," Oliver shot back. The bell stopped tolling. "This morning I was called to a suicide. A man took his life in a car in the parking lot by the Nepomuk curve. And the man was Thies's brother, Lars Terlinden."

"What?" Pia was shocked.

"That's right." Oliver nodded. "What if Lars killed Stefanie and his brother saw it?"

"Lars Terlinden went to study in England right after the girls disappeared." Pia tried to recall the chronology of events in September 1997. The name of Thies's brother had never come up in the old files.

"Maybe that was how Claudius Terlinden kept his son out of the investigation. And then he threatened his other son so that he would keep his mouth shut," Oliver proposed.

"But what did Thies mean when he said that nobody could do anything to Snow White anymore because he would take care of her?"

Oliver shrugged. They didn't seem any closer to resolving the case. In fact it was getting more and more complicated. They walked around the church to the cemetery. The funeral party had gathered under umbrellas, crowding around the open grave. At that moment the white coffin, with a bouquet of white carnations on top, was being lowered. The men from the funeral parlor withdrew, and the pastor began to speak.

Manfred Wagner had obtained a release from custody to attend the funeral for his eldest daughter. With a stony face he stood in the front row beside his wife and two teenagers. The two warders who had accompanied him waited a short distance away. A young woman wearing stiletto heels hurried past Bodenstein and Kirchhoff without looking at them. She had done up her gleaming blond hair in a simple knot, and she wore a tight black suit and big sunglasses despite the gloomy weather.

"Nadia von Bredow," Pia explained to her boss. "She's from Altenhain and was a friend of Laura Wagner's."

"Ah, yes." Oliver was lost in thought. "By the way, I just heard from Dr. Engel that she's worried about Gregor Lauterbach. Cultural minister or not, he rode back home with Terlinden on the Saturday when Amelie disappeared."

Pia's cell began to ring. She quickly took it out and hurried around the corner of the church before she attracted any dirty looks.

"Pia, it's me," Ostermann said. "You told me the other day that interview transcripts were missing from the old file."

"Yes, that's right."

"Listen to this. I don't like telling you this, but it occurred to me that Andreas was pretty interested in those files. He stayed late one evening when I was sick at home, and I . . ."

The rest of his sentence was drowned out by a sudden howl from the siren on the roof of the Black Horse. Pia covered her other ear and asked her colleague to talk louder. Three men left the funeral party when the siren sounded and rushed past Pia toward the parking lot.

". . . I'm wondering . . . prescription . . . but was in our office . . ." was all she could make out. ". . . no idea . . . ask him . . . is it?"

"Can't hear you because of the siren." Pia was straining to hear. "There's a fire somewhere. Okay, give it to me again. What about Andreas?"

Ostermann repeated what he'd said before. Pia listened in disbelief.

"That would be absolutely amazing," she said. "Thanks. We'll see you later."

She put away her phone and walked back to Bodenstein, lost in thought.

Tobias Sartorius walked past the barn and into the former cowshed. All of Altenhain was at the cemetery, so nobody would see him, not even his neighbor Paschke, the old block warden. Nadia had dropped him off up the hill at the rear entrance to the farm and then continued on to the cemetery to attend Laura's funeral. Tobias closed the door of the milk room and went into the house. The feeling that he needed to hide was horrendous. He wasn't suited to such a life. Just as he was about to go upstairs, his father appeared, silent as a shadow, in the kitchen doorway.

"Tobias! Thank God!" he exclaimed. "I've been so worried about you! Where have you been?"

"Dad." Tobias hugged his father. "I was at Nadia's. The cops aren't going to believe me. They'll just lock me up again."

Hartmut Sartorius nodded.

"I came to grab a few clothes. Nadia went to the funeral and will pick me up later."

Only now did it occur to him that his father was at home on a weekday instead of being at work.

"They let me go." Hartmut Sartorius shrugged. "Came up with some sort of flimsy argument. My boss is Dombrowski's son-in-law, after all."

Tobias understood. His throat tightened. Now he was also to blame for his father getting fired.

"I wanted to quit anyway," said Hartmut Sartorius lightly. "I want to do real cooking again, not just thaw out frozen crap and shovel it onto plates." Then he seemed to remember something. "A letter came for you today."

He turned and went into the kitchen. Tobias followed. The letter had no return address. He would have liked to throw it in the trash unopened. Probably another vulgar insult. He sat down at the kitchen table, tore open the envelope, and unfolded the elegant cream-colored sheet of paper. Baffled, he looked at the letterhead of a Swiss bank before he started to read the hand-written text. The very first lines hit him like a fist in the stomach.

"Who's it from?" asked his father. Outside a fire engine thundered past with blue lights flashing and the siren wailing, rattling all the windowpanes. Tobias swallowed. He looked up.

"From Lars," he croaked. "From Lars Terlinden."

The gate to the Terlinden property stood wide open. The acrid smell of smoke penetrated even through the closed car window. The fire department vehicles had driven across the lawn, leaving deep ruts in the marshy ground. It wasn't the villa that was in flames, but a building farther back on the expansive grounds. Pia Kirchhoff left her car in the courtyard in front of the house and approached the site of the fire on foot along with Bodenstein. The thick smoke brought tears to their eyes. The fire department already seemed to have the fire under control. No more flames could be seen, only thick, dark clouds of smoke roiled out of the windows. Christine Terlinden was dressed all in black. Apparently she had been at the funeral or had been just about to drive there, when she noticed the fire. She watched the spectacle in shock, the muddle of fire hoses, the firemen trampling through the flowerbeds and destroying the lawns. Next to her stood her neighbor, Daniela Lauterbach. At the sight of the doctor Bodenstein involuntarily recalled his crazy dreams of the night before. She turned around as if she'd heard his thoughts, and walked over to him and Kirchhoff.

"Hello," she said coolly and without a trace of a smile. Her normally shining, hazelnut-brown eyes today looked like frozen chocolate. "Was your visit with Thies productive?"

"No," Pia replied. "What's going on here? What's the building that's burning?"

"The orangerie. Thies's studio. Christine is very worried about how Thies will react when he finds out that all his paintings have burned."

"Unfortunately we have some more bad news for Mrs. Terlinden," said Bodenstein.

Daniela Lauterbach raised one of her shapely eyebrows. "It can't get much worse," she said, her voice sharp. "I heard that you're still holding Claudius. Why?"

For a moment Bodenstein was tempted to plead for her understanding in order to justify his actions. But Pia spoke first.

"We have our reasons," she said. "Unfortunately we have to report to Mrs. Terlinden that her son has taken his own life."

"What? Thies is dead?" Dr. Lauterbach looked at Pia. Was it relief that flickered briefly in her eyes before consternation spread across her face? How odd.

"No, not Thies," said Pia. "Lars."

Bodenstein let Pia do the talking. It irritated him that he was so eager for Daniela Lauterbach's approval. Was it because of the sympathy that she had shown him? Had he read too much into her kindness because of his own emotional crisis? He couldn't take his eyes off her face and wished absurdly that she would smile at him.

"He died from carbon monoxide poisoning, sitting in his car," Pia said. "We found his body this morning."

"Lars? Good God."

As the doctor realized what terrible news was in store for her friend Christine, the ice in her eyes melted. She seemed suddenly helpless, but then she straightened her shoulders.

"I'll tell her," she said with determination. "It's better that way. I'll take care of her. Call me later."

She turned and went over to her friend, who hadn't taken her eyes off the burning building. Daniela Lauterbach put both arms around her friend's shoulders and spoke softly to her. Christine Terlinden emitted a muted cry and swayed a bit, but Lauterbach held her tight.

"Let's go," said Pia. "They'll manage."

Bodenstein tore himself away from the sight of the two women and followed Pia back through the ravaged park. Just as they reached their car, a woman came walking toward them, but he couldn't immediately place her.

"Hello, Mrs. Fröhlich," Pia greeted Amelie's stepmother. "How are you doing?"

"Not good," the woman admitted. She was very pale but seemed composed. "I wanted to ask Mrs. Terlinden what happened here, since I saw her car. Is there any news? Did your colleague make any headway with those pictures?"

"What pictures?" asked Pia in surprise.

Bewildered, Barbara Fröhlich looked back and forth from Pia to Bodenstein.

"B-but your colleague visited me yesterday," she stammered. "She . . . she said you had sent her. Because of the pictures that Thies gave Amelie."

Bodenstein and Pia exchanged a quick look.

"We didn't send anyone," said Pia with a frown. This whole case was getting stranger and stranger.

"But the woman said . . ." Barbara Fröhlich began, and then stopped helplessly.

"Did you see the pictures?" Bodenstein asked.

"No . . . she looked through the whole room and found a concealed door behind the chest of drawers. And inside there really was a roll of pictures. Amelie must have hidden them there . . . But I didn't see what was in the pictures. The woman took them with her, and even offered to give me a receipt."

"What did she look like, our so-called colleague?" Pia asked. Barbara Fröhlich seemed to grasp that she had made a mistake. Her shoulders slumped forward and she leaned against the fender of the car, a fist pressed to her lips. Pia went over to her and put an arm around her shoulder.

"She . . . she had a police badge," Amelie's stepmother whispered, fighting back the tears. "She was . . . so understanding and friendly. She . . . she . . . said that the pictures would help you find Amelie, and that was all that was important to me."

"Don't worry about it," Pia tried to console her. "Can you remember what the woman looked like?"

"Short dark hair. Glasses. Slim." Barbara Fröhlich shrugged. In her eyes was naked fear. "Do you think Amelie is still alive?"

"I'm sure of it," said Pia, though she had her doubts. "We'll find her. Try not to worry."

"Thies's paintings show the real killer, I'm sure of it," said Pia a little later to her boss as they drove in the direction of Neuenhain. "He gave them to Amelie for safekeeping, but Amelie made the mistake of telling somebody about the pictures."

"Exactly." Oliver nodded darkly. "Namely Tobias Sartorius. And he sent someone over to the Fröhlichs to get the pictures. He's probably already destroyed them."

"It wouldn't matter to Tobias if he was in the pictures," Pia countered. "He served his time. What else could happen to him? No, no, there has to be somebody else who has a vested interest in making sure those pictures never see the light of day."

"And who would that be?"

Pia found it hard to put her suspicions into words. She realized that her first impression of Claudius Terlinden couldn't have been more wrong.

"Thies's father," she said.

"Possibly," Oliver agreed. "But it could also be somebody who isn't even on the list, because we don't know about him. You have to take the next left."

"Where are we going, anyway?" Pia turned on the left turn signal, waited for traffic to clear, and turned into the street.

"To Hasse's," Oliver said. "He lives in the last house on the left side, up near the woods."

Her boss hadn't reacted when Pia told him earlier about Ostermann's call, but he now seemed determined to get to the bottom of the matter. A moment later they pulled up in front of the cottage with a tiny front yard. They knew that Andreas Hasse was planning to have his mortgage paid off on the day he retired. He had mentioned it countless times, full of resentment over the rotten pay that public servants received. They got out and went to the front door. Oliver rang the bell. Hasse himself opened the door. He suddenly turned deathly pale and lowered his head in embarrassment. So Ostermann had scored a bull's-eye with his hunch. Unbelievable.

"May we come in?" Oliver asked. They entered a dark hallway with a worn linoleum floor; the smell of food mixed with cigarette smoke hung in the air. The radio was on. Hasse shut the door to the kitchen. He didn't waste any time trying to lie, but spilled everything out.

"A friend asked me for a favor," he said uncomfortably. "I didn't think it would matter."

"Jeez, Andreas, are you nuts?" Pia was beside herself. "You took transcripts out of the files?"

"How was I to know that old crap would be of any importance?" he protested lamely. "I mean, it's all ancient history, the whole case was closed long ago . . ." He stopped talking when he realized what he was saying.

"You know what that means," Oliver said gravely. "I have to suspend you from the force and take disciplinary action against you. Where are the documents?"

Hasse made a helpless gesture. "I destroyed them."

"Why in the world would you do that?" Pia couldn't believe what she was hearing. Had he really thought nobody would notice?

"Pia, Sartorius killed two girls and tried to cast suspicion on everyone else—even his friends and his teacher. I knew that guy back then. I was on the investigative team from the very beginning! What an ice-cold bastard he was. And now he wants to fan the flames again and—"

"That's not true at all!" Pia interrupted him. "I'm the one who began having doubts. Tobias Sartorius has absolutely nothing to do with it."

"What's the name of your friend who asked you to do this dubious favor?" Oliver asked. Hasse hemmed and hawed a little.

"Gregor Lauterbach," he finally admitted, hanging his head.

The Black Horse was jam-packed. The whole village had gathered there after the funeral. But over their coffee and sandwiches, people were talking less about Laura Wagner and more about the fire at the Terlinden place. Everyone was airing conjecture and speculation. Michael Dombrowski was the captain of the volunteer fire department and had led the operation. On the way back to the firehouse he had gotten off at the Black Horse, and the smell of smoke and fire still clung to his clothes and hair.

"The police think it was arson," he told his friends Felix Pietsch and Jörg Richter as he joined them at a small table in the corner. "I have to ask myself why anyone would set fire to a garden hut." Only now did he notice the oppressive mood of his pals. "What's the matter with you guys?"

"We have to find Tobi," said Jörg. "And end this whole thing once and for all."

Felix nodded in agreement.

"What do you mean?" asked Michael, baffled.

"Don't you see that it's starting all over again? Just like before." Jörg Richter put his half-eaten cheese sandwich back on the plate and shook his head in disgust. "I don't want to go through that again."

"Me neither," Felix agreed with his friend. "We really have no choice about this."

"Are you sure?" Michael looked uncomfortably from one to the other. "You know what that means. For every one of us."

Felix and Jörg nodded. They were aware of the consequences of their plan.

"What does Nadia say?"

"We can't take that into consideration anymore," said Jörg, taking a deep breath. "We can't wait any longer. Otherwise there might be another tragedy."

"Better an end with terror than a terror without end," Felix added in agreement.

"Shit." Michael rubbed his face. "I can't do it! I . . . I mean . . . it was all so long ago. Can't we just let it be?"

Jörg stared at him. Then he shook his head.

"No, we can't. Nadia just told me at the cemetery that Tobi is at home. I'm going over there and put an end to this."

"I'll come with you," said Felix.

Michael still hesitated, desperately searching for a way to stay out of it. "I have to go check the fire site," he finally said.

"You can do that later," said Jörg. "This won't take long. Come on, let's go."

Daniela Lauterbach had crossed her arms, staring at her husband with a mixture of disbelief and contempt. When she came home, he'd been sitting at the kitchen table, gray in the face and looking years older. Even before she could take off her jacket he had started talking—about anonymous threatening letters, about e-mails and photos. The words spilled out of him like a waterfall, bitter, desperate, full of self-pity and fear. Silently and with growing bewilderment she had listened to him without interrupting. His last plea had left her speechless. For a while there was complete silence in the big kitchen.

"What do you expect from me now?" she asked him coolly. "God knows I helped you more than enough back then."

"I wish you hadn't," he replied dully. At these words rage overcame her, a hot, wild rage that had slumbered deep inside her all these years. What hadn't she done for him? This spineless weakling, this phony who couldn't do anything but act like a big shot and make beautiful speeches. As soon as he was in a tight spot, he came crawling to her, whimpering and clinging to her apron strings. She used to like it when he listened to her advice and asked for help whenever he was at his wits' end. He had been her obedient sorcerer's apprentice, her fountain of youth, her masterpiece. When they first met more than twenty years ago, she had instantly seen the talent in twenty-one-year-old Gregor. Back then she was already a successful physician, twenty years older than he was and well-situated thanks to a respectable inheritance. At first she had regarded him only as a diversion in bed, but then she decided to finance the education of the working-class boy, and turned him on to the worlds of art, culture, and politics. Through her contacts she got him a job as a high-school teacher and paved his way into politics. The position of cultural minister was the culmination of her efforts. But eleven years ago, after what happened, she'd wanted to throw him out. He wasn't worth it. An ungrateful weakling who still didn't appreciate all her work and investments even today.

"If you'd listened to me back then and buried the tire iron in the woods instead of grabbing it with your bare hands and throwing it in Sartorius's cesspool, nothing would have happened," she said. "But you wanted to be clever. And because of you Tobias went to prison. Because of you, not because of me!"

He flinched at her onslaught of words as if she'd lashed him with a whip. "I made a mistake, Dani! I was under so much pressure, my God!"

"You fucked an underage schoolgirl," she reminded him in an icy voice. "And now you come here in all seriousness and demand that I get rid of an eyewitness, who happens to be a patient of mine and the son of our neighbor! What kind of person are you, anyway?"

"I'm not demanding that of you," Gregor Lauterbach whispered. "I just want to talk to Thies. That's all. He simply has to continue to keep his mouth shut. You're his doctor, they'll let you in to see him."

"No." Daniela Lauterbach shook her head. "I'm not going to get involved. Leave the boy alone. He's got enough problems. Actually it would be best if you removed yourself from the scene for a while. Go to the house in Deauville until things have settled down here."

"But the police have arrested Claudius," Gregor Lauterbach told her.

"I know." She nodded. "And I ask myself why. What did you really do on Saturday night, you and Claudius?"

"Please, Dani," he pleaded. He slipped off the chair and got down on his knees before her. "Let me talk to Thies."

"He won't answer you."

"Maybe he will. If you're there."

"Not a chance." She looked down at her husband cowering in front of her like a scared little boy. Once again he had lied to her and betrayed her. Her friends had prophesied even before the wedding that it would turn out like this. Gregor was twenty years younger, he was strikingly handsome, an eloquent speaker, and possessed plenty of charisma. Women worshiped him because they saw something in him that he was not. Only she knew how weak he really was. That's where she got her power, as well as from his dependence on her. She had forgiven him under the condition that nothing like that would ever happen again. A relationship with a schoolgirl was taboo. His ever-changing parade of lovers, on the other hand, didn't interest her at all— she found it amusing. Only she knew his secrets, his fears and insecurities. In fact, she knew him much better than she knew herself.

"Please," he continued to beg, looking at her with big, pleading eyes. "Help me, Dani. Don't leave me in the lurch! You know what's at stake for me!"

Daniela Lauterbach heaved a deep sigh. Her determination not to help him dissolved into thin air. As always. She couldn't stay mad at him for long. And this time there really was a lot at stake; he was right about that. She bent down to him, stroked his head, and dug her fingers into his thick, soft hair.

"All right," she said. "I'll see what I can do. But now pack your things and go to France for a few days, until everything is sorted out, okay?"

He looked up at her, grabbed her hand, and kissed it.

"Thank you," he whispered. "Thank you, Dani. I don't know what I would ever do without you."

She smiled. Her anger at him had ebbed away. She felt a deep, peaceful joy rise up inside. Equilibrium had been restored, and she would conquer the threat from outside effortlessly—as long as Gregor was smart enough to appreciate what she was doing for him.

"The cultural minister?" Pia had expected a completely different answer from her colleague and was flabbergasted. "How do you know him?"

"My wife is his wife's cousin," Andreas Hasse explained. "We see each other a lot at family gatherings. Besides, we're both in the men's glee club in Altenhain."

"Oh great," said Bodenstein. "I can't tell you how disappointed I am in you, Hasse."

Andreas Hasse looked at him and stuck out his chin defiantly. "Really?" he replied in a trembling voice. "I had no idea that *I* could disappoint you, since you've never shown any interest in me."

"Excuse me?" Bodenstein raised his eyebrows.

And then it came bubbling out of Hasse, now that he realized his days in K-11 were numbered.

"You've never said more than three sentences to me. I was supposed to become the head of K-11, but then you showed up from Frankfurt, so arrogant and smug. First you turned the whole place upside down, as if it was all rotten—everything that we dumb hick policemen had done before. You don't give a damn about any of us! Just a bunch of stupid cops, far inferior to the noble Herr *von* Bodenstein," Hasse retorted. "You'll find out soon enough where it gets you. People are already planning to pull the rug out from under you."

Bodenstein looked at Hasse as if he'd spit in his face. Pia was the first to come to her senses.

"Are you off your rocker?" she laid into her colleague.

He laughed caustically. "You'd better watch out. At the station everybody has known for a long time that you two have something going on! That's at least as much of a breach of regulations as Frank's moonlighting job."

"Shut your trap!" Pia snarled. Hasse grinned lewdly.

"I knew from the start that something was going on. The others didn't notice it until recently, when you started calling each other by your first names."

Bodenstein turned and left the house without a word. Pia made a couple more furious remarks to Hasse, then followed her boss. He wasn't in the car. She walked down the street and found him over by the woods, sitting on a bench with his face buried in his hands. Pia hesitated, but then went over to him and sat down quietly next to him. The wood of the bench was glittering with moisture from the fog.

"Don't listen to that crazy shit. He's just a bitter, frustrated idiot," she said. Bodenstein didn't answer.

"Am I doing anything right?" he murmured dully after a while. "Hasse is plotting with the cultural minister and stealing transcripts from the files. Behnke has been working in secret for a year in a bar and I didn't even know it. My wife has been cheating on me for months with another guy . . ."

He raised his head, and Pia had to swallow hard when she saw the expression of abysmal despair on his face.

"Why didn't I see any of this? Am I really so arrogant? And how am I supposed to do my job if I can't straighten out my own life?"

Pia regarded the sharp contours of his profile and felt genuine sympathy for him. What Hasse and other people interpreted as arrogance and smugness was just Bodenstein's personality. He didn't get involved, never took advantage of his authority. And even though he might be extremely curious, he would never dream of asking his subordinates indiscreet questions. That was not indifference, it was restraint.

"I didn't know about Behnke's bartending job either," Pia said softly. "And the fact that Hasse stole the transcripts bowled me over too." She grinned. "I didn't even know about our secret relationship."

Bodenstein uttered an inarticulate sound, somewhere between a laugh and a sigh. Then he shook his head, discouraged.

"I have the feeling my whole life is falling apart." He was staring into space. "I can't think about anything but the fact that Cosima is cheating on me with another guy. Why? What was she missing? Did I do something wrong?"

He leaned forward, propping his elbows on his knees and clasping his hands behind his head. Pia bit her lip. What should she say to him? Was there any consolation for him at all in this situation? She hesitated a moment and then put her hand on his arm and squeezed it gently.

"Maybe you did do something wrong," she said. "But when there are problems in a relationship, it's never the fault of just one person. Instead of looking for explanations, you should think about how you can fix things."

Bodenstein rubbed the back of his neck and straightened up.

"I had to look at the calendar to remember when I slept with her last," he said with sudden bitterness. "But it's not easy with a small child who keeps running in."

Pia was uncomfortable talking about this. Even though her own relationship in the past year had become much more intimate than before, she still felt it was embarrassing to talk about such matters with her boss. She got her cigarettes out of her jacket pocket and held out the pack to him. He took a cigarette, lit it, and took a few drags before he went on.

"How long has this been going on? How many nights have I lain beside her like a clueless dope while she was thinking about her other guy? The thought of it makes me sick."

Ah, from despair gradually comes anger. That was good. Pia lit another cigarette.

"Just ask her," she advised him. "It would be best to ask her right away. Then you won't have to keep driving yourself crazy."

"And then what? When she tells me the truth? Oh, shit! I'd like to . . . cheat on her too." He broke off and ground the cigarette under his heel.

"Then do it. Maybe then you'd feel better."

"Are you trying to give me advice?" Bodenstein looked at Pia in surprise, and a hint of a smile played around the corners of his mouth.

"It doesn't seem like anyone else is giving you any," she said. "In school I had a boyfriend who broke up with me. I wanted to kill myself, I was so unhappy. My friend Miriam forced me to go to a party with her, and some guy came over to me. He couldn't stop complimenting me. So, okay. After that I felt better. There are plenty of fish in the sea."

Bodenstein's cell phone rang. At first he ignored it, but finally he took it out of his pocket with a sigh and answered.

"It was Fachinger," he told Pia after he hung up. "Hartmut Sartorius called. Tobias has come home."

He got up from the bench.

"I hope we can still catch him. Sartorius called two hours ago, but the detective on duty just told Fachinger now."

The gate to the Sartorius place was wide open. They crossed the courtyard and rang the doorbell, but nothing happened.

"The door is ajar," said Pia, and pushed it open.

"Hello?" she called into the house. "Mr. Sartorius? Tobias?"

No answer. She went a few steps into the hall and called his name again.

"He must have taken off." Disappointed, she turned around and went back to Bodenstein, who was waiting outside. "And his father isn't home either. What a pisser."

"Let's look around back in the yard." Bodenstein pulled out his cell. "I'll call for backup."

Pia walked around the house. Tobias Sartorius had come back to Altenhain on the day of Laura Wagner's funeral. He wasn't at the cemetery, of course, but during the graveside ceremony the studio of Thies Terlinden had gone up in flames—with the help of an accelerant, as the fire department and the arson squad had determined. Didn't it make sense that Tobias had set fire to the orangerie and then taken off?

". . . no sirens, got it?" Pia heard Bodenstein say. She waited until he stood next to her.

"Tobias knew that the whole village would be at the cemetery and he could set the fire unobserved," she told him her hunch. "I just don't understand why his father called us."

"Me neither," Bodenstein admitted. He glanced around the barnyard. During previous visits the gate and all the doors had been carefully locked, which was understandable given all the threats and the attack on Tobias. How come everything now stood wide open? Just as they turned the corner of the house, they noticed a movement up in the farm area. Two men disappeared through the rear gate and a little later car doors slammed and an engine roared to life. Suddenly Pia had a bad feeling.

"That was probably Tobias and his father." She reached inside her jacket and pulled out her service weapon from her holster. "There's something fishy going on here."

She cautiously opened the door to the milk room and peered inside. Then she went over to the old cowshed. At the open door they both signaled to keep quiet. Pia raised her pistol and went inside the stall. She looked around and froze. On a stool in the corner sat Tobias Sartorius. His eyes were closed and he was leaning against the wall.

"Shit," Pia murmured. "I think we're too late."

Eight steps from the door to the wall. Four steps from the opposite wall to the bookshelf. Her eyes had long since adjusted to the darkness, her nose to the stale, moldy smell. During the day a little light came through a tiny crack above the narrow cellar window that was sealed off with something from the outside. At least she could tell whether it was day or night. The two candles had burned down long ago, but she knew what was in the box on the shelf. Four bottles of water were still left; she had to ration them carefully because she had no idea how long they would have to last. The crackers had slowly dwindled, just like the canned sausage and chocolate. That's all there was. At least she would lose a few pounds while she was here, wherever "here" was.

Most of the time she was so tired, so tired, that she simply fell asleep without being able to fight it off. When she was awake sometimes she'd be overcome by such despair that she'd pound her fists against the door, crying and yelling for help. After that she would fall back into melancholy indifference, lying for hours on the stinking mattress, and try to imagine life outside, the faces of Thies and Tobias. She recited poems to herself from memory, she did pushups and tai chi exercises—not easy to keep her balance in the dark—or sang as loud as she could all the songs she knew, just to keep from going nuts in this dank dungeon.

Eventually somebody would come and get her out of here. She was sure of that. It couldn't be right that the Lord would let her die even before her eighteenth birthday. Amelie curled up on the mattress and stared into the darkness. One of the last pieces of chocolate was slowly melting on her tongue. Simply chewing and swallowing it would have felt like a crime. A leaden fatigue was creeping up inside her, sucking her memories and thoughts into a black hole. Over and over again she brooded about what had actually happened. How did she get to this horrible place? The last thing she remembered was that she had tried in vain to reach Tobias. But she couldn't think of why.

Pia gave a start when Tobias opened his eyes. He didn't move, but simply looked at her without saying a word. The bruises on his face had faded, but he looked tired and sick.

"What happened?" Pia asked, putting away her gun. "Where have you been all this time?"

Tobias didn't respond. There were deep shadows under his eyes, and he looked much thinner than the last time she saw him. Laboriously, as if it took all his strength, he raised one arm and held out a folded piece of paper to her.

"What's this?"

He didn't say a word, so she took the paper out of his hand and unfolded it. Bodenstein stepped up next to her, and they read the handwritten lines together.

Tobi, you're probably wondering why I'm writing to you after such a long time. In the past eleven years not a day has gone by when I didn't think of you and feel guilty. You did my time in prison, and I let it happen. I detest the caricature of a human being I've become. I have not served God as I always wanted to do, but instead have become the slave of an idol. Eleven long years I've been running, and I forced myself not to look back at Sodom and Gomorrah. But now I am looking back. The running is over. I have been defeated. I have betrayed everything that used to mean so much to me. I made a pact with the Devil when I took the advice of my father and lied the first time. I betrayed and sold out you, my best friend. The price for me was eternal torment. Every time I see my face in the mirror I see you before me. What a coward I was! I killed Laura. Not on purpose, it was a stupid accident, but she was dead. I listened to my father and kept my mouth shut, even when it was clear that they were going to convict you for her death. I turned in the wrong direction, and it has led me straight to Hell. Since then I have never been happy. Forgive me, Tobi, if you can. I can't forgive myself. May God be my judge.
—Lars

Pia looked up from the letter. Lars Terlinden had dated his farewell letter the day before and used the bank letterhead where he worked. But what had triggered this confession and his suicide?

"Lars Terlinden committed suicide yesterday," said Bodenstein, clearing his throat. "We found his body this morning."

Tobias did not react, only stared mutely into space.

"Well, then." Bodenstein took the letter from Pia. "Now at least we know why Claudius Terlinden took over the debts of your parents and visited you in prison."

"Come on." Pia touched Tobias's arm. He was wearing only a T-shirt and jeans, and his skin felt cold. "You're going to catch your death out here. Let's go inside."

"They raped Laura when she came out of our house," he said suddenly, tonelessly. "Right here in the stable."

Bodenstein and Pia exchanged a startled look.

"Who?" asked Bodenstein.

"Felix, Jörg, and Michael. My *friends*. They were drunk. Laura had been teasing them all evening. The situation got out of control. Then Laura ran off, straight into Lars's arms. She stumbled, fell, and was dead." He spoke with no emotion, almost indifferently.

"How do you know this?"

"They were just here and told me."

"Eleven years too late," said Pia.

Tobias heaved a sigh. "They loaded Laura's body into the trunk of my car and threw it in the tank at the old airfield. Lars ran away. I never saw him again. My best friend. And then today this letter came . . ."

His blue eyes focused on Pia. Only now did she realize that against all odds her hunch about this man's innocence had actually been right.

"What about Stefanie?" Bodenstein asked. "And where is Amelie?"

Tobias took a deep breath and shook his head.

"I don't know. Honestly. I have absolutely no idea."

Someone came into the cow stable behind them, and the two detectives turned around. It was Hartmut Sartorius. He was deathly pale and could only contain his agitation with the utmost effort.

"Lars is dead, Dad," said Tobias in a low voice. Hartmut Sartorius squatted down in front of his son and embraced him awkwardly. Tobias closed his eyes and leaned on his father. Pia found the sight very moving. Would the suffering these two had endured ever end? The ringtone of Bodenstein's cell phone broke the silence. He took the call and went outside to the barnyard.

"Are you going . . . to arrest Tobias now?" Hartmut Sartorius asked in an uncertain voice, looking up at Pia.

"We have a few questions for him," she replied regretfully. "Unfortunately there is still the suspicion that Tobias had something to do with the disappearance of Amelie Fröhlich. And as long as that's not cleared up . . ."

"Pia!" Bodenstein yelled from the barnyard. She turned and went out to join him. In the meantime the backup they'd ordered had arrived. Two officers got out of their car and walked toward them.

"That was Ostermann," Bodenstein told her, punching a number into his phone. "He deciphered the secret writing in Amelie's diary. In her last entry she writes that Thies showed her the mummy of Snow White in the cellar below his studio . . . Yes? . . . Bodenstein here . . . Kröger, I need you and your team to go out to the Terlinden estate in Altenhain. Where the fire was today. Yes, right away!"

He looked at Pia and she understood what was going on in his head.

"You mean Amelie might be there?"

He nodded, then rubbed his chin pensively and frowned.

"Call Behnke and tell him to get a couple of guys and bring the three men Tobias mentioned down to the station," he instructed Pia. "Send a patrol car to pick up Lauterbach, one to his private residence and another to his office in Wiesbaden. I want to talk to him today. We also have to talk to Claudius Terlinden; he doesn't yet know about his son's suicide. And in case we actually do find the hidden cellar, we need a medical examiner."

"You suspended Behnke from service," Pia reminded him. "But Kathrin could do it. And what about Tobias?"

"I'll tell our colleagues to take him to Hofheim. He'll just have to wait for us there."

Pia nodded and grabbed her phone to relay the instructions. She dictated to Kathrin the names of Felix Pietsch, Michael Dombrowski, and Jörg Richter, then she went back inside the cowshed. She watched as Tobias got to his feet and then leaned heavily on his father.

"My colleagues are going to take you to Hofheim," she told Tobias. "They're waiting in the yard for you."

Tobias Sartorius nodded.

"Pia!" Bodenstein yelled impatiently from outside. "Come on!"

"So we'll see you later." Pia nodded to the two men and left.

•   •   •

A patrol car was parked in front of the Lauterbachs' house when Bodenstein and Pia drove past. A few yards farther on they drove through the open gate into the Terlinden estate, climbed out, and walked across the lawn to the smoldering ruins of the orangerie. The blackened stone walls were still standing, but the roof had partially fallen in.

"We have to get in there right away," Bodenstein told one of the firemen who had stayed behind to watch the fire site.

"Can't be done." The fireman shook his head. "The walls could come down at any minute, and the roof is unstable. Nobody's going in there."

"Yes, we are," Bodenstein insisted. "We've received information that there's a cellar underneath. And the girl who disappeared may be locked in down there."

That changed the situation completely. The fireman conferred with his colleagues and made a phone call. Bodenstein, also on the phone, walked back and forth and around the burned-out building. It was impossible for him to stand still. This damned waiting! The evidence techs arrived and a little later a fire department car pulled in, along with a dark blue vehicle from the Technical Rescue Organization. Pia learned from the patrol officers that the Lauterbachs weren't at home. She got the number of the head secretariat at the Cultural Ministry in Wiesbaden and was told that the cultural minister had been out sick for three days and had not come to the office. So, where was he? She leaned on the fender, lit a cigarette, and waited for Bodenstein to take a break from his telephone marathon for a few seconds. In the meantime the people from the fire department and rescue crew had begun to search through what remained of the roof and walls of the orangerie. Using heavy equipment they carefully cleared away the smoking debris and set up floodlights because it was already getting dark.

Kathrin Fachinger called and reported success: Felix Pietsch, Jörg Richter, and Michael Dombrowski were at the station. None of them had resisted arrest. But there was more news that excited Pia. Ostermann had looked through the five hundred photos on Amelie Fröhlich's iPod and found pictures of paintings that could be the ones Thies had given her. Searching for

Bodenstein, Pia trudged across the mushy lawn that had turned into a muddy mess beneath the tires of the heavy vehicles. Her boss was standing expressionless in front of the orangerie, smoking a cigarette. Just as she was about to show him the pictures from the iPod, the men inside the ruins began to shout and wave. Bodenstein woke from his torpor, dropped the butt, and went inside. Pia followed on his heels, It was still very hot inside the building that had been ablaze only a few hours earlier.

"We found something," the fireman reported who had been leading the work after the captain of the squad had failed to show up. "A trap door. We're trying to get it open."

The street was dry, and the traffic jam on the A5 had dissolved beyond the Frankfurt interchange. Nadia stepped on the gas as soon as the speed limit was lifted and accelerated to 125 miles an hour. Tobias was sitting in the passenger seat. He had closed his eyes and hadn't uttered a sound since they took off. It was all too much for him. His thoughts were circling around what he had learned this afternoon. Felix, Michael, and Jörg. He had thought they were his friends. And Lars, who'd been like a brother to him. They had killed Laura and hidden her body in the tank at the old airfield, but never said a word. They had let him go through hell and kept silent for eleven years. Why had they suddenly decided to come clean? Why now? He felt a deeply upsetting disappointment. Only a few days ago they had drunk beer with him, laughing and exchanging memories from the old days—and the whole time they were fully aware of what they had done, what they had done to *him*! He sighed heavily. Nadia grasped his hand and squeezed. Tobias opened his eyes.

"I can't believe that Lars is dead," he whispered, clearing his throat several times.

"It's all totally incredible," she agreed. "But I've always believed that you were innocent."

He forced a smile. Amid all the disappointments, the bitterness, and the anger, a tiny seed of hope was sprouting. Maybe everything would turn out well for Nadia and him. Maybe they'd both have a chance once the shadows of the past were dispelled and the whole truth had come to light.

"I'm getting pissed off at those cops," he said.

"Oh well," she said, winking at him, "you'll be back in a couple of days. And your father has my cell number, just in case. Everyone will understand that you need some distance about now."

Tobias nodded. He relaxed a little. The ever-present, nagging pain inside him eased a bit.

"I'm so glad you're here," he told Nadia. "Really. You're simply wonderful."

She smiled again, but kept her eyes on the road.

"We're meant for each other, you and I," she replied. "I've always known that."

Tobias put her hand to his lips and kissed it tenderly. Ahead of them were a few days of peace and quiet. Nadia had canceled all her appointments. Nobody would bother them, and he didn't have to be afraid of anyone. The soft music, the pleasant warmth, the soft leather upholstery. He could feel fatigue overwhelming him. With a sigh he closed his eyes and a moment later was deeply and soundly asleep.

The rusty iron stairs were narrow and led steeply downward. He felt the wall for the light switch. Seconds later the 25-watt bulb lit the room with a dim glow. Bodenstein could feel his heart pounding. It had taken hours to secure the ruins enough to go inside safely. The excavator from the rescue crew had pushed the debris aside, and using all their strength the men had pried open the deformed steel trap door. One of the men in a protective suit had climbed down the stairs and found that everything below was okay. The cellar had survived the fire unscathed.

Bodenstein waited until Pia, Kröger, and Henning Kirchhoff had made it down the steep descent and stood beside him in the tiny room. He put his hand on the handle of the heavy iron door. It swung open without a sound. Warm air came toward him, and there was a sweetish smell of wilted flowers.

"Amelie?" called Bodenstein. A flashlight behind him flared up and illuminated a surprisingly large, rectangular room.

"A former bunker," Kröger said. There was a click when he turned on the light switch, and a fluorescent tube on the ceiling sprang to life, humming and flickering. "The electrical lines were laid separately so that in case of damage to the building the cellar would still have power."

The cellar room was sparsely furnished. A sofa, a shelf with a stereo. The rear part of the room had been divided off with an old-fashioned folding screen. But no sign of Amelie. Were they too late?

"Shoot," murmured Kröger. "It's plenty hot in here."

Bodenstein crossed the room. Sweat was running down his face.

"Amelie?"

He moved the screen aside. His gaze fell on the narrow iron bed. He had to swallow. The girl lying there was dead. Her long black hair was spread like a fan over the white pillow. She was wearing a white dress, and her hands were folded over her stomach. The red lipstick seemed grotesque on the dried lips of the mummy. A pair of shoes stood next to the bed. Wilted flowers in a vase on the nightstand, next to it a bottle of cola. It took a couple of seconds before he realized that the girl on the bed could not be Amelie.

"Snow White," Pia said softly next to him. "There you are at last."

It was shortly after nine when they arrived back at the station. In front of the door to the watch room three colleagues were dealing with a rampaging drunk whose female companion was equally inebriated and swearing a blue streak. Pia got herself a diet Coke at the vending machine before she went into the conference room on the second floor. Bodenstein was leaning over the table looking at the photos of the paintings that Kathrin had printed out. Ostermann and Kathrin were sitting across from him. He looked up when Pia came in. She could see the furrows of exhaustion on his face, but she knew that he would not allow himself to take a break right now. Not when they were so close to the goal, and especially now that his private troubles could be pushed aside with all this feverish activity.

"Let's take all three of them at once," Bodenstein decided, casting a glance at the clock. "We also have to talk to Terlinden. And with Tobias Sartorius."

"Where is he?" Kathrin asked in surprise.

"I think he's downstairs, in one of the cells."

"I don't know anything about that."

"Me neither," said Ostermann.

Bodenstein looked at Pia. She raised her eyebrows.

"You told the boys from the patrol at Sartorius's place this afternoon that they should bring him here, didn't you?"

"No. I told them to go to Lauterbach's," said Bodenstein. "I thought you would call another patrol."

"And I thought you'd already done that," said Pia.

"Ostermann, give Sartorius a call," Bodenstein ordered. "He needs to come down here right away."

He grabbed the photos and left the conference room. Pia rolled her eyes and followed him.

"Could I see the pictures before we go in?" she asked him. He handed her the photos without slowing his pace. He was angry because a mistake had escaped his notice. A misunderstanding could always happen when events piled up so rapidly. Nobody was in the interrogation room yet. Bodenstein marched out and came back a moment later.

"Nothing gets done right around here," he growled in annoyance. Pia didn't reply. She was thinking of Thies Terlinden, who had watched over the corpse of Stefanie Schneeberger for eleven years. Why had he done that? Did his father order him to do it? Why had Lars Terlinden chosen this moment to write that letter to Tobias and commit suicide? How come Thies's studio had burned down? Did anyone know about Snow White—or was the arson because of Thies's paintings? If so, the same person who had sent the phony policewoman to see Barbara Fröhlich could be behind the fire. And where was Amelie? Thies had shown her the mummy of Snow White and then let her go; otherwise she wouldn't have been able to write in her diary. What had she told Tobias? Why did she disappear? Did her disappearance have nothing at all to do with the old case?

A thousand thoughts were streaming through her brain, but she couldn't bring any order to this information overload. Bodenstein was on the phone again, this time apparently with Commissioner Engel. He listened with a grim expression on his face and said only "Yes" or "No" occasionally. Pia sighed.

The entire case was turning into a nightmare, and that was due less to the work than to the circumstances under which they had to carry out this investigation. She felt Bodenstein's gaze on her and raised her head.

"When we wrap up this case, she's going to take drastic measures, she said. No, I mean threatened." He put his head back and laughed all of a sudden, but without mirth. "Today she got an anonymous phone call."

"Aha." Pia didn't give a hoot about that. She wanted to talk to Claudius Terlinden and find out what he knew. Each bit of additional information that she received was making it harder to think clearly.

"Somebody told her that you and I are having an affair." Bodenstein ran both hands through his hair. "Allegedly someone saw us together."

"Well, that's no big news," Pia replied dryly. "We do drive around all day together."

A knock at the door ended their conversation. Tobias Sartorius's three "friends" were escorted in. They sat down at the table and Pia took a seat too. Bodenstein remained standing and looked at the three men one by one. Why had they been seized with remorse now, after eleven years? He signaled for Pia to state the formal details of the interview that would be recorded. Then he placed the eight photos on the table. Felix Pietsch, Michael Dombrowski, and Jörg Richter looked at the pictures and turned pale.

"Do you recognize these pictures?"

They shook their heads.

"But you recognize what they depict."

They nodded.

Bodenstein crossed his arms. He seemed relaxed and calm, as he always did. Pia couldn't help admiring his self-control. Anyone who didn't know him well would never have guessed what was really going on inside him.

"Can you tell us who and what we're looking at in the pictures?"

The three men were silent for a moment, then Jörg Richter spoke. He recited the names: Laura, Felix, Michael, Lars, and himself.

"And who is the man in the green T-shirt?" Pia asked. The three hesitated, exchanging brief glances.

"That's not a man," said Jörg Richter finally. "That's Nathalie. Nadia, that is. She used to have really short hair."

Pia picked out the four pictures that showed the murder of Stefanie Schneeberger.

"And who is that?" She tapped her finger on the person Stefanie was embracing. Jörg Richter hesitated.

"That could be Lauterbach. Maybe he went after Stefanie."

"What exactly happened that evening?" Bodenstein asked.

"There was the fair in Altenhain," Richter began. "We were out all day and had drunk a lot. Laura was jealous of Stefanie because she'd been elected Queen of the Fair. Then she probably wanted to make Tobi jealous and flirted with us like crazy. She made us really hot. Tobi was working at the drink stand in the tent, with Nadia. At some point he left; there must have been trouble with Stefanie. Laura ran after him and we ran after her."

He paused.

"We went up the hill, taking Waldstrasse, not the main road. Then we sat around in the back of Sartorius's place. Suddenly Laura came through the milk room into the stable. She was howling and her nose was bleeding. We started pestering her until she got mad and punched Felix. And somehow . . . I don't remember now exactly how . . . the situation escalated."

"You raped Laura," Pia stated in a factual way.

"She had been teasing us nonstop all evening."

"Was the sexual intercourse with her consent or not?"

"Well," said Richter, biting his lower lip. "Probably not."

"Which of you had sexual intercourse with Laura?"

"I did, and . . . and Felix."

"Go on."

"Laura kept hitting and kicking us. Then she ran off. I went after her. And suddenly Lars was standing there. Laura was lying in front of him on the ground, and there was blood everywhere. She probably thought he wanted something from her too. She tripped and hit her head on the rock used to block the gate. Lars was totally shocked; he stammered something and then ran off. We . . . we panicked too and wanted to run away, but Nadia was very cool-headed, as always, and said we should make Laura disappear. Then there wouldn't be any evidence."

"Where did Nadia suddenly come from?" Bodenstein asked.

"She . . . she was there the whole time."

"Nadia watched while you raped Laura Wagner?"

"Yes."

"But why did you want to get rid of Laura's body? Her death was an accident."

"Well, we had . . . raped her, after all. And then she was lying there. All that blood. I don't know why we did it."

"What exactly did you do then?"

"Tobi's Golf was parked there, with the key in the ignition, as always. Felix put Laura in the trunk, and it was my idea to take her to the old airfield in Eschborn. I still had the keys because we'd been there a few days before, doing a little racing. We threw her down the hole and drove back. Nadia waited for us. Nobody at the fair had noticed that we were gone. Everybody was pretty drunk by then. And later we went to Tobi's place and asked him if he was coming back to the fair with us. But he didn't want to."

"And what about Stefanie Schneeberger?"

None of the three knew anything. In the pictures it looked like Nadia had hit Stefanie with the tire iron.

"Anyway, Nadia hated Stefanie like the plague," Felix Pietsch spoke up. "After Stefanie moved to town, Nadia couldn't get anything going with Tobi; he fell for Stefanie like a ton of bricks. And then she also snapped up the lead role that Nadia wanted to play."

"That evening at the fair Stefanie had been flirting a lot with Lauterbach," Jörg Richter recalled. "He was completely nuts about her; anyone with eyes in his head could see that. Tobi had caught the two of them making out near the tent, and that's why he went home. The last time I saw Stefanie was with Lauterbach near the tent."

Felix Pietsch confirmed this with a nod. Michael Dombrowski didn't react at all. He hadn't said a word but just sat there, pale and staring into space.

"Could Nadia have known about these paintings?" Pia asked.

"That's very possible. Tobi told us last Saturday what Amelie had found out. About the pictures and that Lauterbach seems to be in them. Tobi must have told Nadia about it too."

Pia's cell hummed. She recognized Ostermann's number and took the call.

"Excuse me for bothering you," he said. "But I think we've got a problem. Tobias Sartorius has disappeared."

Bodenstein stopped the interview and went outside. Pia gathered together the photos, put them back in the plastic folder, and followed him. He was waiting in the hallway, leaning against the wall with his eyes closed.

"Nadia must know what the pictures show," he said. "She was at Laura's funeral this morning, at the same time Thies's studio burned down."

"She could also be the woman who passed herself off as a policewoman to Barbara Fröhlich," Pia speculated.

"I think so too." Bodenstein opened his eyes. "And to make quite sure that no more paintings would turn up, she set fire to the orangerie while the whole village was at the cemetery."

He pushed off from the wall, walked down the corridor and up the stairs.

"She wouldn't want anyone to know that Amelie had found out the truth about the disappearance of the two girls in 1997," said Pia. "Amelie knew Nadia and had no reason not to trust her. Nadia could easily have thought up some pretext on Saturday night to lure the girl out of the Black Horse and into her car."

Bodenstein nodded, thinking it over. He now considered it highly possible that Nadia von Bredow had killed Stefanie Schneeberger. And now, fearing that what she'd done would be discovered, she had kidnapped and possibly killed Amelie.

When they reached Ostermann's office, they found him holding the phone in his hand.

"I spoke to the father and also sent a patrol over there. Tobias Sartorius drove off with his girlfriend this afternoon. She told old man Sartorius she was taking him to us. But since she hasn't shown up yet, I'm thinking they must have gone somewhere else entirely."

Bodenstein frowned, but Pia was quicker to pick up on what her colleague had said.

"With his *girlfriend*?" she asked. Ostermann nodded.

"Have you got Sartorius's number?"

"Yes." Pia went around his desk and, with a sense of foreboding, she reached for the phone. She pressed the REDIAL button and put it on speaker. Hartmut Sartorius answered after the third ring. She didn't even let him speak before she asked her question.

"Who is Tobias's girlfriend?" she wanted to know, although she had a pretty good idea.

"Nadia. But . . . but she wanted to take him . . ."

"Have you got a cell number for her? Or the license number of her car?"

"Yes, of course. But what's going on?"

"Please, Mr. Sartorius. Give me her cell number." Her eyes met Bodenstein's. Tobias Sartorius was with Nadia von Bredow en route somewhere and probably didn't have a clue what Nadia had done or what she might be planning. As soon as she jotted down the number, Pia hung up and punched it into the phone.

The number you have called is temporarily unavailable . . .

"Now what?" She didn't blame Bodenstein for sending the patrol to Lauterbach's house today. What's done is done.

"We'll send out an APB," Bodenstein decided. "Then we need to track her cell, as far as that's possible. Where does the woman live?"

"I'll find out." Ostermann rolled his chair back to the desk and dialed a number.

"What's going on with Claudius Terlinden?" Pia wanted to know.

"He'll have to wait." Bodenstein went to the coffee machine, shook the pot, which apparently still had coffee in it, and poured himself a cup. Then he sat down in Behnke's empty chair. "Lauterbach is much more important."

On the evening of September 6, 1997, Gregor Lauterbach had kissed Stefanie Schneeberger, his neighbor's daughter, at the fair in Altenhain, and later he was with her in Sartorius's barn. One painting didn't show Nadia fighting with Stefanie, but possibly Lauterbach having sex with the girl. Did

Nadia von Bredow find out about this? And later, when a suitable opportunity presented itself, did she strike her hated rival with a tire iron? Thies Terlinden had seen what happened. Who else knew that Thies was an eyewitness to both murders? Pia's cell phone hummed. It was Henning, who was already in the process of examining the mummified corpse of Stefanie Schneeberger.

"I need the murder weapon." He sounded tired and tense. Pia glanced at the clock on the wall. It was ten thirty and Henning was still at the lab. Had he confessed his juicy problem to Miriam in the meantime?

"You'll have it," she replied. "Do you think you can still get any DNA off the mummy? The girl possibly had sexual relations shortly before her death."

"I can try. The corpse is in very good shape. I estimate she was in that room all these years at stable temperatures, because she hasn't deteriorated much at all."

"How quickly can we get some results? We're under a lot of pressure here." That was certainly an understatement. Not only because they were still searching for Amelie, using all their resources and every available officer, but they were also in the middle of a new investigation of two eleven-year-old murder cases. The latter with only four detectives on it.

"So what else is new?" Henning said. "I'll hurry."

Bodenstein had finished his coffee.

"Come on," he said to Pia. "Let's get moving."

Bodenstein remained sitting behind the wheel for a while when he pulled into the parking area in front of his parents' estate. It was shortly after midnight and he was completely exhausted, but at the same time too wired even to think about going to bed. He had considered sending Felix Pietsch, Jörg Richter, and Michael Dombrowski home after the interview, but then the most important question of all occurred to him: Was Laura already dead when they threw her in the underground tank? The three men were silent for a long time. Suddenly it had dawned on them that it was no longer a matter of a rape or failing to help someone. They could be guilty of something far worse.

Pia had succinctly formulated the charges that might be filed against them: conspiring to cover up the death of an individual to conceal a felony. With that Michael Dombrowski broke down in tears. That was enough to constitute a confession for Bodenstein, and he had instructed Ostermann to prepare a warrant for their arrest. What the three had already told them was more than enough information. It had been years since Nadia von Bredow had contacted any friends from her youth. But shortly before Tobias was due to be released from prison, she had showed up in Altenhain and put major pressure on the three friends from the old days to keep their mouths shut. Since none of them were interested in having the truth come to light eleven years after the fact, they certainly would have continued to keep silent if another girl hadn't vanished. The fact that they bore responsibility for the wrongful conviction of their friend had weighed upon their consciences all these years. Even when the witch hunt directed at Tobias had started up, cowardice and fear of the inevitable consequences had been too great for them to turn themselves in to the police. Jörg Richter hadn't called up Tobias last Saturday simply out of old friendship. Nadia had asked him to invite Tobias that evening and encourage him to drink. And that confirmed Bodenstein's fears. But what got him to thinking most was what Jörg Richter said when asked the question: Why would three grown men listen to Nadia von Bredow?

"Even eleven years ago there was something about her that could throw fear into us." The others had nodded in agreement. "Nadia didn't get to where she is by accident. When she wants something, she gets it. Never mind who loses."

Nadia von Bredow had felt that Amelie Fröhlich was a threat and wanted to gain control over her. The fact that she wouldn't hesitate to kill someone was not a good omen.

Deep in thought, Bodenstein sat in his car. What a day! First the discovery of Lars Terlinden's body, then the fire in Thies's studio, Hasse's incredible admissions, the meeting with Daniela Lauterbach . . . Then he remembered that he was supposed to call her later, after she had told Christine Terlinden the bad news about her son's suicide. He took out his cell phone and searched the inside pocket of his coat until he found the doctor's business card. With heart pounding, Bodenstein waited to hear her voice. But in vain. He got her voicemail. After the beep he asked her to call him back at her convenience. He might have stayed sitting in his car if the coffee he'd drunk hadn't been pressing on his bladder. It was time to go inside anyway. He glimpsed a movement out of the corner of his eye and nearly jumped out of his skin when somebody knocked on the window.

"Dad?" It was Rosalie, his eldest daughter.

"Rosi!" He opened the door and got out. "What are you doing here?"

"I just got off work," she said. "But what are you doing here? Why aren't you at home?"

Oliver sighed and leaned against the car. He was dead tired and had no desire to talk about his problems with his daughter. All day long he'd been distracted from thinking about Cosima, but now the unbearable feeling of failure fell over him.

"Grandma told me that you slept here last night. What happened?" Rosalie gave him a worried look. In the dim glow of the single light her face looked ghostly pale. Why shouldn't he tell her the truth? She was old enough to understand what was going on, and she'd find out sooner or later anyway.

"Last night your mother told me that she's been seeing another man. As a result I preferred to sleep somewhere else for a few days."

"What?" Rosalie's face showed disbelief. "Why, that's . . . No, that's impossible."

Her bewilderment was real, and Bodenstein was relieved to know that his daughter wasn't a secret accomplice of her mother.

"Well," he said with a shrug. "I couldn't believe it at first either. It's going to take me a while."

Rosalie snorted and shook her head. But all at once every grown-up attitude fell away and she was again a little girl, completely overwhelmed by a truth that was just as incredible to her as it was to him. Oliver didn't want to pretend that everything would soon be straightened out. Nothing would ever be the same between him and Cosima. The hurt that she'd caused him was too severe.

"Well, what now? I mean . . . how . . . how . . ." Rosalie broke off. Helpless. All at once tears were running down her face. Oliver took his sobbing daughter in his arms, kissing her hair. He closed his eyes and sighed. How he longed to be able to let his own tears flow—to cry about Cosima, about himself and his life.

"We'll find a solution soon," he murmured, stroking his daughter's hair. "I have to digest it all first."

"But why did she do it?" Rosalie sobbed. "I don't understand it!"

They remained like that for quite a while, and then Oliver took her tear-stained face in his hands.

"Go home, my dear," he said softly. "Don't worry. Your mother and I will get this all straightened out somehow, okay?"

"But I can't just leave you here alone, Papa. And . . . and soon it'll be Christmas, and if you're not there it won't be a family celebration." She sounded desperate and just like herself. Even when Rosalie was little she had felt responsible for everything that happened in her family and her circle of friends—and often took on more burdens than she could cope with.

"It's still a few weeks till Christmas. And I'm not alone," he assured her. "Grandpa and Grandma are there, Quentin and Marie-Louise. It's not so bad."

"But aren't you sad?"

He had no reply.

"At the moment I have so much to do that I don't have time to be sad," he finally told her.

"Really?" Her lips quivered. "I can't stand the thought of you being sad and alone, Papa."

"Don't worry. You can call me anytime or send me a text. But now you have to go to bed, and I do too. Tomorrow we'll talk again, okay?"

Rosalie nodded unhappily and pulled herself together. Then she gave him a wet kiss on the cheek, hugged him one more time, got in her car and turned on the engine. He stood in the parking area and watched her go, until the taillights of her car disappeared in the woods. With a sigh he turned to go inside. Knowing that his children would still love him, even if his marriage broke up, filled him with both relief and solace.

Saturday, November 22, 2008

She sat up with a start. Her heart was pounding loudly, and with wide eyes she looked around, but it was as pitch dark as ever. What had woken her up? Had she really heard a noise or only dreamed it? Amelie stared into the dark and listened tensely. Nothing. She had only imagined it. With a sigh she got up from the musty mattress, grabbed her ankles, and massaged her cold feet. Even though she kept telling herself that they would find her, that she would survive this nightmare, she had secretly given up hope. Whoever had locked her in here never intended to let her out again. Until now Amelie had been able to ward off the recurring panic attacks. But now she was beginning to lose her courage, and she often simply lay there waiting for death. So many times she had told her mother, *I wish I was dead!*—but now she truly comprehended what she had uttered so thoughtlessly. She regretted bitterly how she had treated her mother out of spite and indifference. If only she came out of this alive, she would do everything, absolutely everything, differently. And better. No more talking back, no more running away or being ungrateful.

There had to be a happy ending. There always was. Most of the time, at least. She shuddered as she remembered all the newspaper stories and TV reports that did not have a happy ending. Dead girls buried in the woods, locked inside boxes, raped, tortured to death. Damn, damn, damn. She didn't want to die, not in this shitty hole, in the dark, lonesome and alone. She wouldn't starve very fast, but she could die of thirst. There was very little left to drink, so she was rationing the water to occasional sips.

Suddenly she gave a start again. She heard noises. She wasn't imagining it. Footsteps outside the door. They were coming closer and closer, then stopped. A key turned with a screech in the lock. Amelie wanted to stand up, but her body was stiff with cold and from the dampness that had crept into her bones after so many days and nights of dark imprisonment. A piercing light fell into the room, illuminating it for a few seconds and blinding her. Amelie blinked but couldn't see anything. Then the door closed again, the key turned with another screech, and the footsteps went away. Disappointment clutched at her and held her tight. No fresh water! Suddenly she thought she heard breathing. Was somebody else in the room? The fine hairs on the back of her neck stood up and her heart pounded like mad. Who was it? Was it a person? An animal? Fear threatened to choke off her breathing. She pressed her back against the damp wall.

Finally she gathered her courage together and whispered hoarsely, "Who's there?"

"Amelie?"

In disbelief she gasped for air. Her heart leapt for joy.

"Thies?" she whispered, feeling her way along the wall. It wasn't easy to keep her balance in the dark, although she had tried to memorize every square inch of the room. With outstretched arms she took two steps and flinched when she touched a warm body. She heard his excited breathing as she grasped his arm. Instead of retreating Thies grabbed her hand and held on tight.

"Oh, Thies!" Suddenly Amelie could no longer hold back the tears. "What are you doing here? Oh Thies, Thies, I'm so happy! So happy!"

She flung her arms around him and gave her tears free rein. Her knees felt weak, so great was her relief, finally, finally, not to be alone. Thies let her hug him. In fact, all at once she noticed that he was hugging her too. Cautiously and unpracticed. But then he pulled her close and rested his cheek on her hair. And all of a sudden she was no longer afraid.

Again the cell phone woke him. This time it was Pia, that merciless early riser, telling him at twenty past six that Thies Terlinden had escaped from the psychiatric ward during the night.

"The doctor called me," said Pia. "I'm here in the psych ward now, and I've spoken with the ward doctor and the night nurse. She looked in on him at eleven twenty-seven on her last round, and he was in bed asleep. When she looked the next time at five twelve, he was gone."

"What's their explanation?" Bodenstein was having a hard time getting out of bed. He'd had three hours of sleep at most, and he felt like he could barely move. First Lorenz had called him just as he'd fallen sleep. Then Rosalie, and it took him a great deal of effort to talk her out of getting in her car and coming over to see him. With a suppressed moan he finally succeeded in hauling himself into a vertical position. This time he reached the light switch by the door without running into anything.

"They can't explain it. They searched the whole place and he wasn't hiding anywhere. The door to his room was locked. It looks like he evaporated into thin air, the same as all the others. It's enough to make me sick."

There was no sign of Lauterbach or Nadia von Bredow or Tobias Sartorius, despite a nationwide APB in print, radio, and TV.

Bodenstein staggered into the bathroom, where during the night he had wisely turned up the heat and shut the window that had been open a crack. His face in the mirror was not a pleasant sight. As he listened to Pia talking, his thoughts kept churning. He had foolishly thought that Thies would be safe in the locked psych ward, but he should have known what danger he was in. He should have had a guard posted for Thies's protection. This was Bodenstein's second serious mistake in the past twenty-four hours. If things went on like this, he'd be the next one facing suspension. He said goodbye to Pia, pulled off his sweaty T-shirt and underpants and took a long shower. Time was running away from him. The whole case was threatening to slip out of his grasp. What did it all come down to, first and foremost? Where should he start? Nadia von Bredow and Gregor Lauterbach seemed to be the key figures in this tragedy. He had to find them.

Claudius Terlinden took the news of his son Lars's suicide without a flicker of emotion. After four days and three nights in police custody, his relaxed charm had given way to stubborn silence. On Thursday his lawyer had already lodged a protest, but Ostermann managed to convince the judge there was a danger of possible obstruction of justice. They wouldn't be able to detain him much longer unless there was conclusive evidence that he had no alibi for the time when Amelie disappeared.

"The boy was always too soft, his whole life," was Terlinden's only comment. With an open shirt collar, a three-day growth of beard, and straggly hair he had about as much charisma as a scarecrow. In vain Pia tried to recall what had been so fascinating about him.

"But you," she said sarcastically. "You're tough, right? You're so tough that you don't care about the consequences of all your lies and cover-ups. Lars committed suicide because he could no longer stand his guilty conscience. You stole ten years of Tobias Sartorius's life, and you terrorized Thies to such an extent that he's been looking after a dead girl for eleven years."

"I never terrorized Thies." Claudius Terlinden looked at Pia for the first time this morning. In his bloodshot eyes there was suddenly a vigilant expression. "And what dead girl are you talking about?"

"Oh, come on!" Pia shook her head angrily. "Are you trying to make me believe you don't know what was in the cellar under the orangerie in your garden?"

"No, I don't. I haven't been down there in twenty years."

Pia pulled out a chair from the table and sat down across from Terlinden.

"Yesterday in the cellar under Thies's studio we found the mummified corpse of Stefanie Schneeberger."

"What?" Uncertainty flared in his eyes for the first time. His façade of iron self-control showed its first tiny cracks.

"Thies saw who killed the two girls," Pia went on without taking her eyes off Terlinden. "Somebody found out about it and threatened to have Thies put in a home if he ever said a word. I'm firmly convinced that you were the one who told him that."

He shook his head.

"Last night Thies disappeared from the psychiatric ward after he told me what he'd seen eleven years ago."

"You're lying," Terlinden countered. "Thies never told you anything."

"That's right. His eyewitness account was nonverbal. He painted pictures that show the sequence of events in more detail than photos."

Finally Claudius Terlinden showed some reaction. His eyes shifted back and forth, and his restlessly moving hands betrayed his nervousness. Pia rejoiced inside. Would this conversation finally bring the breakthrough they needed so urgently?

"Where is Amelie Fröhlich?"

"Who?"

"Please! The reason you're sitting here facing me is because the daughter of your neighbor and employee Arne Fröhlich has disappeared."

"Ah yes, that's right. I'd forgotten for a moment. I don't know where the girl is. What interest would I have in Amelie?"

"Thies showed Amelie the mummy of Stefanie. He gave her the paintings that he made about the murders. Amelie was in the process of exposing all the dark secrets of Altenhain. And it's obvious that you wouldn't want that to happen."

"I don't know what you're talking about. What dark secrets?" He managed a scornful laugh. "You really watch too many soap operas. Incidentally, you have to let me go soon. Unless you have some specific charge against me, which I find hard to believe."

Pia didn't allow him to shake her. "Eleven years ago you advised your son Lars not to admit that he had anything to do with Laura Wagner's death, even though it was probably an accident. We're investigating at the moment whether that's enough to extend the detention order."

"Because I wanted to protect my son?"

"No. For obstruction of justice. For perjury. Take your pick."

"All that is ancient history." Claudius Terlinden scrutinized Pia coolly. He was a tough nut to crack, and Pia's confidence was fading.

"Where were you and Gregor Lauterbach after you left the Ebony Club?"

"That's none of your business. We didn't see the girl."

"Where were you? Why did you commit a hit-and-run?" Pia's voice grew sharper. "Were you so sure that nobody would dare turn you in?"

Claudius Terlinden didn't answer. He wasn't going to let himself be provoked into making a rash statement. Or was he perhaps really innocent? The evidence techs had been unable to find any trace of Amelie in his car. A hit-and-run accident was no grounds to hold the man any longer, and he was unfortunately right about the statute of limitations regarding the facts of the old case. Damn it.

Bodenstein drove along the now familiar main street, past Richter's grocery store and the Golden Rooster, and at the kindergarten turned left onto Wald-strasse. The streetlights were on; it was one of those days when it never really got light. He was hoping to find Lauterbach at home on an early Saturday morning. Why had the cultural minister incited Hasse to destroy the old transcripts? What role had he played in September 1997? He stopped in front of Lauterbach's house and saw to his dismay that, contrary to his orders, there were no patrol cars or even a plainclothes vehicle to be seen. Before he could telephone the station and voice his anger, the garage door opened and the backup lights of a car turned on. Bodenstein climbed out and walked over to the driveway. His heart skipped a beat when he saw Daniela Lauterbach behind the wheel of the dark-gray Mercedes. She stopped next to him and got out. He could see from her face that she hadn't gotten much sleep.

"Good morning. What brings you here so early?"

"I wanted to ask you how Mrs. Terlinden is doing. I've been thinking about her all night." It was a lie, but Daniela Lauterbach would surely take a sympathetic interest in her neighbor. He was right. Her brown eyes showed concern and the smile faded from her weary face.

"She's not doing well. Losing a son that way is beyond terrible. And then the fire in Thies's studio and the corpse in the cellar of the orangerie—it was all too much for her." She shook her head sadly. "I stayed with her until her sister arrived to help out."

"I really admire the way you support your friends and patients," Bodenstein said. "People like you are rare."

His compliment seemed to please her. She smiled again, that warm, motherly smile that seemed to trigger an almost irresistible need in him to throw himself into her arms, seeking comfort.

"Sometimes I care more about the fate of others than is good for me." She sighed. "But I simply can't hold back. When I see somebody suffering, I have to help."

Bodenstein shivered in the icy morning air. She noticed at once.

"You're cold. Let's go in the house, if you have any more questions for me."

He followed her through the garage and upstairs into a big entry hall, a relic of the eighties in all its uselessness.

"Is your husband home?" he asked in passing, looking around.

"No." For a fraction of a second she hesitated. "My husband is on a business trip."

If that was a lie, Bodenstein accepted it for the moment. Maybe she didn't know the game her husband was playing.

"I have to speak with him, urgently," he said. "We found out that he had an affair with Stefanie Schneeberger eleven years ago."

The warm expression vanished abruptly from her face, and she turned away.

"I know," she admitted. "Gregor told me about it then, although not until after the girl disappeared." It was obviously difficult for her to speak about her husband's infidelity.

"He worried that he'd been seen during his . . . bit of hanky-panky in Sartorius's barn and the police might consider him a suspect." There was bitterness in her voice and her gaze was somber. The betrayal still hurt, and it reminded Bodenstein of his own situation. Daniela Lauterbach may have forgiven her husband after eleven years, but she had definitely not forgotten the humiliation.

"But why is that important now?" she asked in confusion.

"Amelie Fröhlich was looking into those past events and must have found out about the affair. If your husband knew about it, he may have considered Amelie a threat."

Daniela Lauterbach stared at Bodenstein in disbelief.

"Surely you don't suspect my husband of having anything to do with Amelie's disappearance?"

"No, he's not a suspect," Bodenstein assured her. "But we urgently need to talk to him. He did something that could have legal implications for him."

"May I ask what that might be?"

"Your husband convinced one of my colleagues to remove the 1997 interview transcript from the official police records."

This news obviously gave her a shock. She turned pale.

"No." She shook her head resolutely. "No, I can't believe that. Why would he do such a thing?"

"That's what I'd like to ask him. So, where can I find him? If he doesn't get in touch with us immediately we'll have to launch a search for him. And I'd rather save him that embarrassment, given his position."

Daniela Lauterbach nodded. She took a deep breath, keeping her emotions under control with iron self-control. When she looked at Bodenstein again, another emotion was visible in her eyes. Was it fear or rage—or both?

"I'll call him and let him know," she said, trying with difficulty to lend her words a casual tone. "I'm sure there must be some kind of mistake."

"I think so too," Bodenstein agreed with her. "But the sooner we get this matter cleared up, the better."

It had been a long time since Tobias had slept so soundly and blissfully, without a single dream. He turned over on his back and sat up with a yawn. It took him a moment to realize where he was. Last night they had arrived here quite late. In spite of a heavy snowfall Nadia had exited the autobahn at Interlaken. Somewhere she had stopped, put chains on her car, and then drove on undaunted, up the steep switchback road, higher and higher. He was so tired and exhausted that he hardly noticed what the inside of the cabin looked like. He hadn't been hungry either, just followed her up a ladder and got into the bed, which took up the entire area of the loft. His head barely touched the pillow before he was asleep. No doubt the deep sleep had done him good.

"Nadia?"

No answer. Tobias hunched down to look out the tiny window by the bed. It took his breath away when he caught sight of the deep-blue sky, the snow, and the impressive mountain panorama in the distance. He had never been to the mountains; there had been no ski vacations in his childhood, just as there had been none to the sea. Suddenly he could hardly wait to touch the snow. He climbed down the ladder. The cabin was small and cozy, with wooden walls and ceiling, a corner bench with a table set for breakfast. It smelled like coffee, and logs crackled in the fireplace. Tobias smiled. He slipped on jeans, a sweater, jacket, and shoes, opened the door and stepped outside. For a moment he paused, blinded by the gleaming brightness. He inhaled the crystal-clear, icy air deep into his lungs. A snowball hit him right in the face.

"Good morning!" Nadia laughed, waving. She was standing a couple of yards below the steps, and her radiance competed with the snow and sunshine. He grinned, ran down the steps, and sank in up to his knees in powder snow. She came toward him, her cheeks red, her face more beautiful than ever under her fur-trimmed hood.

"Wow, is it great here!" he shouted enthusiastically.

"Do you like it?"

"Oh yeah! I've only seen something like this on TV."

He trudged all the way around the cabin, which nestled against the steep slope with its A-frame roof. The four feet of snow squeaked under his shoes. Nadia grabbed his hand.

"Look," she said. "Over there, those are the most famous peaks in the Bernese Alps: the Jungfrau, the Eiger, and the Mönch. I love the sight of them."

Then she pointed down into the valley. Way down there, hardly visible to the naked eye, houses stood tightly packed together, and a little farther off a long lake glittered blue in the sun.

"How high up are we here?" he asked.

"Fifty-nine hundred feet. Above us are only glaciers and chamois."

She laughed, threw her arms around his neck, and kissed him with her cold, soft lips. He held her tight and returned her kiss. He felt so light and free, as if he had left all the troubles of the past years somewhere far below, down in the valleys.

The case demanded so much of his attention that he had no time to worry about his own troubles. He was glad about that. For years Bodenstein had been confronted almost daily with the dark abysses of human nature, and for the first time he recognized parallels with himself that he had previously ignored. Daniela Lauterbach seemed to know as little about her husband as he knew about Cosima. It was shocking, but apparently it was possible to live with someone for twenty-five years, sleeping in the same bed and having children, without really knowing that person. Often enough there had been cases in which clueless relatives had lived with murderers, pedophiles, and rapists and were flabbergasted when they learned the awful truth.

Bodenstein drove past the Fröhlichs' house and the rear entrance to the Sartorius farm to the turnaround at the end of Waldstrasse and continued up the drive of the Terlindens' estate. A woman opened the front door. She had to be Christine Terlinden's sister, although he couldn't see much resemblance. The woman was tall and thin; the look she gave him testified to her self-confidence.

"Yes?" Her green eyes were direct and searching. Bodenstein introduced himself and told her that he wished to speak with Christine Terlinden.

"I'll go get her," said the woman. "I'm Heidi Brückner, by the way, Christine's sister."

She had to be at least ten years younger and, unlike her sister, seemed completely without pretensions. She wore her shiny brown hair in a braid, and her face, with the lovely complexion and high cheekbones, bore no trace of makeup. She let him in and closed the front door behind him.

"Please wait here."

She left and was gone for quite a while. Bodenstein studied the paintings on the walls, which were doubtless also done by Thies. They resembled the pictures in Daniela Lauterbach's office in their ghastly apocalyptic gloom: contorted faces, screaming mouths, chained hands, eyes full of fear and torment. Footsteps approached and he turned around. Perfectly coiffed blonde hair, a vacant smile on a face that showed no sign of her age.

"My deepest sympathy," said Bodenstein, holding out his hand.

"Thank you. That's very kind of you." She seemed not to bear a grudge that the police had been holding her husband for days. Nor had the suicide of her son, the fire in the studio, or the discovery of Stefanie Schneeberger's mummy left any visible traces. Astounding. Was she a master of repression or was she taking such strong tranquilizers that she hadn't yet taken it all in?

"Thies has been missing from the hospital since this morning," he said. "He didn't happen to come home, did he?"

"No." She sounded worried, but not excessively concerned. Bodenstein hadn't yet told her about what he found so strange. He asked her to tell him more about Thies, and was taken downstairs to his basement room. Heidi Brückner followed at a distance, silent and wary.

Thies's room was friendly and bright. Since the house was built on a slope, big picture windows gave him a great view of the village. There were books on the shelves and stuffed animals sitting on a couch. The bed was made and nothing had been left carelessly lying around. The room of a ten-year-old boy, not of a thirty-year-old man. Only the pictures on the walls were extraordinary. Thies had painted portraits of his family. And here it was evident what a wonderful artist he was. In the portraits he had captured not only the faces of the people but also their personality in a subtle way. Claudius Terlinden had a friendly smile at first glance, but his body language, the expression in his eyes, and the colors in the background lent the painting an ominous tone. His mother was painted rosy and bright, and at the same time flat and two-dimensional. A picture without depth for a woman with no real personality. Bodenstein thought the third picture was a self-portrait until he remembered that Lars was Thies's twin brother. It was painted in a totally different style, almost blurred, and showed a young man with still unfinished features and uncertain eyes.

"He's helpless," Christine Terlinden replied to Bodenstein's question of how Thies got along. "He can't cope with the world on his own, and he never carries any money. He can't drive a car either. Because of his illness he shouldn't have a driver's license, and it's also better that way. He can't assess danger."

"And people?" Bodenstein looked at Christine Terlinden.

"How do you mean?" She smiled in bewilderment.

"Is he able to assess people? Can he tell who is sympathetic to him and who isn't?"

"That . . . is not something I can judge. Thies doesn't speak. He avoids contact with other people."

"He knows very well who means him well and who doesn't," said Heidi Brückner from the doorway. "Thies is not mentally handicapped. Actually we don't really know the full extent of his abilities."

Bodenstein was surprised. Christine Terlinden didn't answer. She was standing at the window looking out at the cloudy gray of the November day.

"Autism," her sister went on, "can manifest itself in a wide range of ways. You simply stopped challenging him at some point, and instead stuffed him full of medications so that he'll stay calm and not cause any problems."

Christine Terlinden turned around. Her already motionless face now seemed completely frozen.

"Excuse me," she said to Bodenstein. "I have to let the dogs out. It's already eight thirty."

She left the room, her heels clicking on the stairs.

"She's escaping back to her everyday routines," Heidi Brückner noted with a hint of resignation in her voice. "She's always been like that. And she'll probably never change."

Bodenstein looked at her. There seemed to be little love lost between the two sisters. So why was she here?

"Come on," she said. "I want to show you something."

He followed her upstairs to the entry hall. Heidi Brückner stopped to make sure that her sister was nowhere to be seen, then strode over to the wardrobe and took out a purse that was hanging on a hook.

"I intended to give this to a pharmacist friend of mine," she explained softly. "But under the circumstances it seems better that the police have it."

"What is it?" Bodenstein asked curiously.

"A prescription." She handed him a folded piece of paper. "They've made Thies take this stuff for years."

Pia sat with a gloomy face at her desk typing the report about the interview with Pietsch, Dombrowski, and Richter into her computer. She was angry because she hadn't been able to keep Claudius Terlinden in custody any longer. His lawyer had lodged another complaint, insisting on the immediate release of his client. After consulting with Commissioner Engel, Pia had finally had to let him go. Her telephone rang.

"The girl's temple was definitely crushed by a blow with this tire iron," said Henning Kirchhoff in a sepulchral voice, without bothering to say hello. "And we did find foreign DNA in her vagina. But it'll take a while before we can narrow it down further."

"Okay, great," said Pia. "And what about the tire iron? Can you do another analysis of the traces left back then?"

"I'll check to see how busy our lab is." He paused briefly. "Pia . . ."

"Yes?"

"Did Miriam get in touch with you?"

"No. Why should she?"

"Because that stupid cow called her yesterday and told her I'd gotten her pregnant."

"Oh, shit. Now what?"

"Well." Henning heaved a sigh. "Miriam was completely calm. She asked me if that was possible. When I had to admit it was, she didn't say another word. She just picked up her purse and left."

Pia was careful not to give him a lecture about faithfulness and adultery. He didn't sound like he could cope with that at the moment. Although it was none of her business, she did feel sorry for her ex-husband.

"Have you considered that this Löblich woman might be trying to take you for a ride?" she asked. "If I were you, I'd make inquiries. Is she really pregnant? And if so, couldn't another man be involved?"

"That's not the point," he replied.

"What is the point then?"

Henning hesitated with his reply.

"I cheated on Miriam, fool that I am," he said after a while. "And she'll never forgive me for it."

Bodenstein looked at the private prescription that Dr. Lauterbach had written for Thies, and glanced at the names of the drugs. Ritalin, droperidol, fluphenazine, fentanyl, and lorazepam. Even as a layman he knew that autism was not a disease that could be treated with psychopharmaceuticals and sedatives.

"It's simply easier to solve problems with a chemical sledgehammer than via the difficult path of therapy." Heidi Brückner spoke in a muted voice, but the fury in her words was unmistakable. "My sister has taken the path of least resistance all her life. When the twins were small, she preferred traveling with her husband to looking after the kids. Thies and Lars experienced extreme neglect in their early childhood. Housemaids who spoke not a word of German were hardly the correct substitute for a mother."

"What are you trying to say?"

Heidi Brückner's nostrils flared.

"That Thies's problems were created at home," she said. "It quickly became clear that he had difficulties. He was aggressive, had a tendency to angry outbursts, and didn't obey. Until he was four or five he didn't speak a word. But who would he speak to? His parents were practically never home.

Claudius and Christine never tried to help the boy with therapies, they always relied on drugs. Thies would spend weeks completely sedated, just sitting around listlessly. As soon as they discontinued the medication he would flip out. They put him in the children's psychiatric clinic and left him there for years. What a nightmare. The boy is sensitive and highly intelligent and was forced to live with mentally handicapped patients!"

"Why didn't anyone intervene?" Bodenstein wanted to know.

"Who would have done that?" She sounded sarcastic. "Thies never had contact with normal people or with teachers who might have noticed what was wrong with him."

"You mean, he's not autistic after all?"

"No, he certainly is. But autism is not a clearly defined disease. It ranges from really serious mental handicaps to the mild manifestations of Asperger's syndrome, where the patient is perfectly capable of living an independent, though limited life. Many autistic adults learn to cope with their idiosyncrasies." She shook her head. "Thies is a victim of his egotistical parents. And Lars became one too."

"Oh?"

"As a child and teenager Lars was extremely shy. He hardly dared open his mouth to speak. In addition he was deeply religious, and wanted to be a pastor," said Heidi Brückner matter-of-factly. "Since Thies obviously couldn't take over the firm, Claudius pinned all his hopes on Lars. He refused to let him study theology, sent him to England, and made him take a degree in business administration. Lars was never really happy. And now he's dead."

"Why didn't you intervene, if you knew all this?" asked Bodenstein, disconcerted.

"I tried for many years." She shrugged. "Since I couldn't talk about it with my sister, I spoke to Claudius. It was 1994, I remember that very clearly, because I had just returned from Southeast Asia where I was working as a development aide. A lot had changed here. Wilhelm, my brother-in-law's older brother, had died a couple of years earlier; Claudius had taken over the firm and moved into this gigantic box of a house. I would gladly have stayed for a while to help out Christine a little."

She snorted contemptuously.

"Claudius didn't think that was a good idea. He never could stand me, because he couldn't intimidate and control me. I stayed two weeks and observed the whole scene. My sister would spend her days at one golf course after another, leaving the boys in the care of a housemaid from the village and this Daniela. One day Claudius and I got into an awful fight. Christine had gone to Mallorca, as she so often did. Fixing up the house there." Heidi Brückner laughed contemptuously. "That was more important than her sons. I had gone for a walk and came back in the house through the downstairs. I couldn't believe my eyes when I entered the living room and surprised my brother-in-law with the daughter of the housekeeper. The girl was no more than fourteen or fifteen . . ."

She broke off, shaking her head in disgust at the memory of this incident. Bodenstein was paying close attention. Her account jibed with what Claudius Terlinden himself had said—up to one decisive point.

"He had a full-blown erection when I came into the living room and screamed at him. The girl ran away. Claudius stood before me with his pants down, beet-red in the face. Denial was no longer possible. And suddenly Lars was standing there too. I'll never in my life forget the expression on his face. You can imagine why I haven't been welcome here since then. Christine never had the guts to rebel against her husband. She refused to believe me when I phoned her at once to tell her what I'd seen. She called me a liar and said I was just jealous. Today is the first time we've seen each other in fourteen years. And to be honest, I don't plan to stay long."

She heaved a sigh.

"I've always tried to make excuses for my sister," she went on after a moment. "Maybe it was a way to ease my guilty conscience. I've always secretly feared that one day things would end in disaster, but I never expected anything like this."

"And now?"

Heidi Brückner understood what Bodenstein meant.

"This morning I finally realized that having family ties to someone doesn't mean you have to defend their actions. My sister leaves everything to that Daniela, as she always has. What good am I here?"

"You don't like Dr. Lauterbach?" Bodenstein asked.

"No. I used to think there was something wrong with her. All that exaggerated concern for everyone. And the way she mothers her husband—I found that strange, almost sick." Heidi Brückner swept a stray lock of hair out of her face. Bodenstein saw a wedding ring on her left hand. For an instant he felt disappointed and then wondered why he had such an absurd reaction. He didn't know this woman at all, and after the investigation was over he would probably never see her again.

"After I saw those piles of medicines I thought even less of her," Heidi Brückner went on. "I'm no pharmacist, but I've extensively researched Thies's symptoms. That woman doesn't have to tell me a thing."

"Did you see her this morning?"

"Yes, she was here briefly to check on Christine."

"When did you arrive?"

"Last night around nine thirty. I left home at once after Christine called and told me what had happened. It takes me an hour to drive here from Schotten."

"You mean, Dr. Lauterbach wasn't here all night?" Bodenstein asked in surprise.

"No. She arrived a little while ago, around seven thirty, stayed for a cup of coffee, and then left. Why?" Her green eyes were inquisitive, but Bodenstein didn't reply. The pieces of the puzzle were falling into place as if by themselves. Daniela Lauterbach had lied to him. And certainly not for the first time.

"Here's my number." He handed her his business card. "And thank you so much for your candor. You've helped me a great deal."

"You're welcome." Heidi Brückner nodded and held out her hand. Her handshake was warm and firm. Bodenstein hesitated.

"Oh, in case I have another question—how can I reach you?"

A tiny smile flitted across her serious face. She pulled out her wallet and took out a card for him.

"I probably won't be here for much longer," she said. "As soon as my brother-in-law comes home, he'll undoubtedly throw me out."

•   •   •

After breakfast they had plodded through the deep snow for a couple of hours, enjoying the magnificent view of the Bernese Alps covered with snow. Then the weather suddenly changed, which was typical of the high mountains. Within minutes the radiant blue sky clouded over, and without warning a blizzard moved in. Hand in hand they returned to the cabin, breathlessly got out of their soaking wet clothing and climbed up the ladder to the loft stark naked. Heat from the wood stove had risen to the ceiling. Cuddled close together they lay on the bed while the wind howled around the cabin and the windowpanes rattled. They looked at each other. Her eyes were close to his and he could feel her breath. Tobias pushed the hair out of his face and shut his eyes when she slid down his naked body, licking his skin, teasing him with her tongue. All his pores broke out in a sweat as he panted, and his muscles tensed to the breaking point. With a moan he pulled her onto him and saw her face filled with lust. She began to move with more intensity, full of desire for him, and her sweat dripped onto him. Ecstatic joy flooded through him, then broke with unexpected force over him, and he felt as if the walls were swaying and the floor shaking beneath him. For a while they lay there, exhausted and happy, panting and waiting for their heartbeats to return to normal. Tobias took her face in his hands and gave her a long, tender kiss.

"That was wonderful," he said softly.

"Yes. That's how it will be forever and ever," Nadia whispered, her voice husky. "Just you and me."

Her lips brushed his shoulder, and smiling she snuggled up closer to him. He pulled the covers up over them and closed his eyes. Yes, that's how it would be. His muscles relaxed and he felt how tired he was.

But suddenly he pictured Amelie's face. It felt like he'd been punched in the face, and in a flash he was wide awake. How could he lie here so calmly while she was still missing and possibly fighting for her life somewhere?

"What is it?" Nadia murmured sleepily. It wasn't a good idea to talk about another woman in bed, but Nadia was also worried about Amelie.

"I was just thinking about Amelie," he replied honestly. "Where could she be? I hope nothing's happened to her."

He wasn't prepared for Nadia's reaction. She stiffened in his arms, jumped up and shoved him violently away from her. Her beautiful face was contorted with rage.

"Are you crazy?" she yelled, beside herself. "You fuck me and then start babbling about some other woman? Aren't I enough for you?"

She clenched her fists and pounded on his chest with a strength he wouldn't have believed possible. Tobias had a hard time defending himself. Panting and stunned by this outburst, he stared at her.

"You fucking asshole!" Nadia screamed, the tears gushing from her eyes. "Why do you always think about other women? I always had to listen to you talking about what you'd said and done with some other girl! Haven't you ever thought how that might hurt me? And now you're lying here with me in bed and jabbering about that . . . that little slut!"

The thick, damp fog lifted and completely dissipated in the Taunus. Driving on the B8, bright sunshine greeted them as they left the woods beyond Glashütten. Oliver flipped the sun visor down.

"Lauterbach will turn up," he said to Pia. "He's a politician and concerned about his reputation. His wife probably called him long ago."

"Well, I hope so." Pia didn't quite share the optimism of her boss. "Claudius Terlinden is being watched, at any rate."

The phone lines between K-11, the district attorney's office, and the court were jammed up since Jörg Richter's confession that Laura was still alive when he and his friends threw her into the underground tank. She had begged for her life, crying and screaming, until they had rolled the lid over the hole. It was clear that in the case of Laura Wagner the proceedings would have to be reopened, and that Tobias Sartorius would be exonerated. If he ever showed up. As of now there had been no sign of him.

Oliver turned left and drove through the village of Kröftel toward Heftrich. Just before the entrance to Heftrich stood the farm which Stefanie Schneeberger's parents had purchased ten years ago. A big sign pointed the way to the farm store, where only organic produce from their own fields that they had grown themselves was sold. Oliver pulled in at the farm, which was spick and span. They got out and looked around. There was hardly anything left of the dreary functionality of the former homestead farm, one of many that had been set up en masse in the sixties for returning Germans from eastern Europe. The Schneebergers had added on buildings and remodeled those that already existed. Under the new awning of the middle building, in which the farm store was located, fall flower arrangements waited for buyers. The roofs of the buildings were covered with solar and photovoltaic panels. Two cats were lolling on the steps of the farmhouse, enjoying the rare sunshine.

The store was closed for lunch, and no one answered the door at the house either. Oliver and Pia went into the bright barn where large stalls housed cows with calves, standing knee-deep in straw or lying contently chewing their cuds. What a sight, compared with the usual animal husbandry with its narrow pens. In the rear courtyard two eight- or nine-year-old girls were currying a horse that patiently submitted to their affectionate grooming.

"Hello!" Pia said to the two girls. They were as alike as two eggs and were unmistakably the younger sisters of the dead Stefanie. The same dark hair, the same big brown eyes. "Are your parents home?"

"Mom is over there in the horse stable," one of them replied, pointing to the long building behind the cow barn. "Dad is hauling away the manure with the tractor."

"All right. Thank you."

Beate Schneeberger was just sweeping the stable aisle when Oliver and Pia came inside. She looked up when the Jack Russell terrier that had been rummaging after mice in an empty stall began to bark.

"Hello?" Bodenstein called and then stopped. The terrier was small but still shouldn't be underestimated.

"It's all right to come closer." The woman gave him a friendly smile without interrupting what she was doing. "Bobby makes a lot of noise, but that's all. What can I do for you?"

Bodenstein introduced himself and Kirchhoff. Beate Schneeberger stopped. The smile vanished from her face. She was a beautiful woman, but care and sorrow had left clear traces on her even features.

"We came to tell you that your daughter Stefanie's body has been found," Bodenstein said.

Mrs. Schneeberger looked at him with big brown eyes and nodded. Like Laura's mother, she reacted calmly and with composure.

"Let's go in the house," she said. "I'll call my husband. He'll be here in a few minutes."

She leaned the broom on one of the stall doors and got her cell out of the pocket of her down vest.

"Albert," she said. "Can you please come to the house? The police are here. They've found Stefanie."

Amelie woke up because in her dream she thought she'd heard a light splashing sound. She was thirsty. She had a terrible, torturous thirst. Her tongue stuck to her palate and her mouth was as dry as paper. A couple of hours ago she and Thies had eaten the last couple of crackers and then drank the last of the water. Amelie had heard that people had saved themselves from dying of thirst by drinking their own urine. The narrow strip of light under the ceiling told her that outside their prison it was daytime. She could make out the contours of the bookshelf on the other side of the cellar room. Thies lay curled up next to her on the mattress, his head in her lap, sleeping soundly. How did he get here? Who had locked them both in? And where were they, anyway? Amelie's despair grew. She would have liked to cry, but she didn't want to wake up Thies, even though her leg had gone to sleep under the weight of his head. She licked her dry tongue over her chapped lips. There it was again. That gurgling and splashing sound. As if somewhere a faucet was running. If she got out of here she swore that she would never waste water again. She used to pour out whatever was left in a half-full bottle of soda if it had gone flat. What she wouldn't give now for a swallow of lukewarm, flat Coke.

Her gaze roamed over the room and stopped at the door. She couldn't believe her eyes when she saw that water was actually trickling through the gap. Excitedly she pushed Thies off her lap, swearing as her numb leg refused to obey. On all fours she crawled across the floor, which was already wet. Like a dog she greedily licked up the water, moistening her face and laughing. God had heard her desperate prayers. He wasn't going to let her die of thirst after all. More and more water was coming in under the door, splashing down the three steps like a lovely little waterfall. Amelie stopped laughing and straightened up.

"That's enough water, dear Lord," she whispered, but God didn't hear her. The water kept on coming, already forming a big puddle on the bare cement floor. Amelie's whole body began to tremble with fear. She had never wished for anything more ardently, but now that her wish for water had come true, this wasn't exactly what she had hoped.

Thies had woken up. He was sitting on the mattress with his arms wrapped around his knees, rocking back and forth. She frantically considered going over to the bookshelf and shaking it. It was rusty but seemed stable enough. Whoever had locked her and Thies in here must have turned on the water. This room was apparently deeper than the rest of the cellar. There was no drain in the floor, and the narrow light coming from outside was right under the ceiling. If the water kept running it would eventually flood the room. They would drown like rats. Amelie looked around wildly. Damn! She had survived this long without flipping out, without starving to death or dying of thirst, so she had no intention of drowning. She leaned over Thies and took his arm in a firm grip.

"Get up!" she ordered him. "Come on, Thies! Help me put the mattress on top of the bookshelf!"

To her amazement he stopped rocking back and forth and stood up. Together they managed to heave the heavy mattress onto the top of the bookshelf. Maybe the water wouldn't reach that far, then they'd be safe up there. And with each hour that passed the likelihood that someone would find them increased. Somebody would have to notice the running water—a neighbor, the water company, or someone else. Cautiously Amelie climbed up onto the bookshelf so that it wouldn't fall over. When she reached the top she stretched out her hand to Thies. She hoped the old rusty thing would hold both of them. A moment later he was sitting next to her on the mattress. In the meantime the water had covered the floor of the cellar room and was still flowing through the crack under the door. Now all they could do was wait. Amelie shifted her weight and carefully stretched out on the mattress.

"So," she said with a hint of gallows humor. "I guess that's what you get from wishing. When I was a kid I always wished for a bunk bed. Now I finally have it."

Beate Schneeberger led Oliver and Pia into the dining room and offered them seats at the massive table, right next to the huge tile stove radiating a pleasant warmth. From the many tiny rooms of the former farmhouse they had made a single huge room, and only the load-bearing beams remained. The result seemed modern and yet was surprisingly cozy.

"Please wait until my husband gets here," said Mrs. Schneeberger. "I'll make us some tea."

She went into the kitchen, which was also open on all sides. Oliver and Pia exchanged a glance. Unlike the Wagners, whose lives had fallen apart when their daughter disappeared, the Schneebergers seemed to have managed to survive the pain and start over. And then they had the twin girls.

Not five minutes later a big, gaunt, white-haired man in a checked shirt and blue work pants entered the dining room. Albert Schneeberger shook hands with Kirchhoff first, then Bodenstein. He too had a calm and serious demeanor. They waited until Mrs. Schneeberger had served the tea, then Bodenstein cautiously told them all the details. Albert Schneeberger stood behind his wife's chair, his hands resting lightly on her shoulders. Their sadness was palpable, but also the relief at finally learning the fate of their child.

"Do you know who did it?" asked Beate Schneeberger.

"No, we're not sure yet," said Bodenstein. "We only know that it could not have been Tobias Sartorius."

"Then he was convicted unjustly?"

"Yes, it looks that way."

For a while they said nothing. Albert Schneeberger looked thoughtfully out the big picture windows at his daughters, who were peaceably grooming the horse.

"I never should have let Terlinden talk me into moving to Altenhain," he said suddenly. "We had an apartment in Frankfurt but were looking for a house in the country, because in the city Stefanie had fallen in with the wrong crowd."

"How did you know Claudius Terlinden?"

"I actually knew Wilhelm, his older brother. We had studied together and later became business partners. After his death I got to know Claudius. My firm was one of his suppliers. Something developed between us that I falsely assumed was friendship. Terlinden rented us the house near his on the same street." Albert Schneeberger heaved a deep sigh and sat down next to his wife. "I knew that he was very interested in my company. Our know-how and patents were an ideal match for his concept and very important to him. At that time he was working on forming a corporation and going public. Eventually he made me an offer. There were several interested parties. Terlinden had a lot of competition at the time."

He paused and sipped his tea.

"Then our daughter disappeared." His voice sounded matter-of-fact, but they couldn't help noticing how difficult it was for him to recall those horrible events. "Terlinden and his wife were very sympathetic and attentive. Real friends, as we thought at first. I was hardly in a position to worry about my business. We did everything we could to search for Stefanie, got involved with various organizations, the radio, the TV. When Terlinden made me a new offer, I took it. The company didn't matter to me; I could only think of Stefanie. I always hoped that she would turn up someday."

He cleared his throat, struggling to maintain his composure. His wife put her hand on his and squeezed it gently.

After a while Schneeberger went on. "We had agreed that Terlinden would not change the structure of the company and would keep all the employees on. But what happened was the direct opposite. Terlinden found a loophole in the contracts. He went to the stock exchange, broke up my company, sold everything he didn't need, and laid off eighty of a hundred and thirty employees. I was in no position to defend myself. It was . . . horrible. All those people that I knew so well, were suddenly unemployed. None of it would have happened if I'd been able to think straight back then."

He rubbed his hand over his face.

"Beate and I decided to leave Altenhain. It had become intolerable to live next door to that . . . that man. The way he put pressure on the people in his company and in the village and manipulated them, and all under the pretense of his benevolence."

"Do you think that Terlinden did something to your daughter so he could get at your company?" Kirchhoff asked.

"Since they found Stefanie's ... corpse on his property, it seems quite possible." Schneeberger's voice faltered, and he pressed his lips together. "To be honest, my wife and I could never really imagine that Tobias would do anything to our daughter. But there was all that circumstantial evidence and all that testimony from witnesses. In the end we no longer knew what to believe. At first we suspected Thies. He used to follow Stefanie around like a shadow ..."

He shrugged helplessly.

"I don't know whether Terlinden would have gone that far," he said then. "But he exploited our situation without batting an eye. The man is an evil speculator and a liar with no conscience. He will literally trample on corpses to get whatever he wants."

Oliver's cell phone rang. He had turned over the wheel to Pia so he took the call without looking at the display. When he unexpectedly heard Cosima's voice, he gave a start.

"We have to talk," she said. "Reasonably."

"I don't have time right now," he replied. "We're in the middle of an interview. I'll call you later."

With that he punched off the conversation without saying good-bye. He'd never done that before.

They had left the valley and the bright sunshine was cut off. Gloomy gray fog surrounded them again. In silence they drove through Glashütten.

"What would you do in my place?" Oliver asked abruptly. Pia hesitated. She vividly remembered her disappointment when she learned about Henning's affair with District Attorney Valerie Löblich. By that time they had already been separated for more than a year. But Henning had continued to deny it until Pia caught him and Löblich in flagrante. Had her marriage not already been in pieces, that would have been the last straw. In Oliver's place she would never be able to trust Cosima again. When it came down to it, she had consistently lied to him. An affair was also something other than getting a little on the side, which under certain circumstances was excusable.

"You should talk to her," she advised her boss. "After all, you do have children together. And twenty-five years of marriage can't be swept away so easily."

"A super piece of advice," said Oliver mockingly. "Thanks a lot. So what do you really think?"

"Do you really want to know?"

"Sure. Otherwise I wouldn't have asked."

Pia took a deep breath.

"When something is broken, it's broken. And even if you patch it up, it'll never be whole again," she said. "That's my opinion. Sorry if you were expecting something different."

"I wasn't." To her astonishment Oliver even smiled, although not very happily. "Your honesty is what I especially appreciate about you."

His cell rang again. This time he looked at the display first to save himself another unpleasant surprise.

"It's Ostermann," he said, and took the call. He listened for a few seconds and nodded. "Call Dr. Engel. She should be there when we talk to him."

"Tobias?"

"No." Bodenstein took a deep breath. "The cultural minister has turned up and is waiting for us, along with his lawyer."

They conferred outside the door to the interview room in which Bodenstein had placed Gregor Lauterbach and his lawyer. He didn't want a friendly, casual atmosphere; Lauterbach had to be made aware that he couldn't expect special treatment.

"How do you want to play this?" Commissioner Engel asked.

"I'm going to put him under massive pressure," said Bodenstein. "We don't have any time to lose. Amelie has been gone for a week now, and if we expect to find her alive we can't handle anybody with kid gloves."

Nicola Engel nodded. They entered the sparsely furnished room, one wall of which was taken up by a one-way mirror. At a table in the middle sat Cultural Minister Lauterbach and his attorney, whom Bodenstein and Kirchhoff knew well; he was not going to make things pleasant for them. Dr. Anders defended prominent citizens, almost without exception, who were involved in murder and manslaughter cases. It didn't bother him to lose trials, because he wanted most of all to get his name in the papers and hopefully bring his cases up for appeal before the federal supreme court.

Gregor Lauterbach recognized the seriousness of the situation and had decided to cooperate. Pale and visibly shaken, he related in a low voice the events of September 6, 1997. On that evening he had met his pupil Stefanie Schneeberger in the barn of the Sartorius farm to explain to her that he did not intend to start anything with a pupil. Then he went home.

"The next day I heard that Stefanie and Laura Wagner had vanished without a trace," said Lauterbach. "Someone called us and said the police would direct their suspicions at Stefanie's friend, Tobias Sartorius, for the murder of both girls. My wife found a bloody tire iron in our garbage can. I then told her that I had spoken with Stefanie because she had been pestering and flirting with me all evening at the village fair. It was clear to both of us that Tobias must have thrown the tire iron into our garbage can after he killed Stefanie in a fit of anger. Daniela wanted to prevent any gossip from focusing on me. She told me to bury the tire iron somewhere. I don't know why I did it—it was probably a knee-jerk reaction—but I threw the tire iron into Sartorius's cesspool."

Bodenstein, Kirchhoff, and Nicola Engel listened quietly. Even Dr. Anders said nothing. With his arms crossed and his lips pursed he stared as if uninvolved into the mirror across from him.

"I . . . I was convinced that Tobias had beaten Stefanie to death with it," Lauterbach went on. "He had seen us together, and then she broke up with him. By throwing the tire iron into our garbage can he wanted to cast suspicion on me. Out of revenge."

Bodenstein looked at him sharply. "You're lying."

"No, I am not." Lauterbach swallowed nervously. He looked over at his lawyer, but Anders was still raptly studying his own image in the mirror.

"We've discovered in the meantime that Tobias Sartorius had nothing to do with the murder of Laura Wagner." Bodenstein spoke more aggressively than was his habit. "We found the mummified corpse of Stefanie. And we have retrieved the tire iron from our evidence room and sent it to the lab. They can probably still get fingerprints off it. In addition, the medical examiner has found traces of foreign DNA in the body. Semen. If it turns out that it's yours, you'll be in a hell of a mess, Mr. Lauterbach."

Gregor Lauterbach fidgeted on his chair and licked his lips nervously.

"How old was Stefanie at the time?" Bodenstein asked.

"Seventeen."

"And how old were you?"

"Twenty-seven." Lauterbach was almost whispering. His pale cheeks flushed blood-red and he lowered his eyes.

"Did you have relations with Stefanie Schneeberger on September 6, 1997, or not?"

Lauterbach was petrified.

"You're bluffing," said his lawyer, finally coming to his aid. "The girl could have slept with anyone."

"What clothes were you wearing on the evening of September 6, 1997?" Bodenstein didn't let himself be put off, and he didn't take his eyes off Lauterbach, who looked at him in bewilderment and shrugged.

"I submit to you that you were wearing jeans, a light blue shirt over a green T-shirt from the fair committee, and light brown shoes."

"What does that have to do with the case?" Lauterbach's lawyer wanted to know.

"Here." Bodenstein paid no attention to him. He took the printouts of Thies's paintings from the file and laid them out for Lauterbach, one after the other. "These pictures were painted by Thies Terlinden. He was an eyewitness to both murders, and this was his way of communicating what he saw."

He tapped his finger on one of the figures.

"Who could that be?" he asked. Lauterbach stared at the pictures and shrugged.

"That's you, Mr. Lauterbach. You kissed Stefanie Schneeberger at the fair and then you had sexual relations with her."

"No," Gregor Lauterbach murmured, white in the face. "No, no, that's not right, you have to believe me!"

"You were her teacher," Bodenstein went on, unperturbed. "Stefanie was in a subordinate position to you. What you did is punishable by law, and you

suddenly realized that. You had to be afraid that Stefanie would tell someone about it. A teacher who has sex with his underage pupil is finished."

Gregor Lauterbach shook his head.

"You beat Stefanie to death, threw the tire iron into the cesspool, and
went home. There you confessed everything to your wife, and she advised
you to keep your mouth shut. Her prediction of what would happen worked,
but not entirely. The police did hold Tobias responsible for the murder, and
he was arrested and convicted. There was only one small problem: Stefanie's
body had disappeared. Someone must have seen you with Stefanie."

Lauterbach was still shaking his head.

"You suspected Thies Terlinden of being an accessory. So that he would
keep his mouth shut, your wife—as Thies's doctor—administered drugs to the
young man on a regular basis and exerted intense intimidation. That worked
fine for eleven years. Until Tobias Sartorius was released from prison. You
learned from your acquaintance Andreas Hasse, a member of K-11, that we
were interested in the old case, yes, that we had even gotten hold of the old
files. And then you persuaded Hasse to remove the relevant interview transcripts from the files."

"That's not true," Lauterbach whispered hoarsely. Beads of sweat glistened on his forehead.

"Yes, it is," Kirchhoff now said. "Hasse has already admitted it and as a
result has been suspended from duty. If you hadn't done that, you wouldn't
be sitting here."

"What is the point of all this?" Dr. Anders put in. "Even if my client had
sexual relations with his pupil, the statute of limitations on the assault expired
long ago."

"But not on the murder."

"I didn't murder Stefanie!"

"Then why did you talk Mr. Hasse into destroying the interview transcripts?"

"Because . . . because I . . . I . . . I thought it would be better if I kept my
name out of all this," Lauterbach admitted. The sweat was now running
down his cheeks. "Could I have something to drink?"

Nicola Engel stood up without a word, left the room, and returned a moment later with a bottle of water and a glass. She set both in front of Lauterbach and sat down. Lauterbach unscrewed the cap, poured himself a glass of water, and drank the whole thing.

"Where is Amelie Fröhlich?" Kirchhoff asked. "And where is Thies Terlinden?"

"How should I know?" said Lauterbach.

"You knew that Thies witnessed everything back then," Kirchhoff replied. "You also found out that Amelie was interested in the events of 1997. Both of these facts presented a threat to you. So it's not hard to imagine that you had something to do with their disappearance. At the time Amelie vanished, you and Terlinden were at the very spot where she was last seen."

In the harsh fluorescent light Gregor Lauterbach looked like a zombie. His face glistened with sweat, and he was rubbing his palms nervously on his thighs until his lawyer put his hand on his arm.

"Mr. Lauterbach." Bodenstein stood up, rested his hands on the tabletop, and leaned forward. "We're going to compare your DNA with that found in the vagina of Stefanie Schneeberger. If it's a match, you will be charged with statutory rape of an underage pupil, regardless of what your lawyer here says about the time limit running out. Based on these accusations that will be the end of your tenure as cultural minister. I will do my best to bring you to trial, I promise you that. I don't have to tell you what the press will do when it comes out that because of your silence an innocent young man, a former pupil of yours at that, had to serve ten years in prison!"

He fell silent and let his words sink in. His threatening tone had its effect, and Gregor Lauterbach was shaking all over. What did he fear more—the punishment he was facing or a possible public execution by the press?

"Tonight I'm going to give you one more chance," said Bodenstein, now in a calm voice. "I will refrain from instigating legal proceedings with the district attorney's office if you help us find Amelie and Thies. Think it over and discuss it with your lawyer. We'll now take a ten-minute break."

"That bastard," said Pia, glaring at Lauterbach through the one-way glass. "He did it. He killed Stefanie. And now he's snatched Amelie, I'm sure of it."

They couldn't hear what Lauterbach was discussing with his lawyer, because Dr. Anders had insisted that they turn off the microphone.

"Together with Terlinden." Oliver frowned in thought as he sipped water from a paper cup. "But how did he find out that Amelie might know something?"

"No idea." Pia shrugged. "Maybe Amelie mentioned something about the paintings to Terlinden? But no, I don't think so."

"Me neither. There's still a piece missing. Something must have happened to scare Lauterbach."

"Hasse?" Nicola Engel suggested from the background.

"No, he didn't know about the paintings," said Pia. "We didn't find them until he was out of the picture."

"Hmm. Then we're actually missing a connection here."

"Just a moment," Oliver said. "What's the deal with Nadia von Bredow? She was there when the boys raped Laura. And she's in one of the pictures with Stefanie and Lauterbach in the background."

Dr. Engel and Pia gave him a quizzical look.

"What if she was in the barnyard the whole time? She didn't ride off with the boys to hide Laura's body. And Nadia knew about the paintings, because Tobias told her about them."

Dr. Engel and Pia instantly understood what Oliver was getting at. Had Nadia von Bredow blackmailed Lauterbach with what she knew and forced him to act?

"Let's go back in." Oliver tossed the cup into the trash can. "I think we've got him."

The water was rising. Inch by inch. In the last light of day Amelie had seen that it was up to the third step. Her attempt to block the water from coming in with a thick woolen blanket worked until the water pressure pushed the blanket away. Now it was pitch dark, but she could hear the steady rush of water in the pipes. In vain she sought to calculate when the water would reach the top of the bookshelves. Thies lay close beside her, and she could feel his chest rising and falling. Now and then he coughed and wheezed. His skin was feverishly hot, and the cold dampness in this hole would finish him off. Amelie remembered that he'd been looking ill lately. How was he going to survive all this? Thies was so sensitive. A couple of times she had tried talking with him, but he hadn't answered.

"Thies," she whispered. It was hard for her because her teeth were chattering so hard that she could hardly open her mouth. "Thies, say something."

Nothing. And then she finally lost heart. Her iron self-control, which had kept her from flipping out in the dark over all these days and nights, had vanished. She broke down in tears. There was no hope left. She was going to die in here, drowning miserably. Snow White had never been found either. Why should she have any better luck? Fear overpowered her. Suddenly she flinched. She felt something touch her back. Thies put his arm around her, slipped his leg over hers, and held her tight. The heat radiating from his body warmed her.

"Don't cry, Amelie," he whispered in her ear. "Don't cry. I'm here."

"How did you learn of the existence of these pictures?"

Bodenstein didn't dwell on a long introductory speech. He could easily see the condition Gregor Lauterbach was in. The minister was not a particularly strong man, and the pressure was really getting to him. After the trying events of the last few days he wouldn't be able to hold out much longer.

"I've received anonymous letters and e-mails," replied Lauterbach, silencing his lawyer with a feeble motion of his hand when he tried to protest. "That evening in the barn I had lost my keys, and in one of the letters there was a photo of the key ring. Then it was clear to me that somebody had seen Stefanie and me."

"Seen you doing what?"

"You know." Lauterbach looked up, and Bodenstein read in his eyes nothing but self-pity. "Stefanie had been tantalizing me the whole time. I . . . I didn't want to . . . sleep with her, but she badgered me so much that I . . . simply couldn't do anything else."

Bodenstein waited silently until Lauterbach spoke again in a whiny voice.

"When I . . . when I noticed that I'd lost my key ring, I wanted to go look for it. My wife would have ripped my head off, because the keys to her office were on it too."

He looked up, pleading for understanding. Bodenstein had to force himself to conceal his growing contempt for this man.

"Stefanie said I'd better leave. She would look for the keys and bring them to me later."

"And did she do that?"

"Yes. I'd gone home by then."

Bodenstein left it at that for the moment.

"So you received letters and e-mails," he said. "What was in them?"

"That Thies knew everything. And that the police would not find out if I kept my mouth shut."

"What were you supposed to keep your mouth shut about?"

Lauterbach shrugged and shook his head.

"Who do you think wrote these letters to you?"

Again a helpless shrug.

"You must have some sort of idea. Come on, Mr. Lauterbach!" Bodenstein leaned forward again. "Keeping silent now is the worst possible solution."

"But I really have no clue!" said Lauterbach in impotent despair which was obviously not faked. Alone and backed into a corner, he showed his true colors: Gregor Lauterbach was a weak man, and without his wife's protection he shrank to a spineless homunculus. "I don't know anything else! My wife told me that there were pictures, but Thies couldn't have written the letters and e-mails."

"When did she tell you about the paintings?"

Lauterbach rested his forehead on his hands, shook his head. "I don't remember exactly."

"Try to remember," Bodenstein pressed. "Was it before or after Amelie disappeared? And how did you wife know about them? Who could have told her?"

"My God, I don't know!" Lauterbach wailed. "I really don't know!"

"Think!" Bodenstein leaned back. "On the Saturday evening that Amelie disappeared, you went to dinner with your wife and the Terlindens at the Ebony Club in Frankfurt. Your wife and Christine left for home at nine thirty, and you rode back with Claudius. What did you do after you left the Ebony Club?"

Gregor Lauterbach paused to think. He seemed to realize that the police knew a lot more than he'd assumed.

"Okay, I think my wife told me on the way to Frankfurt that Thies had given the neighbor girl some sort of pictures and I was in them," he admitted reluctantly. "She found out about them that afternoon, from an anonymous phone call. We didn't have time to discuss it further. Daniela and Christine left at nine thirty. I asked Andreas Jagielski about Amelie Fröhlich; I knew that she waited tables at the Black Horse. Jagielski called his wife and she told him that Amelie was at work. So Claudius and I drove to Altenhain and waited for the girl in the parking lot at the Black Horse. But she never showed up."

"What did you want to find out from Amelie?"

"Whether she was the one who had written those anonymous e-mails and letters to me."

"And? Did she?"

"I didn't get a chance to ask her. We waited in the car, it was about eleven or eleven thirty. Then Nathalie showed up. I mean Nadia. Nadia von Bredow she calls herself now."

Bodenstein looked up briefly and met Pia's gaze.

"She ran around the parking lot," Lauterbach went on, "looking in the bushes, and finally she went across the street to the bus stop. That was when we first noticed a man sitting there. Nadia tried to wake him up, but she couldn't. Finally she drove off. Claudius called the Black Horse on his cell and asked for Amelie, but Mrs. Jagielski told him she'd left a long time ago. Then Claudius and I drove to his office. He was afraid the police would come snooping around. The last thing he needed was a police search, so he wanted to store some incendiary documents somewhere else."

"What sort of documents?" asked Bodenstein.

Gregor Lauterbach resisted a bit, but not for long. Claudius Terlinden had secured his position of power over the years by bribery on a grand scale. Of course he'd always been wealthy, but he didn't come into the big money until the late nineties, when he expanded his firm and took it public on the stock exchange. That was how he acquired major influence in the worlds of business and politics. He had done the best deals with countries against which an official trade embargo had been imposed, such as Iran and North Korea.

"He wanted to get rid of those documents that evening," Lauterbach concluded. Now that he was no longer the immediate target, he had regained some of his self-confidence. "Since he didn't want to destroy them, we took them to my house in Idstein."

"I see."

"I have nothing to do with the disappearance of Amelie or Thies," Gregor Lauterbach declared. "And I haven't murdered anyone."

"That remains to be seen." Bodenstein gathered up the pictures and put them back in the file. "You can go home now. But you're under police surveillance, and we'll be monitoring your telephone. I would also like to ask you to remain available. In any event, let me know before you leave your house."

Lauterbach nodded meekly. "Could you at least keep my name out of the media for the time being?" he pleaded.

"That's not something I can promise you." Bodenstein held out his hand. "The key to your house in Idstein, please."

Sunday, November 23, 2008

Pia had spent a sleepless night and was already on her feet when the call came at 5:15 A.M. from the surveillance team: Nadia von Bredow had just returned to her apartment at the West Harbor in Frankfurt. Alone.

"I'll be right there," said Pia. "Wait for me."

She tossed the hay that she was holding under her arm over the door of the horse stall and put away her cell phone. The case wasn't the only thing that had kept her awake. Tomorrow at three thirty in the afternoon she had an appointment for an inspection at Birkenhof by the zoning office of the city of Frankfurt. If they didn't cancel the demolition order, she, Christoph, and the animals would soon be homeless.

In the last few days Christoph had been worrying himself sick about the matter, and his former optimism had swiftly evaporated. The seller of

Birkenhof had failed to mention to Pia that there was a construction ban on the land where the house stood because of the high-tension lines from the power plant. The seller's father had erected a hut sometime after the war and had expanded it over the years without a building permit. For sixty years no one had noticed until she had applied for a building permit, ignorant of the illegality.

Pia quickly fed the poultry, then she phoned Bodenstein. When he didn't answer, she wrote him a text and then, lost in thought, walked back to the house, which suddenly seemed foreign to her. On her tiptoes she crept into the bedroom.

"Do you have to go?" asked Christoph.

"Yes. Did I wake you?" She turned on the light.

"No. I couldn't sleep either." He looked at her, his head propped on his hand. "I've been wondering for half the night what we can do if they're serious."

"Me too." Pia sat down on the edge of the bed. "Anyway, I'm going to sue the shitheads that sold me this property. It was malicious fraud, most definitely."

"We'll have to prove it first," Christoph noted. "I'm going to discuss it today with a friend of mine who knows about these things. Until then we won't do anything."

Pia sighed. "I'm so glad you're here," she said softly. "I don't know what I would have done alone."

"If I hadn't come into your life, you would never have applied for a building permit, and nothing would have happened." Christoph gave her a crooked grin. "Now don't get discouraged. Go do your job and I'll worry about all this, okay?"

"Okay." Pia managed a smile. She bent over and gave Christoph a kiss. "Unfortunately I have no idea when I'll be home tonight."

"Don't worry about me." Christoph smiled too. "I have to work at the zoo."

Bodenstein recognized her familiar figure from far away. She was standing in the light of the streetlamp next to her car in the parking lot, her red hair the only spot of color in the misty darkness. He hesitated a moment before he strode over to her. Cosima was not a woman who would allow anyone to hang up on her. Actually he should have known that sooner or later she would waylay him, but the case he was working on had monopolized his attention. So now he felt unprepared and at a disadvantage.

"What do you want?" he asked gruffly. "I don't have time for this."

"You didn't call me back," said Cosima. "I have to talk with you."

"Jeez, right now?" He stood in front of her, studying her pale, composed face. His heart was pounding and it took a real effort to remain calm. "You haven't felt the need to talk to me in weeks. Go find your Russian friend if you're in the mood to talk."

He pulled out his car key, but she didn't budge from the spot where she was standing next to the car door.

"I want to explain—" she began.

"I don't want to hear it. And I really don't have time right now," Oliver interrupted her. He had barely slept all night and had to get going urgently, which made for rather poor conditions for an important talk like this.

"Oliver, please believe me, I didn't want to hurt you!" Cosima reached out her hand to him, but let it drop when he shrank back. Her breath stood like a white cloud in the cold morning air. "I didn't want to go that far, but—"

"Just stop!" he shouted. "You did hurt me! More than any person ever has! I don't want to hear any excuses or justifications from you, because no matter what you say, you've ruined everything! Everything!"

Cosima didn't say a word.

"Who knows how many times you've cheated on me before? The way you've played me for a fool and lied to me is such a cliché," he went on through clenched teeth. "What did you do on all those business trips? How many beds did you waltz through while your stupidly naïve and trusting bourgeois husband dutifully stayed home with the kids and waited for you? Maybe you even had a laugh at my expense because I was dumb enough to trust you!"

Like poisonous lava these words erupted from the depths of him; finally all the bottled-up disappointment came pouring out. Cosima let his anger wash over her without batting an eye.

"Maybe Sophia isn't even my child—maybe she's the brat of one of those shaggy, dubious film types you like to hang out with!"

He stopped talking when he realized how monstrous this reproach was. But now that he'd said it, he couldn't take it back.

"I would have bet my life on our marriage," he said in a strained voice. "But you've lied to me and betrayed me. I'll never be able to trust you again."

Cosima straightened her shoulders.

"I thought you'd react like this," she responded coolly. "Self-righteous and uncompromising. You see the whole thing only from your own egotistical point of view."

"How else would I see it? From the point of view of your Russian lover?" He snorted. "You're the one who's selfish. For twenty long years you never once asked me how I was doing. You went off traveling for weeks at a time. I never liked it, but I accepted it because your work is important to you. Then you got pregnant. You never asked me if I wanted another child, you made the decision all on your own and presented me with the facts. You should have known that with a little baby you wouldn't be able to go globetrotting. Then out of sheer boredom you plunged into an affair—and now you want to accuse me of being selfish? If it wasn't all so sad, I'd have to laugh!"

"When Lorenz and Rosi were small, I was still able to work. And sometimes you did take over the responsibility," Cosima argued. "But that's not what I want to discuss with you. What's past is past. I made a big mistake, but I'm certainly not going to go around in sackcloth and ashes until you decide to forgive me."

"So why are you here?" The cell phone in his coat pocket rang and vibrated, but he ignored it.

"After Christmas I want to accompany Gavrilow's expedition through the Northwest Passage for four weeks," Cosima informed him. "You'd have to take care of Sophia while I'm gone."

Speechless, Oliver stared at his wife as if she'd just slapped him. Cosima hadn't come to ask his forgiveness—no, she had long ago made up her mind about her future. A future in which he was relegated to the job of babysitter. His knees felt as soft as butter.

"You can't be serious," he whispered.

"Oh yes I am. I signed the contract a couple of weeks ago. It was clear to me that you wouldn't approve." She shrugged. "I'm sorry it had to come up this way, honestly. But I've been doing a lot of thinking the past few months. I would regret it to the end of my days if I don't make this film . . ."

She kept on talking but her words no longer registered with him. He'd understood the most important thing: In her heart she had left him long ago, rejecting the life they had shared. Actually he'd never really been sure of her. All these years he had thought that the contradictory side of her personality was what made their relationship special, like adding salt to the soup. But now he realized that they just didn't fit together. He felt a painful pang in his heart.

And now she was doing the same thing she'd done so many times before: She had made a decision that he was forced to accept. She was the one who always determined the direction of their lives. She had the money. She had bought the property in Kelkheim and paid for the house to be built. He could never have afforded all that. It hurt, but on this gloomy November morning he saw for the first time that Cosima was no longer the beautiful, self-assured, exciting companion he wanted at his side. Instead she was the woman who ruthlessly pushed through her will and her plans. How stupid and blind he'd been all this time!

The blood was roaring in his ears. She had stopped talking and looked at him unmoved, as if waiting for a reply. He blinked. Her face, the car, the parking lot—it all blurred before his eyes. She wanted to leave him for another man. She wanted to live her life, and there was no longer any room for him in it. Suddenly jealousy and hatred overwhelmed him. He took a step toward Cosima and grabbed her wrist. Shocked, she tried to pull away, but he held her hand tight, as if in a vise. Her cool superiority vanished abruptly, and she opened her eyes wide in fear. Then she opened her mouth to scream.

At six thirty Pia decided to go to Nadia von Bredow's condo without her boss. Bodenstein wasn't answering his cell and hadn't responded to her text.

Just as she was about to press the doorbell, the front door opened and a man came out. Pia and her two plainclothes colleagues who'd been staked out at the apartment started to slip past him to enter the building.

"Stop!" The slightly graying man in his mid-fifties and wearing round horn-rims blocked their way. "This is not allowed! Who are you looking for?"

"None of your business," Pia snapped back.

"It certainly is." The man took up position in front of the elevator, crossed his arms, and scrutinized her arrogantly. "I'm the chairman of the owners' association. You can't just walk right in here."

"We're from the criminal police."

"Oh yeah? Have you got an ID?"

Pia was boiling with fury. She pulled out her ID and shoved it in front of the man's nose. Without another word she started for the stairs.

"You can wait down here," she told one of her colleagues. "The two of us will go up."

They had barely reached the door of the penthouse apartment when it opened. A brief look of fear was evident on the face of Nadia von Bredow.

"I told you to wait downstairs," she said curtly. "But as long as you're here you can take the suitcases."

"Are you going away?" Pia realized that Nadia von Bredow didn't recognize her and probably took her for the cab driver. "But you just got home."

"What business is it of yours?" she replied irritably.

"Quite a bit, I think." Pia held out her ID. "Pia Kirchhoff, Hofheim Criminal Police."

Nadia von Bredow looked her up and down and stuck out her lower lip. She was wearing a dark-brown Wellensteyn jacket with a fur collar, jeans, and boots. She had pulled back her blonde hair in a tight knot, but even her carefully applied makeup couldn't hide the shadows under her red-rimmed eyes.

"You're coming at a bad time. I have to rush to the airport."

"Then you'll have to take a later flight," said Pia. "I have a few questions for you."

"I don't have time for this right now." She pushed the button for the elevator.

"Where have you been?" asked Pia.

"Traveling."

"I see. And where is Tobias Sartorius?"

Nadia von Bredow gave Pia an astounded look with her grass-green eyes.

"How should I know?" Her surprise seemed genuine, but she wasn't one of the best-paid actors in Germany for nothing.

"Because you drove off with him after Laura Wagner was buried instead of dropping him off with us for questioning."

"Who said that?"

"Tobias's father. So?"

The elevator arrived and the door slid aside. Nadia von Bredow turned to Pia and gave her a mocking smile.

"I hope you don't believe everything he tells you." She looked at Pia's colleague. "The police: to serve and protect. Would you mind helping me get my luggage into the elevator?"

The man actually made a move to grab her suitcase, but at that instant Pia blew her top.

"Where is Amelie? What did you do with the girl?"

"Me?" Nadia von Bredow's eyes widened. "Not a thing! Why would I do anything with her?"

"Because Thies Terlinden gave paintings to Amelie that clearly prove that you were not only present when your friend Laura was raped, but you also watched as Gregor Lauterbach had sex with Stefanie Schneeberger in Sartorius's barn. Afterward, you beat Stefanie Schneeberger to death with a tire iron."

To Pia's surprise Nadia von Bredow began to laugh.

"Where did you hear such nonsense?"

Pia made an effort to control herself. She really wanted to grab the woman and give her a slap.

"Your friends Jörg, Felix, and Michael have confessed," she said. "Laura was still alive when you gave them orders to get rid of her. You must have been afraid that Amelie had found out the truth through Thies and his paintings. That's why it was in your interest to get rid of her too."

"My God." Nadia remained totally unmoved. "Even screenwriters couldn't think up such an outrageous story. I saw that girl Amelie only once, and I have no idea where she is."

"You're lying. You were in the parking lot of the Black Horse and you threw Amelie's backpack in the bushes."

"Oh, really?" Nadia von Bredow looked at Pia with raised eyebrows, as if she were unbearably bored. "Who says so?"

"You'll see."

"I know how to do a few things," she replied sarcastically. "But being two places at the same time, that's something I haven't mastered. I was in Hamburg on that Saturday, and I have witnesses."

"Who?"

"I can give you their names and phone numbers."

"What were you doing in Hamburg?"

"Working."

"Not true. Your manager told us that you had no shoot that evening."

Nadia von Bredow glanced at her expensive watch and made a face, as if she'd wasted enough time.

"I was in Hamburg to MC a gala together with my colleague Torsten Gottwald for around four hundred guests, and it was taped by North German TV," she said. "I can't give you the phone numbers of all the guests that were present, but I can give you those of the director, Torsten, and several others. Would that be proof enough that I couldn't have been running around in a parking lot in Altenhain at the same time?"

"Save your sarcasm," Pia snapped back. "If you're worried about your suitcase, my colleague will gladly carry it for you to our car."

"Oh, that's rich. The police are offering taxi service now."

"With the greatest of pleasure," Pia replied coldly. "And it takes you straight to your cell."

"That's ridiculous!" Nadia von Bredow seemed to be slowly realizing that she was in serious trouble. A deep furrow appeared between her carefully plucked eyebrows. "I have an important appointment in Hamburg."

"Not anymore. For now you're under arrest."

"Why, if I may ask?"

"Because you willingly collaborated in the death of your classmate Laura

Wagner." Pia smiled smugly. "You must know that from your film scripts. It's also called accessory to murder."

The two plainclothes colleagues put Nadia von Bredow in the back seat and drove off in the direction of Hofheim. Then Pia tried once more to reach Bodenstein. Finally he picked up.

"Where the heck are you?" Pia asked with annoyance. She was clamping her cell phone between her ear and shoulder as she fished for the seatbelt. "I've been trying to reach you for an hour and a half. You don't have to come to Frankfurt. I just arrested Nadia von Bredow and sent her off to the station."

Bodenstein said something, but his voice was so indistinct that she couldn't understand him.

"I can't hear you," she said peevishly. "What's going on?"

". . . had an accident . . . waiting for the tow truck . . . fairgrounds exit . . . gas station . . ."

"Oh no, that's all we need. Just wait there, I'll pick you up."

Swearing, Pia punched off the call and raced off. She felt like she was standing all alone in a big hall, at the precise moment when she couldn't allow herself any mistakes or lose her perspective. One tiny slipup and the case would be ruined. She floored it. The city streets were nearly empty of traffic on this early Sunday morning, and it barely took her ten minutes to navigate the distance through the Gutleut district to the main train station and from there out to the fairgrounds. It would have taken her half an hour on a weekday.

On the radio Amy MacDonald was singing a song that Pia had initially liked. But the station had been playing it around the clock and now it made her want to puke. Just before eight o'clock she spied the orange warning lights of the tow truck flashing on the opposite side of the road in the gradually brightening gray light of morning. What was left of Bodenstein's BMW was being loaded onto the flatbed. She turned around at the Westkreuz and a couple of minutes later pulled up in front of the tow truck and a patrol car. Bodenstein sat on the crash barrier, his face pale and his elbows propped on his knees as he stared into space.

"What happened?" Kirchhoff asked one of the uniformed officers after she introduced herself. She was watching her boss out of the corner of her eye.

"Apparently he swerved to avoid an animal," replied the officer. "The car is totaled, but he doesn't seem to be hurt. At least he doesn't want to go to the hospital."

"I'll take care of him. Thanks a lot."

She turned around. The tow truck moved off, but Bodenstein didn't even raise his head.

"Hey." Pia stopped in front of him. What should she say to him? He certainly wouldn't want to go home—wherever that might be these days. Apart from that, now was not the time to be absent from the investigation. Bodenstein heaved a deep sigh. There was a forlorn expression on his face.

"She's going with him on a trip around the world, right after Christmas," he said tonelessly. "Her work is more important than me or the kids. She already signed the contract in September."

Pia hesitated. A dumb cliché like *It'll turn out all right* or *Chin up* would be out of place here. She felt really sorry for him, but there was no time to waste. Nadia von Bredow was waiting at the station, along with every available officer in the Regional Criminal Unit.

"Come on, Oliver." Although she would have liked to grab him by the arm and drag him into the car, she forced herself to be patient. "We can't stay here sitting on the side of the road."

Bodenstein closed his eyes and rubbed the bridge of his nose with his thumb and forefinger.

"Twenty-six years I've been dealing with murderers and killers," he said in a hoarse voice. "But I could never really imagine what would drive a person to kill someone else. This morning I understood for the first time. I believe I would have strangled her in the parking lot if my father and brother hadn't intervened."

He hugged himself as if he were freezing, and looked at Pia with bloodshot eyes. "In my whole life I've never felt so shitty."

●   ●   ●

The conference room could barely hold all the officers that Ostermann had ordered to come in to the Regional Criminal Unit. After his accident Bodenstein didn't seem in any shape to take over the lead of the team, so Pia took the floor. She asked for quiet, outlined the situation, enumerated the facts, and reminded her colleagues of their highest priority, which was to find Amelie Fröhlich and Thies Terlinden. Since Behnke wasn't there nobody questioned Pia's authority, and everyone listened attentively. Pia's gaze fell on Bodenstein, who was leaning against the wall in the back of the room next to Commissioner Engel. She had gotten him coffee at the gas station and added a little bottle of cognac. He drank it without protest, and now he seemed to be doing somewhat better. But he was obviously still in shock.

"The prime suspects are Gregor Lauterbach, Claudius Terlinden, and Nadia von Bredow," Pia now said, stepping over to the screen on which Ostermann had projected a map of Altenhain and vicinity. "These three people have the most to lose if the truth comes out about what really happened in Altenhain in 1997. Terlinden and Lauterbach came from this direction last Saturday evening." She pointed to the Feldstrasse. "Before that they were in Idstein, but we've already searched that house. We're concentrating now on the Black Horse. The owner and his wife are in cahoots with Terlinden, so it's entirely possible that they did him a favor. Possibly Amelie didn't leave the restaurant at all. In addition, every resident around the parking lot has been questioned again. Kai, do you have the arrest warrants?"

Ostermann nodded.

"Good. Jörg Richter, Felix Pietsch, and Michael Dombrowski will be brought here; Kathrin will handle that, along with several colleagues from the patrol units. Two two-man teams will question Claudius Terlinden and Gregor Lauterbach simultaneously. We also have arrest warrants for both of them."

"Who's going to take on Lauterbach and Terlinden?" asked one of the officers.

"Detective Superintendent Bodenstein and Commissioner Engel will take Lauterbach," Pia replied. "I'll go see Terlinden."

"With whom?"

Good question. Behnke and Hasse weren't around any longer. Pia looked at the colleagues sitting before her, then made a decision.

"Sven will go with me."

The officer from SB-21 who had been selected opened his eyes wide in surprise and pointed at himself. Pia nodded.

"Any more questions?"

There were none. The meeting adjourned with the hubbub of voices and scraping chairs. Pia jostled her way over to Bodenstein and Nicola Engel.

"Was that okay, that I included you?" she asked Engel.

"Yes, of course." The commissioner nodded and then took Pia aside.

"Why did you pick DI Jansen?"

"Spontaneous inspiration." Pia shrugged. "I've often heard the boss say how pleased he is with Sven's work."

Nicola Engel nodded. Her inscrutable expression might have made Pia doubt her decision under other circumstances, but there was no time for that now. DI Sven Jansen came over to join them. As they all made their way downstairs, Pia quickly explained what she expected to achieve from the simultaneous questioning of the two suspects and how she intended to proceed. In the parking lot they separated. Bodenstein held Pia back for a moment.

"Well done," he said. "And—thank you."

Bodenstein and Nicola Engel waited quietly in the car until Pia's call came in, saying that she and Jansen were standing at Terlinden's front door. Then they got out and rang the Lauterbachs' doorbell at the same second Pia rang the Terlindens' bell. It took a moment before Gregor Lauterbach opened the door. He was wearing a terrycloth bathrobe, and on the chest was the logo of an international hotel chain.

"What do you want?" he asked, studying them with swollen eyes. "I've already told you everything."

"We like to ask questions multiple times," Bodenstein replied politely. "Isn't your wife at home?"

"No. She's at a conference in Munich. Why do you ask?"

"Just wondering."

Nicola Engel was still holding her cell phone to her ear and now nodded to Bodenstein. Pia and Sven Jansen were standing in the foyer of Terlinden's villa. As they had all agreed, Bodenstein now asked the cultural minister the first question.

"Mr. Lauterbach," he began. "We're still interested in the evening when you and your neighbor waited for Amelie in the parking lot of the Black Horse."

Lauterbach nodded uncertainly. His eyes shifted to Nicola Engel. It seemed to bother him that she was on the phone.

"You saw Nadia von Bredow."

Lauterbach nodded again.

"Are you quite sure?"

"Yes, I am."

"How did you recognize Ms. von Bredow?"

"I . . . I don't know. I just recognized her."

He swallowed nervously as Engel now handed her cell to Bodenstein. Bodenstein scanned the text message that Jansen had written. Claudius Terlinden claimed—unlike Lauterbach—that on the Saturday evening in question he hadn't seen any specific person in the parking lot of the Black Horse. Several people had entered the restaurant, and others came out. In addition, he had seen someone sitting on the bus stop bench but didn't recognize who it was.

"I see." Bodenstein took a deep breath. "You and Mr. Terlinden perhaps should have correlated your stories better. Unlike you, Mr. Terlinden says he didn't recognize anyone."

Lauterbach turned a deep red. He stammered for a bit, insisting he had seen Nadia von Bredow, and he would even swear to it.

"She was in Hamburg that evening," Bodenstein cut him off. Gregor Lauterbach had something to do with the disappearance of Amelie. He was almost positive of that now. But at the same moment doubts popped up in his mind. What if Nadia von Bredow was lying? Had the two of them perhaps joined forces to get rid of the potential threat? Or was Claudius Terlinden lying? Thoughts whirled around in Bodenstein's head, and suddenly he was filled with the shattering certainty that he'd overlooked something extremely important. He met Engel's eyes as she gave him a quizzical look. What the hell was it he wanted to say? As if she sensed his hesitation, the commissioner took over.

"You're lying, Mr. Lauterbach," she said coolly. "Why? How did you decide that it was Nadia von Bredow who was supposedly in the parking lot?"

"Without my lawyer present I won't answer any more questions." Lauterbach's nerves were frazzled, and he alternated between turning red and going pale.

"That is your right." Dr. Engel nodded. "Call a car to take him to Hofheim. We're taking you with us to the station."

"You can't just arrest me like this," Lauterbach protested. "I have immunity."

Bodenstein's cell rang. It was Kathrin Fachinger. She sounded like she was on the verge of hysteria.

". . . don't know what to do! He suddenly had a gun in his hand and he shot himself in the head! Shit, shit, shit! Everyone here is going crazy!"

"Kathrin, just stay calm." Bodenstein turned away as Dr. Engel presented Lauterbach with the arrest warrant. "Where are you now?"

In the background he could hear yelling and all sorts of commotion.

"We were going to arrest Jörg Richter." Fachinger's voice was shaking. She was totally out of her depth in this situation, which was obviously escalating. "Went to his parents' house, showed him the arrest warrant. And all of a sudden the father went to a drawer, took out a pistol, held it to his head and pulled the trigger! And now the mother has the pistol in her hand and is trying to prevent us from taking her son! What should I do now?"

The panic in the voice of his youngest colleague yanked Bodenstein out of his own confusion. Suddenly his brain started working again.

"Don't do a thing, Kathrin," he said. "I'll be there in a few minutes."

The main road through Altenhain was blocked. In front of the Richters' store stood two ambulances with lights flashing, and several patrol cars were parked nearby. Onlookers crowded up to the crime scene tape. Bodenstein found Kathrin Fachinger in the yard. She was sitting on the back steps, white in the face and unable to move. He briefly put his hand on her shoulder and made sure that she wasn't wounded. Inside the house there was utter chaos. An emergency doctor and EMTs were looking after Lutz Richter, who lay in a pool of blood on the tile floor in the hall. Another medic was taking care of his wife.

"What happened?" Bodenstein asked. "Where's the weapon?"

"Here." A patrol officer handed him a plastic bag. "A gun that fires blanks. The husband is still alive, but the wife is in shock."

"Where is Jörg Richter?"

"On the way to Hofheim."

Bodenstein looked around. Through the etched glass of a closed door he could vaguely make out the orange and white of the EMTs' uniforms. He opened the door and froze for a moment at the sight of the living room. It was stuffed full almost to the ceiling; on the walls hung hunting trophies and all sorts of militaria—sabers, antique rifles, helmets, and other weapons— piled on the sideboard, in the open cupboard, on the coffee table, several end tables, and on the floor were pewterware, cider pitchers, and so much junk that it briefly took his breath away. In one of the plush easy chairs Margot Richter was sitting with a stunned look on her face, an IV in her arm. Next to her stood a female EMT holding the drip bag.

"Is she lucid?" Bodenstein wanted to know. The medic nodded.

"Mrs. Richter." Bodenstein squatted down in front of the woman, which wasn't easy in the middle of all that junk. "What happened here? Why did your husband do that?"

"You can't arrest my boy," Mrs. Richter murmured. All energy and malice seemed to have drained from her body, and her eyes were sunk deep in their sockets. "He didn't do anything."

"Then who did?"

"My husband is the guilty one." Her gaze wandered here and there, briefly brushing Bodenstein and then moving off into space. "Jörg wanted to pull the girl back out, but my husband said he should leave her there, it would be better that way. Then he went and dragged a plate over the tank and shoveled dirt on top of it."

"Why did he do that?"

"So that we'd have peace again. Laura would have ruined the boys' lives, when nothing really happened. It was all just in fun."

Bodenstein couldn't believe his ears.

"That little slut wanted to turn in her friends, go to the police. So it was all her own fault. She'd been teasing the boys the whole evening." With no transition she switched from the past to the present day. "Everything was fine, but then Jörg just had to tell somebody what happened back then! What an idiot!"

"At least your son has a conscience," Bodenstein retorted coolly, getting up. Any sympathy he may have had for the woman had been extinguished. "Absolutely nothing was fine—on the contrary! What your son did was no trivial offense. Rape and accessory to murder are capital crimes."

"Bah!" Margot Richter made a scornful gesture and shook her head. "Nobody was talking about that old story anymore," she said bitterly. "And then they got scared because Tobias showed up again. Nothing would have come of it if they'd only kept their traps shut, those . . . those weaklings!"

Nadia von Bredow merely nodded indifferently when Pia told her that her alibi for that Saturday evening had been checked and verified.

"Very good." She cast a glance at her watch. "So I can go now."

"No, not yet." Pia shook her head. "We still have a few more questions."

"All right then, shoot." Nadia looked at Pia with her big bored eyes, as if trying to suppress a yawn. She didn't seem in the least nervous, and Pia couldn't shake the impression that she was playing a role. What was the real Nathalie like, hidden behind the beautiful, flawless façade of the fictional character Nadia von Bredow? Did she still exist?

"Why did you tell Jörg Richter to ask Tobias over that evening and to make sure that he stayed as long as possible?"

"I was worried about Tobi," Nadia replied smoothly. "He didn't seem to take the attack on him in the barn seriously. I wanted to know that he was safe."

"Really?" Pia opened the file and searched until she found what Ostermann had deciphered from Amelie's diary. "Do you want to hear what Amelie wrote about you in her last diary entry?"

"I suppose you're going to read it to me anyway." Nadia rolled her eyes and crossed her long legs.

"That's right." Pia smiled. "*I found it comical the way this blondie has been falling all over Tobias. And the way she looked at me! Sheer jealousy, as if she wanted to eat me alive. Thies totally panicked when I mentioned the name Nadia to him. There's something not quite right about her . . .'*"

Pia looked up.

"You didn't like it that Amelie was so familiar with Tobias," she said. "You used Jörg Richter to watch him and then saw to it that Amelie disappeared."

"Nonsense!" The indifferent smile had vanished from Nadia's face. Her eyes suddenly sparked with anger. Pia recalled Jörg Richter's comment that even as a young girl Nadia had been able to terrify other people. He'd called her ruthless.

"You were jealous." Pia remembered what Amelie's diary said. "Maybe Tobias told you that Amelie visited him now and then. I think you were afraid that something was brewing between Tobias and Amelie. To be honest, Ms. von Bredow, Amelie looks a lot like Stefanie Schneeberger. And Stefanie was the love of his life."

Nadia von Bredow leaned forward a little.

"What do you know about true love?" she whispered in a dramatically lowered voice and wide-open eyes, as if she'd received a director's instructions. "I've loved Tobias ever since we were kids. Ten long years I waited for him. He needed my help and my love to get back on his feet after being in prison."

"Then you're probably fooling yourself. Your love obviously isn't reciprocated," Pia jabbed, and saw with satisfaction that her words had hit home. "Especially if you couldn't even trust him for twenty-four hours."

Nadia von Bredow pressed her lips together. Her beautiful face contorted for a fraction of a second.

"The relationship that Tobias and I have is none of your business!" she

replied vehemently. "What's the point of this shitty questioning about Saturday night? I wasn't there, and I don't know where the girl is. Period."

"So where is your great love then?" Pia kept needling her.

"No idea." Blazing green eyes looked into hers without blinking. "I do
love him, but I'm not his nursemaid. So, may I go now?"

Pia was starting to feel disappointed. She couldn't prove that Nadia von
Bredow had anything to do with Amelie's disappearance.

"You posed as a police officer and went to see Mrs. Fröhlich," Bodenstein
said from the background. "That's called unauthorized assumption of authority. You stole the paintings that Thies gave to Amelie. And later you set fire to
the orangerie to make sure that there would be no more pictures."

Nadia von Bredow didn't look around at Bodenstein.

"I admit that I did use the police badge and a wig from the prop department to find the paintings in Amelie's room. But I did not set the fire."

"What did you do with the pictures?"

"I cut them into little pieces and fed them through the shredder."

"Makes sense. Because the pictures would have exposed you as a murderer."
Pia took the photocopies of the paintings out of the file and placed them on
the table.

"Quite the opposite, actually." Nadia von Bredow leaned back with a
cold smile. "The pictures prove my innocence. Thies is really an amazing observer. Unlike you detectives."

"How so?"

"For you, green equals green. And short-haired means short-haired. Take
a closer look at the person who killed Stefanie Schneeberger. Compare her
with the person who watched while Laura was raped." She leaned over, briefly
looked at the pictures, and tapped on one of the figures. "Here, look at this.
The person next to Stefanie clearly has dark hair, and if you look at this
picture with Laura—the hair is much lighter and curly. I can tell you that on
that evening in Altenhain almost everybody was wearing a green T-shirt
from the Fair Association. There was some sort of text printed on the front,
if I remember correctly."

Bodenstein compared the two pictures.

"You're right," he conceded. "So who is the second person?"

"Lauterbach," said Nadia von Bredow, confirming what Bodenstein already suspected. "I was waiting for Stefanie in the yard behind the barn, because I wanted to talk to her about the Snow White role. She didn't really care about playing the part, she only took it so she could officially spend more time with Lauterbach."

"Just a moment," Bodenstein interrupted. "Mr. Lauterbach told us that he'd only had sex with Stefanie once. On that evening."

"Then he was lying." Nadia snorted. "The two of them were having an affair all summer long, even though everybody thought she was with Tobi. Lauterbach was completely crazy about her, and she thought that was cool. So I was standing by the barn when Stefanie came out of Sartorius's house. Just as I was about to go over and talk to her, Lauterbach showed up. I hid in the barn and couldn't believe my eyes when they came in and got it on together in the hay, only a yard away from where I was hiding. I had no chance to escape, and had to watch them go at it for half an hour. And listen to them both tearing me down."

"And then you were so furious that you killed Stefanie," Bodenstein concluded.

"Oh no. I didn't say a word. Suddenly Lauterbach realized that he'd lost his key ring while they were screwing. He crawled around on all fours, practically hysterical, almost howling. Stefanie couldn't stop laughing at him. Then he got mad as hell." Nadia von Bredow laughed spitefully. "He was in a gigantic panic because of his wife, who was the one with the money; even the house belonged to her. He was nothing but a pathetic little horny teacher who liked to play the big man to his pupils. At home he had nothing to say!"

Bodenstein had to swallow. It sounded all too familiar to him. Cosima had the money and he had nothing to say. And this morning, when she confirmed she was having an affair, he'd felt like killing himself.

"At some point Stefanie got pissed off. She had probably imagined everything being much more romantic and finally saw what a timid creep her wonderful lover really was. She suggested getting his wife to help him look for the keys. Of course it was meant as a joke, but Lauterbach was beyond joking. Stefanie probably thought she had the situation under control. She kept on teasing him and threatened to tell everyone about their affair, until he finally flipped out. As they were leaving the barn he grabbed her. Then they really started fighting. She spit in his face and he slapped her. Stefanie got mad and Lauterbach caught on that she was actually going to do it—march right over to his wife and tell her everything. He grabbed the nearest thing he could get his hands on and hit her with it. Three times."

Pia nodded. The mummy of Stefanie Schneeberger exhibited three skull fractures. But that wasn't enough to prove Nadia's innocence, because she could also have been an accessory.

"Then he ran off as if he'd been stung by a scorpion. Wearing a green T-shirt, by the way. He'd taken off his cool denim shirt when they were fucking. I found the key ring. And when I came out of the barn Thies was kneeling on the ground beside Stefanie. I told him, 'Take good care of your dear Snow White,' and then I left. I tossed the tire iron into Lauterbach's garbage can. That's exactly what happened. Swear to God."

"So you knew that Tobias didn't kill either Laura or Stefanie," Pia said. "How could you let him go to prison if you loved him so much?"

Nadia von Bredow didn't answer right away. She sat stock still, her fingers fidgeting with one of the photocopies.

"At that time I was totally pissed at him," she said softly at last. "For years I'd had to listen to him telling me what he'd said to this girl or that one, how much in love he was or wasn't anymore. He asked for my advice on the best way to get his chicks into bed or how to dump them. I was his *best friend,* ha!"

She gave a bitter laugh.

"As a girl I was uninteresting. I was someone he took for granted. Then he started dating Laura, and she didn't want me to come along when they went to the movies or the swimming pool or to parties. I was the third wheel, and Tobi never even noticed!"

Nadia von Bredow pressed her lips together and her eyes were swimming in tears. Suddenly she was once again the hurt, jealous girl, the stopgap, who as the confidante of the coolest guy in town had no prospect of winning him for herself. Despite all the success she'd had since then, those disappointments had left scars on her soul that she would carry for the rest of her life.

"And all of a sudden that stupid Stefanie came to town." Her voice was toneless, but her fingers, which had ripped one of the photos to tiny shreds, showed what was going on inside her. "She forced her way into our clique and snapped up Tobi. Everything was suddenly different. And then she also turned Lauterbach's head and got the Snow White role that he had promised to me. There was no talking to Tobi anymore. He didn't want to hear anything from anybody, because for him there was only Stefanie, Stefanie, Stefanie!"

Nadia's face was distorted with hatred and she shook her head.

"None of us could have foreseen that the police would be so stupid and that Tobi would really have to do time. I thought a couple of weeks in juvie would have served him right. By the time I realized that he was really going to trial it was far too late to say anything. We had all lied and kept silent for too long. But I never left him in the lurch. I wrote him regularly and I waited for him. I wanted to make up for everything he'd been through. I wanted to do everything for him. And keep him from going back to Altenhain, but he was so stubborn!"

"You didn't *want* to keep him from going back," Bodenstein noted, "you *had* to keep him from going back. Because it was possible that he'd seen through your role in this sad drama. And that couldn't be allowed to happen. So you played the role of the faithful friend."

Nadia von Bredow smiled frostily and said nothing.

"But Tobias went back to his father's house," Bodenstein went on. "You couldn't stop him. And then Amelie Fröhlich showed up, who bears a fateful resemblance to Stefanie Schneeberger."

"That stupid little bitch stuck her nose into things that are none of her fucking business." Nadia ground her teeth angrily. "Tobi and I could have started a new life anywhere in the world. I have enough money. Someplace where Altenhain was only a bad memory."

"And you would have never told him the truth." Pia shook her head. "What a crazy basis for a relationship."

Nadia didn't even deign to look at her.

"You saw Amelie as a threat," Bodenstein said. "So you wrote the anonymous letters and e-mails to Lauterbach. Because you could count on him to do something to protect himself."

Nadia von Bredow shrugged.

"By doing that you set terrible events in motion."

"I wanted to prevent Tobias from being hurt again," she said. "He has suffered enough, and I—"

"Bullshit!" Bodenstein interrupted her. He came over to the table and sat down facing her so that she'd have to look at him. "You wanted to stop him from finding out what you had done in 1997—or to put it more precisely: what you didn't do! You were the only one who could have spared him the conviction and kept him out of prison, but you didn't. Because of injured pride and childish jealousy. You watched as his family was humiliated and destroyed, you stole ten years of your great love's life out of pure selfishness, only so that one day he would belong to you completely. That has got to be the lowest motive I've come across in a long time."

"You don't understand!" Nadia von Bredow countered with sudden bitterness. "You have no idea what it's like to be constantly rejected!"

"And now he has rejected you again, right?" Bodenstein watched her face sharply, registered the play of emotions ranging from hatred to self-pity to furious spite. "He feels deeply indebted to you, but that's not enough. He loves you as little today as he did then. And you can't keep hoping that someone will get rid of your competition for you."

Nadia von Bredow stared at him, full of hate. For a moment it was dead quiet in the interview room.

"What have you done to Tobias Sartorius?" asked Bodenstein.

"He got what he deserved," she replied. "If I can't have him, nobody else will either."

"She's a total nut case," said Pia, stunned, as Nadia von Bredow was taken away by several officers. She had thrown a fit and started screaming when she realized that they weren't going to let her go. Bodenstein had justified the arrest warrant with flight risk, since Nadia von Bredow did own houses and apartments abroad.

"She's a psychopath," he said now. "No doubt about it. When she realized that Tobias Sartorius still didn't love her despite everything she'd done for him, then she killed him."

"You think he's dead?"

"I'm afraid he is." Bodenstein got up from his chair as Gregor Lauterbach was escorted in by an officer. His lawyer appeared seconds later.

"I want to speak with my client," Dr. Anders demanded.

"You can do that later," said Bodenstein, assessing Lauterbach, who was looking miserable as he sat hunched on the plastic chair. "So, Mr. Lauterbach. Now let's talk turkey. Nadia von Bredow has just seriously incriminated you. On the evening of September 6, 1997, in front of the barn on the Sartorius farm you killed Stefanie Schneeberger with a tire iron, because you were afraid that she was going to tell your wife about your affair. Stefanie had threatened to do just that. What do you say about that?"

"He has nothing to say," his lawyer replied in place of Lauterbach.

"You suspected Thies Terlinden of being an eyewitness to what you'd done and put pressure on him to keep quiet."

Pia's cell phone rang. She glanced at the display, got up, and moved away a few yards from the table. It was Henning. He had analyzed the medications that Dr. Lauterbach had been prescribing for Thies for years.

"I spoke with a colleague from psychiatric cardiology," said Henning. "He is very familiar with autism and was shocked when I faxed him the prescriptions. These drugs are absolutely counterproductive for the treatment of a patient with Asperger's."

"In what way?" Pia asked, plugging her other ear with her finger because her boss had raised his voice and was firing all his cannons at Lauterbach. His lawyer kept shouting, "No comment!" as if he were already in the middle of a press conference in front of the courthouse.

"Combining a benzodiazepine with other centrally active pharmaceuticals such as neuroleptics and sedatives will amplify their effects reciprocally. These neuroleptics on the prescription are actually used for acute psychotic disorders with delusions and hallucinations; the sedatives are used for calming; and benzodiazepines are used for relief of anxiety. But the latter have another effect that could be interesting for you: they work as an amnesic. That means that the patient has no memory while the drug is in his system. Any physicians who have prescribed these medications to an autistic patient over a lengthy period should have their license revoked, at the very least. Such action is tantamount to causing grievous bodily harm."

"Can your colleague write a report for us?"

"Yes, certainly."

Pia's heart began to pound from excitement when she grasped what all this meant. Dr. Lauterbach had stuffed Thies full of consciousness-altering drugs for over eleven years in order to keep him under control. His parents might have believed that the prescribed medications would benefit their son. Why Daniela Lauterbach did this was perfectly obvious; she wanted to protect her husband. But suddenly Amelie showed up, and Thies stopped taking his medications.

Bodenstein opened the door; Lauterbach had hidden his face in his hands and was sobbing like a child, while Dr. Anders packed his briefcase. An officer came in and led the weeping Gregor Lauterbach away.

"He confessed." Bodenstein seemed extremely pleased. "He murdered Stefanie Schneeberger. Whether it was in the heat of the moment or with premeditation really isn't important. Tobias is innocent in any event."

"I knew that the whole time," Pia said. "We still don't know where Amelie and Thies are, but it's clear to me who was trying to get rid of both of them. We were on the wrong track the whole time."

It was cold, cold, cold. The icy wind howled and raged, the snowflakes stung his face like tiny needles. He could no longer see a thing, everything around him was white, and his eyes were watering so badly that he was almost blind. He could no longer feel his feet, nose, ears, or fingertips. He staggered through the snowstorm from one reflective road marker to the next to keep from losing his orientation entirely. He had no more sense of time and just as little hope that a snowplow might come by. Why did he keep walking at all? Where did he want to go? He could hardly pull his feet out of the snow, they were frozen to clumps of ice in the thin gym shoes. It took a superhuman effort to fight his way step by step through this white hell. He fell again and landed on all fours in the snow. Tears ran down his face and turned to ice. Tobias fell forward and just lay there. Every fiber of his body was in pain; his left forearm which she had struck with the iron poker was completely numb. She had attacked him like a madwoman, hitting and kicking him, spitting on him in an apoplectic, hate-filled frenzy. Then she ran out of the cabin and simply drove away, leaving him behind in the middle of nowhere in the Swiss Alps. For hours he had lain naked on the floor, unable to move, as if in shock. At the same time he had hoped and feared that she would come back and get him. But that didn't happen.

What had actually happened? They had spent a wonderful day in the snow under a steel-blue sky, had cooked and eaten a meal together and then made passionate love. Out of the blue Nadia had suddenly blown her top. But why? She was his friend, his best, closest, oldest friend, who had never abandoned him. Suddenly the memory shot through him like a bolt of blinding lightning. "Amelie," he mumbled with stiffened lips. He had mentioned Amelie's name because he was worried about her, and that was what made Nadia blow up. Tobias pressed his fists to his temples and forced himself to think. Gradually his foggy brain came up with the connections that he had been unwilling to acknowledge until now. Nadia had long been in love with him, but he had never realized it. How painful it must have been for her to listen to him recounting his numerous infatuations in minute detail. She had never let it show as she gave him tips and advice the way a good pal does. Tobias lifted his head in a daze. The storm had died down. He resisted the temptation to remain lying in the snow and hauled himself up to a standing position, his knees stiff. He rubbed his eyes. Impossible! Down there in the valley he could make out lights! He forced himself onward. Nadia had been jealous of his girlfriends, especially Laura and Stefanie. And when she had casually asked him at the edge of the forest whether he liked Amelie, he had guilelessly answered "yes." But how could he have known that Nadia, the famous actress, would be jealous of a seventeen-year-old girl? Had Nadia done something to Amelie? Good God! The thought got him moving faster, sending him down toward the valley. Nadia had a head start of a night and a day. If anything happened to Amelie, then he would be to blame, because he had told Nadia about Thies's paintings and that Amelie wanted to help him. He stopped and opened his mouth in a wild, angry wail that echoed off the mountains. He screamed until his vocal cords hurt and his voice gave out.

•　•　•

Dr. Daniela Lauterbach seemed to have been swallowed up by the earth. At her office they thought she was at the physicians' conference in Munich, but inquiries showed that she had never arrived there. Her cell phone was turned off and her car could not be found. It was so frustrating. At the psychiatric hospital they considered it possible that Dr. Lauterbach had picked up Thies. She was one of the doctors on call, and no one would have paid any attention if she entered a ward. But on that Saturday night she had not been on call for emergencies. She had faked the call so she could leave and then waited outside the Black Horse. Amelie knew her and had probably voluntarily gotten into her car. To throw suspicion onto Tobias, Dr. Lauterbach had shoved Amelie's cell phone into his pants pocket when she drove him home later. It was a perfect setup, and other coincidences helped her out as well. The probability of finding Amelie Fröhlich or Thies Terlinden alive was tending toward zero.

That evening at ten o'clock Bodenstein and Kirchhoff were sitting in the conference room watching the *Hessen Journal* news on TV, which had announced that the police were looking for Dr. Daniela Lauterbach and that Nadia von Bredow had been arrested. Reporters and two television teams were still hanging around outside the police station, greedy for news of Nadia von Bredow.

"I think I'll go home." Pia yawned and stretched. "Can I drive you somewhere?"

"No, no. You go ahead," said Bodenstein. "I'll take one of the official cars."

"Are you okay so far?"

"So far, yes." Bodenstein shrugged. "Life goes on. Somehow."

She gave him another dubious glance, then grabbed her jacket and purse and left. Bodenstein got up and turned off the TV. All day long he had managed to banish the unpleasant encounter with Cosima from his mind through hectic activity, but now the memory came back in a nasty, galling wave. How could he have lost control like that? He switched off the fluorescent lights and slowly walked down the hall to his office. The guest room at his parents' house tempted him as little as a tavern. He might as well spend the night at his desk. He closed the door behind him and hesitated for a moment in the middle of the room, which was bathed in a weak glow from the streetlights outside. He was a failure as a husband and a police officer. Cosima preferred a thirty-five-year-old to him, and Amelie, Thies, and Tobias were probably long dead because he hadn't found them in time. The past lay in ruins, and the future didn't look much rosier.

If she leaned down and stretched out her arm, she could touch the surface of the water with her fingertips. The water was rising much faster than Amelie had thought it would, and obviously there was no drain anywhere. Not much longer and they'd be sitting in the water up here on the bookshelf. And even if they didn't drown, because the water would flow out through the sliver of a window near the ceiling, they would die from hypothermia. It was cold as hell. And Thies's condition had worsened dramatically. He was shivering and sweating, his body hot with fever. Mostly he seemed to sleep, his arm wrapped around her, but when he was awake, he talked. What he said was so scary and sinister that Amelie wanted to cry.

As if someone had pulled aside a black curtain in her mind, her memory was again crystal clear and she knew how she had ended up in this hole of a cellar. The Lauterbach woman must have put some kind of drug in the water and in the crackers, because she had fallen asleep every time she ate or drank anything. But now she could remember what happened. Dr. Lauterbach had called her and waited in the parking lot, friendly and concerned, begging her to come along to visit Thies, since he was having such a hard time. Without hesitation Amelie got into the doctor's car—and woke up in this cellar. In the condemned buildings in Berlin, the homeless shelters, and on the streets of the city, she thought she'd seen all the evil that existed in this world, but it had only been a pale glimmer of how cruel people could be. Living in Alten-hain, this idyllic little village that she had considered so boring and desolate, were merciless, brutal monsters, disguised behind masks of bourgeois re-spectability. If she ever got out of this cellar alive, she would never trust any-one again for the rest of her life. How could a human being do something so horrific to someone else? Why hadn't Thies's parents ever realized what the nice, friendly neighbor woman had done to their son? How could a whole village look on in silence as an innocent young man was sentenced to ten years in prison while the true criminals got off scot-free? In the long hours of darkness Thies had gradually told her everything he knew about the gruesome events in Altenhain, and that was a lot. No wonder Dr. Lauterbach wanted him dead. The instant she had this thought, Amelie was filled with the shattering certainty that the two of them were going to die. The Lauterbach woman wasn't stupid. She would have made sure that nobody would find them here. Or at least not until it was too late.

Bodenstein rested his chin in his hand and stared at the empty cognac glass. How could he have been so wrong about Daniela Lauterbach? Her husband had murdered Stefanie Schneeberger in the heat of the moment, but she was ice cold. She had covered up what he'd done and threatened Thies Terlinden for years afterward, doping him up with drugs and intimidating him. She had allowed Tobias Sartorius to go to prison and sat by as his parents went through hell.

Bodenstein reached for the bottle of Rémy Martin that he'd once received as a gift and which had stood unopened for over a year in his cabinet. He loathed the stuff, but he was in the mood for something alcoholic. All day long he hadn't eaten a bite, drinking way too much coffee. In one gulp he emptied the third glass of cognac in fifteen minutes and grimaced. The liquor kindled a small, agreeable fire in his stomach, flowed through his bloodstream, and relaxed him. His gaze wandered to the framed photograph of Cosima next to the telephone. She was smiling at him, as she had done for years. He didn't hold it against her that this morning she had ambushed him and provoked him to say and do despicable things. He still regretted having lost control that way. Although she was the one who had ruined everything, he felt himself in the wrong. And that bothered him at least as much as his arrogant belief that he'd had a perfect marriage. Cosima had chosen to cheat on him with a younger man because he no longer satisfied her as a man. She had been bored with him and so she sought out another man, an adventurer like herself. This thought drove his feeling of self-worth to sink even lower than he would have thought possible. There was a knock on the door as he downed his fourth cognac.

"Yes?"

Nicola Engel stuck her head in the door.

"Am I disturbing you?"

"No. Come in." He rubbed the bridge of his nose with his thumb and forefinger. She entered his office, closed the door behind her, and came closer.

"I've just gotten word that Lauterbach has been stripped of his immunity. The court has approved the arrest warrant for him and Ms. von Bredow." She remained standing in front of his desk and eyed him. "My God, you look terrible. I didn't realize this case was taking such a toll on you."

What should he say to that? He was too tired to give a tactically intelligent answer. He still couldn't really read Nicola. Was she asking out of genuine human interest or because she wanted to use his failures as the final nail in the coffin and put an end to his role as the head of K-11?

"The attendant circumstances have been getting to me," he finally admitted. "Behnke, Hasse. This stupid talk about Pia and me."

"There's nothing to it, is there?"

"No, of course not." He leaned back. His neck was sore, and he grimaced again. Her eyes fell on the cognac.

"Have you got another glass?"

"In the cabinet. Bottom left."

She turned around, opened the cabinet door, took out a glass, and sat down on one of the visitors' chairs facing his desk. He poured her a finger's width, then filled his own glass almost to the brim. Nicola Engel raised her eyebrows but said nothing. He said "Cheers" and drank without putting the glass down.

"What's really wrong?" she wanted to know. She was a sharp observer, and she'd known him for a long time now. Before he met Cosima, whom he married soon afterward, he and Nicola had been a couple for two years. Why try to fool her? Soon everybody would find out anyway, especially when he gave them his new address.

"Cosima has found somebody else," he said, trying to make his voice sound as calm as possible. "I'd had my suspicions for a while, and a couple of days ago she admitted it."

"Oh." It didn't sound like schadenfreude. But she couldn't bring herself to say she was sorry. He didn't care. He grabbed the bottle, filled his glass again. Nicola looked at him without saying a word. He drank. Felt the effect of the alcohol on an empty stomach and understood why people, under certain circumstances, turned into alcoholics. Cosima retreated all the way to the back of his consciousness, and his worries about Amelie, Thies, and Daniela Lauterbach went up in smoke.

"I'm not a good cop," he said. "Or a good boss. You should look for somebody else to do my job."

"Not on your life," she answered firmly. "When I started here last year, that was my intention, I admit. But now I've had a year to watch your management style and the way you lead your team. I could use a few more people like you."

He didn't say anything to this, and wanted to pour himself another cognac, but the bottle was empty. He casually tossed the bottle in the wastebasket and followed it with Cosima's photo. When he picked up the basket, he met Nicola's searching look.

"I think you should call it a day," she said, glancing at her watch. "It's almost midnight. Come on, I'll drive you home."

"I don't have a home anymore," he reminded her. "I'm living with my parents again. Funny, right?"

"Better than a hotel. So, come on. Let's go."

Bodenstein didn't budge. He didn't move his gaze from her face. Suddenly he remembered the first time he'd met her, more than twenty-seven years ago, at a party given by a fellow student. He'd been standing around in the tiny kitchen with a couple of guys drinking beer. He hadn't really noticed the girls at the party, because the disappointment over breaking up with Inka was still too fresh in his mind for him to consider a new relationship. In front of the door to the toilet he met Nicola. She had looked him over from head to toe and in her inimitable direct way said something to him that caused him to leave the party with her on the spot, without even saying good-bye to the host. That time he had also been drunk and in pain, the way he was today. Unexpectedly a wave of heat raced through his body and shot into his abdomen like glowing lava.

"I like you," he repeated her words from back then in a hoarse voice. "Do you feel like having sex?"

Nicola looked at him in surprise, and a smile tugged at the corners of her mouth.

"Why not?" She hadn't forgotten their first conversation either. "I just have to make a quick trip to the toilet first."

Monday, November 24, 2008

"You wore this same shirt and tie yesterday," Pia noted with a sharp look when Bodenstein joined her in the still empty conference room. "And you haven't shaved."

"Your powers of observation are truly phenomenal," he replied dryly, heading for the coffee machine. "In my hasty departure I unfortunately couldn't take my whole wardrobe with me."

"Right." Pia grinned. "I always took you for somebody who would put on fresh clothes every day, even in the trenches. Or did you happen to take my advice?"

"Please, let's not jump to conclusions." Bodenstein's expression was unreadable as he poured milk in his coffee. Pia was just about to reply when Ostermann appeared in the doorway.

"What bad news do you have for us today, Mr. Detective Superintendent?" asked Bodenstein. Ostermann gave first his boss, then Pia an annoyed look. They just shrugged.

"Tobias Sartorius called his father last night. He's in a hospital in Switzerland," said Ostermann. "Still no news of Amelie, Thies, or Dr. Lauterbach."

Behind him Kathrin Fachinger appeared, followed by Nicola Engel and Sven Jansen.

"Good morning," said the commissioner. "I'm bringing the reinforcements I promised. DI Jansen will work temporarily with the K-11 team, Bodenstein. If you have no objections."

"That's fine." Bodenstein nodded to their colleague from the burglary division. He had accompanied Pia yesterday to interview Terlinden. Everyone sat down at the table. Only Nicola Engel excused herself and headed for the door. There she turned around and said, "Could I have a word with you in private?"

Bodenstein got up, followed her out to the hall, and closed the door behind him.

"Behnke obtained a temporary court order appealing his suspension and at the same time reported in sick," said Nicola Engel in a low voice. "His legal adviser is a lawyer from the firm of Dr. Anders. How can he afford that?"

"Anders will take a case like that pro bono," said Bodenstein. "All he cares about are the headlines."

"Okay, we'll wait and see what happens." Nicola Engel looked Bodenstein up and down. "I also learned something else this morning. Actually I wanted to tell you this at a better moment, but before you hear it from someone else through a leak . . ."

He gave her a wary look. It could be anything, beginning with his suspension to the news that she would be taking over leadership of the National Criminal Police. It was typical of Nicola never to show her cards too soon.

"Congratulations on your promotion," she announced to him to his surprise. "First Chief Detective Inspector Oliver von Bodenstein. Including a raise in your pay grade. What do you say to that?"

She smiled at him expectantly.

"Does this mean that I've slept my way to the top?" he replied. The commissioner grinned, but then turned serious.

"Do you regret last night?" she wanted to know.

Bodenstein cocked his head. "I wouldn't say that," he answered. "What about you?"

"Me neither. Although I don't usually care for reheated food."

He grinned, and she turned to go.

"Oh, Ms. Commissioner . . ."

She stopped.

"Perhaps . . . we could repeat it occasionally?"

Then she grinned too.

"I'll think it over, Mr. Chief Detective. See you later."

He watched her go until she turned the corner, then reached for the door handle. Suddenly and unexpectedly he was filled with an almost painful feeling of happiness. Not because he had avenged himself by cheating on Cosima—and with his boss to boot, whom she despised with all her heart—but because at this moment he felt freer than he'd ever felt in his life. Last night his future had unfolded before him with breathtaking clarity, revealing undreamt-of possibilities, after he'd been trudging around for a week feeling deeply hurt and full of self-pity. Not that he had ever felt trapped at Cosima's side, but now he sensed that even though his marriage had failed, it didn't mean that his life was over. Quite the opposite. Not everyone at the age of fifty got another chance.

Amelie's legs felt like they had frozen to ice, yet she was sweating all over. With all her might she tried to keep Thies's head above water. The buoyancy of the water, which had now risen to a good sixteen inches above the top shelf, had made it possible for her to shift his body to a sitting position. Fortunately the bookshelf was screwed solidly into the wall, or it probably would have tipped over long ago. Gasping, Amelie inhaled and tried to ease her cramped muscles. With her right arm she held Thies tight while with her left she tried to touch the ceiling. A foot and a half of air was left, no more.

"Thies!" she whispered urgently, shaking him. "You have to wake up, Thies!"

He didn't react. She couldn't possibly move him higher, she wasn't strong enough. But in a couple of hours his head would be underwater. Amelie was close to giving up. It was so cold! And she had such a terrifying fear of drowning. Images from *Titanic* kept popping up in her mind. She had seen that movie half a dozen times and had blubbered when Leonardo DiCaprio slipped off the plank and sank into the deep. The waters of the North Atlantic could hardly be any colder than this shit-brew here.

With quivering lips she kept talking to Thies, begging him, shaking him, pinching him on the arm. He simply had to wake up.

"I don't want to die," she sobbed, leaning her head against the wall in exhaustion. "I don't want to die, damn it!"

The cold was paralyzing her movements and her thoughts. With the greatest effort she thrashed her legs up and down in the water. Eventually she wouldn't be able to manage even that. She mustn't fall asleep. If she let go of Thies, he would drown and she with him.

Claudius Terlinden looked reluctantly at the documents that lay before him on the desk, as his secretary escorted Oliver von Bodenstein and Pia Kirchhoff into his office.

"Have you found my son?" He didn't get up from his chair and made no effort to conceal his displeasure. From close up Pia could see that the events of the past few days had left their mark on Terlinden, although he seemed emotionally unaffected. He was pale and had dark shadows under his eyes. Was he taking refuge in his daily routine in order to forget his worries?

"No," Bodenstein said regretfully. "Unfortunately we haven't. But we know who abducted him from the psychiatric ward."

Claudius Terlinden gave him an inquisitive look.

"Gregor Lauterbach has confessed to the murder of Stefanie Schneeberger," Bodenstein went on. "His wife kept silent about it in order to protect him and his career. She knew that Thies had been an eyewitness to the crime. She has consistently threatened your son and treated him for years with psychopharmaceuticals that he didn't need at all. Because she feared that Amelie Fröhlich and your son could be dangerous to her husband and herself, she decided to take action. We're afraid that she may have done something to both of them."

Terlinden stared at Bodenstein, his face was a mask of frozen surprise.

"Who did you think murdered Stefanie?" Pia asked. Claudius Terlinden took off his glasses and rubbed his hand over his face. He took a deep breath.

"I actually thought it was Tobias," he admitted after a moment. "I assumed that he saw Gregor with the girl and then flipped out with jealousy. It was clear to me that my son Thies must have witnessed something, but since he never spoke I didn't know what he saw. Now, of course, some things make more sense. That's why Daniela was always so concerned about him. And that's why Thies was so terrified of her."

"She threatened to send him to an institution if he ever breathed a word," Pia explained. "But even she didn't know that Thies was keeping Stefanie's body concealed in the cellar of the orangerie. She must have found that out from Amelie. Because of that, Dr. Lauterbach set the fire. It wasn't the painting she wanted to destroy, but the mummy of Snow White."

"Good Lord!" Terlinden got up from his chair, went over to the wall of windows, and looked out. Did he have any idea how thin the ice was under his feet? Oliver and Pia exchanged a glance behind his back. He would be held accountable for numerous offenses, not least for the extensive bribery incidents that Gregor Lauterbach had revealed in his cowardly attempt to clear his own name. Terlinden as yet knew nothing about that, but surely he realized what a gigantic burden of guilt he carried because of his policy of silence and cover-ups.

"Lutz Richter tried to commit suicide yesterday when our colleagues arrested his son," Bodenstein said, breaking the silence. "Eleven years ago he established a sort of militia to hush up what really happened. Laura Wagner was still alive when Richter's son and his friends threw her into the empty underground tank at the airfield in Eschborn. Richter knew that but he covered up the tank with dirt."

"And when Tobias came back from prison, Richter took matters into his own hands and organized the attack on him," Pia added. "Did you order him to do that?"

Terlinden turned around.

"No. In fact, I expressly forbade the assault," he replied hoarsely.

"Manfred Wagner was the one who shoved Tobias's mother off the bridge," Pia went on. "If you hadn't forced your son Lars to keep quiet about the truth, none of this would have happened. Your son might still be alive, the Sartorius family wouldn't be destitute, and the Wagners would have learned what happened. Do you realize that you must bear the sole blame for the suffering these families have endured? Not to mention that because of your cowardice your own family has gone through hell!"

"Why me?" Terlinden shook his head, baffled. "I was only trying to contain the damage."

Pia couldn't believe her ears. Obviously Terlinden had found some sort of justification for his actions and omissions, and had been deluding himself for years.

"How could the damage have been any worse?" she asked sarcastically.

"The very fabric of the village community was threatening to break apart," Terlinden replied. "My family has borne a great responsibility in this village for decades, if not centuries. I had to live up to it. The boys did something stupid when they were drunk, and the girl had provoked them."

He had begun in an uncertain voice, but now he spoke in a tone of utter conviction.

"I thought that Tobias killed Stefanie. So he would be going to prison in any event. What did it matter if he was convicted of one crime or two? Because he kept his four friends out of trouble, I supported his family and always made sure that—"

"Now you shut up!" Bodenstein interrupted the man. "All you wanted was to keep your son Lars out of it! You were concerned solely with protecting your own name, which inevitably would have ended up in the newspapers if Lars had been connected to the murders. The young people and the villagers meant nothing to you. And it's glaringly obvious how unimportant the Sartorius family was to you because you opened the Black Horse to compete with the Golden Rooster and even hired Sartorius's cook to manage your restaurant."

"In addition, you exploited the circumstances with ice-cold determination," Pia took over. "Albert Schneeberger never wanted to sell you his company, but you put such massive pressure on him in this terrible situation that he finally did. Then, contrary to your agreement, you fired his employees and broke up the company. You are the only one who profited from the whole sad affair—in every respect!"

Claudius Terlinden glared daggers at Pia.

"But now everything has turned out very differently than you ever thought possible." Pia refused to be intimidated. "The people in Altenhain didn't wait for further orders from you, but decided to take action on their own. And then Amelie showed up and began investigating on her own initiative, putting half the village at risk. But your power had diminished to such an extent that you couldn't stop the avalanche that was triggered by Tobias's return."

Terlinden's expression darkened. Pia crossed her arms and returned his infuriated look without batting an eye. She had nailed his sore spot with absolute precision.

"If Amelie and Thies die," she said with an ominous undertone, "you will bear sole responsibility for their deaths!"

"Where could those two be?" Bodenstein took over. "Where is Dr. Lauterbach?"

"I don't know," Claudius Terlinden said between clenched teeth. "God damn it, I really don't know!"

The dark gray clouds hovering low over the Taunus promised snow. In the past twenty-four hours the temperature had dropped by almost eighteen degrees. This time the snow would stick. Pia was driving down the pedestrian street in Königstein, ignoring the angry looks from the few people who were out. She parked in front of the jewelry store above which Dr. Lauterbach had her practice. There a receptionist was bravely holding the fort, patiently fielding the incessant phone calls, and rescheduling indignant patients who had appointments that day.

"Dr. Lauterbach is not in," she replied to Bodenstein's inquiry. "And I haven't been able to reach her by phone."

"But she's not at the conference in Munich."

"No, that was only on the weekend." The woman raised her hands helplessly as the phone rang again. "Actually she wanted to be back today. You can see what's going on here."

"We presume that she's cleared out," said Bodenstein. "We think she's responsible for the abduction of two people, and she knows that we're on her trail."

The receptionist shook her head, wide-eyed.

"But that can't be," she protested. "I've been working for the doctor for twelve years. She would never hurt anyone. I mean, I . . . I *know* her."

"When was the last time you saw Dr. Lauterbach or spoke with her? Has she been acting differently in the past few days, or has she been away more than usual?" Bodenstein glanced at the name tag on the right breast pocket of the woman's starched white smock. "Mrs. Wiesmeier, please think! Your boss may have made a mistake, although she meant well. You could help her now, before things get any worse."

Bodenstein's personal plea and the urgent tone of his voice had an effect. Waltraud Wiesmeier paused to think, a frown on her face.

"I've been wondering why Dr. Lauterbach canceled all her appointments for people to look at Mrs. Scheithauer's villa last week," she said after a while. "She's been trying for months to find a buyer for that big old place, and finally somebody was interested and wanted to come down from Düsseldorf on Thursday. But I had to call and cancel the appointment with him and two real estate agents. It was strange."

"What kind of house is it?"

"An old villa on Grüner Weg with a view of the Woogtal. Mrs. Scheithauer was one of our patients for years. She had no heirs, and when she died in April she left her estate to a foundation and the villa to Dr. Lauterbach." She gave an embarrassed smile. "I think the boss would have preferred it the other way around."

"At a press conference this morning a spokesman for the cultural ministry announced the surprising resignation of Cultural Minister Gregor Lauterbach, stating personal reasons . . . ," said the news reporter on the car radio as Pia turned from Ölmühlweg down Grüner Weg. She slowly drove past the new construction and turned onto a cul-de-sac that ended at a huge wrought-iron gate.

"There has been no official reaction from the state chancellery. The government spokesman . . ."

"This must be it." Bodenstein undid his seatbelt and got out almost before Pia had stopped the car. The gate was secured by a chain and a brand-new padlock, and only the roof of the villa could be seen. Pia shook the bars of the gate and looked to the left and right. The wall was over six feet tall with iron spikes on top.

"I'll call for backup and a locksmith." Bodenstein pulled out his cell. If Dr. Lauterbach was inside the villa, she probably wouldn't give up without a fight. In the meantime Pia walked along the wall of the spacious estate but found only a smaller locked gate that was overgrown with thorny brush.

Minutes later a locksmith showed up. Two patrol cars from Königstein parked farther up the street, and the officers approached on foot.

"The villa has been empty for a few years," said one of the officers. "Old Mrs. Scheithauer lived at the Rosenhof retirement home in Kronberg. She was way over ninety when she died in April."

"And then she left the whole place to her doctor," Pia noted. "Why do some people have all the luck?"

The locksmith had finished his job and wanted to leave, but Bodenstein asked him to wait a moment. The first tiny snowflakes came floating down as they walked up the gravel path. The castle ruins on top of the hill had vanished in the clouds; the whole world around them seemed to have ceased to exist. Another patrol car caught up with them and stopped in front of the entrance. The front door was also locked, and the locksmith got to work.

"Do you hear that?" asked Pia, who had eyes and ears like a lynx. Bodenstein listened, but he heard only the rustle of the wind in the tall firs in front of the villa. He shook his head. The door was opened and he stepped into a large, dim entry hall. It smelled deserted and musty.

"Nobody here," he said, disappointed. Pia went past him and touched the light switch. It made a bang and sparks flew out of the switch. The two officers from Königstein grabbed their weapons. Bodenstein's heart was in his throat.

"Just a short circuit," said Pia. "Sorry."

They moved on from room to room. The furniture was covered with white sheets, the shutters closed in front of the tall windows. Bodenstein crossed the big room that opened off the entry hall on the left side. The parquet floor creaked under his feet. He pulled aside the damp, moth-eaten velvet curtains, but the room didn't get much brighter.

"I hear a rushing noise," said Pia from the doorway. "Everybody be quiet!"

The officers fell silent. And now Bodenstein actually heard it too. There was water running down in the cellar. He went back and followed Pia to a door underneath the curved stairway.

"Has anybody got a flashlight with them?" she asked, trying to open the door, but it wouldn't budge. One of the patrol officers handed Pia a flashlight.

"It's not locked but it won't open." Pia bent down and shone the light at the floor. "Look at this. Somebody put silicone under the door. Why would they do that?"

The colleagues from Königstein knelt down and dug out the silicone with their pocket knives. Pia yanked on the door until it sprang open. The sound of running water was louder now. Five or six dark shapes hurried past her and into the depths of the house. "Rats!" Bodenstein jumped back and bumped into one of the officers so hard that he almost fell over.

"You don't have to KO me just for that," the uniformed colleague complained. "You almost landed on my foot."

Pia ignored them. She was lost in her own thoughts.

"Why was the cellar door sealed with silicone?" she asked as she went down the stairs, shining the flashlight in front of her. After ten steps she stopped in her tracks.

"Shit!" she swore. She was standing up to her ankles in icy water. "A water line broke! That's why we got a short circuit. The circuit breaker must be down here."

"I'll call the water company," said one of the officers. "They'll have to shut off the main line."

"And they'd better call the fire department too." Bodenstein was keeping a wary eye out for more rats. "Come on, Pia. Lauterbach isn't here."

Pia wasn't listening to him. Alarm bells were going off in her head. The house was empty and belonged to Daniela Lauterbach, who in the past week had suddenly canceled appointments for potential buyers to see the house. And not because she wanted to hide out here herself. Since her shoes and stockings were already wet anyway, Pia went farther down the steps. The water glugged and the cold hit her like a shock.

"What are you doing?" Bodenstein called after her. "Come on out of there!"

Pia bent over and shone the light around the corner in the dark. The water was up to less than ten inches below the ceiling. Pia went down another step, holding on to the railing with one hand. Now she was up to her hips in water.

"Amelie!" she yelled, teeth chattering. "Amelie? Hello?"

She held her breath and strained to listen; the cold was bringing tears to her eyes. Suddenly she froze. A jolt of adrenaline shot violently through her body, as if from an electric shock.

"Help!" she heard over the steady rush of the water. "Help! We're in here!"

Smoking impatiently, Pia paced up and down in the entry hall. She hardly noticed her wet clothes and shoes, she was so excited. Bodenstein preferred to wait outside in the falling snow until the flooded cellar was accessible. The thought of spending any time under the same roof with an armada of rats gave him the creeps. The water company had turned off the main line, and the men from the Königstein Volunteer Fire Department were pumping out the cellar with all the hoses they had, sending the water down the hill into the overgrown park. Thanks to an emergency generator they now had lights. Three ambulances had arrived, and the police had cordoned off the property.

"All the air shafts through which the water could have drained out were blocked and sealed with silicone," the fire captain reported. "Incredible."

But true. For Bodenstein and Pia there was no doubt who had done it.

"We're going in now," announced one of the firemen, who like two of his colleagues was wearing waterproof waders that reached to his navel.

"I'm coming with you." Pia tossed her cigarette carelessly on the parquet floor and stamped it out.

"No, stay here," Bodenstein called from the doorway. "You'll catch your death."

"At least put on some rubber boots." The captain turned around. "Wait, I'll get you some."

Five minutes later Pia followed the three firemen through the knee-high standing water into the cellar. In the light from the flashlight they opened one door after another until they found the right one. Pia turned the key in the lock and shoved against the door, which opened into the room with a piercing screech. Her heart was pounding hard enough to burst, and her knees buckled from relief when the cone of light from the flashlight revealed the pale, dirty face of a girl. Amelie Fröhlich blinked, blinded. Pia stumbled down the last two steps into the lower room, held out her arms, and grabbed hold of the hysterically sobbing girl.

"Calm down now," she murmured, stroking Amelie's matted hair. "Everything is going to be all right, Amelie. You don't have to be scared anymore."

"But . . . but Thies," Amelie gasped. "I . . . I think he's dead!"

Everyone at the Regional Criminal Unit felt enormous relief. Amelie Fröhlich had come through her ten days in the cellar of the old villa in Königstein without serious injury. She was exhausted, dehydrated, and had lost a lot of weight. But from a physical point of view she hadn't suffered any ill effects from the terrible ordeal. She and Thies were taken to the hospital. The prognosis for Terlinden's son was not good. He was in poor condition and was suffering from severe withdrawal symptoms. After the meeting in K-11 Bodenstein and Pia drove to the hospital in Bad Soden and were rather surprised to encounter Hartmut Sartorius and his son Tobias in the lobby.

"My ex-wife came out of her coma," Sartorius declared. "We were able to talk with her briefly. She's doing well, considering."

"Oh, that's great." Pia smiled. Her gaze fell on Tobias, who seemed years older. He looked ill, and there were dark circles under his eyes.

"Where have you been?" asked Bodenstein, turning to Tobias Sartorius. "We've been very worried about you."

"Nadia left him behind in a mountain cabin in Switzerland," Hartmut Sartorius replied. "My son had to walk through the snow to the next village." He put his hand on Tobias's arm. "I still can't believe that I was so wrong about Nadia."

"We've arrested Ms. von Bredow," Bodenstein said. "And Gregor Lauterbach has confessed to murdering Stefanie Schneeberger. In the next few days we're going to demand that proceedings against you be reopened. You will be acquitted of any wrongdoing."

Tobias Sartorius merely shrugged. It didn't matter at all to him. The ten years he'd lost and the ruin of his family could never be repaired by any belated acquittal.

"Laura was still alive when the three boys threw her in the underground tank," Bodenstein went on. "When they suddenly developed scruples and wanted to pull her back out, Lutz Richter stopped them by covering the tank with dirt. He was also the one who started a militia in Altenhain and made sure that everyone kept their mouths shut."

Tobias didn't react, but his father turned deathly pale.

"Lutz?"

"Yes." Bodenstein nodded. "Richter also organized the attack on your son in the barn, and he and his wife were behind the graffiti on your house and the anonymous letters. They used all means possible to prevent the truth from coming out. When we arrested his son, Richter shot himself in the head. He's still in a coma, but he'll survive, and then he'll be called to account in court."

"And Nadia?" Hartmut Sartorius whispered. "I suppose she knew about all of this, didn't she?"

"Yes, she did," said Bodenstein. "She was an eyewitness when Lauterbach killed Stefanie. And earlier she had convinced her friends to throw Laura in the tank. She could have averted Tobias's conviction, but she said nothing. For eleven years. When he got out of prison, she wanted to make sure he didn't come back to Altenhain."

"But why?" Tobias's voice sounded hoarse. "I don't understand. She . . . she always wrote to me and waited for me and . . ."

He fell silent, shaking his head.

"Nadia was in love with you," said Pia. "But you always rejected her. She found it very convenient that Laura and Stefanie vanished from the scene. She probably didn't think they would actually convict you. When you were sent to prison, she decided to wait for you and win you for herself. But then Amelie showed up. Nadia saw her as a rival, but more than that, she was a genuine threat, because Amelie had obviously found out about something. Nadia disguised herself as a police officer so she could look for Thies's paintings at the Fröhlichs' house."

"Yes, I know. But she didn't find them," said Tobias.

"Oh yes, she did," Bodenstein replied. "Anyway, she destroyed the paintings, because you would have realized at once that Nadia had lied to you."

Stunned, Tobias stared at Bodenstein, then swallowed hard when he realized the full scope of Nadia's lies and deceit. It was almost more than he could cope with.

"Everyone in Altenhain knew the truth," Pia went on. "Claudius Terlinden didn't talk, because he wanted to protect his own name and his son Lars's reputation. Since he had a guilty conscience, he supported you and your parents financially and—"

"That wasn't the only reason," Tobias interrupted her. His rigid expression became animated again, and he cast a glance at his father. "But now I'm slowly beginning to get it. All he cared about was his power and . . ."

"And what?" asked Hartmut.

Tobias just shook his head mutely.

His father swayed. The truth about his neighbors and former friends was shattering for him. The whole village had kept silent and lied and selfishly watched as his livelihood, his marriage, his good reputation, yes, his very life were ruined. He sank down onto one of the plastic chairs next to the wall and buried his face in his hands. Tobias sat down next to him and put his arm around his father's shoulders.

"But we also have some good news." Only now did it occur to Bodenstein why he and Pia had come to the hospital. "Actually we were just on our way to see Amelie Fröhlich and Thies Terlinden. We found both of them today in the cellar of a house in Königstein. Dr. Lauterbach kidnapped them and hid them there."

"Amelie is alive?" Tobias straightened up as if he'd had an electric shock. "Is she okay?"

"Yes. Come with us. Amelie will be glad to see you."

Tobias hesitated a moment but then stood up. Even his father looked up and smiled timidly. But seconds later his smile disappeared, and his expression contorted with hatred and fury. He jumped up and dashed with a speed that surprised Pia toward a man who had just entered the lobby of the hospital.

"No, Dad, no!" they heard Tobias shout, and only then did they recognize Claudius Terlinden, accompanied by his wife and the Fröhlichs. Obviously they were on their way to see their children. Hartmut Sartorius grabbed Terlinden by the throat, trying to choke him, while Christine Terlinden and Arne and Barbara Fröhlich stood by as if paralyzed.

"You pig!" Sartorius snarled full of hate. "You lying bastard! You have my family on your conscience!"

Claudius Terlinden's face was flushed and he was desperately flailing his arms and kicking at his attacker. Bodenstein grasped the situation and moved to take action. Pia too wanted to intervene, but she was shoved roughly aside by Tobias. She collided with Barbara Fröhlich, lost her balance, and fell to the floor. People had stopped, gaping at what was going on. Tobias had reached his father and tried to grab his arm, but at that instant Claudius Terlinden managed to escape from Hartmut's grip. The fear of death lent him super-human strength. He shoved Sartorius away. Pia got back on her feet and watched as if in slow motion as Hartmut Sartorius stumbled backward from the violent shove and crashed into an open fire door. Tobias started yelling and threw himself over his father. Suddenly there was blood everywhere. Pia reacted instinctively. She tore the scarf from Barbara Fröhlich's neck, knelt down next to Sartorius, ignoring the pool of blood that was fast becoming a lake. In the desperate hope of being able to stop the bleeding somehow, she pressed the bright blue pashmina scarf against the gaping wound on the back of Sartorius's head. The man's legs twitched convulsively and he made a gur-gling sound.

"We need a doctor! Quick!" Bodenstein shouted. "Damn it, there must be a doctor here somewhere!"

Coughing and choking, Claudius Terlinden crawled a short distance away, his hands at his throat. His eyes were bulging out of his head.

"I didn't mean to do it," he kept stammering over and over. "That's ... that's not what I wanted. It was ... it was an accident ..."

Pia heard footsteps and yelling as if from far away. Her jeans, her hands, her jacket were all soaked with blood. White shoes and pants legs appeared in her field of vision.

"Step aside!" somebody yelled. She scooted back a little, looked up, and met Bodenstein's eyes. It was too late. Hartmut Sartorius was dead.

"I couldn't do a thing." Pia shook her head in shock. "It all happened so fast."

She was still shaking all over and could barely hold the bottle of Coke that Bodenstein had pressed into her blood-smeared hands.

"Don't blame yourself," said Oliver.

"But I do, damn it. Where's Tobias?"

"He was still there." Bodenstein looked around, searching. The lobby was cordoned off, and yet there was a throng of people. Police, doctors with tense, shocked expressions, and the officers in their white overalls looked on as the body of Hartmut Sartorius was lifted into a zinc coffin. "Just stay right here." Bodenstein put his hand briefly on Pia's shoulder and got up. "I'm going to look for Tobias and make sure he's okay."

Pia nodded and stared at the sticky, dried blood on her hands. She straightened up and took some deep breaths. Gradually her heartbeat calmed down and she could think clearly again. Her gaze fell on Claudius Terlinden, who sat slumped on a chair, staring into the distance. In front of him stood an officer who was apparently trying to take down an account of what happened. The death of Hartmut Sartorius was an accident, there was no doubt about that. Terlinden had acted in self-defense and with no malice aforethought, and yet he seemed to be gradually comprehending the weight of guilt on his shoulders. A young female doctor squatted down in front of Pia.

"Shall I give you something to calm your nerves?" she asked with concern.

"No, I'm okay," replied Pia. "But could I maybe wash my hands somewhere?"

"Yes, of course. Come with me."

Her knees shaking, Pia followed the doctor. She kept an eye out for Tobias Sartorius, but didn't see him anywhere. Where was he? How would he cope with this horrible occurrence, seeing his father die right before his eyes? Pia was usually able to keep a cool head and remain composed even in a crisis, but the fate of Tobias Sartorius had shaken her to her core. Little by little he had lost everything that a human being can lose.

"Tobi!" Amelie sat up in bed and smiled in disbelief. She had thought of him so often during the past horrible days and nights; she had talked to him in her mind, imagining how it would be to see him again. The memory of the warmth in his sea-blue eyes had kept her from going crazy, and now he was right here in the room. Her heart skipped wildly with joy. "Oh, I'm so happy that you came to visit me! I've wanted so much . . ."

Her smile faded when in the dim light she noticed Tobias's expression.

He closed the door of the hospital room behind him and came closer with hesitant steps to stand at the foot of her bed. He looked terrible, deathly pale, with swollen, bloodshot eyes. Amelie could tell that something dreadful must have happened.

"What happened?" she asked softly.

"My father is dead," he whispered. "It just happened . . . down in the lobby. Terlinden was coming toward us . . . and my father . . . and he . . ."

Tobias fell silent. His breathing was ragged, and he pressed his fist against his mouth, fighting for self-control. In vain.

"Oh God." Amelie stared at him in horror. "But how . . . I mean, why . . ."

Tobias grimaced and doubled up, his lips quivering.

"Dad tried to . . . attack that . . . bastard." His voice was toneless. "And Terlinden shoved him . . . against a glass door . . ."

He broke off. Tears were streaming down his haggard face. Amelie tossed back the covers and held out her arms to him. Tobias sat down on the edge of the bed and allowed Amelie to pull him close. He pressed his face against her neck, his body shaking with wild, desperate sobs. Amelie held him tight. Her heart ached for him as she realized that Tobias had nobody left in the world—she was the only one he could turn to in his boundless grief.

Tobias Sartorius had vanished without a trace from the hospital. Bodenstein sent a patrol to his parents' house, but so far he hadn't shown up there. Claudius Terlinden had gone home with his wife. He was not directly responsible for Hartmut's death; it had been an accident, an unfortunate accident with a tragic result. Bodenstein glanced at his watch. Today was Monday, so Cosima would be at her mother's. The bridge nights at the Rotkirch house were a dependable ritual going back decades, so he was pretty sure he wouldn't run into her when he picked up some fresh clothes before he drove back to the station. Dirty and sweaty, he was longing for a good long shower.

To his relief the house was dark, only the little lamp on the chest in the hall was burning. The dog greeted him with effusive joy. Oliver petted him and looked around. Everything seemed so normal and so painfully familiar, but he knew this wasn't home anymore. Before he could get sentimental he determinedly climbed the stairs to the bedroom. He turned on the light and was shocked to see Cosima sitting in the easy chair by the window. His heart skipped a couple of beats.

"Why are you sitting here in the dark?" he asked, because he couldn't think of anything better to say.

"I wanted to think in peace and quiet." She squinted in the glare of the light, then stood up and stepped behind the chair as if seeking protection.

"I'm sorry that I lost my temper like that this morning," Oliver began after a brief pause. "It . . . was all a bit too much for me."

"That's all right. It was my fault," Cosima replied. They looked at each other without a word until the silence turned awkward.

"I just came by to pick up some clothes," he said, and left the bedroom. How could he suddenly feel nothing at all for someone for whom he had felt nothing but love for twenty-five years? Was he fooling himself by resorting to some sort of emotional defense mechanism? Or was this simply proof that his feelings for Cosima had long since become nothing but habit? He realized that over the past few weeks and months they'd had numerous minor quarrels, and each time more of his love had faded. Oliver was surprised that he was able to analyze the situation with such clarity. He opened the hall closet and studied the suitcases standing there. He didn't want to take any of the luggage that Cosima had used in her trips around the world. That's why he decided on two dusty but brand-new hardshell suitcases that Cosima found too unwieldy.

As he was passing the door of Sophia's room, he stopped. There should be time for a brief look in at the little one. He set down the suitcases and went into the room, which was illuminated by a small night-light next to the bed. Sophia was sleeping peacefully with her little thumb in her mouth, surrounded by her stuffed animals. Oliver looked at his youngest daughter and sighed. He bent over the bed, reached out his hand, and lightly touched the sleep-warm face of the child.

"I'm sorry, sweetheart," he whispered softly. "But even for your sake I can't pretend that everything is fine."

The way the female police officer had knelt down in the huge pool of blood was a sight that Tobias would never forget. He had sensed that his father was dead even before anyone uttered those most final of words. As if turned to stone he had stood there, speechless and empty of all feeling, letting himself be pushed aside by doctors, medics, and police officers. In his heart there was no more room for emotion after so much horrible news. As in a ship that was filling up with water, the last protective bulkheads had closed to prevent the vessel from sinking.

Tobias left the hospital and took off walking. Nobody tried to stop him. He marched straight through the dark Eichwald, and the cold gradually cleared his thoughts. Nadia, Jörg, Felix, Papa. They had all left, betrayed, or disappointed him, and now he had no one else he could turn to. Mixed in with the paralyzing gray of his helplessness were mixed bright red sparks of anger. With each step he took his resentment grew toward the people who had destroyed his life, squeezing all the air out of him and leaving him to stop and gasp for breath. His heart cried out for revenge because of everything that they had done to him and his parents. Now he had nothing more to lose. In his mind more and more loose ends were coming together, and suddenly it all made sense. In a flash he realized that with his father's death he was now the last person who knew the secret of Claudius Terlinden and Daniela Lauterbach. Tobias clenched his fists as he recalled what happened twenty years ago—an event that his father had helped the two of them conceal.

He had been seven or eight years old at the time, and had spent the evening in the side room of the restaurant, as he did so often. His mother wasn't there, so nobody had thought about putting him to bed. At some point he woke up on the couch in the middle of the night. He got up, crept to the door, and overheard a conversation that he couldn't understand. Only Claudius Terlinden and old Dr. Fuchsberger, who ate at the Golden Rooster almost every night, were still sitting at the bar. Tobias had seen drunks often enough to recognize that the honorable notary public Dr. Herbert Fuchsberger was completely plastered.

"So what's the problem?" Claudius Terlinden said, giving Tobias's father a sign to refill the notary's glass. "My brother doesn't give a damn. He's dead."

"I'll be in deep shit," Fuchsberger had muttered indistinctly, "if it ever gets out!"

"Why would it get out? Nobody knows that Willi changed his will."

"No, no, no! I can't do it," Fuchsberger moaned.

"I'll raise the fee," Terlinden countered. "In fact, I'll double it. A hundred thousand. How's that?"

Tobias had seen how Terlinden motioned to his father for more drinks. Things went on like this for a while until the old man finally gave in.

"All right," he said. "But you stay here. I don't want anyone seeing you in my office."

After that Tobias's father had disappeared with Dr. Fuchsberger in tow while Claudius Terlinden remained sitting at the bar. Tobias would probably never have understood what went on that night if years later he hadn't been searching for the car insurance papers in his father's office and found a will in the safe. At the time he hadn't given much thought to why Wilhelm Terlinden's will would be in his father's safe. Getting his very first car registered was much more important. And Tobias hadn't thought about it since then, pushing the discovery aside and finally forgetting all about it. But the shock of his father's death seemed to have opened a secret chamber in his brain, and suddenly it all came back to him.

"Where are we going?"

Amelie's voice pulled Tobias out of his gloomy reveries. He looked at her, put his hand on hers, and it warmed his heart. Her dark eyes were full of genuine care for him. Without all that metal piercing her face and that crazy hairdo she was beautiful. Much more beautiful than Stefanie had ever been. Amelie hadn't hesitated a second to sneak out of the hospital with him when he said that he still had a score to settle. Her gruff, prickly manner was only a façade; he had seen that at their first meeting in front of the church. Since people had so often disappointed and betrayed Tobias, he was continually astounded at Amelie's selfless honesty and lack of guile.

"First we're driving to my house, and then I have to talk to Claudius Terlinden," he now replied. "But you'll have to wait in the car. I don't want anything to happen to you."

"I'm not leaving you alone with that fucker," she argued. "If we're together he won't dare do anything to you."

In spite of everything Tobias had to smile. She was certainly brave enough. A tiny gleam of hope flickered inside him like a candle whose light was seeking a path through the fog and darkness. Maybe there would be a future for him when all of this was over.

Cosima hadn't budged. She was still standing behind the easy chair and now watched Oliver open the suitcase and pack it with the contents of his wardrobe.

"This is your house," she said after a while. "You don't have to move out."

"But I'm going to." He didn't look at her. "It was our house. I don't want to live here anymore. I can use the apartment in the old carriage house at the estate, it's been empty for a while. That's the best solution. Then when you're traveling, my parents or Quentin and Marie-Louise can take care of Sophia."

"Well, that was fast," Cosima said sharply. "So you've already written off the whole marriage."

Oliver sighed.

"No, it wasn't me," he said. "It was you. I merely accepted your decision, the way I've always done. And now I'm trying to figure out the new situation. You've chosen another man, and I can't do anything about that. But I intend to keep on living in spite of it."

For a second he considered telling Cosima about spending the night with Nicola. He remembered some pointed remarks that Cosima had made about Nicola, since she knew he was working with his ex. But that would have been a cheap shot and beneath him.

"Alexander and I work together," Cosima said. "I haven't 'chosen' him, as you put it."

Oliver continued stacking his shirts in the suitcases.

"But maybe he's a better fit for you than I ever was." He looked up. "Why, Cosima? Have there been so few adventures in your life?"

"No, that's not it." She shrugged. "There isn't any reasonable explanation. And no excuse for it either. Alex simply crossed my path at the wrong time. I was so pissed off at you on Mallorca."

"So you just jumped into bed with him. Because you were pissed off at me." Oliver shook his head and closed one of the suitcases. He straightened up. "Well, that's just great."

"Oliver, please don't throw everything away." Cosima pleaded. "I made a mistake, I know. And I'm truly sorry. But there are so many things that still bind us."

"And even more that divide us," he replied. "I will never be able to trust you again, Cosima. And I cannot and will not live without trust."

Bodenstein left her standing there and went into the bathroom across the hall. He closed the door behind him, undressed, and got in the shower. Under the hot water his cramped muscles relaxed and the tension eased a bit. His thoughts drifted to the previous night and then to the many nights to come in his life. Never again would he lie awake tormenting himself with worry about what Cosima was doing on the other side of the globe, whether things were going well, whether she was in danger, had had an accident, or was even in bed with another guy. It surprised him that this new scenario did not make him feel melancholy, only deeply relieved. He could no longer live according to Cosima's rules of the game. In fact, he decided at this very moment never to live according to any rules but his own.

He hoped that they hadn't arrived too late, but they had been waiting for less than fifteen minutes in the car when the black Mercedes drove up and stopped briefly in front of the spike-topped gate of the Terlinden plant. As if by magic the gate slid to one side. The brake lights of the Mercedes went out as it moved forward.

"Okay, go!" said Tobias. They jumped out of the car, ran like mad, and just made it through the gate before it closed. The gatehouse was empty. At night only the cameras watched the grounds. There hadn't been any security service for quite a while, as Tobias had learned from his friend Michael, who worked at the Terlinden plant. Had worked, he corrected himself. Now Michael was in the slammer, just like Jörg and Felix and Nadia.

A light snowfall had started. Silently they followed the tire tracks that Terlinden's Mercedes had left. Tobias slowed down a bit. Amelie's hand felt ice cold in his. During the days of her imprisonment she had lost a lot of weight, and was really too weak to take part in an escapade like this. But she had insisted on coming with him. Without speaking they walked past the big workshops. When they turned the corner they saw the lights go on in the top floor of the administration building. Near the front entrance stood the black Mercedes in the orange glow of the portal's lights. Tobias and Amelie dashed across the unlit parking lot and reached the entrance of the building.

"The door isn't locked," Amelie whispered.

"I'd rather you wait here," said Tobias and looked at her. Her eyes seemed gigantic in her sharp, pale face, but she shook her head firmly.

"No way. I'm coming with you."

"All right then." He took a deep breath and then gave her a big hug. "Thanks, Amelie. Thanks for everything."

"Stop screwing around," she answered gruffly. "Let's go in."

A smile flitted across his face and he nodded. They crossed the big lobby, went past the elevator, and entered the stairwell, which was also unlocked. Claudius Terlinden didn't seem to be afraid of break-ins. By the time they reached the fifth floor Amelie was out of breath and had to lean on the banister for a moment. The heavy glass door clacked when Tobias opened it. He paused briefly and listened in the dark hallways, which were only dimly lit by tiny lamps near the floor. Hand in hand they crept along the hallway. Tobias could feel his heart hammering with tension. He stopped when he heard the voice of Claudius Terlinden coming from the half-open door of a room at the end of the hall.

". . . hurry. If it starts snowing any harder the plane might not even start."

Tobias and Amelie exchanged a glance. Terlinden seemed to be on the phone. Apparently they had arrived in the nick of time, because it sounded as though he wanted to take off in a plane for parts unknown. They went closer. Suddenly they heard a second voice. Amelie gave a start when she heard it and grabbed Tobias's hand.

"What's wrong with you?" asked Dr. Daniela Lauterbach. "Why are you just standing around like this?"

The door opened all the way and bright light flooded into the hallway. Tobias managed to open the door of an office behind him just in time. He shoved Amelie into the dark and stood next to her, his heart pounding.

"Shit, what's she doing here?" Amelie whispered in bewilderment. "She tried to kill me and Thies! And Terlinden knows that!"

Tobias nodded nervously. He was trying to figure out how he could stop the two. He had to prevent them from getting on that plane and disappearing forever. If he were alone he would have simply confronted them. But there was no way he was going to put Amelie in any danger. His eyes fell on the desk in the room.

"Hide under there," he said softly. Amelie tried to protest, but Tobias insisted. He waited until she had crept under the desk, then he lifted the receiver of the telephone and pressed it to his ear. In the faint glow from the exterior lighting he could hardly see a thing. He pressed a button and hoped that it would get him an outside line. And it did. With shaking fingers he dialed the police.

Terlinden was standing in front of the open safe, absentmindedly massaging his sore neck with one hand and staring into space. He hadn't really recovered from the accident at the hospital. He still felt like his heart was going to stop for a couple of beats. Could it be the result of having his supply of oxygen cut off for a few moments? Hartmut Sartorius had attacked him like a madman, choking him with unexpected power until he saw flashes of light before his eyes. For a few seconds he was sure that his last hour had come. He had never been physically attacked before, and the idea of being "scared to death" had been an empty cliché until today. But now he knew how it felt to look death in the eye. He couldn't remember how he managed to escape from the viselike grip of that maniac, but suddenly Sartorius was lying on the floor in a pool of blood. It was horrible, absolutely horrible! Claudius Terlinden realized that he was still in shock.

His gaze fell on Daniela, who was kneeling under his desk and screwing the computer housing back together with an expression of concentration. The hard drive, which she had replaced with another one, was already in one of the suitcases. Daniela had insisted on doing this, although he thought it was unnecessary. He hadn't saved anything on his computer that would interest the police. Everything was turning out differently than he had planned. In hindsight Claudius Terlinden had to acknowledge that the cover-up of Lars's involvement in the murder of Laura Wagner had been a grave mistake. He hadn't sufficiently considered what the consequences might be if he took

the boy out of the line of fire. This single decision, which he'd thought so
insignificant, had made dozens of others necessary. The web of lies had become
so tangled and confused that it had resulted in regrettable but unavoidable
collateral damage. If those stupid farmers had only listened to him instead of
taking matters in their own hands, nothing would have happened. Then the
tiny rip in the fabric that occurred after the return of Tobias Sartorius rapidly turned into a huge hole, a yawning black abyss. Terlinden's whole life,
his rules, the daily rituals that gave him security—all of it was swept along
by this maelstrom of infernal events.

"What's wrong with you? Why are you just standing there?"

Daniela's voice tore him out of his musings. With a groan she got to her
feet and looked him up and down with a contemptuous expression on her face.
Claudius Terlinden noticed that he was still holding his throat, and he
turned away. She must have realized long ago that everything might fall
apart one day. Her escape plan was perfect and had been worked out to the
tiniest detail. But it left him cold. New Zealand? What would he do there?
This was the center of his life, here in this village, in this building, in this room.
He didn't want to leave Germany, even if the worst-case scenario meant he'd
spend a couple of years in jail. The thought of sitting in some foreign country
with a false identity made him uncomfortable, even afraid. Here he was
somebody, people knew him and respected him, and he was sure that everything would eventually calm down. In New Zealand he would be a nothing,
a nameless refugee, forever and ever.

He looked around the big room. Was he really seeing all this today for
the last time? Never again to walk into his house, visit the graves of his parents and grandparents in the cemetery, look out at the familiar panorama of
the Taunus? The prospect was unbearable and actually brought tears to his
eyes. He had fought so hard to take the life work of his forefathers to even
greater heights. Could he really leave it all behind and walk away?

"Come on, Claudius, let's get out of here!" Daniela's voice had a piercing
sound. "It's snowing even harder outside. We have to go."

He shoved the documents that he wanted to leave into the safe. His
hand happened to touch the box in which he kept the pistol.

I don't want to leave, he thought. *I'd rather kill myself.*

He froze. Where had that thought come from? He had never understood how anyone could be so cowardly as to see suicide as the only way out. But everything was different now that death had grinned in his face.

"Is there anyone besides us in the building?" Daniela asked.

"No," Terlinden croaked and took the box with the gun out of the safe.

"Then why is the outside line busy?" She bent over the telephone in the middle of his desk. "Extension twenty-three."

"That's bookkeeping. There's nobody there."

"Did you lock the door behind us when we came in the building?"

"No." He snapped out of his paralysis, opened the box, and looked at the Beretta.

The restaurant above the Opel Zoo was crowded. The place was dark, warm, and loud, just the way Pia liked it, and she and Christoph were sitting at a table right by the front window. At the moment Pia was no longer hearing in her mind what the people from the zoning office had said, nor was she seeing the lights of Kronberg or the glittering skyline of Frankfurt in the distance. She could smell the enticing aroma of the perfectly grilled filet mignon on her plate, but her stomach seemed to be tied in knots.

She had driven straight home from the hospital and stuffed all her clothes in the washing machine. Then took such a long shower that she used up all the hot water, but she still felt dirty. Pia was used to corpses, but not to watching someone die right before her eyes. Especially not a man she knew, with whom she'd been talking only a minute before, and for whom she had felt a deep sympathy. She shuddered.

"Would you rather go home?" Christoph asked at that moment. The concern in his brown eyes nearly caused Pia to lose her self-control. Suddenly she was fighting back tears. Where could Tobias be? She hoped he hadn't done anything to harm himself.

"No, it's all right." She forced herself to smile, but the sight of the juicy steak on the plate before her made her nauseous. She shoved the plate away. "I'm sorry I'm not better company today. I just can't help blaming myself."

"I know. But what else could you have done?" Christoph leaned forward, reached out his hand, and touched her cheek. "You said yourself that everything happened incredibly fast."

"Yes, of course. It's bullshit. I couldn't have done anything, not a thing. But still . . ." She heaved a big sigh. "In moments like that I hate my job with all of my heart."

"Come on, sweetie. We'll go home, open a bottle of red wine, and . . ."

The ring of Pia's phone cut him off. She was on call.

"Whatever was coming after 'and' interests me a lot." Pia grinned feebly, and Christoph raised his eyebrows meaningfully. She grabbed her cell and took the call.

"A Tobias Sartorius called in an emergency seven minutes ago," the dispatcher from the operations center told her. "He's in the admin building of the Terlinden company in Altenhain and he says that a Dr. Lauterbach is there. I've already sent a patrol car—"

"Oh shit," Pia interrupted her colleague. Her thoughts were racing. What was Daniela Lauterbach doing with Claudius Terlinden? Why was Tobias there? Did he want to take revenge? Without a doubt Tobias was a ticking time bomb after all he'd been through. She jumped up. "Radio the guys right away. And for God's sake tell them not to go in with flashing lights and sirens. Tell them to wait for me and Bodenstein!"

"What happened?" asked Christoph. Pia explained it to him in a few words as she punched Bodenstein's number into her cell. To her relief she reached him only seconds later. In the meantime Christoph signaled the restaurant owner, who knew him well since he was the director of the neighboring zoo. He promised to come by later and pay the bill.

"I'll drive you," he said to Pia. "It'll take me three seconds to get our jackets."

She nodded, went out front, and waited impatiently, staring at the snowstorm. Why had Tobias called in an emergency? Had something happened to him? She hoped they wouldn't be too late.

"Damn," Tobias whispered in helpless fury. Claudius Terlinden and Daniela Lauterbach had left the office. Loaded down with luggage and briefcases they were walking down the hall to the elevator. What could he do to stop them? How long would it take the cops to get here? Damn, damn! He turned to Amelie, who was peeking out from under the desk.

"Stay here," he said in a voice rough with tension.

"Where are you going?"

"I have to get them involved in a conversation to stall for time until the police get here."

"No, please don't do that, Tobi!" Amelie slipped out from her hiding place. In the faint glow from the exterior lights her eyes looked huge. "Please, Tobi, let them go. I'm scared."

"I can't just let them take off after everything they've done. You have to understand that," he replied vehemently. "Stay here, Amelie. Promise me that."

She crossed her arms and nodded. He took a deep breath and put his hand on the door handle.

"Tobi!"

"Yes?"

She went over to him and touched her palm to his face.

"Be careful," she whispered. A tear rolled down her cheek. Tobias stared at her. For a fraction of a second he was tempted to take her in his arms, kiss her, and simply stay with her. But then the fierce wish for revenge, which was what had brought him here, took precedence. He couldn't let Terlinden and Lauterbach escape.

"I'll be right back," he murmured. Before he could have second thoughts he stepped out into the hall and took off running. The elevator was already on the way down, so he tore open the fire door and dashed down the stairs, taking three or four steps at a time. He reached the lobby at the very moment they were getting out of the elevator.

"Stop!" he shouted, and his voice echoed through the lobby. As if stunned they both spun around and stared at him in disbelief. Terlinden dropped his suitcase. Tobias was shaking all over. Although he would have liked to hurl himself at them, he had to control himself and stay calm.

"Tobias!" Claudius Terlinden was the first to recover. "I . . . I'm terribly sorry about what happened. Really, you have to believe me, I didn't mean to—"

"Shut up!" Tobias screamed, fixing his eyes on them as he slowly moved in a semicircle. "I'm not going to listen to any more of your shitty lies. You're to blame for everything. You and this . . . this devious bitch."

He pointed his finger accusingly at Daniela Lauterbach.

"The two of you have always pretended to be so understanding, but you knew the truth all along. And you let me go to prison. And now you're probably trying to make your escape, right? But there's no chance in hell I'm going to let that happen. I've already called the police, and they'll be here any minute."

He saw the quick look that Terlinden and Lauterbach exchanged.

"I'm going to tell you everything that I know about you. And it's a lot, believe me. My father is dead so he can't be a witness anymore, but I know what you did in 1997."

"Now just calm down," said Daniela Lauterbach, giving him the friendly smile that always fooled people. "What exactly are you talking about?"

"I'm talking about your first husband." Tobias came closer and stood right in front of her. Her cold brown eyes bored into his. "About Wilhelm, Uncle Willi, Claudius's older brother, and what he put in his will."

"I see." Daniela Lauterbach kept smiling at him. "And why do you think the police would be interested in any of this?"

"Because it wasn't his real will," said Tobias. "Dr. Fuchsberger gave the real one to my father after Claudius got him drunk and promised him a hundred thousand marks."

The smile on Daniela Lauterbach's face froze.

"Your first husband was deathly ill, but he wasn't happy about the fact that you'd cheated on him with his brother Claudius, so he changed his will two weeks before he died. He disinherited both of you. Instead he stipulated that the daughter of his chauffeur would be his sole heir, because shortly before his death he found out that Claudius had gotten her pregnant in May 1976. And that on his orders you made her abort the child."

"Did your father tell you this nonsense?" Claudius Terlinden broke in.

"No." Tobias didn't take his eyes off Daniela Lauterbach. "He wasn't supposed to tell anyone. Dr. Fuchsberger gave my father the will and he was supposed to destroy it, but he never did. He kept it hidden in his safe, until today."

Now he looked at Claudius Terlinden.

"That's why you made sure my father stayed in Altenhain, isn't it? Because he knew everything. Actually the company doesn't belong to you, or the villa either. And Dr. Lauterbach would never have inherited her house or all the money from her first husband. According to the will, it all belongs to the daughter of Wilhelm Terlinden's former chauffeur, Kurt Cramer . . ." Tobias snorted. "Unfortunately, my father never could bring himself to tell anyone about the real will. It's a shame, really."

"Yes, what a shame," said Daniela Lauterbach. "But that gives me an idea."

Terlinden and Dr. Lauterbach were standing with their backs to the stairwell and couldn't see Amelie, who had come into the lobby, but they did notice that Tobias's attention was distracted for a moment. Daniela Lauterbach grabbed the box that Terlinden had stuck under his arm, and Tobias suddenly found himself looking into the barrel of a gun.

"I'd almost forgotten about that dreadful evening, until you reminded me of it. You remember, Claudius, the way Wilhelm suddenly stood in the doorway of the bedroom, holding this very pistol and aiming at us?" She smiled at Tobias. "Thank you for giving me the idea, you little idiot."

Without hesitating another second, Daniela Lauterbach fired the gun. An ear-splitting boom shattered the silence. Tobias felt a violent jolt and then his chest seemed about to explode. In disbelief he stared at the doctor, who had already turned away. He heard Amelie desperately calling his name in a shrill voice. He wanted to speak but couldn't get any air, and his legs gave way. Tobias Sartorius hit the granite floor but didn't feel it. Everything around him was black and deathly still.

They were discussing how to get onto the hermetically sealed grounds of the Terlinden factory when from the other side of the gate a dark limousine approached with its high beams on. The gate slid silently to the side.

"There he is!" shouted Pia, motioning to her colleagues. Claudius Terlinden, behind the wheel of the Mercedes, had to brake abruptly as two patrol cars suddenly blocked his way.

"He's alone in the car," said Bodenstein. Pia stepped up next to him, her weapon drawn, and motioned to Terlinden to roll down the window. Two uniformed officers lent weight to her demand as they took up position on the other side of the car, weapons at the ready.

"What do you want from me?" Terlinden asked. He was sitting stock still, his hands gripping the steering wheel. Despite the cold, his face glistened with sweat.

"Step out of the vehicle, open all the doors and the trunk," Bodenstein ordered. "Where is Tobias Sartorius?"

"How should I know?"

"And where is Dr. Lauterbach? Now get the hell out!"

Terlinden didn't move. Naked panic showed in his wide-open eyes.

"He's not getting out," said a voice from inside the car behind tinted windows. Bodenstein leaned forward and saw Daniela Lauterbach in the back seat. She was holding a gun pressed to the back of Terlinden's neck.

"Now clear the road at once, or I'll shoot this man," she threatened. Bodenstein began to sweat. He had no doubt that Daniela Lauterbach would do as she said. The woman had a gun in her hand and nothing left to lose—an extremely dangerous combination. The doors of the Mercedes had automatically locked by the time the car reached the gate, so neither Bodenstein nor the officers on the other side could have yanked open the doors to overpower the doctor.

"I think she means it," Terlinden whispered tensely. His lower lip was quivering, and he was obviously in a state of shock. Bodenstein was frantically considering the options. There was not much chance they could escape. In this weather even an S-Class Mercedes couldn't do more than seventy-five miles an hour with snow tires.

"I'll let you go," he said at last. "But first tell me where Tobias is."

"Probably with his daddy in heaven," replied Daniela Lauterbach with a cold laugh.

Bodenstein and a patrol car followed the black Mercedes as it left the company grounds and drove up the hill to the B8, while Pia called for backup on the radio and ordered an ambulance. Terlinden turned right on the highway that had recently been widened to four lanes, heading for the Autobahn. At

Bad Soden two more patrol cars joined them, and a few kilometers farther on they picked up three more. Luckily rush hour was over. If they got into a traffic jam the situation could escalate rapidly, but Lauterbach would hardly shoot her driver in the head while they were moving. Bodenstein looked in the rearview mirror. Now a dozen emergency vehicles were following them, blue lights flashing and blocking all three lanes for the traffic behind them.

"They're heading for the city," said Pia as the black Mercedes took a right at the Eschborn Triangle. Ignoring the smoking ban in all service vehicles, she lit up a cigarette. Various voices were squawking from the radio. Their colleagues in Frankfurt had been informed and would attempt to keep the roads clear if Terlinden actually headed into the city.

"Maybe they're going to the airport," Bodenstein mused aloud.

"I hope not," said Pia, who was waiting for news of Tobias. Bodenstein took a quick glance at his colleague, whose face was white with tension. What a day. The immense pressure of the past few weeks had barely subsided after Thies and Amelie were found. A whole new chain of events suddenly started, coming thick and fast. Had it really only been this morning that he woke up in Nicola's bed?

"They're heading into the city!" Pia yelled into the radio as Terlinden shot straight through the Westkreuz interchange instead of taking the Autobahn 5. "What are they up to?"

"They want to lose us downtown," Bodenstein guessed. The wipers on high were flicking over the windshield. The snow had changed to pounding rain, and Terlinden was driving way above the speed limit. He wouldn't be stopping at any red lights, and the last thing they needed right now was for some pedestrian to get run over.

"Now he's passing the fairgrounds, turning right on Friedrich Ebert Boulevard," Pia reported. "He's doing at least fifty, keep the streets clear!"

Bodenstein needed to concentrate. The streets were wet with rain and reflected the taillights of the cars that had pulled over to the side, as well as the blue lights of the police cars that were blocking all the side streets.

"I think I'm going to need glasses soon," he muttered, stepping harder on the gas so he wouldn't lose Terlinden, who had just blown through his third red light. What was Lauterbach planning? Where was she going?

"Have you ever thought that maybe she—" Pia began, but then yelled, "Turn right! He's going right!"

Suddenly, without warning, Terlinden took a right at Platz der Republik down Mainzer Landstrasse. Bodenstein also spun the wheel to the right and clenched his teeth as the Opel skidded around the corner and just missed hitting a streetcar.

"Damn, that was close," he hissed. "Where'd he go? I can't see him."

"Left! Left!" Pia forgot the name of the street in her excitement, although she'd worked for years at the old police headquarters across the street. She was pointing frantically. "He went in over there!"

"Where?" the radio squawked. "Where are you?"

"Turned down Ottostrasse," said Bodenstein. "But I don't see them. Damn!"

"Tell the others to keep going straight to the train station!" Pia shouted into the radio. "Maybe he's just trying to shake us off."

She leaned forward.

"Right or left?" said Bodenstein as they crossed Poststrasse on the north side of the train station. He had to brake hard as a car came shooting out from the right. Swearing mightily, he stomped on the gas and decided intuitively to turn left.

"Jeez," said Pia without taking her eyes off the street. "I didn't know you even knew such words."

"I have kids," said Bodenstein, slowing down to a crawl. "Do you see the car anywhere?"

"There are hundreds of cars parked around here," she complained. She had rolled down her window and was peering out into the darkness. Farther up ahead they saw patrol cars with blue lights flashing. Passersby had stopped to stare despite the pouring rain.

"There!" Pia shouted, and Bodenstein jumped. "There they are! Coming out of that parking space!"

She was right. Seconds later the black Mercedes was in front of them, racing south on Baseler Strasse so fast that it was all Bodenstein could do to keep up. They zoomed across Baseler Platz toward the Friedensbrücke, and Bodenstein started praying silently. Pia kept reporting their position over the radio. At seventy-five miles an hour the Mercedes raced down Kennedyallee followed by a column of patrol cars. The police up ahead didn't try to stop them.

They crossed the bridge and Pia said, "They're heading for the airport after all" as they passed the Niederräder racetrack. She had barely gotten those words out when Terlinden whipped his car all the way to the left across three lanes and jumped the curb to skid along the streetcar tracks. Pia could hardly talk fast enough to keep up as Terlinden changed direction. The patrol cars in front were already on the airport approach road and couldn't turn around, but Bodenstein and Pia stayed behind the Mercedes as it turned onto the Isenburger cutoff in a breakneck maneuver. On the straightaway Terlinden stomped on the gas, and Bodenstein was sweating blood as he was forced to do the same. All of a sudden brake lights lit up in front of him, and the heavy Mercedes fishtailed and wound up in the oncoming lane. Bodenstein braked so hard that his car skidded too. Had Lauterbach shot her hostage at full speed?

"The back tire blew!" yelled Pia, who had grasped the situation at once. "Now they're not going anywhere."

After the frantic, crazy chase Terlinden hit his blinker and turned left onto Oberschweinstiege. He chugged along doing twenty-five through the woods, crossed the railroad tracks and pulled into the parking lot a couple of hundred yards farther on. Bodenstein stopped too, and Pia jumped out of the car and motioned to her colleagues in the patrol cars to surround the Mercedes. Then she got back inside. Bodenstein instructed everybody via radio to stay in their cars. Daniela Lauterbach was still armed. He didn't want to run any unnecessary risk and place his colleagues' lives in danger, especially since a SWAT team would arrive shortly. But then the driver's side door of the Mercedes opened. Bodenstein held his breath. Terlinden got out. He staggered slightly, held on to the open car door and looked around. Then he raised his hands in the air. He stood there motionless in the beam of the headlights.

"What's happening?" the radio squawked.

"He stopped the car and got out," said Bodenstein. "We're going over there."

He nodded to Pia, and they got out and approached Terlinden. Pia had her weapon aimed at the Mercedes, ready to fire at the slightest movement.

"Don't shoot," said Claudius Terlinden, dropping his arms. Pia's nerves were tensed to the breaking point as she tore open the rear door of the Mercedes and aimed inside. Then she lowered her gun, feeling only boundless disappointment. The back seat was empty.

"All of a sudden she was standing there in my office with a pistol aimed at me." Claudius Terlinden was speaking haltingly. Slumped and pale, he sat at the narrow table in one of the police vans. He was obviously in shock.

"Go on," Bodenstein urged him. Terlinden wanted to rub his hand over his face, but then he remembered that he was wearing handcuffs. Despite his allergy to nickel, thought Pia cynically, watching him without sympathy.

"She . . . she forced me to open the safe," Terlinden went on in a shaky voice. "I can't remember exactly what happened. Down in the lobby Tobias showed up all at once. With the girl. He—"

"With what girl?" Pia interrupted.

"With that . . . that . . . I can't remember her name."

"Amelie?"

"Right. Yes, I guess that's her name."

"Good. Keep talking."

"Daniela shot Tobias without hesitating. Then she forced me to get into the car."

"What about Amelie?"

"I don't know." Terlinden shrugged. "I don't know anything anymore. I just had to drive and keep driving. She told me which way to go."

"And she got out at the train station," said Bodenstein.

"Yes. She yelled 'Now turn right!' and then 'Now left!' I did exactly as she said."

"I can understand that." Bodenstein nodded, then leaned over. His voice turned sharp. "What I don't understand is why you didn't get out at the train station too. Why lead us on a dangerous chase through the city? Do you have any idea how easily you could have caused an accident?"

Pia chewed her lip and kept her eyes on Terlinden. Just as Bodenstein turned to her, Claudius Terlinden made a mistake. He did something that nobody in shock would do: He glanced at his watch.

"You're lying through your teeth!" Pia shouted at him. "It was all a prearranged plot. You were just playing for time. Where is Lauterbach?"

For a couple more minutes Terlinden tried to keep up the pretext, but Pia wouldn't let up.

"You're right," he finally admitted. "We were going to run away together. The plane leaves at eleven forty-five tonight. If you hurry maybe you can catch her."

"Where's it going? Where did you want to fly to?" Pia had to control herself not to grab the man by the shoulders and give him a good shake. "You'd better start talking. That woman shot someone. That's called murder. And if you don't start telling the truth, I promise you're going to be charged as an accomplice. So, which flight is Daniela Lauterbach planning to take? And under what name?"

"The one to São Paulo," Terlinden whispered, closing his eyes. "As Consuela la Roca."

"I'm going to the airport," Bodenstein decided as they stood outside next to the police van. "You keep grilling Terlinden."

Pia nodded. It really made her nervous that she hadn't heard anything yet from their colleagues in Altenhain. What happened to Amelie? Had Lauterbach shot her too? She asked one of the patrol officers to find out about Amelie and then climbed back into the VW bus.

In the interrogation room at the station Pia asked, "How could you do such a thing? Daniela Lauterbach almost killed your son Thies, after she'd been pumping him full of drugs for years."

Terlinden shut his eyes for a moment.

"You don't understand the situation," he replied wearily as he averted his eyes.

"Then explain it to me," Pia said. "Tell me why Daniela Lauterbach mistreated Thies so badly and why she set fire to the orangerie."

Claudius Terlinden opened his eyes and stared at Pia. A minute passed, then two.

"I fell in love with Daniela when my brother brought her to the house for the first time," he said. "It was a Sunday, the fourteenth of June, 1976. It was love at first sight. But a year later she married my brother, even though they weren't at all suitable for each other. They were absolutely miserable together. Daniela was very successful in her career, and she overshadowed my brother. He started hitting her more and more often, even in front of the servants. In the summer of 1977 she suffered a miscarriage, a year later another one, and then a third. My brother wanted an heir; he was furious and blamed her. When my wife had twin sons, that was the last straw."

Pia listened in silence, careful not to interrupt.

"Eventually Daniela might have asked for a divorce, but a couple of years later my brother was diagnosed with cancer. Terminal. So she no longer wanted to leave him. He died in May 1985."

"How convenient for the two of you," Pia remarked sarcastically. "But that doesn't explain why you wanted to help her escape. This is the woman who kidnapped Amelie and Thies and locked them in a cellar. If we hadn't found them they would have drowned, because Lauterbach flooded the cellar."

"What are you talking about?" Claudius Terlinden looked up in annoyance.

Suddenly it dawned on Pia that Terlinden really might not know what Daniela Lauterbach had done. Earlier in the day he had come to the hospital to visit his son, but the tragic death of Hartmut Sartorius may have postponed any further conversation. Besides, Thies probably wouldn't have wanted to tell his father what happened. So Pia now told Claudius Terlinden in detail about Daniela Lauterbach's devious attempt to murder Amelie and Thies.

"That can't be true," he kept whispering in growing bewilderment.

"Yes, it is. Daniela Lauterbach wanted to kill Thies because he was an eyewitness when her husband murdered Stefanie Schneeberger. And Amelie had to die because she had figured out the secret that Thies had kept all these years."

"My God." Terlinden buried his face in his hands.

"It seems to me that you didn't know the love of your life very well if you actually wanted to flee with her." Pia shook her head.

Terlinden was now staring into space.

"What an idiot I am. Everything is my fault! I was the one who offered that house to Albert Schneeberger."

"What does Schneeberger have to do with it?"

"Stefanie totally turned Thies's head. He was crazy about her, and then he happened to see how she and Gregor . . . well . . . you know. He had a fit of rage and attacked Gregor, and we had to put him in the psychiatric ward. A week before the girls died, he came back home. He was acting rationally again. The medications had worked wonders on him. And then Thies saw Gregor kill Stefanie."

Pia caught her breath.

"Gregor wanted to run away, but suddenly Thies stood in front of him. The boy was just standing there, staring at him, not saying a word, as usual. Gregor ran home in a panic, howling like a baby." Terlinden's voice took on a scornful tone. "Daniela called me and we met at Sartorius's barn. Thies was sitting next to the dead girl. At that moment it seemed best to hide the body somewhere, so I thought of the old bunker underneath the orangerie. But we couldn't get Thies to leave. He refused to let go of Stefanie's hand. Then Daniela had the idea of telling him that he should take care of Stefanie. It wasn't an ideal situation, but it worked. For eleven years. Until Amelie showed up. That nosy little twit ruined everything."

He and Daniela Lauterbach had known the truth about Laura and Stefanie all these years and never said a word. How could they have lived with such a terrible secret? Pia wondered.

"So who did you think kidnapped the girl and your son?" she asked.

"Nadia," Claudius Terlinden replied dully. "On the night that Gregor killed Stefanie, I saw her in the barn, but I never told anyone."

He sighed heavily.

"Later I had a talk with her about it," he went on. "She was quite reasonable, and when I offered to use my contacts to get her into television, she promised me never to breathe a word about what happened that night. She left Altenhain as she had always planned to do, and made a marvelous career for herself. After that, order was restored. Everything was fine." He rubbed his eyes. "Nothing would have happened if everyone had played by the rules."

"People aren't chess pieces," Pia replied sharply.

"Yes they are," Terlinden contradicted her. "Most people are happy to have somebody else take on the responsibility for their puny lives and make the decisions that they're unable to make. Somebody has to keep an eye on the big picture and pull the strings if necessary. And that someone is me." A smile appeared on his face, revealing a trace of pride.

"Wrong," said Pia soberly. She now understood all the connections in the story. "It wasn't you, but Daniela Lauterbach. You were only a pawn in her game, and she pushed you here and there at will."

Terlinden's smile vanished.

"You'd better hope that my boss catches her at the airport. Otherwise you're the only one who'll get the big headlines and you'll spend the rest of your life in prison."

"Unbelievable." Ostermann shook his head and looked at Pia. "If I understand things correctly, it means that Tobias's mother legally owns half of Altenhain."

"Precisely." Pia nodded. Before them on the table lay the three-page last will and testament of Wilhelm Julius Terlinden, signed and notarized on April 25, 1985, in which he disinherited his wife Daniela Terlinden, née Kroner, and his brother Claudius Paul Terlinden. Amelie had handed the document in a thick envelope to an officer before she got into the ambulance that would take Tobias Sartorius to the hospital. The young man had been very lucky. The gun Daniela Lauterbach had used to shoot him hadn't caused a fatal wound because of its low penetration power. Still, Tobias had lost a lot of blood, and even after the emergency operation he was not entirely out of danger.

"I don't really understand completely why Wilhelm Terlinden's will was in Hartmut Sartorius's possession," said Pia. "It was drafted only a couple of weeks before he died."

"That's probably when Wilhelm first learned that the two had been cheating on him for years."

"Hmm." Pia did her best to suppress a yawn. She had lost all sense of time and was dead tired, yet in high spirits. Tobias and his family had been the victims of evil intrigues and the greedy lust for money and power. But thanks to the will that Hartmut Sartorius had kept in his safe, Tobias and his mother could look forward to a relatively happy ending, at least financially.

"Go on, get out of here," Ostermann told Pia. "The paperwork can wait till tomorrow."

"Why didn't Hartmut Sartorius ever make this will public?" asked Pia.

"He was probably afraid of the consequences, or maybe he had skeletons of his own in the closet. Somehow he'd gotten hold of this will—most likely not in a legal manner," Ostermann replied. "Besides, in a village like that, other laws apply. I know all about it."

"What do you mean?"

Ostermann grinned and stood up.

"Don't tell me you want to hear my life story now, at three thirty in the morning."

"Three thirty? My God . . ." Pia yawned and stretched. "Did you know that Frank's wife left him? Or that Hasse was friends with the cultural minister?"

"Yes to the first one, no to the second," said Ostermann, turning off his computer. "Why do you ask?"

"I don't know." Pia shrugged. "But we seem to spend more time with our colleagues than with our partners, and yet we know nothing about each other. Why is that?"

Her cell rang with the special ringtone reserved for Christoph. He was waiting for her down in the parking lot. Pia got up with a groan and reached for her purse.

"I'm really having a tough time with this."

"Now, don't go getting all philosophical," Ostermann said from the doorway. "Tomorrow I'll tell you everything about me that you need to know."

Pia gave him a weary grin.

"Everything? Really?"

"Sure." Ostermann switched off the light. "I've got nothing to hide."

•   •   •

On the short ride from Hofheim to Unterliederbach, Pia's eyes closed from exhaustion. She didn't notice when Christoph got out to open the gate. When he shook her shoulder gently and kissed her cheek, she opened her eyes in confusion.

"You want me to carry you inside?" Christoph offered.

"Not a good idea." Pia yawned and grinned. "Then I'd have to drag the feed sacks myself all next week because you gave yourself a hernia."

She got out and staggered to the front door. The dogs greeted her with happy barking, demanding to be petted. After she hung up her jacket and pulled off her boots, she suddenly remembered the appointment with the zoning office.

"What actually happened at the meeting today?" she asked Christoph. He turned on the light in the kitchen.

"Nothing good, I'm afraid," he answered seriously. "Neither the house nor the barn were approved when they were built. And it's next to impossible to obtain retroactive approval because of the overhead power lines."

"But that can't be!" Pia felt like the rug was being pulled out from under her feet. This was her house, her home! Where was she supposed to go with all these animals? She stared at Christoph, shocked. "Now what? What happens now?"

He came over to her and took her in his arms.

"The demolition order still stands. We can file an appeal that will delay it for a while, but unfortunately not forever. And there's also another little problem."

"Oh, please no," Pia murmured, close to tears. "What else?"

"Actually the state of Hessen has the right of first refusal for the property, because at one time an autobahn exit was supposed to be built here," Christoph told her.

"Oh great. Then I'm going to be dispossessed." Pia wriggled out of his arms and sat down on the kitchen table. One of the dogs nudged her with his nose, and she patted his head absentmindedly. "All that money I paid goes down the drain."

"No, no, listen to me." Christoph sat down facing her and took her hand. "There's actually some very good news too. You paid three euros per square meter. The state will pay you five."

Pia looked up in disbelief.

"Who told you that?"

"Well, I happen to know a lot of people. And today I made a lot of phone calls." He smiled. "And I learned something interesting."

Then Pia had to smile too.

"If I know you, you've already found us a new farm," she said.

"You do know me well, I'll admit," Christoph said, amused, but then turned serious. "The thing is, the vet who used to take care of our animals at the zoo wants to sell his former horse clinic in the Taunus. I went out to see the place a while back, because we were looking for someplace to house new animals under quarantine. The farm isn't suited for that, but . . . for you and me and for your animals it would be a dream. I picked up the key today. If you want, we can drive out and see it tomorrow. What do you think?"

Pia looked into his brown eyes. Suddenly she felt overcome by a deep, warm surge of happiness. It didn't matter what happened. Even if they had to tear down the house and leave Birkenhof. Because she wasn't alone. Christoph would always stand by her, the way Henning had never done. He would never leave her in the lurch.

"Thank you," she said quietly and reached out her hand to him. "Thank you, my darling. You're simply incredible."

He took her hand and held it against his rough cheek.

"I'm only doing all this because I want to move in with you," he said with a smile. "I hope you realize that you can't get rid of me that easily."

Tears welled up in Pia's eyes.

"As if I'd ever want to," she whispered, smiling too.

Tuesday, November 25, 2008

It was a little after five in the morning when Bodenstein left the hospital. He felt deeply moved by the sight of Amelie patiently keeping watch by Tobias

Sartorius's bed until he woke up from the anesthesia. He put up the collar of his coat and made his way to the service vehicle. At the last second he had managed to arrest Daniela Lauterbach. She wasn't on the plane going to South America, but on the one headed for Australia. Bodenstein walked around the hospital building, lost in thought. The fresh snow creaked under his shoes. It occurred to him that almost three weeks had passed since the day the skeleton of Laura Wagner had been found at the Eschborn airfield. Previously in his career he had viewed every case from the sober perspective of an outsider who was getting a look inside the lives of complete strangers, but this time he felt like he'd been personally involved in events. Something in his attitude had changed, and he knew that he would never again feel the way he had before.

He stopped when he reached the car. He felt as though on the slow, calm river of life he'd suddenly gone crashing over a waterfall and was now sailing on stormy waters in a whole new direction. This image was alarming and yet exciting at the same time.

Bodenstein got into the car, started the engine, and waited until the windshield wipers had shoved the snow aside. Yesterday he had promised Cosima to drop by for breakfast and talk over everything in peace and quiet, if his work permitted. He was astounded to realize that he no longer harbored any anger toward her and felt fully able to discuss the whole situation objectively. He drove out of the parking lot and took the Limesspange expressway toward Kelkheim. His cell phone, which hadn't worked inside the hospital, beeped. He took it out of his pocket and pressed the message symbol. A callback from 3:21 A.M. with a cell number he didn't recognize. He pressed the number on the display at once.

"Hello?" said a sleepy female voice he didn't recognize.

"Bodenstein," he said. "Please excuse me for bothering you so early, but I had a callback number on my cell and thought it was urgent."

"Oh . . . hello," said the woman. "I went with my sister to see Thies at the hospital and got home really late. But I wanted to thank you."

Now he finally realized who he was talking to, and his heart leaped with joy.

"Thank me for what?" he asked.

"You saved Thies's life," said Heidi Brückner. "And probably my sister's too. We saw on the TV that you've arrested my brother-in-law and the Lauterbach woman."

"Hmm. Yes."

"Well then." She sounded suddenly embarrassed. "That was what I wanted to tell you. You . . . you've been working hard, and you're probably tired so . . ."

"No, no," Bodenstein said quickly. "I'm wide awake. But I haven't eaten anything in ages and was about to get some breakfast."

There was a brief pause, and he was afraid the conversation might have been cut off.

"I could do with a little breakfast myself," she replied. Bodenstein could imagine her smiling, and he smiled too.

"Why don't we meet for coffee somewhere?" he suggested, hoping it sounded casual enough. Inside he was all nerves. He thought he could feel his heart beating in his fingertips. He almost felt like he was doing something forbidden. How long had it been since he had made a date with an attractive woman?

"That would be nice," Heidi Brückner said to his relief. "But I'm already at home. In Schotten."

"Better than in Hamburg." Bodenstein grinned and waited in suspense for her reply. "Although for coffee I'd be willing to drive all the way to Hamburg."

"Then why don't we meet here in Vogelsberg?" she said. Bodenstein slowed down for a snowplow in front of him. In one kilometer the B8 veered to the right. To Cosima.

"It's a big area," he said, although he actually had her address on her business card. "I could drive all over Vogelsberg looking for you."

"Oh, it'd be a shame to waste your time like that." She laughed. "Schlossgasse 19. In the middle of the old town."

"Okay. I'll find it," he said.

"Great, I'll be expecting you. And drive carefully."

"I will. See you soon." Bodenstein ended the call and sighed. Was this a good idea? There was a pile of paperwork waiting at the office, and Cosima was waiting at home. The snowplow was still crawling along in front of him. Right turn to Kelkheim.

There would be plenty of time for the paperwork later. And the discussion with Cosima could wait too. Bodenstein took a deep breath and put on his blinker. To the left. Toward the autobahn.

Acknowledgments

From the initial idea to the finished book is always a long, yet exciting process. I'd like to thank my husband Harald for his understanding, my sisters Claudia Cohen and Camilla Altvater, my niece Caroline Cohen, Simone Schreiber, Anne Pfenninger, Vanessa Müller-Raidt, and Susanne Hecker for reading the manuscript and offering helpful suggestions at various stages of its genesis. I thank Christa Thabor and Iska Peller for their wonderful collaboration.

My thanks to Professor Hansjürgen Bratzke, director of the Center for Forensic Medicine at the University of Frankfurt, for advice and support in all matters of forensic medicine.

I also have to thank the team from K-11 of the Regional Criminal Unit in Hofheim, which kindly allows Bodenstein, Pia & Co. to make use of their workplace. Without the advice of KOR Peter Öhm, EKHK Bernd Beer, KOK Jochen Adler, and above all KOK Andrea Schulze, I could not present the work of the criminal police as realistically as I here tried to do.

Many thanks also to all the residents of Altenhain. I hope they won't hold it against me for making their village the setting for this book. I can assure everyone that all characters and events arose from my own imagination.

My most heartfelt thanks go to my German editors Marion Vazquez and Kristine Kress. Marion because she encouraged me to write this book and followed the entire process, and Kristine Kress because she gave the book its final polish. Working with you both was extremely enjoyable.

And last but not least I would like to thank all my wonderful readers and booksellers who enjoy my books and have motivated me to keep writing.

—Nele Neuhaus, November 2009

Turn the page for a sneak peek at
Nele Neuhaus's next novel

Available January 2014

Prologue

He set down the shopping bag and put away his purchases in the tiny refrigerator. The ice cream, her favorite flavor of Häagen-Dazs, had almost melted, but he knew that was exactly the way she liked it, so creamy and rich with the crunchy bits of cookies. It had been weeks since he'd seen her. Although it was hard for him, he never pressured her. He knew he really shouldn't rush her; he had to be patient. She had to want to come to him on her own. Yesterday, she had finally gotten in touch, sending a text message. And soon she would be here. The anticipation made his heart beat faster.

He looked around the trailer, which he'd given a good cleaning the night before. He glanced at the clock over the narrow kitchen counter. Already twenty past six. He had to hurry, because he didn't want her to see him like this, all sweaty and unshaven. After work, he'd stopped at the barbershop for a quick trim, but the rancid smell of the lunch stand still clung to every pore. He tore off his clothes, which were reeking of sweat and deep-fry oil, stuffed them into the empty shopping bag, and jumped into the mini-shower next to the kitchen. Even though it was cramped and the water pressure was low, he preferred the confines of his trailer to the unhygienic public bathrooms at the trailer park, which weren't cleaned very often.

He soaped up from head to toe, shaved carefully, and then brushed his teeth. Sometimes he had to force himself to do these things because it was so tempting to let himself go and sink into self-pity and lethargy. Maybe that's what would have happened if she hadn't been around.

A couple of minutes later, he slipped into fresh underwear and a clean polo shirt, then took a pair of jeans out of the dresser. Finally, he strapped his watch to his wrist. A couple of months ago, a pawnbroker at the train station had offered him one hundred and fifty euros for it—an outrageously paltry sum, considering that thirteen years ago he'd paid eleven thousand D-marks for this masterpiece from a Swiss watch company. He was keeping this watch. It was the last reminder of his former life. One more look in the mirror and then he opened the door and stepped out of the trailer.

His heart skipped a beat when he saw her sitting outside on the rickety garden chair. He'd been looking forward to this moment for days and weeks. He stood there, allowing the sight of her to sink in completely.

How beautiful she was, how tender and delicate! A sweet little angel with soft blond hair falling over her shoulders; he knew what it felt like and how it smelled. She was wearing a sleeveless dress that revealed her lightly tanned skin and the fragile vertebrae of her neck. She had a rapt expression on her face as she busily thumbed a text on her cell phone, and she didn't notice him. He didn't want to frighten her, so he cleared his throat. She looked up and her eyes met his. Her smile began at the corners of her mouth and then spread over her whole face. She jumped to her feet.

He had to swallow hard as she came over and stopped right in front of him. The look of trust in her dark eyes gave his heart a pang. Good God, how sweet she was! She was the only reason why he hadn't thrown himself in front of a train long ago, or in some other affordable way had put a premature end to his miserable life.

"Hello, sweetie," he said hoarsely, putting his hand on her shoulder—only briefly. Her skin felt silky and warm. At first, he always felt shy about touching her.

"Where did you tell your mother you were going?"

"She and my stepdad went to some party tonight, at the firehouse, I think," she replied, sticking her cell into her red backpack. "I told her I was going to Jessie's place."

"Good."

With a glance, he made sure that no curious neighbor or chance passerby was watching them. He was tingling inside with excitement, and his knees felt weak.

"I bought you your favorite ice cream," he said softly. "Shall we go inside?"

Thursday, June 10, 2010

She felt like she was tipping over backward. As soon as she opened her eyes, everything started spinning around. And she felt sick. No, not sick; she felt ghastly. She could smell the vomit. Alina groaned and tried to raise her head. Where was she? What had happened, and where was everybody else?

They had all been sitting together under the tree, Mart beside her, with his arm around her shoulders. It felt good. She laughed, and he kissed her. Katharina and Mia kept on complaining about the mosquitoes, and they'd been drinking this sweet stuff—vodka and Red Bull.

Alina sat up with an effort. Her head was pounding. She opened her eyes and was shocked to see the sun was about to set. How late was it anyway? And where was her cell phone? She couldn't remember how she'd gotten here, or where exactly she was. The past few hours were a blank, a total blackout.

"Mart? Mia? Where are you?"

She crawled over to the trunk of the huge weeping willow. It took all her strength to get to her feet and look around. Her knees felt as soft as butter, everything was spinning around her, and she couldn't see clearly. She'd probably lost her contact lenses when she was throwing up. And she'd certainly done a lot of that. The taste in her mouth was disgusting, and she could feel vomit on her face. The dry leaves crackled under her bare feet. She looked down. Her shoes were gone, too.

"Shit, shit, shit," she muttered, fighting to hold back the tears. She was going to be in big trouble if she showed up at home looking like this.

From a distance, she could hear voices and laughter drifting toward her, along with the aroma of grilled meat, which made her feel even more nause-ated. At least she hadn't landed somewhere out in the boonies; there were other people close by.

Alina let go of the tree trunk and took a couple of tentative steps. Every-thing around her was spinning round like a carousel, but she forced herself to keep walking. What a bunch of assholes they all were. Some friends! They'd just let her lie here drunk, with no shoes and no phone. Maybe fat Katharina and that stupid cow Mia were having a good laugh at her expense. She was really going to let them have it when she saw them tomorrow at school. And she would never speak to Mart again in her life.

At that moment, Alina happened to look at the steep bank leading down to the river and stopped short. There was somebody lying down there, in the stinging nettles, right next to the water. Dark hair, a yellow T-shirt—it was Alex. Damn, how had he gotten down there? What had happened? Cursing, Alina made her way down the bank. The nettles stung her bare calves, and she stepped on something sharp.

"Alex!" She squatted down next to him and shook his shoulder. He stank of vomit, too, and was groaning softly. "Hey, wake up!"

She waved away the mosquitoes that kept buzzing around her face.

"Alex! Wake up! Come on!" She tugged on his legs, but he was as heavy as lead and didn't budge.

On the river, a motorboat passed by. The wake sloshed up on shore, mak-ing the water gurgle in the reeds and lap against Alex's legs. Alina gasped in terror. Right in front of her eyes, a pale hand emerged from the water and seemed to reach out for her.

She recoiled and uttered a frightened cry. Among the reeds—not six feet away from Alex—Mia was lying in the water. Alina thought she could see her face just below the surface. In the diffuse half-light of dusk, she could see long blond hair and wide-open, dead eyes that seemed to be looking straight at her.

As if paralyzed, Alina stared at the gruesome sight, her mind reeling in confusion. What the hell had happened here? Another wave rolled in, Mia's body moved, and her arm stuck out of the dark water as pale as a ghost, as if she were begging for help.

Alina was shaking all over, even though it was still intolerably hot. Her stomach rebelled, and she staggered, turning around to throw up in the nettles. But instead of vodka and Red Bull, only bitter gall came up. Sobbing desperately, she crawled up the steep bank on all fours, scratching her hands and knees on the stubbled slope. Oh, if only she were home in her room, in bed, safe and sound! All she wanted was to get away from this horrible place and forget everything she'd seen.

Pia Kirchhoff was typing into her PC the final report on the investigation into the death of Veronika Meissner. Since early morning, the sun had been baking the flat roof of the building where the offices of Kommissariat 11 of the Criminal Police were located, and the readout on the digital weather station sitting on the windowsill next to Kai Ostermann's desk showed it was eighty-eight degrees. Room temperature. Outside, it was probably a good five degrees hotter. Schools had canceled lessons because of the heat. Although the doors and windows were open wide, there was no hint of a breeze to bring any relief. Pia's forearm stuck to the desktop as soon as she leaned on it. She sighed and pressed PRINT, then added the report to the slim folder. All that was missing was the autopsy report, but where had she put it? Pia got up and searched through her out-box, eager to be done with this case at last. Since yesterday, she'd been holding down the fort alone at K-11. Her colleague Kai Ostermann, with whom she shared the office, was attending a course at the National Criminal Police office in Wiesbaden. Kathrin Fachinger and Cem Altunay were taking part in a nationwide seminar in Düsseldorf, and the boss had been on vacation since Monday at an undisclosed location. Commissioner Nicola Engel had granted Pia some time off when she was promoted to detective superintendent, but that, too, had fallen by the wayside because the department was so short-staffed. Pia didn't really mind. She hated for anyone to make a fuss over her; the change in her rank was no more than an administrative formality.

"So where's that damn report?" she muttered in annoyance. It was almost five already, and she was planning to go to her class reunion in Königstein at seven. The construction work they were doing on her farmhouse, the Birkenhof, often left her no time for any social life, but she was looking forward to seeing the girls from her old school after twenty-five years.

A knock at her open door made her spin around.

"Hello, Pia."

Pia couldn't believe her eyes. It was her former colleague Frank Behnke, but he was totally transformed. He had changed his usual look—jeans, T-shirt, and worn cowboy boots—for a light gray suit with shirt and tie. He wore his hair a little longer than before, and his face no longer looked as haggard, which was an improvement.

"Hello, Frank," she replied, amazed. "Long time no see."

"But you did recognize me," he said with a grin, shoving his hands into his pants pockets and giving her the once-over. "You're looking good. I heard you stumbled up another rung of the career ladder. I suppose you'll be taking over from the old man soon, eh?"

As always, Frank Behnke lost no time pushing her buttons, and he did it effortlessly. Her polite query as to how things were going for him stuck in her throat.

"I didn't 'stumble up' the career ladder, no way. My rank was changed, that's all," she responded coolly. "And whom are you referring to as 'the old man'? You mean Bodenstein?"

Behnke just shrugged it off with a grin and kept on chewing his gum. That was one thing he hadn't managed to give up.

After his inglorious departure from K-11 two years earlier, he'd lodged a complaint about his suspension and been lucky enough to be reinstated. At any rate, he'd been transferred to the National Criminal Police office in Wiesbaden, and nobody at the Regional Criminal Unit in Hofheim had been sorry to see him go.

He slipped past her and sat down in Ostermann's chair.

"Everybody flew the coop, I see."

Pia muttered to herself as she kept on looking for that autopsy report.

"To what do I owe the honor of this visit?" she then asked.

Behnke clasped his hands behind his head.

"Well, what a shame that you're the only one here to share my happy news with," he said. "But the others will find out soon enough."

"What is it?" Pia gave him a suspicious look.

"I got fed up with working the streets. I've done that shit long enough," he replied without taking his eyes off her. "The Special Assignment Unit, K-11, all that's behind me now. I always got the best evaluations, so they forgave me my minor indiscretion."

Minor indiscretion! Behnke had punched their colleague Kathrin Fachinger in a fit of uncontrolled rage and committed enough other transgressions to warrant a suspension.

"I was having personal problems back then," he went on. "That was taken into account. At the State Police office, I passed a couple of additional qualifications, and now I'm at K-134, the Office of Internal Affairs, responsible for investigating and bringing charges against police personnel and preventing corruption."

Pia couldn't believe her ears. Frank Behnke as an Internal Affairs investigator? That was utterly absurd.

"Along with my colleagues from the other federal states, in the past few months we've developed a strategic concept that will go into effect on July first nationwide. Improvement of services and professional oversight within subordinate departments, sensitivity training for personnel, and so on...." He crossed one leg over the other and jiggled his foot. "Dr. Engel is a competent manager, but occasionally we get reports from the individual investigative offices about transgressions committed by colleagues. I can vividly recall certain incidents in this very office that were quite disturbing: failure to administer punishments in the office, not following up on misdemeanors, unauthorized IT queries, passing internal documents to third parties ... just to mention a few examples."

Pia abruptly stopped searching for the autopsy report.

"What are you getting at?"

Behnke's smile turned malicious, and his eyes took on an unpleasant glint. Pia had a bad feeling about all this. As always, he was enjoying demonstrating his superiority and power with regard to his opponent, a character trait of his that she despised. As a colleague, with his envy and perpetually rotten temper, Behnke had been a veritable torment, but as a representative of internal investigations, he could be a disaster.

"You, of all people, should know best." He stood up and came around the desk to stand close to her. "But you're the obvious favorite of the old man."

"I have no idea what you're talking about," Pia replied icily.

"Oh, don't you? Really?" Behnke moved so close that it made her uncomfortable, but she resisted the urge to step back. "Starting Monday, I'm going to start an authorized internal investigation in this building, and I probably won't have to dig very deep to bring a few corpses to light."

Pia was shivering despite the tropical heat in the office, but she remained outwardly calm, even though she was boiling inside; she even managed to smile. Frank Behnke was an unforgiving and petty person who forgot nothing. Old frustrations were still eating at him and seemed to have multiplied tenfold in recent years. And he was contemplating revenge for the injustice and humiliation he imagined he'd suffered. It wouldn't be smart to make an enemy of him, but Pia's anger was stronger than her good sense.

"Well then," she said sarcastically, resuming her search. "I wish you much success in your new job as . . . a cadaver dog."

Behnke turned to go.

"Your name isn't on my list yet. But that could change at any time. Have a nice weekend."

Pia didn't react to the unambiguous threat contained in his words. She waited until he was gone, then grabbed her cell and punched the hot key for Bodenstein. The call went through, but nobody picked up. Damn. She was sure that her boss hadn't the slightest idea what a nasty surprise was waiting for him here. She knew pretty much what Behnke was insinuating. And it could have very unpleasant consequences for Oliver von Bodenstein.

The deposit on three returnable bottles was enough for a pack of noodles. Five more would buy veggies to go with it. That was the currency he dealt in these days.

Before, in his former life, he hadn't paid any attention to collecting the deposit, but had blithely tossed empty bottles into trash cans. That was exactly the sort of person who ensured his basic needs today. He'd received twelve euros and fifty cents from the kiosk dealer for the two bags of empty bottles. He got paid six euros an hour under the table by the greedy cheapskate

for standing all day in this tin box at the edge of an industrial zone in Fech-
enheim, grilling hot dogs and burgers and deep-frying potatoes. If the cash
register didn't add up perfectly, the amount was docked from his pay. Today,
everything had come out even, and he hadn't had to beg for his money like
he usually did. Fatso was in a good mood and had paid him what he was
owed for the past five days.

Combined with the money from collecting bottles, he had about three
hundred euros in his wallet: a small fortune. That was why, feeling suddenly
flush, he'd splurged not only on a haircut but also a shave from the Turkish
barber across from the train station. After a visit to Aldi, he had enough left
to pay the rent on his trailer space for two months in advance.

He parked his rickety motor scooter next to the trailer, pulled the hel-
met off his head, and took the shopping bag out of the carrier.

The heat was driving him crazy. It didn't even cool off at night. In the
morning, he would wake up soaked with sweat. In the miserable lunch stand
of thin corrugated iron, it could get up to one hundred and forty degrees,
and the stifling humidity made the stench of sweat and rancid fat settle in
his hair and pores.

The dilapidated trailer in the RV park in Schwanheim was supposed to
have been a temporary solution, back when he still believed he could make a
go of it and restore his financial situation. But nothing in his life had turned
out to be as long-lasting as this temporary arrangement—he'd already been
living here for seven years.

He unzipped the awning, which must have been dark green decades ago,
before the weather had faded it to a nondescript pale gray. A puff of hot air
gusted toward him. Inside the trailer, it was several degrees hotter than outside, with a stifling and stuffy smell. No matter how much he scrubbed and
aired out the place, the odors had settled into the upholstery and every nook
and cranny. Even after seven years, it still filled him with disgust, but for him
there was no other option.

Ever since his plunge into the abyss, and as a convicted criminal, he belonged to the underclass, even among the residents of the slum on the outskirts
of the metropolis. Nobody wandered in here on vacation or to admire the
glitzy skyline of Frankfurt, the concrete and glass symbols of big money across

the river. His neighbors were mostly blamelessly impoverished retirees or failures like himself who had landed on the down escalator. Alcohol often played a leading role in the story of their lives, which were depressingly similar. As for himself, he drank no more than one beer in the evening, he didn't smoke, and he paid attention to his weight and grooming. He didn't bother with the Hartz IV law of 2005, which combined unemployment insurance with social welfare, because he couldn't stand the thought of having to show up as a supplicant and kowtow to the bigoted whims of indifferent bureaucrats.

A tiny scrap of self-esteem was the last thing he possessed. If he lost that, he might as well kill himself.

"Hello?"

A voice outside the awning made him turn around. A man was standing behind the half-desiccated hedge that divided the property of his tiny plot from the neighbor's.

"What do you want?"

The man came closer, hesitated. His piggy little eyes flicked angrily from left to right.

"Somebody told me you would help anyone who was having trouble with the authorities." The high-pitched falsetto was a grotesque contrast to the massive figure of the man. Sweat was beading on his balding head, and the smell of garlic overpowered the even less pleasant body odors.

"Oh, really? Who says that?"

"Rosi, from the kiosk. She told me, 'Go see Doc. He'll help you.'" The sweating hunk of lard glanced around again, as if he was afraid to be seen there. Then he took a roll of bills out of his pocket. Hundreds, even a couple of five hundreds. "I'll pay you well."

"Come on in."

Right off, the guy seemed kind of disagreeable, but that didn't matter. He couldn't be picky about his clientele, his address was not in any phone book, and he certainly didn't have a Web site. Still, there were limits to what he'd do, no matter how much money was offered, and people knew that. With his previous conviction and the probation that was still in force, he couldn't get involved in anything that might send him back to the slammer.

But word on the street was that he'd already helped tavern owners and operators of lunch stands who had come into conflict with official regulations, desperate pensioners who'd been bilked on promotional shopping trips or by door-to-door salesmen, unemployed people or immigrants who couldn't understand the complex bureaucracy in Germany, and young people who were seduced early by the temptations of a life on credit and had fallen into the debt trap. Anyone who asked for help knew that he worked only for cash.

He had long since gotten over any feelings of sympathy. He was no Robin Hood; he was a mercenary. For cash in advance, he would fill out official forms on the scratched-up Formica table in his trailer, translate complicated bureaucratic German into understandable everyday language, and offer legal advice for any situation in order to augment his income.

"What's the problem?" he asked his visitor, who cast an appraising glance at the obvious indicators of poverty and seemed to gain confidence.

"Man, it's sure hot in here. Have you got a beer or a glass of water?"

"No." He made no effort to be friendly.

Long gone were the days of mahogany-veneer conference tables in air-conditioned rooms, trays holding little bottles of water and fruit juice, and glasses arrayed upside down.

With a snort, the fat man pulled out some rolled-up papers from the inside pocket of his greasy leather vest and handed them over. Recycled paper, small print. The tax office.

He unfolded the papers, which were damp with sweat, smoothed them out, and scanned the text.

"Three hundred," he demanded without looking up. Rolls of cash stuffed in pants pockets always signified illegal earnings. The sweaty fat man could afford to pay a bit more than the usual rate he charged seniors and the unemployed.

"What?" the new client protested, as anticipated. "For a few pages?"

"If you can find someone to do it cheaper, be my guest."

The fat man muttered something unintelligible, then reluctantly peeled off three banknotes and laid them on the table.

"Do I at least get a receipt?"

"Sure. My secretary will make it out later and give it to your chauffeur," he replied. "Now have a seat. I'll need some information from you."

Traffic was backed up at Baseler Platz leading to the Friedensbrücke. For a couple of weeks now, the city had been one big construction zone, and Hanna was annoyed that she'd forgotten all about that and driven into downtown instead of taking the route via the Frankfurter Kreuz and Niederrad to Sachsenhausen. As she drove along at a snail's pace behind a bunch of rusty pickup trucks with Lithuanian license plates crossing the bridge over the Main River, Hanna replayed the unsatisfying conversation with Norman that morning. She was still pissed off about his stupidity and his lies. It had been hard for her to fire him with no notice after eleven years, but he'd left her no choice. Before he stomped off in a huff, he'd fired off a series of nasty curses and issued several vile threats.

Hanna's smartphone hummed, and she grabbed it and opened her mail app. Her assistant had sent her an e-mail. The header said "Catastrophe!!!" Instead of a message, there was a link to FOCUS online. Hanna clicked the link with her thumb, and her stomach lurched when she read the headline.

Hanna Heartless, it said in bold letters, and beside it was a rather unflattering photo of her. Her pulse began to race and she felt her right hand trembling uncontrollably. She gripped her phone harder. *All she cares about is profit. The guests on her TV show have to sign a nondisclosure agreement before they're allowed to speak. And whatever they say is scripted in advance by Hanna Herzmann, 46. Bricklayer Armin V., 52, wanted to speak during the show about his hassle with his landlord (the topic was "My Landlord Wants to Evict Me"), but with the cameras rolling, he was labeled a transient renter by the moderator. When he protested after the broadcast, he discovered another side of the supposedly sympathetic Hanna Herzmann, and of her lawyer. Now Armin V. is unemployed and homeless after his landlord finally succeeded in evicting him. Something similar happened to Bettina B., 34. The single mother was a guest on Hanna Herzmann's program in January (topic: "When Fathers Hit the Road"). Contrary to preliminary arrangements, Bettina B. was portrayed as an overtaxed mother and alcoholic. For her, too, the broadcast had unpleasant consequences: She received a visit from Child Welfare.*

"Shit," Hanna muttered. Once something was on the Internet, it was impossible to delete. She bit her lip and thought hard.

Unfortunately, the article was close to the truth. Hanna had a real knack for finding interesting topics, and she wasn't afraid to ask embarrassing questions and stir up dirt. In doing so, she basically couldn't care less about the people and their often tragic fates. She secretly had nothing but contempt for most of them and their urge to bare all in return for fifteen minutes of fame. Hanna managed to coax the most intimate secrets out of people in front of the camera, and she was a master at pretending to be sympathetic and interested.

Besides, the true story was often insufficient, so a little dramatization was necessary. And that had been Norman's job. He had cynically called the show *Pimp My Boring Life* and was happy to distort reality, regardless of how painful it might prove to be. Whether that was morally acceptable or not wasn't Hanna's concern; in the end, the show's success in the ratings validated his tactics. Of course, the letters of complaint from disgruntled guests filled several file folders. They often didn't understand until later, when they were subjected to public mockery, what sort of embarrassing things they'd said in front of a television audience. As a matter of fact, complaints arose only seldom, and that was due to the polished, absolutely airtight legal contracts that each person who wanted to speak on her broadcast had to sign in advance.

A car honked behind her, startling Hanna out of her reverie. The traffic was moving again. She raised her hand in apology and stepped on the gas. Ten minutes later, she turned down Hedderichstrasse and then into the back courtyard of the building where her company was located. She put her smartphone in her shoulder bag and stepped out of the car. In the city, it was always several degrees warmer than out in the Taunus region; the heat built up between the buildings until it felt like a sauna. Hanna fled into the air-conditioned foyer and stepped into an elevator. On the way to the sixth floor, she leaned against the cool wall and took a critical look at herself in the mirrored surface.

In the first weeks after her breakup with Vinzenz, she had looked terribly harried and exhausted, and the girls in Makeup had had to muster all their professional skill to make her look the way the television viewers expected. But now Hanna found her appearance quite passable, at least in the dim light of the elevator. She'd colored her hair to cover the first silver strands, not out of vanity, but from a sheer instinct for self-preservation. The TV business was unforgiving: men could have gray hair, but for women, that would mean eventual banishment to the afternoon cultural and cooking shows.

Hanna had hardly stepped out of the elevator on the sixth floor when Jan Niemöller appeared out of nowhere. In spite of the tropical weather outdoors, the manager of Herzmann Productions was wearing a black shirt, black jeans, and even a scarf around his neck.

"All hell has broken loose!" Niemöller trotted along beside her excitedly, waving his skinny arms. "The phones are ringing off the hook, and nobody can reach you. And how come I have to hear from Norman that you fired him with no notice? Why didn't you tell me? First you give Julia the boot, now Norman—who do you think is going to do the work?"

"Meike is going to fill in for Julia during the summer; that's already been set up. And we're going to be working with an independent producer."

"And you don't even ask me about it?"

Hanna looked Niemöller up and down.

"Hiring and firing is my job. I took you on to deal with the business stuff so I wouldn't have to worry about it."

"Oh, so that's how you see it?" He was insulted, of course.

Hanna knew that Jan Niemöller was secretly in love with her, or, rather, with all the glory surrounding her, which also spilled over onto him as her associate. But she viewed him solely as a business partner—as a man, he was not her type. Besides, he'd been acting so possessive lately that she needed to put him in his place.

"That's not just the way I see it; that's the way it *is,*" she said with a tad more coolness. "I appreciate your opinion, but I'm the one making the decisions."

Niemöller opened his mouth to protest, but Hanna cut him off with a wave of her hand.

"The network hates this sort of publicity. We're no longer in a very strong position. With the shitty ratings in recent months, I had no choice but to kick Norman out. If they take us off the air, all of you can go scrambling for another job. Do you get it?"

Irina Zydek, Hanna's assistant, appeared in the hallway.

"Hanna, Matern has called you three times. And almost every newspaper and TV news desk, except for Al Jazeera." Her voice had an anxious undertone.

The rest of the staff appeared in the doorways of their offices, and their concern was palpable. The news had obviously gotten around that she'd fired Norman without notice.

"We're meeting in half an hour in the conference room," Hanna said as she walked by. First, she had to call Wolfgang Matern back. She couldn't afford any trouble with the network at the moment.

She stepped into her office at the end of the corridor; it was flooded with light. She dropped her shoulder bag on one of the visitors' chairs and sat down behind her desk. As her computer booted up, she leafed quickly through the callback messages that Irina had written on yellow Post-its, then picked up the phone. She never liked to put off unpleasant tasks for long. She hit the speed-dial number for Wolfgang Matern and took a deep breath. He picked up in a matter of seconds.

"It's Hanna Heartless," she said.

"Good to hear you've still got a sense of humor," the CEO of Antenne Pro replied.

"I've just fired my producer without notice because I learned that for years he's been doctoring the bios of my guests if he found the truth too boring."

"You mean you didn't know that?"

"No!" She put all the indignation she could into this lie. "I'm stunned. I couldn't check out every story, so I had to depend on him. That is—or was—his job."

"Please tell me that it won't turn into a bloodbath," said Matern.

"Of course not." Hanna leaned back in her chair. "I already have an idea for how we can turn this thing around."

"What is it?"

"We'll admit everything and apologize to the guests."

There was a moment's silence.

"Retreat disguised as an advance," Wolfgang Matern said at last. "That's precisely why I admire you. You don't run and hide. Let's talk about it tomorrow over lunch, okay?"

Hanna could almost hear his smile, and a weight lifted off her heart. Sometimes her spontaneous ideas were the best.